Beautiful women are disappearing. Will Sloane Burbank be next?

"LACED WITH ROMANCE AND SUSPENSE."
JAMES ROLLINS

"ANDREA KANE EXPERTLY JUGGLES SUSPENSE AND ROMANCE."
IRIS JOHANSEN

"KANE IS AN ADROIT MASTER AT ROMANTIC SUSPENSE, AND SHE KEEPS THE READER GUESSING TO THE VERY END."
BOOKLIST

"ANDREA KANE DELIVERS THE KIND OF EDGY SUSPENSE AND ROMANTIC TENSION THAT WILL REV UP YOUR PULSE AND KEEP YOU TURNING THE PAGES."
JAYNE ANN KRENTZ

ANDREA KANE

TWISTED

AVON
An Imprint of HarperCollinsPublishers

This book was originally published in hardcover April 2008 by William Morrow, an Imprint of HarperCollins Publishers.

AVON BOOKS
An Imprint of HarperCollins*Publishers*
10 East 53rd Street
New York, New York 10022-5299

First Avon Books paperback printing: August 2009
First William Morrow hardcover printing: April 2008

10 9 8 7 6 5 4 3 2 1

For Rascal, with all my love.

And to Rhonda, with thanks for being there
during a time of insurmountable grief,
for offering me a unique depth of understanding,
honesty, and compassion, and for being
    a kindred spirit—
one I'm proud to call my friend.

ACKNOWLEDGMENTS

The creation of *Twisted* involved an extensive learning experience for me. I always spend months on research before and during the writing of a novel, but this time I did far more in-the-trenches detailed field research than I can begin to describe. And I've never been more fascinated. My writing took me into the world of the FBI, where I met and spoke with some of the most dedicated professionals I've ever had the good fortune to consult with. Without their cooperation and their generosity—sharing their time and expertise with me—I could never have infused *Twisted* with the level of depth and realism I did, nor could I have brought my characters and their stories so vividly to life. I'm immensely grateful to everyone at the Bureau who went out of their way to help me. I hope I did you all proud.

Specifically, I'd like to thank the following:

Angela Bell, public affairs specialist at FBI Headquarters. Angela, working with you was a true privilege. You coordinated every aspect of my Bureau-related research thoroughly, intuitively, and in record time—and you were *always* spot-on with every contact you put me in touch with. You are awesome!

SA Steve Siegel and the Newark field office, including SSA Bill Evanina, SA Laura Robinson, and an enormous special thank-you to SA Sherri Evanina, who just made things happen. Sherri, you either knew the answers to my million and one questions, or produced someone who did. You're a real miracle worker.

SA James Margolin of the New York field office, who connected me up with all the right people, and made the necessary meetings happen no matter how busy the most densely populated FBI field office in the country was. Included in that list of outstanding contacts were SA Rich DeFilippo, SA Leslie Berens, SABT Pete Licata, and SSA Konrad Motyka, the supervisor of C-6, who, along with all the members of his squad, taught me what I needed to know about the Asian Criminal Enterprise Task Force in order to bring the squad to life in *Twisted*. He also educated me in various Chinese dialects (including how to curse in each of them, which was necessary to the book), and in the workings of Enhanced SWAT. Konrad, your knowledge base is extensive—thank you for taking so much time to share it with me.

The two principal firearms instructors at Fort Dix: SA Jody Roberson and SA Mike Adams, who allowed me the opportunity to watch a Pistol Qualification Course (PQC) firsthand. Mike also skillfully (and patiently) taught me how to load and shoot a Glock 22, working on my grip, aim, and accuracy, until I was hitting every target. I was very proud, but very sore. Trust me, it's not as easy as it looks on TV.

Kurt Crawford, who escorted me through the FBI Academy at Quantico, and showed me where qualified men and women evolve into Special Agents.

And an overwhelming, special thank you to the awe-inspiring agents at CIRG who helped me create the heart and soul of this book:

CNU Unit Chief John Flood, who took me through an entire day of crisis (hostage) negotiation training with his unit and his trainees, so I could witness and experience firsthand the astounding skills and strategies employed by real FBI crisis negotiators. The commitment and solidarity of the CNU is a tribute to Unit Chief Flood's skill and team-building efforts. He is a true leader in every sense of the word, and I have tremendous admiration and respect for him, his team, and their contribution to our country.

SSA James McNamara of the BAU, who exemplifies the term *the real deal*. Extensively published and a true expert in his field, he taught me so much about psychological and behavioral techniques used by the BAU in order to understand who and what a person is—including the ability to analyze the mind and actions of a serial killer.

My thanks also to SA Al Tribble, SSA Russ Atanasio, and SSA Bob Holley for taking the time to explain so many Bureau nuances to me— from the different squad responsibilities and how things are broken down, to the additional training that's necessary for various ancillary responsibilities, to what it's like to be a retired Army Ranger who becomes an FBI agent.

If I've inadvertently omitted anyone, I apologize. I talked with so many Bureau professionals, each of whom was a unique learning experience unto him- or herself. Each field-office visit, each trip to Quantico and Fort Dix, was filled with amazing agents, technical staff, and media contacts/specialists, who were more than willing to answer all my questions, and explain the many, many roles of the FBI.

In addition, many of the special agents I've acknowledged were also kind enough and thorough enough to read the finished manuscript of *Twisted* for accuracy, and to then provide their feedback. I thank them all for that.

To that end, I take full responsibility for any unintentional errors that might have slipped by me, and for any literary license I took. I only did so when absolutely necessary.

With the NYPD being such a vital part of *Twisted*, I must thank my constant, smart-as-a-whip consultant, Detective Mike Oliver, who knows the NYPD like the back of his hand, and who, as always, spent hours helping me— this time dissecting and understanding federal and local jurisdiction so I could accurately depict where the FBI's and the NYPD's jurisdiction began and ended.

After working with two of the finest law enforcement organizations in the world—the FBI and the NYPD—I have a newfound appreciation for all they do on our behalf.

In addition to law enforcement, my research required consulting with a highly regarded expert in orthopedic surgery of the hand and upper extremities, and an equally effective hand therapist, so that I could accurately portray Sloane's injuries, her surgeries, and the stages of her recovery. I had the good fortune of being put in touch with Dr. Daniel Mass, an expert in his field, and a professor at the University of Chicago Pritzker School of Medicine. Dr. Mass spent hours educating me, through text, visuals, and lengthy telephone conferences, answering my numerous layperson questions, until I could describe the surgeries and complications Sloane endured.

Through Dr. Mass, and in conjunction with the medical education he provided me, I was introduced to Candice Brattstrom, an experienced and knowledgeable hand therapist, who's an important member of Dr. Mass's team. Candice taught me the intricate occupational-therapy regimen Sloane would have to adhere to, as well as the tools she would have to use, to recover the mobility and use of her hand. Candice, you were an excellent, thorough, and patient teacher—and a pleasure to get to know.

In conjunction with the above, I want to thank Saurabh Agarwal, soon-to-be MD, of the University of Chicago Pritzker School of Medicine, for introducing me to Dr. Mass. I very much appreciate your spotting such an outstanding surgeon, and for arranging our initial contact.

While I'm thanking medical consultants, my thanks, as always, goes to Hillel Ben-Asher, MD, who reviewed each medical and drug-administering scenario of *Twisted* with me, and helped me orchestrate the details as authentically as possible.

Last (but definitely not least) on my medical consultant

list is Dr. Paul Sedlacek, DVM, who educated me in ketamine—its effects and dosages—and spent a good part of his vacation answering my frantic e-mails about drugging people versus drugging animals.

My appreciation to Adam Cuddyer, head instructor at ATA Black Belt Academy, Hillsborough, New Jersey, for teaching me the complex Krav Maga techniques that were an integral part of Sloane's life and an exciting addition to the plot of *Twisted*.

I want to thank everyone at HarperCollins who believes in me, and who works tirelessly on my behalf proving it, particularly: Brian Grogan, Rhonda Rose, Donna Waitkus, Lisa Gallagher, Lynn Grady, Tavia Kowalchek, Liate Stehlik, Adrienne DiPietro, Pamela Spengler-Jaffee, Tom Egner, and Rich Aquan.

A special thank-you to my editor at HarperCollins, Lucia Macro, for recognizing this book as "the one," and for touting it as such. An additional thanks to Lucia's assistant, Esi Sogah, for all she does to facilitate the process we work so hard to perfect.

I can't close without thanking Andrea Cirillo, whose caring and commitment know no bounds.

And, most of all, thank you to my family, for loving and supporting me and one another. I'm proud of your accomplishments, and grateful for your ever-present involvement and input—all of which prevailed despite the pain of loss. We're still the best team there is, and I continually treasure the unique bond we share. I could never have done this without you.

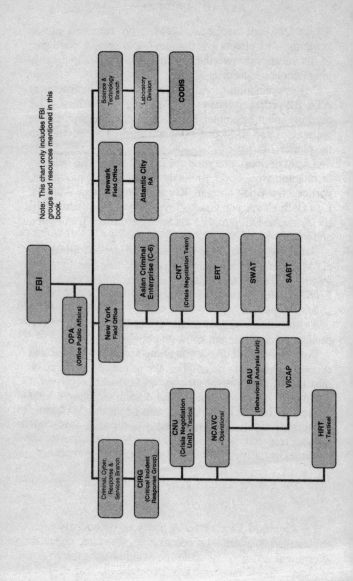

Note: This chart only includes FBI groups and resources mentioned in this book.

FBI

OPA
(Office Public Affairs)

Criminal, Cyber, Response & Services Branch

CIRG
(Critical Incident Response Group)

CNU
(Crisis Negotiation Unit) - Tactical

NCAVC
- Operational

BAU
(Behavioral Analysis Unit)

VICAP

HRT
- Tactical

New York Field Office

Asian Criminal Enterprise (C-6)

CNT
(Crisis Negotiation Team)

ERT

SWAT

SABT

Newark Field Office

Atlantic City RA

Science & Technology Branch

Laboratory Division

CODIS

DEFINITIONS OF ACRONYMS AND TERMS

Please refer to the accompanying chart for information on how groups and resources mentioned in this book interrelate.

ADIC *Assistant Director in Charge:* Of the fifty-six FBI field offices nationwide, only the three largest are headed up by ADICs. Those are the New York, Los Angeles, and Washington field offices. Each of the remaining field offices is headed up by a SAC (Special Agent in Charge).

BAU *Behavioral Analysis Unit:* One of the three components of the National Center for the Analysis of Violent Crimes (NCAVC), the BAU provides behavioral-based investigative and operational support through case experience, research, and training to complex and time-sensitive crimes, usually involving acts or threats of violence.

CCTV *Closed Circuit Television:* Utilized for surveillance.

CE *Criminal Enterprise:* A group of individuals with an identified hierarchy, or comparable structure, engaged in criminal activity similar to the infamous organized-crime groups. The New York field office squad that deals with

Asian Criminal Enterprise is designated C-6. C-6 is, in fact, a task force, including members both of the FBI and of the NYPD.

CIRG *Critical Incident Response Group:* Facilitates the FBI's rapid response to, and the management of, crisis situations. Contains three main branches: (1) Operations Support Branch, (2) Tactical Support Branch (Hostage Rescue Team, or HRT, and Crisis Negotiation Unit, or CNU, are components of this CIRG branch), and (3) National Center for the Analysis of Violent Crime (BAU is a component of this CIRG branch).

CNT *Crisis Negotiation Team:* The specific team members, trained by the CNU, and located at individual field offices, who handle crisis negotiations in their respective territories.

CNU *Crisis Negotiation Unit:* An integral part of the Operations Support Branch of CIRG. The CNU is responsible for the Crisis (Hostage) Negotiation Program, including operations, training, research, and program management.

CODIS *Combined DNA Index System:* Allows federal, state, and local crime labs to exchange, share, and compare DNA profiles electronically, linking crimes to one another and to convicted offenders.

Dai Lo *"Elder Brother":* A Cantonese term referring to the gang leader. The term is accepted by all Asian gangs, regardless of which dialect is spoken by their members.

Enhanced SWAT: Of the fifty-six FBI field offices, nine have enhanced SWAT teams. Those enhanced teams are larger in number than the regular SWAT teams, and have more extensive tactical equipment. They are also the immediate backup to HRT (Hostage Rescue Team—the third branch of CIRG [the Tactical Support Branch]—which is the full-time national-level tactical team based in Quantico, Virginia).

ERT *Evidence Response Team:* Special agents who collect, identify, manage, and preserve crime-scene evidence. (Note: ERT is the federal counterpart of [and sometimes coordinates their efforts with] local Crime Scene Investigation [CSI] Units.) There are ERT members in each of the FBI's fifty-six field offices.

ICE *Immigration and Customs Enforcement.*

M.E. *Medical Examiner.*

NCAVC *National Center for the Analysis of Violent Crimes:* This branch of CIRG combines investigative and operational support functions, research, and training to assist federal, state, local, and foreign law enforcement agencies investigating unusual or repetitive violent crimes.

NSA *National Security Agency.*

OPA *Office of Public Affairs:* Located at FBI headquarters, OPA is the office that supplies the media with up-to-the-minute access to breaking news, vital information, latest press releases, stories, congressional testimony and speeches, etc.

RA *Resident Agencies:* Smaller satellite branches of each field office, responsible for a portion of the field office's territory. For example, the Newark Field Office (in New Jersey) has five RAs in its jurisdiction: Atlantic City, Franklin Township, Garret Mountain, Trenton, and Red Bank.

ROTC *Reserve Officer Training Corps:* College-based, officer commissioning program for all branches of the U.S. Armed Forces (with the exception of the Coast Guard).

RTCC *Real Time Crime Center (NYPD):* Conducts rapid analysis of citywide crime to provide a real-time assessment of emerging crime, crime patterns, and emerging criminal suspects citywide. Originally just for homicides and shootings, now expanded to include other major crimes.

SA *Special Agent:* Trainees who complete the intensive twenty-one-week training program at the FBI Academy in Quantico graduate and become Special Agents.

SABT *Special Agent Bomb Technicians:* Special agents who go through additional training to become specialists in finding, assessing, and disrupting incendiary and explosive devices.

SSA *Supervisory Special Agent:* Special agents who are promoted and have a managerial role in a squad or at FBI headquarters.

SWAT *Special Weapons and Tactics:* Special agents specifically trained in extended weaponry and tactical expertise in order to be able to intervene in high-risk events such as arrests, search warrants, barricades, and hostage situations.

Unsub *Unknown Subject:* Just as *perp* is police lingo for perpetrator, *subject or offender* is FBI lingo for the same. If the identity of the subject is not known, he/she is referred to as the Unsub.

VICAP *Violent Criminal Apprehension Center:* Another of the three components of NCAVC, VICAP is a nationwide data information center to collect, collate, and analyze violent crimes, particularly murder.

One final note: The fictitious artificial-intelligence software program created by Dr. Elliot Lyman in *Twisted,* along with its crime analysis capabilities, were inspired by some cutting-edge law enforcement research, the Classification System for Serial Criminal Patterns (CSSCP). CSSCP was developed by Professor Thomas Muscarello at DePaul University, working with detectives from the Chicago Police Department.

CHAPTER ONE

DATE: 19 March
TIME: 2100 hours
OBJECTIVE: Athena

She was a true warrior.

Subduing her had required all my skill and training. Even the weapon hadn't been enough to make her submit. Not like the others. Not until she'd felt the prick of the blade, sensed drops of her own blood trickling down her neck. At that point she'd quivered, then gone still. She was too smart not to. She wanted to fight. I could see it in her eyes. But she didn't. In the end, I'd won. I injected her with the Nembutal, and in five minutes her eyes went dull and her body went limp.

I had her.

Her warm, drugged body slumped against my shoulder. It felt good. My timing and execution had been perfect. It was spring break. She wouldn't be missed for days.

By then it would be too late.

John Jay College of Criminal Justice
New York City
March 20, 4 P.M.

The auditorium crackled with anticipation.

It was the final seminar of the two-day "Crimes Against Women: How Not to Become Another Statistic" conference. The panel of experts included Jimmy O'Donnelly, an NYPD detective from the Special Victims Unit; Sharon McNally, a psychologist who specialized in counseling victims of violent crimes; Dr. Charles Hewitt, a professor of statistics and mathematics right here at John Jay; Dr. Lillian Doyle, also a John Jay professor but in the sociology department; Lawrence Clark, a retired supervisory special agent from the FBI's Behavioral Analysis Unit, a component of the NCAVC—the investigative branch of the Bureau's Critical Incident Response Group.

And Sloane Burbank, the final name on this impressive list of experts.

All of them had spoken. Now it was her turn.

The moderator ran through Sloane's impressive credentials, which included a year in the Manhattan D.A.'s Office before joining the FBI full-time, where she was trained as a crisis negotiator by the CNU, the operational branch of the FBI's CIRG division. Currently, she was an independent consultant who worked with law enforcement, corporations, and educational institutions, training them in crisis management and resolution. She was also a certified Krav Maga instructor. And all at thirty years old.

With an admiring nod in her direction, the moderator stepped away from the mike and turned the room over to Sloane.

Amid enthusiastic applause, Sloane rose from behind the speaker table, thinking for the dozenth time how good she sounded on paper. And she *was* good—just not as good as she'd been a year ago. Then again, perception outweighed reality. She was the only one who'd know the difference.

Exuding her usual energy and self-assurance, Sloane unbuttoned her blazer and tossed it over the back of her chair. She wasn't surprised by the skepticism she saw on some of the faces in the audience. Their reaction was nothing new. And it was something she'd used to her advantage more times than not.

Despite her impressive résumé, she was a fine-boned woman with a delicate frame and the fresh-scrubbed features of a college student. That made people doubt her abilities—enough so that many of them wrote her off.

Let them. It gave her the advantage. And having the advantage gave her power.

As Sloane knew, power came in many forms.

She pulled on her protective gloves and walked to the front of the room, dead center, with the aisle stretching before her, and the two sections of the auditorium split on either side of her.

"So far tonight, you've heard about coping with the aftermath of a physical attack, ways to avoid one, and some profiles of typical victims and assailants," she began. "Every bit of what you learned is true. But there's another truth. We can't always control the circumstances in which we find ourselves. So what happens when you wind up in a parking lot alone at night, your car is ten rows back, and a creepy guy who's built like a Hummer is lying in wait?"

She held out her gloved hands, palms up, to show she was unarmed, then pointed at her pocketless and holsterless black turtleneck and slacks. "I'm dressed just like you would be. No weapon. No handy object to act as one. And no purse, although if I had one, I wouldn't have time to grab for my cell phone or, even better, for a can of pepper spray. That's why I learned Krav Maga."

A spark of interest flickered in the audience's eyes—even those who'd been Doubting Thomases.

"Brief background," she began. "Krav Maga is a whole different breed of self-defense. Its roots trace back to Czechoslovakia during the rise of Nazi terrorism. It was founded by Imi Lichtenfeld, who refined his street-fighting skills protecting his and other Jewish families from attack. Lichtenfeld later emigrated to Israel, further developed those techniques, and then taught them as chief instructor for the Israeli Defense Forces. In Hebrew, *Krav Maga* means 'contact combat'—training designed for the unpredictable nature of street fighting. There are no rules. No trophies for good form. Only survival."

As Sloane spoke, a brawny man wearing a ski mask crept out from behind the curtains at the front of the room, visible to the audience, but not to Sloane.

He whipped a knife out of his pocket and charged forward, leaving Sloane no time to prepare and the audience no time to react.

Grabbing Sloane's left shoulder, he pressed the knife to her back. "Get in my car," he ordered in a gravelly voice.

It was like someone flipped a switch.

Sloane whipped around in a quick body turn. Her left forearm shot forward, locking against his right wrist to deflect the knife attack, and propelling her into the offensive strike of delivering a forward horizontal punch to his throat with her right elbow. As he gasped for air and recoiled from the simulated blow to his throat, her left hand snapped up, pinching his knife-wielding arm in a vise grip between her upper arm, forearm, and chest. The nut-cracking pressure caused the knife to fall from his hand.

Threat obliterated.

Sloane then trapped her assailant's head with her right forearm, grabbed his shoulder with her left hand, and yanked his upper torso down, jerking her knee upward in a lighting strike to his groin.

She stifled a smile as she felt him inadvertently tense and arch away from her, even as he responded on cue, doubling up and crying out as if he'd been castrated. She finished him off with a downward elbow strike to the back of his neck, then pushed him away as he collapsed on the floor, writhing in mock agony.

It was all over in ten seconds.

"I'm crushed by your lack of faith," Sloane murmured as she helped him up, applause filling the auditorium. "I barely tapped your windpipe. Did you really think I'd kick your balls through your nose?"

"Never crossed my mind." His reply was drowned out by the applause. "I know you're a pro. Pure reflex on my part."

"I'll try not to take it personally." Sobering, Sloane turned to address the room. "That was just one example of using Krav Maga in self-defense," she explained. "There are dozens of moves, for whatever threatening situation you may find yourself in. Read the tip sheet I passed out. In it you'll find contact information on local Krav Maga programs. I can't stress training enough. It's empowering, it's practical, and it works." She turned to her attacker, gesturing for him to remove his ski mask. "How about a round of applause for John Jay's own Dr. Elliot Lyman. He was a great demo partner and a good sport."

More applause as Elliot complied.

"Even if you *are* still a chicken," Sloane added under her breath. "Back in high school, you ducked every time I slammed one of your lobs back at you, even though you had seven inches and two years on me. Nothing's changed."

"Then I was a computer geek," he reminded her. "Now I'm a computer-science professor. A nerd who plays with algorithms. Not a kick-ass FBI agent like you."

"*Ex*–FBI agent," she reminded him.

"For now. That'll change."

"Maybe. Maybe not. We'll see." Sloane's jaw tightened in a way that declared the subject closed.

She finished her presentation, answered a slew of questions, and then chatted with her copresenters for a while after the seminar broke up. She knew the John Jay faculty participants from previous workshops they'd given here, and from her visits to Elliot. They'd known each other since her freshman year in high school when she'd tutored him in Spanish and he'd tutored her in computers. They'd stayed in touch afterward, and resumed their friendship when Sloane left the Bureau and moved back east.

An hour later, she was heading for her car, reflecting on the disparate opinions voiced by law enforcement professionals and academicians. Watching silver-haired Lillian Doyle explain the roots of violence in modern-day civilization to Jimmy O'Donnelly, a retired NYPD detective who'd seen every heinous form of violence imaginable, was like watching two people talking two different languages. The louder they spoke, the less they understood each other.

Still, the eclectic composition of the panel was good for the attendees. They'd gotten a varied perspective on the subject of crimes against women. It was also good for the speakers. Neither Jimmy O'Donnelly nor Larry Clark was the type to retire. As for the professors, they reveled in the debates. Especially Lillian Doyle, who, according to Elliot, needed the mental distraction. Her cancer was no longer in remission, and this semester had been a tough one on her.

Sloane herself enjoyed doing these workshops. They were good for her in more ways than one.

She turned up the collar of her coat as a stiff breeze blasted across her face, reminding her that winter wasn't quite over. A throbbing pain shot through her palm, triggering the same vivid flashback as always. The knife, slicing through her flesh. The blood. The pain. It was an image she couldn't escape. It had changed the course of her life.

It had changed her.

Now she winced, belatedly realizing she should have put on her street gloves before venturing outside. Her occupational therapist would be royally pissed if she knew. Well, no point in fishing for them now. She was practically at her car.

A few minutes later, she hopped into her Subaru Outback. It took her extra time to turn the key in the ignition, and she gritted her teeth against the discomfort.

The engine had just turned over when her cell phone rang.

The caller ID read *private*. Not unusual. Most of her clients chose to protect their privacy.

"Sloane Burbank," she said into the mouthpiece.

"Sloane?" a women's tentative voice replied. "This is Hope Truman. Penny's mother. I don't know if you remember me."

"Mrs. Truman—hello—of course I remember you." Sloane's brows arched in surprise. It had been a dozen years since she'd spoken to the Trumans, although she and Penny had been inseparable friends in elementary and middle school. Even afterward, when Penny had gone on to attend a private high school, they'd still gotten together for shop-till-you-drop days and sleepovers. Then social lives, college applications, and life had kicked in, and they'd eventually grown apart and ultimately lost touch. But the memories of their antics, their secret codes, and shared adolescence were the kind that lasted forever, like cherished diaries.

"How are you?" Sloane asked. "And how's Penny? Last I heard she was working her way up the editorial ladder at *Harper's Bazaar.*"

"Then you don't know."

"Know what?"

"That's why I'm calling." Mrs. Truman took a deep breath. "Penny disappeared almost a year ago."

Sloane's spine straightened. "When you say disappeared . . ."

"I mean vanished into thin air. Without a trace. And without a word to Ronald and me. No contact whatsoever."

"No contact from Penny—or from anyone?" Sloane's trained mind kicked into gear. The Trumans were wealthy and high-visibility. Ronald Truman was a renowned cardiologist at Mount Sinai. He was always making medical headlines. And recently his self-help books on keeping your heart healthy had topped the bestseller lists.

Making the Trumans ideal candidates for extortion.

"No contact from anyone," Mrs. Truman was answering.

"You never received a ransom call or note?"

"Never. And God knows, we waited. Trust me, Sloane, we went through every channel and considered every option. Including the unthinkable—that it was a kidnapping gone wrong. But Penny's body was never found." A shaky sigh. "I'm aware of how slim the odds are. It's been eleven months. But she's my daughter. I can't let it go."

"I understand."

Sloane knew a lot more about the odds than Mrs. Truman did. And what she knew made her sick.

"I just read the newspaper article about you and the conference you're speaking at," Mrs. Truman continued. "I had no idea you were an FBI agent, or that you'd left to apply your skills as a private consultant. When I saw those words—it was the first glimmer of hope I've felt in months. We've exhausted all avenues. I remember what close friends you and Penny were. You were inseparable for years. I'm asking you—no, I'm begging you—before you leave Manhattan, would you stop by my apartment? I realize I'm asking a great deal, and with absolutely no notice. I'm willing to pay anything you ask—double or triple your normal rates. I'll have my driver pick you up at the campus and drop you off there afterward. Whatever it takes to—"

"That's not necessary," Sloane interrupted. There were a hundred questions running through her mind. But this situation had to be probed in person. "Penny was a big part of my life. If there's anything I can do, I'll do it. The conference just ended. I'm in the parking lot with my motor running. I'll swing by now, before I head home."

"God bless you." There were tears of gratitude in the older woman's voice.

"What's your address?"

"One twenty-five East Seventy-eighth, between Park and Lex. Apartment 640."

"I'm on my way."

CHAPTER TWO

DATE: 20 March
TIME: 1800 hours
OBJECTIVE: Athena

Finally. She's awake.

This time there's awareness in her eyes. Not like the other times she came to, when she was groggy and disoriented. This time she sees me—*really* sees me. She's quivering. Afraid.

She should be. She knows she's mine.

I can feel that adrenaline rush begin. I'm used to it now, although the first time it caught me by surprise. Not anymore. Now I anticipate it. It feels good. Power. Control. She's resisting, but her struggles are futile. This time I took extra precautions because of her strength and intelligence. Thicker ropes binding her wrists and ankles. Duct tape securing the ropes. The door of her room double-locked.

I didn't gag her. I will when I go out. But no one can hear her. Not from this place.

Breaking her is going to be harder than the last one. But I'll do what I must.

They demand it.

125 East Seventy-eighth Street, Apartment 640

Sloane perched at the edge of the Trumans' elegant antique mahogany-and-damask sofa, sipping the tea that Penny's mother had insisted on brewing. Setting down her cup, she adjusted her pen in a style she'd gotten used to—one that guarded her injury—and flipped open her notebook.

She waited patiently while Hope Truman fluttered about, arranging a plate of ladyfingers.

Ladyfingers. That brought back a slew of memories. Snack time at Penny's, after they'd played Barbies for hours. Penny would stylize her Barbie, choosing fashionable outfits for her, then color- and style-coordinating all her accessories. Sloane would pretend her Barbie was She-ra, Princess of Power, and body parts would fly. It was lucky for Ken that he wasn't anatomically correct.

Back then, ladyfingers had represented a treat. Now they were Hope Truman's way of releasing a burst of nervous energy—desperation and procrastination combined. Sloane recognized the signs. A loved one who wanted results, but was terrified of what they'd be. And after nearly a year? There was nothing to cling to but prayers, nothing to hope for but a miracle.

Sloane was supposed to be that miracle.

Subtly, she studied Penny's mother. At fifty-seven, she'd aged gracefully. Still slender. Well put together. Hair and makeup perfect. Brown cashmere turtleneck sweater and camel slacks that made her a walking ad for Bergdorf.

But it was obvious that this crisis had taken a huge toll.

There were tight lines on her face that had nothing to do with age, and a haunted look in her eyes that Sloane had seen too many times to misread.

"So how are your parents?" Mrs. Truman asked, grasping for chitchat to accompany the normal motions of hostessing.

"They're fine," Sloane replied. "They retired and moved

to Florida—although I use the word *retired* loosely. My mother still works with a few of her favorite authors who were clients at her literary agency, and my dad still handles an occasional art deal if he has an affinity for the piece involved."

"Yes, I remember how much he used to travel abroad—and how often you went with him."

"I loved it. That's how I learned so many languages. It's probably one of the main reasons the Bureau became so interested in recruiting me." Sloane cleared her throat, and gently steered the conversation to where it needed to be. "Do you want to tell me about Penny?"

With an unsteady nod, Mrs. Truman stopped fussing over the refreshments and sank onto the edge of a wingback chair, her fingers tightly interlaced as she spoke. "I apologize for rambling."

"Don't. You're frightened. Striking up ordinary conversation is a natural reaction under circumstances like these."

"Thank you. And thank you for coming," Mrs. Truman repeated. "I can't tell you what it means to me."

"You don't have to." Sloane leaned forward. "Mrs. Truman . . ."

"Hope," the older woman corrected. Her lips curved ever so slightly. "You're not a child anymore. I think we can dispense with the formalities."

Sloane returned the faint smile. "Okay—Hope. I can only imagine what an ordeal this has been for you and your husband. You said Penny disappeared a year ago?"

"As of April fourteenth, yes, it will be a year. Although we didn't find out she was missing until several days afterward."

"Tell me all the details you can."

Hope nodded, resorting to autopilot as she retold a story she'd probably told a dozen times before. "The fourteenth was a Saturday. She didn't show up at work on the sixteenth or the seventeenth. She didn't call in either day. Her assistant at the magazine tried to reach her at home and on her cell. No answer. The morning of the seventeenth, she was scheduled to meet her friend Amy for breakfast. Amy and Penny roomed together after college graduation for two or three years. Ronald and I have met Amy many times. She's lovely. When Penny didn't keep their breakfast date, and Amy had no luck finding her at her office or with any of her friends, she called us."

"And you called the police."

Hope nodded. "They ran down every lead they could. Eventually, they learned that a woman matching Penny's description had bought a bus ticket to Atlantic City on April fourteenth. At that point, they brought in the FBI."

"Which field office handled the case—New York or Newark?"

"New York, although they worked closely with Newark. It didn't matter. Neither turned up anything. Either the woman they thought was Penny never arrived in Atlantic City or there were no witnesses who remembered seeing her."

"What about a credit-card receipt for the ticket?"

"Another dead end. Whoever bought that ticket paid cash."

Sloane's brow furrowed. "This doesn't sit right. I realize Penny and I hadn't been in touch in ages, but she wanted to write for a fashion magazine since we were eleven. Plus, she was always conscientious. Unless she made a complete one-eighty—"

"She didn't."

"Then didn't the fact that she missed work for two days without so much as a phone call raise any red flags at *Harper's Bazaar*?"

"Yes . . . and no." Hope took a shaky sip of tea. "It seems Penny was going through a rough patch at work. Something about being passed over for a promotion. It was a rocky time for her. Not just professionally, but personally. According to Penny's assistant, Rosalinda, Penny had been seeing someone and the relationship had just broken up. So when Penny didn't come in, Rosalinda covered for her. She told everyone at the magazine that Penny was working at home. When the FBI questioned her, she admitted that Penny had left the office the previous day in tears, saying something about what a mess her life was and how she was ready to pack it in."

"At that point, did Penny get in touch with you?" Sloane asked carefully.

"No, not that day. We spoke about a week earlier." Hope Truman cleared her throat. "If you're asking if we were close, I'd say we were—as a mother and daughter. We weren't girlfriends. She was a private person. She didn't confide in me about her personal life. So if she went through a breakup, she didn't mention it. But splitting up with a boyfriend can hardly be compared to dropping off the face of the earth. If Penny had planned on doing that, she would never have done so without a word to her father and me. Nor would she have done so without taking her personal belongings or making final arrangements with her landlord, her bank, and her utility companies. Plus, none of her credit cards has been used since her disappearance."

"What was the FBI's theory on all that?"

"That the combination of personal issues in her life might have overwhelmed her. That she might have become depressed. And that severe depression sometimes causes people to behave in ways that are inconsistent with their personalities."

Sloane hid her skepticism. Translated, the investigators were saying that Penny either lost it and ran off to start a new life, severing all ties with her old one, or she committed suicide. Well, suicide would have produced a body and probably a note. And fleeing to start over? That theory was extreme. Especially since a year had passed. By now, Penny would have contacted her family, let them know she was okay.

None of that reasoning cheered Sloane up. Because the alternatives were far more gruesome.

"I know all the terrifying thoughts that are going through your mind right now," Hope said. "I've agonized over every one of them for almost a year. None of this fits. But I have nowhere to turn. I check in with the FBI periodically. The agent at the New York field office who's handling the case is always polite, always willing to check out anything Ronald and I come up with. But I'm not a fool. They've put this case on the back burner. Unless some new lead materializes . . ."

"Let me talk to them," Sloane suggested. "I have contacts in the New York field office. I'll explain the situation and tell them you've hired me. They'll set up a meeting between me and the special agent in charge of your case. He or she will bring me up to speed. That'll help me decide on the best course of action." Sloane's pen poised over the page. "What's his or her name?"

"His. Special Agent Parker."

Sloane's chin came up. "Derek Parker?"

A nod. "Why? Do you know him?"

"Yes. I know him." Sloane went back to writing. "We worked together in the Cleveland field office." She shut her notebook and set aside her teacup. "I'll contact New York first thing tomorrow and set up a meeting with him. I'll call you right afterward and fill you in. We'll take it from there."

Mrs. Truman's lips trembled. "Thank you, Sloane."

"Thank me when I have some answers." *And pray that those answers aren't what I expect.*

Sloane rose. She wasn't looking forward to this. The whole situation sucked. Her objectivity was compromised on both sides. The odds that Penny was alive stunk. And given who the agent in charge was, the cooperation would stink, too.

She'd have to pull a few favors, set up this meeting without Derek knowing about it in advance. That would take away his home-court advantage and give her an edge—at least going in.

After that, all bets were off.

CHAPTER
THREE

Where am I?

Oh my God. Where is he?

It's been hours since he left. Or does it just feel that way? He gagged me. I begged him not to. I promised not to scream. I couldn't if I tried. My mouth is so dry. My throat is raw. But he said the gag was a test. A test for what?

My mind is fuzzy. I can't remember how I got here or how long it's been. Snatches of memory flicker, then scatter like dust. It must be the drugs.

What does he want?

He won't tell me. All he says is that I'll know when the time is right, and that if I'm good, he'll leave off the gag and untie the ropes.

The mattress I'm on smells stale. So does the blanket. It's scratchy, but at least it's something to wrap myself in to stave off the chill. I thanked him when he gave it to me. He looked pleased.

Still, I'm so cold. My whole body aches. A rough blanket and a musty mattress do little to cushion this hard, bare floor. It feels like concrete. The room's small, like a child's bedroom. I can't see much. He keeps it dimly lit. There's a tiny window, but the curtains are drawn. It's like I'm locked in some kind of a cage. By myself. Earlier today, I heard another voice through the wall. A woman's voice. At least I thought I did. Maybe I was hallucinating. I can't focus.

What is he going to do to me?

I'm not sure what's more terrifying—finding out his plan, or lying here, helpless and waiting.

Footsteps. Coming toward the room. A key turning.

Please, God, let someone have found me. Let this nightmare end.

No. Oh no. It's him. He's back.

And he's back for me.

FBI New York Field Office
26 Federal Plaza, New York City
March 24

It had taken some doing, but the Asian Criminal Enterprise Task Force—C-6 as the squad was designated in the New York field office—had finally gotten a Title III so they could wiretap Chen Long Hua's phone. A damn good thing, too, considering what they'd intercepted and pieced together from his cryptic Friday-night call. A third prostitute had been killed. Same MO, different location, according to what the Bureau had learned from the NYPD. The second prostitute had been killed in Manhattan, the first and third in Queens. No tangible link between them other than their occupation and the fact that they were Asian. Except that they all had been taken to an abandoned building, drugged, and subjected to repeated, violent sex, then killed, their throats slit with a combat knife. In all three cases, the only thing left behind had been a copper coin with a python on one side and a Greek goddess on the other. Probably the killer's sick idea of payment for services rendered.

And there was one other connection. All three women worked at one of three Fukienese brothels the Bureau had linked to Chen—who was known on the streets as Xiao Long or "Little Dragon," the leader, or Dai Lo, of the Red Dragons.

Chen had been ripping mad in his Friday-night phone

call to his enforcer. He was convinced that Lo Ma, a.k.a.
"Old Horse" and his gang, the Black Tigers, were responsible for killing his girls and trying to put him out of business. He wanted revenge. And he wanted it now.

Special Agent Derek Parker took a gulp of lukewarm
coffee and turned back to his computer. His squad had kept
an eye on the Red Dragons all weekend. The gang had been
suspiciously quiet. That meant they were planning something. If C-6 wasn't all over this like white on rice, an all-
out turf war could erupt. Proactive measures had already
been taken. Derek had alerted the NYPD's Fifth Precinct
in Chinatown and the 109th Precinct in Flushing to flood
the areas with patrol cars. Reinforcements were ready to
move in if Chen's guys showed up in numbers.

Scanning his monitor, Derek continued typing up the
FD-302 that detailed Friday night's surveillance. He ignored the *bing* that announced the arrival of another e-mail.
He'd already made a conscious decision to ignore all of
them, even though his in-box was exploding in typical
Monday-morning fashion. What he was doing took prece-
dence over everything else. He was working a volatile case,
with links to international organized crime. This pissing
match between Xiao Long and Lo Ma could screw up years
of hard work.

The Bureau had invested a lot in this investigation.
They'd sent Derek down to Quantico for two weeks of specialized training. When he returned to the New York field
office, he was reassigned to C-6. With one special agent out
on maternity leave and another two transferred to counterterrorism, C-6 was short-staffed at a time they couldn't afford to be.

Derek had been a logical choice to move to that squad.
He'd worked just about every kind of violent crime, from
kidnapping and extortion to bank robberies and murder for
hire. His previous investigations had led him to cross paths
with the key gang members currently under surveillance.
He knew the players. He knew the turf.

And now he knew the drill.

With a quick glance at his watch, Derek saw he was running right on schedule. Eight-thirty. Early for this squad, who worked the streets till all hours of the night. Not for him. His Ranger training had taken care of that. The army had taught him leadership, respect, loyalty, and discipline. Those traits had stayed with him—discipline included. Up at six-thirty. Workout from seven to eight. Shower and dress. Grab a quick, high-protein breakfast. Then report for duty.

"Derek, good, you're at your desk."

Derek swiveled around to see his squad leader, SSA Antonio Sanchez, standing beside his cubicle, elbow perched on the divider.

"Hey, Tony," he greeted him. "I didn't know you were in yet."

"Ditto. I thought you might show up a little late, since you worked half the weekend. Besides, your targets are first heading off to bed."

"Yeah, but after what we heard Friday night and an eerily quiet weekend, it feels like we're perched on a keg of dynamite. We can't afford a full-scale gang war. I'm getting things in order for the U.S. attorney's office. Early this afternoon, I've got a couple of interviews with our informants. They'll be wired and hitting the streets to pick up on any neighborhood vibes. The NYPD is doing their thing. And the squad and I will rotate shifts in the van, listening."

Tony gave an emphatic nod. At forty-five, he'd been with the Bureau for sixteen years. He was tight with his squad, but he was every bit a leader. He was shrewd. He was intense. And he knew his team. Including its newest member.

"There's no doubt that a strike is imminent. Do what you have to. But plan on a short interruption around ten. There's a meeting I need you to take."

Derek's brows rose. "When did this come up?"

"Over the weekend. It'll only chew up half an hour of your time."

"What's it about, and who's it with?"

"It's about the Penelope Truman case. You're the case agent of record. The Trumans requested that you meet with the new consultant her parents just hired."

The Truman case? That was the last thing Derek had expected. That case had been cold for nearly a year. Plus, it was a missing persons case, unrelated to anything handled by C-6. So why was Tony inserting himself, especially when it wasn't his style to volunteer one of his team members without any forewarning?

"I don't get it," Derek stated bluntly. "Is there some new lead I don't know about? Did the Trumans hear from their daughter?"

"I wasn't given any specifics." Tony straightened and turned back toward his office. "Just call up the file, print out the related paperwork, and take the meeting. Answer whatever questions you can, as cooperatively as you can." A pause. "Consider it a personal favor."

"A personal favor," Derek repeated slowly. "For who?"

"Me. The Trumans. And a couple of our people down in CIRG."

It was almost time.

Sloane wandered around the table in the small meeting room on the twenty-second floor, rolling her bottle of Poland Spring between her palms and steeling herself.

The next half hour was *not* going to be fun. Then again, at least she knew who'd be walking through that door in— she glanced at her watch, aware that Derek was always punctual—precisely three minutes. He, on the other hand, was about to be coldcocked.

She'd called in a favor from Tony Sanchez, who'd mentored her during her hostage negotiation training in Quantico. He'd been kind enough to set things up, no questions asked, even when she requested that her name be withheld during the orchestration of the meeting.

Maybe he knew about the history between her and Derek. Maybe not.

Her bottle of water hit a tender spot in the curve between her thumb and forefinger, and Sloane winced at the contact. She used her left hand to set the bottle on the table and cap it, grimacing as the throbbing in her right hand continued. It wasn't just the injury. The scars themselves were really bothering her today. Her physical-therapy session this afternoon was going to hurt like hell.

She began performing some simple pain-relief exercises, bending and straightening her fingers, then stretching them to relax the muscles.

The conference room door blew open, and Derek strode into the room. He had a file folder tucked under his arm, and that same cocky walk Sloane remembered all too well. It had been thirteen months, but one quick glance told her he hadn't changed—at least not intrinsically. The surface was another matter entirely. His dark hair was longer than before and his attire was a one-eighty. Derek had always been a suit-and-tie kind of guy. Now he was wearing jeans and a navy T-shirt. Sloane couldn't help but do a slight double take on that one.

Even without knowing who he was about to cross paths with, he clearly didn't want to be here. His entire body language told her that.

It got worse. His probing stare found her, and his midnight-blue gaze went from brooding to glacial.

"Sloane." He said her name as if seeking confirmation that this wasn't really happening.

"Hello, Derek." Sloane had rehearsed her opening. No physical contact. Not even a handshake. No proximity. She stayed where she was, letting the table act as a barrier between them. "Right on time, as always. Excellent. I appreciate your taking this meeting. I see you printed out file information. That'll give me a jump start. Shall we begin?" She gestured for him to take a seat.

"You're the Trumans' consultant?" he demanded.

"Guilty as charged."

"And you asked Tony not to mention that."

Clearly, he wasn't going to make this easy.

"Guilty again. I couldn't risk your refusing to come. So I asked Tony not to mention my name."

"Obviously nothing's changed. You're still a coward."

"And you're still a judgmental hard-ass. Adhering to a new dress code, I see. But otherwise the same."

"The dress code's part of the job. You can't blend into the gang world wearing a suit."

"Point taken. And, hey, the jeans and T-shirt are as crisp and wrinkle-free as your suits. Different uniform, same Army Ranger."

"Ditto for the Manhattan A.D.A.," Derek countered, referring to her pre-FBI days as a New York City prosecutor.

"Touché." Sloane acknowledged his dig with a tight nod. "Now that we've gotten the cutting remarks out of the way, can we talk about Penny Truman?"

"Why? Do you have a new lead?"

"I won't know until you run through your case file with me."

"I'm sure you already have all the facts. And unless you've become psychic, there's nothing for you to find. I realize the Trumans are desperate for answers, and that they have the money to pay an outside consultant to find them. But you're wasting your time. I covered all the bases, and then some."

Sloane gripped the back of her chair and leveled a hard stare at Derek. "Leave your ego at the door, Derek. This isn't about your skills as an agent. Yes, the Trumans are desperate. But they didn't just call me because I'm good and because I can devote more time and resources to their case than the Bureau can. They called me for personal reasons. Penny and I were once close friends. We went through school together. I had no idea she was missing until her mother called me last week. If you need to justify my involvement in the case, use that. Spin it any way you want to. All I want is to find Penny."

The tension in Derek's jaw slackened a bit. "I wasn't aware of any of this. Fine. Have a seat."

Simultaneously, they pulled out chairs and sat down, facing each other across the table.

"Why didn't the Trumans mention you when I questioned them?" Derek asked.

"Because Penny and I hadn't been in touch for a while." Sloane filled him in on the background of their friendship. "But I did know her—well. And there's no way she'd just take off like that, not because of a job, not because of a guy. She's either being held against her will, or dead."

One dark brow rose.

"Yes, I'm aware the odds favor the latter," Sloane responded. "That doesn't mean I'm ready to call it quits—not without a fight."

"I guess some things are worth fighting for. Others aren't."

Sloane gritted her teeth as the pointed barb found its mark. She'd throw it right back in his face, if his implication didn't have merit. Plus, she wasn't here to fight. She was here for Penny.

On that thought, she stuck to the case. "When you interviewed Penny's friends, coworkers, ex-boyfriend, did your gut tell you anything the evidence couldn't support?"

"Nope." Derek's reply was terse. "No red flags. I got the usual—apprehension over what happened to Penelope, jitters over talking to the FBI, and alibis that all checked out."

"Including the one provided by Penny's ex-boyfriend?"

"Yup. He was in Honolulu all week—with the colleague he dumped your friend for." Derek slid the file across the table. "Read it for yourself. It's all there. Copies of everything—a list of everyone Penelope knew, my interviews with each of them, details of her life during the months preceding her disappearance. Also, the names and phone numbers of the agents I worked with in the Newark field office. Take the file. Dig as deep as you want to. But after eleven months, I'd steel myself for the worst."

"That's par for the course these days. Steeling myself for the worst is the only way to survive." Sloane picked up the file, pausing as she gazed down at it. "How long have you been in New York?" she heard herself ask.

"A year."

"So you got the transfer right away?"

"We both knew I would. This field office was my first assignment out of Quantico. I spent seven years here before Cleveland. And with so many Bureau members transferring to counterterrorism since 9/11, and so few new agents requesting assignments in New York over the sunny south, a seasoned agent who'd worked Violent Crimes and kidnappings looked pretty damned good."

"Still on SWAT?"

"Enhanced SWAT," he corrected. "A bigger team. More sophisticated equipment. New York's not Cleveland. Ten percent of the Bureau works here."

"Including you now. You've also done some internal transferring since you got back. You moved from Violent Crimes to C-6."

"My cases shifted. The subjects were into narcotics and gangs. So my transfer to C-6 was a logical step."

"Tony spoke highly of you. He also mentioned that you just got back from a CE training course at Quantico. You're building quite a diverse résumé."

"Diversity's good. It keeps you challenged and in demand." Derek leaned forward, and Sloane could feel his hard stare without looking up. "What about you—enjoying the life of a high-paid consultant?"

"It keeps me challenged and in demand," she parroted back, her chin coming up. "Plus, being my own boss is gratifying—no red tape." Inadvertently, she gripped the file folder more tightly, causing the edge to dig into her palm right where the scars were. She flinched, and released the file.

Derek's glance flickered from her hand to her face. His expression didn't change. "Still in pain?"

"Yeah, well, a two-inch knife slash will do that to you. So will three surgeries, and thirteen months of physical therapy." Sloane wasn't looking for sympathy, nor did she expect any—not from Derek. "That's another reason being in my own business makes sense. I need the time flexibility. My hand therapist and I see a lot of each other."

"*Three* surgeries?" Derek's eyes narrowed in puzzlement. He'd only been in her life for the first—the emergency surgery that had been performed to stop her from bleeding to death. "Why?"

"Complications," Sloane replied tersely. "Excess scarring, grafting a ruptured tendon, nerve damage—let's just say it's been a busy year." Gathering up Penny's file, Sloane rose, her body language declaring the subject closed. "I've taken up enough of your time. I appreciate your candor and your thoroughness. If I pick up the slightest lead on Penny's whereabouts, I'll advise you immediately."

"Here's my direct contact information." Still scrutinizing her, Derek came to his feet, handing her the familiar Bureau card with the official FBI logo on it, along with his own private extension and cell-phone number.

"Thanks." Sloane responded in kind, whipping out one of her business cards and passing it across the table. "There you go. I doubt you'll have any cause to reach me, but just in case, everything you need is on there."

Derek glanced down at the card, which had her office and cell-phone numbers on it, but was devoid of a street address, listing Sloane's office only as a PO box in Hunterdon County, New Jersey. "You're working out of your parents' vacation house," he surmised.

"Living there, too. My folks retired to Florida. I bought the house from them. It's perfect for my needs. Small, airy, with an extra room for my office, and four country acres to explore. My hounds like that. So does my archery course."

"You're shooting again."

"Just recently. And just a bow and arrow."

"Why? Target practice is target practice. A bow, a gun— what's the difference?"

"About four pounds of trigger-finger pressure and a lot of dexterity and control. Right now I have none of those. It's possible I never will." Sloane walked around the table, passing Derek without a backward glance, and heading for the door. "But, like I said, it's good to see you haven't changed. Same empathetic guy. Always ready to cut a person some slack. I'll be in touch."

CHAPTER FOUR

DATE: 24 March
TIME: 2200 hours

I crave my time in this room.

Peace, solitude, fulfillment. There's nothing but me, my thoughts, and her. Being here renews my focus and my strength. And it keeps the demons away.

But only when I'm behind these doors.

I spent hours with Athena tonight. As I suspected, preparing her is harder than the others. She's young. Intelligent. An unwelcome obstacle. Especially now. I must finish. But it exhausts me.

When I left her, I had to come here. I needed the relief—and the reminder. My resolve has to win out over my weariness. She reminds me of that. She reminds me that I have to channel my energy, even when they scream for justice. Justice delivered by my hand. And she'll be my muse.

I don't want to leave here. I want to shut my eyes and breathe, inhale her scent, visualize her beauty. Then I'll sleep—maybe for an hour or two. It's the only time I do, the only place I can.

The demons are lying in wait just outside. Once I open the door, leave this sanctuary, they'll consume me again.

And I'll do exactly as they command.

Hunterdon County, New Jersey
March 25, 10:15 A.M.

It was that kind of cold, drizzly morning that made you want to pull the comforter over your head and go back to sleep.

Unfortunately, Sloane didn't have that option. Not only was she buried in work, but her hounds, as she lovingly called them, wanted no part of sleeping in, or in allowing her to do so.

The term *hounds,* albeit accurate, seemed like a misnomer when it came to Sloane's three troublemakers. Moe, Larry, and Curly were three miniature dachshunds Sloane had adopted from animal rescue two years ago, as puppies. Moe—short for Mona—was long-haired and the sole female of the trio, Larry was wire-haired, and Curly was a sleek, bald frankfurter—the traditional smooth, short-haired variety. All three of the pups had boundless energy, strong personalities, and were loving and loyal—except when they were fighting.

Today, like every other day, they'd leaped up at daybreak, badgered Sloane until she let them out to do their "business"—which they did as quickly as possible to escape the rain. They then raced through the house and jumped all over the bed, wreaking havoc with Sloane and her bedding until she relinquished any idea of going back to sleep.

It was just as well. Penny's case was weighing heavily on her mind. She had a lot to accomplish in very little time. Two days, to be exact. After that, she was heading up to Boston, where she was conducting a two-day crisis management and resolution training program at the corporate headquarters of a multinational bank. She was catching a 6 A.M. flight up to Logan Airport on Thursday. Which gave her just today and tomorrow to make some headway.

Settled on the cushy lounge in her home office, with Moe, Larry, and Curly sprawled around her, Sloane reread Derek's report on Penny's alleged Atlantic City trip—again.

Then she shoved the papers aside and sank back into the cushion. She'd read the file cover to cover three times. No red flags. Still, she kept being drawn back to Atlantic City. It didn't make sense. Why would Penny go there? She'd grown up wealthy, but practical. Her philosophy about money was simple: spend, but only on those things that mattered. Which to Penny meant her appearance, her education, and anything relating to a career in fashion writing.

Sloane could still remember their annual Christmas outings to FAO Schwarz, when they were kids. She herself was a stuffed-animal freak; she'd run from display to display, unable to decide, wanting to buy everything. Penny would stand off to a side, sizing up the inventory and eventually choosing the stuffed toy that matched her room and conveyed an aura of elegance.

Gambling? Never—not when Sloane knew her. Penny would think that was wasteful and stupid.

Just in case her friend's habits had changed, Sloane had scrutinized Penny's credit-card statements. Nope. Same old Penny. Itemized charges for a designer wardrobe and accessories that were in sync with someone climbing the corporate ladder at *Harper's Bazaar*. Also, charges for extracurricular courses in everything from modern art to ancient philosophy. No surprises there either. Penny always prided herself on being cultured and well rounded. She loved to learn.

None of those charges was beyond the scope of what her salary could cover. As for gambling, there was absolutely no indication of it in her financial records or the behavioral descriptions provided by her friends and colleagues—and not even a single lottery ticket found in her apartment.

Maybe Penny had planned to meet someone in Atlantic City. But, if so, wouldn't that person have called when she didn't arrive? Sloane had checked Penny's cell-phone records, which had been retrieved by court order. They indicated that no calls had been made or received since April 14—the day of her disappearance.

One dead end after another. Derek hadn't lied. He'd been every bit as thorough as he'd claimed, leaving no stone unturned.

Sloane would have to rely on her knowledge of Penny to spot a tiny, unnoticed stone and flip it over, hoping to find something beneath it.

Grabbing a pad and pen, she made a list of the people Penny was closest to at the time of her disappearance. It was time to reinterview every one of them—starting with the ex-boyfriend. Maybe if Sloane asked the right questions, she'd provoke an answer, however innocent, that held the filaments of a clue.

She was still writing when her cell phone rang.

Preoccupied with what she was doing, she picked up the phone automatically and punched it on, anchoring it in the curve of her shoulder and pressing it to her ear. "Sloane Burbank."

"Hey, Sloane. It's Bob Erwin."

"Bob . . . hi." Sloane put down her pen. Bob was a sergeant with the NYPD's Midtown North Precinct. He'd consulted with Sloane several times in the past, and attended two of her daylong workshops on workplace violence. "What's up?"

"I'm not sure." Bob cleared his throat. "Evidently, we've got a missing college student. Name's Cynthia Alexander. Twenty years old. Last seen on her college campus a week ago Sunday. But that's not necessarily the day she disappeared. It was spring break. The school was pretty deserted. She was supposed to fly home this past Thursday night for a long weekend. She bought the ticket—round-trip. But she never showed, so her parents called the cops. She could be a runaway. She could be a kidnapping victim. Or she could be a free-spirited college junior who took some chill-out time and is going to show up any minute. Who the hell knows? I've got a team of detectives looking into it."

Sloane's brows knit. The scenario Bob had just presented was all too commonplace. College students often took off on a whim, then returned when they were ready. But even if the NYPD suspected foul play, there'd be no reason to call her. Not unless there was more to this than what she'd just been told.

"Okay, Bob, what aren't you saying?" she asked bluntly. "Is this girl from a prominent or political family? Did she take someone with her when she vanished into thin air—possibly against that someone's will? Is the president of the university putting pressure on you that would be relieved by your being able to say you're working with a consultant? Is the precinct trying to up its conviction numbers, or feeling squeezed to resolve this before turning it over to Missing Persons?" A pause. "Did I leave anything out?"

A tight chuckle. "I keep forgetting you used to be a kick-ass prosecutor. Remind me never to get on your bad side. No to all the above. Average girl, average family, disappeared alone and without hostages, and no internal pressure. Although Missing Persons is swamped and I'd love to solve this case in a week so I don't have to dump it in their laps. On the other hand, if Cynthia Alexander was kidnapped en route, it's an interstate matter, since she's from Ohio. So it might be the FBI we'll have to call in."

"Well, since I'm no longer FBI, why are you calling me?"

"Cynthia's from Cleveland. In which case it's possible the case might fall into the jurisdiction of your old FBI field office. I'd want a rundown on your contacts there so I could direct this to whoever would be most helpful. But more immediately, I'm hoping you can narrow down the time frame of Cynthia's disappearance. The campus she vanished from was John Jay. She was registered for that two-day workshop you were a panelist on, which is why she didn't leave earlier for spring break. I'm trying to ascertain whether or not she actually attended the conference. We're talking to all the speakers. But when I saw your name on that list, I was thrilled. I know you had an auditorium filled with people, but I also know you have a mind like a steel trap. I don't expect you to remember her by name. But I'd like to show you some photos. Maybe something will click."

Sloane blew out a breath. "When did you want to do this?"

"Today, if possible. The sooner the better. Are you completely tied up?"

"Always. But how about this—let me make some calls, set up a few interviews on a case I'm working on. Then I'll drive into Manhattan. We can meet at John Jay. Two of my other workshop presenters are professors there. With class back in session, they should be available. In the meantime, you contact the rest of the panelists. The more of us that can look at those photos, the better chance you'll have of someone recognizing Cynthia Alexander."

"I've already put in those calls. How does two o'clock sound? We can meet in the same auditorium you spoke in. There's no lecture going on in there until four-thirty."

"Sounds like a plan. Count me in."

John Jay College of Criminal Justice
New York City
2 P.M.

As it worked out, this timing was perfect, Sloane thought as she hurried into the building. She'd arranged a meeting with a group of Penny's colleagues at *Harper's Bazaar* at four-fifteen, a quick drink with Penny's old roommate, Amy, at five-thirty, and a dash down to Wall Street for a cup of coffee with Doug Waters, Penny's ex, at seven. That gave her an hour plus now to help out the NYPD on this missing college kid, then do some in-depth interviews probing Penny's state of mind at the time of her disappearance.

Tomorrow, she'd pore over the interviews, follow up on any leads she might spot, then call Hope Truman with an update. After that, she had a hand-therapy session, some romp time with the hounds before she brought them over to her neighbor, and an evening of putting the finishing touches on her latest presentation before she packed a bag and fell into bed.

The bank execs wanted the works—including a simulated barricade with hostages. Well, they'd be getting one. By the time Sloane hopped onto the plane for her return flight, the staff would be able to handle whatever was thrown their way.

Practically vibrating with energy, Sloane took the stairs at John Jay at a dead run, yanking off her gloves and scarf, and unbuttoning her coat as she dashed through the auditorium door.

She spotted Sergeant Erwin right away. In his early forties, he was tall and thin, with salt-and-pepper hair and the kind of pleasant face that often gave perps a false sense of security—enough to talk freely about things they shouldn't without an attorney present, and wind up behind bars.

Right now he was perched at the edge of the table Sloane had sat behind last week, reviewing photos with her fellow "Crimes Against Women" speakers.

"Hi, Bob."

"Sloane, great, you're here." He beckoned her over. "Take a look at some of these and see if they ring any bells."

Tossing a general wave of greeting to the rest of the group, Sloane inclined her head in Bob's direction. "Anything yet?"

"Not from me." SVU detective Jimmy O'Donnelly scrutinized the last photo and the police report and pushed both of them away.

"I can't offer anything either," Sharon McNally said apologetically.

The two of them stood up, said their good-byes, and prepared to leave.

"Thanks, anyway." Bob turned back to watch Sloane scan the photos. "I appreciate your taking the time to come in. I could have e-mailed all this to you, but I was hoping that if the bunch of you got together, maybe one of you would notice something that would jog the others' memories."

Sloane was only half listening. Chewing her lower lip, she was concentrating on the photos of Cynthia Alexander. An all-American girl. Pretty, tall, with long dark hair, green eyes, and a firm, athletic figure. Not a surprise, given that the police report said she was captain of the swim team. In two of the photos she was wearing a varsity jacket and in another she was dripping wet but proudly brandishing a team trophy. Sloane got it. She herself had been captain of the swim team and the tennis team back in her undergrad days at Penn State. The adrenaline high of a win, the thrill of competing—it was a rush. She could see that mirrored in Cynthia's eyes.

"Do you recognize her?" Bob asked.

"Unfortunately, no. Have you talked to her swim coach yet?"

"Yup. Cynthia has never missed a practice. She's cool under pressure. She doesn't drink—not even beer. And there's no signs she's into drugs."

"Not a surprise. Not a great omen either—not in this case." Sloane frowned. "It contradicts the theory that she's off on some who-gives-a-damn weeklong bash. Lack of discipline and varsity sports don't mesh."

"I know. Neither does the background info we're getting on Cynthia Alexander and the idea of her being a spring-break party girl. According to everyone we've interviewed, she's a loner—into school, sports, and music. From a close-knit family. No emotional baggage. No boyfriend, no tight crowd of girlfriends, no car. Hangs out in the library or with her fellow swim-team members. Responsible and punctual. And frugal when it comes to money. Not exactly someone who'd register for a workshop, buy plane tickets to go home, and chuck both."

Sloane tilted her head in Bob's direction. "What about Cynthia's parents? Where are they now?"

"Her father's camped out at the Cleveland police station, and her mother's camped out at ours."

"Right." Sloane recognized the scenario. It was the ultimate expression of hope. Cynthia's parents needed to believe that their daughter was alive and would magically reappear, unharmed, with a perfectly logical explanation. At the same time, they were realistic enough to understand that if something traumatic had happened to their child, she'd need a loved one there to comfort and support her when she resurfaced.

"The Alexanders are playing it smart," Sloane concluded aloud. "By splitting up and posting themselves on either end, they're making sure that whichever city Cynthia surfaces in, she won't be alone. This way, they can offer maximum help to the authorities and to their daughter." Pausing, Sloane blew out her breath. "I don't have a good feeling about this. If you and the Cleveland police decide to bring in the FBI, I can contact my old field office for you. In the meantime, you mentioned that it's *Mrs.* Alexander who's in Manhattan. I'd like to talk to her. I know you have many competent female detectives, and I'm not trying to step on any toes, but . . ."

"But you have a special way with people," Bob finished for her. "I've seen it firsthand. So, if our investigation goes nowhere and Cynthia doesn't show up in the next few days, I'll take you up on both your offers." An uneasy pause. "Which my instincts tell me I'll be doing."

"This scenario never gets easier." Sloane picked up the paperwork Bob had brought, flipping through the police report until she found Cynthia's spring schedule. "Most of the courses Cynthia's registered for are literature and social sciences."

"Which is why Dr. Hewitt didn't recognize her. He teaches math and stats. Cynthia's major is Humanities and Justice. Dr. Doyle would be a better bet, since she teaches sociology and Cynthia took two of her classes—one last year, one last semester. We're waiting for Dr. Doyle to arrive. Her son is driving her in."

Sloane's brow furrowed. "She's not on campus?"

"Doctor's appointment," Bob supplied.

"Ah." Sloane nodded sympathetically. "From what Elliot told me, her cancer is no longer in remission, and the prognosis doesn't look good. I feel terrible about that. Lillian is an intelligent, caring woman." Something in Cynthia's academic schedule caught Sloane's eye. "Speaking of Elliot, have you spoken with him? Cynthia took a computer course last semester. He might have been her professor."

"Elliot?" Bob spread his hands in a questioning gesture.

"Dr. Lyman. He's a computer-science whiz. He teaches here. Primarily on the graduate level, but he does teach one or two undergrad courses."

"He wasn't on the list of panelists at your workshop."

"He wasn't actually a panelist. He helped me with a demonstration. But he was definitely there through my whole presentation."

"Great. I'll send for him now."

While Bob was contacting the computer-science department, the door to the lecture hall opened and Lillian Doyle made her way in. She looked as if she'd had a trying day. Her step was a trifle unsteady, and she was leaning on her son's arm. She was visibly more peaked than she'd been last Thursday at the seminar.

"Hello, Sloane." Depleted or not, Lillian was obviously determined to conceal her limitations to the best of her ability. She straightened her spine and smiled as she approached Sloane. "I hope I haven't held up the process. The police said something about a missing student?"

"Yes." Sloane felt a wave of sadness. It didn't take a doctor to see that Lillian was going downhill rapidly. "But I'm sure Sergeant Erwin will keep his interview with you brief." She turned, giving a sympathetic glance to the man standing beside Lillian. "Hi, Luke."

"I'm sorry. Where are my manners?" Lillian murmured. "You two remember each other, right?"

"Right, Mother." Luke's smile was weary. "Sloane's been back in New York for a year now. We've managed to grab an occasional cup of coffee together, despite her busy schedule. How are you, Sloane?"

"Overworked, but fine." She smiled back, thinking that Luke had aged even in the couple of months since she'd seen him. He looked as drained as his mother. Clearly, he was suffering as he watched her deteriorate. "How about you?"

"Can't complain. Bellevue's been great about rearranging my shifts. So I've had more time to fine-tune my chess and other board-game skills in order to take on my mother. Although she's still the reigning champ. I can't touch her when it comes to the Book Lover's edition of Trivial Pursuit, or the Age of Mythology."

Lillian pooh-poohed him, but Sloane could see that Luke's praise had lifted her spirits. He was the same reserved, gentle guy Sloane had met seven years ago. Clean-cut and ruggedly built, he had a reassuring demeanor and a solid presence that emanated comfort and strength—even at a time of personal crisis. He was obviously Lillian's caretaker. Well, no one was better suited for the job. Sloane had seen that firsthand on the day they met: 9/11—the day the world had changed forever.

She'd been at Bellevue Hospital in her capacity as an A.D.A., interviewing a witness for the prosecution. Luke was employed at Bellevue as a medical assistant—a job he was well qualified for. He'd served as a combat medic in the army, stationed overseas in South Korea at Camp Casey.

When the chaos of the terrorist attacks erupted, Sloane had run into the corridor to see what was going on. She literally collided with Luke. The badge on his white uniform and the photo ID clipped to his pocket told Sloane who and what he was.

He'd worked tirelessly. She'd helped as best she could.

And together they'd endured the fallout from the day's heinous events. That kind of shared experience forged a bond that was hard to explain.

It was certainly motivation enough to stay in touch.

"How's your hand doing?" Luke was asking.

"Some good days, some bad," Sloane replied, snapping back to the present. "I take it one baby step at a time."

As she spoke, Sloane noticed that Lillian was leaning more heavily on Luke's arm. It was time to get the poor woman's input on Cynthia Alexander and let her go home. "Sergeant Erwin is over there," Sloane told her, pointing in his direction. "Why don't we get you settled in a comfortable chair and let him talk to you."

"Thank you." Flanked by Luke and Sloane, Lillian made her way over to the cluster of chairs and the table where the photos were laid out. Beside it, Sergeant Erwin had snapped his cell phone shut and was watching their approach.

"Who's the missing student?" Lillian asked Sloane.

"Cynthia Alexander. I don't know if you remember her. But she took a couple of your courses."

"Cynthia?" Lillian looked surprised. "Of course I remember her. A bright girl. Very conscientious. She did A work even after the swimming season got under way and she was inundated with practice."

"Dr. Doyle." Bob Erwin inserted himself in the conversation, having heard Lillian's response. "Thank you for coming in. Please, have a seat." He pulled out a chair and waited until she was settled. "Obviously, you're acquainted with Cynthia Alexander. Just to be on the safe side, is this the girl you're thinking of?" He offered her two close-up photos.

"Yes, Sergeant." Lillian glanced at the pictures and handed them back. "That's Cynthia." She met his gaze, visibly comprehending his motives. "My illness hasn't affected my mental faculties. That's definitely the young woman I'm referring to."

"I didn't mean to imply—"

"Please, don't apologize. I understand. You have to be sure." Lines of concern creased Lillian's brow. "When you say missing, do you mean taken?"

"That's what we're trying to figure out." Bob dragged over a chair and sat down directly across from Lillian. "Professor Doyle, do you recall if you saw Cynthia at the workshop you participated in last Thursday?"

"I . . ." Lillian frowned in concentration. "No, I don't think so. That doesn't mean she wasn't there. The topic is one that would definitely have interested her. Partly because she was a student of human behavior and partly because she was a loner. There were just so many attendees, and I wasn't feeling one hundred percent. All I recall is a sea of faces."

"I understand." Bob's tone was compassionate. It was clear he was frustrated about striking out again, especially since Lillian was his most promising John Jay lead. But it was equally clear how upset she was about failing to provide concrete details, and about her limited energy level. "Do you feel up to sitting for a few minutes and telling me everything you can about Cynthia?" he asked.

"Of course. Anything I can do to help."

"Thank you." Bob whipped out a pad.

At that moment, Elliot entered the lecture hall and strode over. "Hey," he greeted Sloane. "I was told to come here on a police matter. What's going on?"

Sloane pulled him aside, quietly filling him in on the situation. "I'm the one who suggested Sergeant Erwin send for you. You were at the workshop with the rest of us. And from Cynthia's transcript, it looks like she took one of your courses."

A thoughtful pause, and then a nod. "She did. Comp 201. I remember her, but only vaguely. It was a pretty big intro course. I'm not sure how much help I can be."

"Do you have a visual of her in your mind's eye? Because the sergeant has photos."

"I'll check them out. But from what I recall, she was tall, dark hair, kind of fresh-scrubbed looking."

"That's Cynthia. Do you remember if you saw her at our workshop last Thursday or anytime over the course of that two-day seminar? The cops are trying to establish a more exact time for her disappearance."

Elliot shook his head. "I didn't see her at all." A pause. "You think she was kidnapped?"

"I think it's a distinct possibility."

"Ransom?"

"Nope. She comes from a middle-class family. If she was taken, it was for something uglier than cash."

Elliot looked a little green around the gills. "Besides verifying that she was my student, how can I help the police?"

"Sergeant Erwin's talking to Lillian now. She knew Cynthia better than any of the rest of us who spoke at the workshop. When they're finished, he'll ask you some questions. Anything that pops into your head—even the smallest detail—might mean something. Her work ethic, the classmates she hung around with—something the sergeant asks might trigger a memory. If it does, sing out. It could make a difference." Sloane shot a quick glance at her watch. "Damn. It's ten of four. I've got to get going. I've got three interviews to conduct."

She went over to where Bob was questioning Lillian. "Excuse me for interrupting, but I've got to get to my next appointment. Bob, my offers stand. I'll be out of town Thursday and Friday, but you have my cell number. Say the word and I'll get in touch with the Cleveland field office. And, when I get home, I'll have a talk with Mrs. Alexander." She crossed her fingers and held them up. "Let's hope it's not necessary and Cynthia will be back by then."

"Yeah. Let's. Thanks, Sloane."

"No problem. Lillian, be well." She waved at Luke, then headed off, pausing only when Elliot caught her arm.

"You sure you can't stay?" he asked, rubbing his palms together nervously. "I'm not exactly a pro at being interrogated."

"You're not being interrogated, just questioned. And you don't have to be a pro. Just be honest." Sloane's mind was already shifting back to Penny's disappearance and how much she had to accomplish before she left for Boston. "I wish I could hang around for moral support, Elliot, but I can't. I'll give you a call later, see how it went."

"How about dinner instead? You want to grab a bite?"

"Only if you don't mind eating late. My last interview's at seven down on Wall Street. I can meet you around eight. Eight-thirty if you want to meet in midtown."

"Eight-thirty it is. We'll go to Jake's. My treat."

A teasing spark lit Sloane's eyes at the mention of Jake's Saloon. It was Elliot's favorite haunt, just minutes away from John Jay. "Burgers or steak?" she inquired.

He chuckled. "Steak. It's only fair. You're putting in extra-long hours for my sake. The least I can do is spring for your favorite—filet mignon."

"You're on. See you then."

CHAPTER FIVE

DATE: 25 March
TIME: 2300 hours

I enjoyed my customary cup of Earl Grey tea and my single lemon square before I retired for the night. But rather than have them at the coffee table, as I usually do, tonight I enjoyed my bedtime ritual in Aphrodite's acquiescent presence.

It was a wise choice.

Not that I needed the company. I actually prefer eating my late-night snack alone. But, after the past days with Athena, and the unexpected upset of today, I needed something calming. Aphrodite's serenity was the perfect balm to my edginess. I brought her fresh rose petals, scattered them around the room. Then I handed her the silver comb-and-brush set I'd purchased especially for her, together with the matching hand mirror, and watched with pleasure as she obeyed my instructions and preened herself.

She was beautiful—a carbon copy of the illustration and story that lay on her mattress. She was my consummate validation, the reinforcement that all my pain and hard work has paid off, and will continue to.

I am a success.

Soon will come her final rituals.
How I envy her peace.

Canal Street, New York City
March 26, 1:15 A.M.

Lower Manhattan at night was like an outdoor flea market—except the merchandise in the booths was either hot, counterfeit, or both.

Wearing well-worn jeans, a black T-shirt, and a cheap parka, Derek lingered at one of the numerous kiosks, turning a Samsung MP3 player over in his hands and studying it with intense concentration, as if he were deciding whether or not to buy.

"Looks like the real thing and a helluva deal," he muttered. "Too bad it's really a piece of crap worth about two bucks."

The seller—an Asian-American in his early twenties named John Lee, whose scrawny build was swallowed up by his navy ski jacket—stared back at Derek, his black almond eyes unblinking, his features inscrutable.

"If you say so," he answered in unaccented English. "I say otherwise. And I have the warranty and user manual to prove it."

"Yeah, well, let's say I'm a skeptic."

"Then it's good you're not here to buy. I save my sales pitch for serious shoppers."

"Gullible shoppers, I think you mean."

"That's your take, not mine. Cash is cash."

Derek leaned forward, pointing at the MP3 player as if he were asking a question about how it worked. "So what's the word on the street?" He kept his voice low, although the corner they were on was fairly deserted.

Lee looked around furtively before replying. "The meeting's happening tomorrow night."

"Where and when?"

"Nom Wo Club. Two A.M."

No surprise there. The Nom Wo Club was one of Lo

Ma's most profitable gambling parlors. "And the agenda? Property damage or bloodshed?"

"Depends on how it goes. Could be either. Could be both."

"Who's showing up?"

"Enforcers on both sides, the Red Dragons and the Black Tigers. Plus backup. I'm not sure how many. But I do know it's not just the kids."

"And you're sure you can get in?"

"No sweat. I'm a regular. I play there three nights a week."

"Only this time you'll play with an electronic listening device." Derek reached into his pocket. "Come to the field office at one o'clock tomorrow afternoon. I'll prep you and set you up."

Lee wet his lips with the tip of his tongue. "I can't be seen at your offices."

"Give me a break, Lee." Derek counted out two tens and a five. "Your crowd doesn't hang out at Federal Plaza. Plus, they're not even awake until two in the afternoon. You'll be long gone by then."

"And this listening device?"

"Tiny. And too well concealed to be spotted. You're cool."

A pause, as Lee considered his options. "Yeah, okay," he agreed. He eyed the bills in Derek's hand, his gaze shifting to the MP3 player. "You buying that?"

"Hell, yeah." Derek's tone was laced with sarcasm as he tossed Lee the bills. "A Samsung MP3 player with an OLED display for twenty-five bucks? That's a steal."

Lee shoved the money into his pocket.

"Don't forget the warranty and user manual," Derek reminded him. "You can't be too careful these days. Everyone's out to rip you off."

With a grunt, Lee handed over the fake papers. "Sucks, doesn't it?"

85 West Cocktail Bar
Marriott Hotel World Financial Center
Vesey Street, New York City
1:30 A.M.

Sloane shifted on the bar's leather stool and took another careful sip of her raspberry cocktail. She'd been nursing it for the past half hour, making sure to keep a clear head. Not only for the drive home, but for the interview she was about to conduct.

After Doug Waters had blown her off at the last minute because of some major deal he was negotiating, she'd called his bluff, determined to speak to him today, while she was in Manhattan. Her interviews with Penny's friend Amy and coworkers at *Harper's Bazaar* had yielded nothing. But they'd all mentioned Doug, and the fact that Penny had seemed to take the breakup hard. So Sloane was hell-bent on getting Doug's side of the story—tonight, before he had time to spin the facts in his favor.

She'd decided to wait him out. Even investment bankers went home eventually. So, after hearing the time commitment involved in his negotiations, she'd suggested they meet between 1 and 2 A.M. right here at the Marriott, walking distance from Merrill Lynch's investment-banking headquarters. Doug had been audibly surprised by how far she'd bend to make this meeting happen. He'd lost his smooth edge, tripped over an attempted excuse, and then finally realized he sounded like a man with something to hide. He'd agreed to meet her at the bar.

Sloane had made some quick arrangements. She'd called her neighbor, Elsa Wagner, an elderly woman who lived alone, except for her Pomeranian, Princess Di, and her son, Burt, who'd practically moved in since his recent divorce. Between Elsa and Burt, Sloane had constant and reliable backup for her beloved hounds when she was out of town or working long hours.

Having made plans for her "babies," Sloane then pro-

longed her dinner with Elliot—although she knew she was
less than stellar company, given how drained and preoccupied she was. She made sure to fortify herself with three
leaded cups of coffee. Those were all the reinforcements
she needed to be sharp as a tack for her meeting with Doug.
Her time at the Bureau had conditioned her well for the
long days and bizarre hours that were the mainstay of investigative work.

Now she took a healthy swallow of water to dilute the
effects of the alcohol, then returned to her drink, stirring it
with the little straw. There were just a handful of stragglers
left at the cocktail bar. Most of them were cramming for
early-morning meetings.

Sloane didn't envy them.

Not ten minutes later, a good-looking guy in his midthirties wearing a dark navy Zegna suit and carrying a sleek
Ferragamo briefcase approached the counter. He looked
exhausted. "Excuse me," he said to the bartender, who was
in the process of cleaning up. "I'm supposed to be meeting
someone. My name is Doug Waters. Has someone—a
woman—asked for me?"

"That would be me," Sloane informed him from the
quiet corner she was sitting in.

He turned, and did a double take. "*You're* Sloane Burbank?"

"Guilty as charged."

"Can I get you something?" the bartender interrupted
to ask.

"Scotch. Neat." Doug waited for his drink, then walked
over to Sloane and perched on the stool beside her.

"You're obviously surprised," Sloane noted. "What were
you expecting?"

Doug put down his briefcase. "Let's put it this way.
There are five women in this bar. I'd narrowed down the
possibilities to three. You weren't even on the list of candidates."

Sloane's lips twitched. "And why would that be?"

"You're kidding, right? You said you were an ex–FBI agent. I figured you were solid, muscular, and intimidating."

"I am."

"Right. What are you—five foot two? A hundred pounds?"

"Five three and one-ten. And if you want proof that I'm intimidating, let's step over there." Sloane pointed to a deserted, semidarkened corner of the lounge. "This way you won't have to suffer the embarrassment of people seeing me toss you on your ass. Or worse, if you're still not convinced."

His brows rose, and he gave a quiet chuckle. "Never mind. I believe you. Plus I wouldn't be much of a challenge. I'm about to fall on my ass anyway. I just worked forty hours straight."

He wasn't lying. Sloane could see that. He looked haggard, with dark circles under his eyes and a five o'clock shadow that said he hadn't shaved since at least yesterday. So he hadn't been blowing her off. He'd really been putting together some major deal.

"I appreciate your meeting me," she said. "I'll make this brief so you can go home and get some sleep."

"Sleep? Right." He grimaced. "Three hours tops. I've got to be back at my desk by seven." He drank some of his scotch. "You said you were a friend of Penny's and that her parents hired you to conduct a last-ditch investigation on her disappearance. But you also said there were no new developments. And Penny's been missing for a year. So how do I factor into your investigation? I've already told the police and the FBI everything I know."

"I realize that." Sloane nodded. She took an intentional sip of her drink, then crossed her legs and propped an elbow on the counter, conveying a relaxed, informal demeanor. "This isn't an interrogation, Doug. It's a review of facts. You and Penny were very close right before her disappearance. I just want to make sure there isn't some nuance—something she might have said or done—that you didn't stress to the authorities that I'll pick up on because of how well I knew Penny. No hidden agenda. No accusatory tone. You have an alibi. I'm not questioning it—or your motives. I'm just looking for a miracle to give to Penny's parents."

Her soft-pedaling paid off.

Doug visibly relaxed, downing a little more of his scotch. "Penny's a terrific person. We were good together for a long time. But two ambitious workaholics can't last indefinitely as a couple unless one of them is ready to take a backseat to the other's career. Neither of us was willing to do that. So we broke things off. The decision was mutual, and it was amicable. No fighting, screaming, throwing things. Just a mature parting."

"Your alibi—the woman you were in Hawaii with—was that a new relationship?"

A muscle worked in Doug's jaw. "If you're asking if I was being unfaithful to Penny, the answer is yes. I'm not proud of it. Nor was it going on for long. Things were unraveling between Penny and me. I work round the clock. So does my new girlfriend, Sandy. We're both at Merrill Lynch, so we're together all the time. It just happened. And, for the record, Penny knew. I told her about it around a month before we ended things."

"How did she take it?"

"She wasn't surprised. But she was hurt and angry. We were a couple. She felt betrayed. I think that's pretty normal."

If Doug was looking for Sloane's opinion, he wasn't getting it. Any sign that she was judging him negatively would mark the end of this interview.

Instead, she stuck with the facts. "You say she felt angry and betrayed. But she didn't end things then."

"Not officially. But, like I said, the breakup was gradual, not sudden. We were already in the talking phases. My relationship with Sandy just accelerated things. Penny and I called it quits a few weeks later."

"Yet she called you the day before she disappeared."

"Mm-hmm, around four o'clock," Doug confirmed. "And before you ask, I'll give you the same explanation I gave the FBI, because it's the truth. The reason Penny called was to make arrangements for a mutual swap of our belongings. I'd left some things at her place, and she'd done the same at mine."

"She called to set up a time for you to meet." Sloane took a sip of her drink, intentionally knitting her brows in puzzlement. "That doesn't sound to me like someone who was planning to vanish into thin air."

"Nor to me. She sounded a little down, or maybe intro-spective's a better word. But nothing dire. Plus, Penny's not the impulsive type. I can't imagine her just taking off and leaving her entire life behind."

"You told that to the FBI?"

"Twice. Special Agent Parker grilled the hell out of me. Believe me, if I had the slightest clue that that call from Penny was a prelude to this, I would have said or done something. I certainly wouldn't have hung up and boarded an evening flight to Hawaii."

"Did you work out a time and place to get together once you got back from your trip?"

"I wasn't sure of my schedule. We left it that I'd call her a week from Monday and we'd work out the details."

"Penny liked things nailed down," Sloane murmured. "She wasn't a hang-loose kind of person."

Doug gave a half smile. "You did know her well. No, she was anything but hang loose. She was decisive and get it done now. If it wasn't for my vacation and her weekend plans, she would have pushed to get it done ASAP."

Sloane's head came up. "How do you know Penny had weekend plans? Did she mention she had something on tap?"

"Hmm?" Doug looked startled, as though the conversa-tion had jolted a thought he'd long since forgotten. "Not during that phone call she didn't. But she didn't have to. I knew about that seminar since she registered for it a couple of months earlier."

"What seminar?"

"I don't remember the topic. But it was part of a Classical Humanities lecture series. They were held one Saturday afternoon a month. Penny went to several of them. She was really into the whole academic scene."

"Did you tell this to Special Agent Parker?"

"I doubt it. To be frank, it slipped my mind until now. The lecture series was Penny's thing, not mine. I never went with her. I worked most Saturdays. Special Agent Parker was focused on my alibi and my recollections of Penny's state of mind. So was I. A lecture that she might or might not have attended just didn't seem important." Doug paused, studied Sloane's face. "Why? Does it mean something?"

"That depends. Where were the lectures held?"

"Richard Stockton College."

Sloane set down her glass with a thud. Did that mean something? Hell, yes.

CHAPTER
SIX

He's crazy.

I can see the madness in his eyes.

God, I'm so terrified. I've begged, pleaded, struggled to break his hold. But it's futile. When that insanity glitters in his dark stare, he doesn't hear me. If I keep fighting, he hits me.

I know what's coming next—the only thing that stops my struggles entirely.

The sting of the hypodermic needle. I feel it pierce my skin. Then the room starts spinning around me. I hate that sense of slipping away, of losing touch with reality. And I hate the sick and disoriented way I come to—groggy, nauseated, and with no clue about how much time has passed.

He visits me soon after I come to. On those visits, he's different.

The rage in his eyes is gone. He looks almost normal. He's polite, even considerate. He'll bring me a meal, sit silently and read while I eat. His reading material is scholarly—classics, philosophy, mythology. I look around while I force down the food. I don't comprehend anything I see. There's a fabricated gold shield hanging on the wall, statuettes of an owl and an olive tree flanking it on either side, and a photocopied story of Athena—complete with illustrations, like a chapter out of a children's book—that he's placed at the foot of my mattress. I don't understand any of it, but I don't dare ask questions.

Once I've finished eating, he escorts me to the bathroom. The dichotomy is bizarre. He keeps a combat knife at my throat to assert his domination, yet holds my arm while we walk, since I'm so unsteady on my feet. That's the only time he touches me. And he never intrudes on my privacy. He waits outside the bathroom until I come out.

Escape is impossible.

Beneath the curtains, there are bars on the window, and he's fitted it with a heavily tinted glass pane so I can't see outside my prison.

Earlier, I requested fresh air. He refused. I then requested a bath. He surprised me by agreeing. He's agreed to pick up some toiletries and have them for me tonight.

It's a luxury to anticipate.

I so want to meet the other women. I hear their voices, their weeping. Maybe they can explain to me why we're here.

Or maybe I don't want to know.

March 26
12:05 P.M.

Richard Stockton College was about a twenty-minute ride from Atlantic City, and a little over two hours from Sloane's house.

She didn't have the time to drive there and back. Not today.

She did it anyway.

One thing she'd learned years ago is that you got a lot more out of people when you talked to them in person than you did when you talked to them over the phone.

She arrived on campus around eleven, and was directed to the office of special affairs. She waited at the desk for Doris Hayden, who administered the lecture series. Her instincts told her that she was on the verge of finding the first new and viable lead in this case.

That meant forward motion. It didn't mean a happy ending.

Sloane was a realist. If her theory was correct, she'd leave with a new venue to explore, and more ammunition to support her belief that Penny's disappearance involved foul play rather than free will.

Which meant she'd be one step closer to giving Hope Truman the closure she needed. However, it also suggested that that closure would involve facing the loss of her daughter.

On that sober thought, Sloane conducted her business. After seeing Sloane's credentials and hearing why she was there, Doris had cooperated fully. She'd pulled up the on-line registration forms of all twenty-five attendees. Only four, including Penny, were from Manhattan—the rest were locals.

Doris had immediately e-mailed everyone on the list with a brief explanation of the situation and an electronic photo of Penny that Sloane provided via her laptop.

Sloane had thanked her profusely. Then, time being of the essence, she began her follow-up on campus, tracking down five Stockton students who'd attended the seminar. All of them had received Doris's e-mail. None of them recognized Penny's photo, or remembered seeing anyone who matched her description at the seminar that day.

Not a good sign.

Next, Sloane left urgent voice-mail messages on the cell phones of the other six Stockton undergrads who were on the registration sheet, asking them to check their e-mails and get back to her ASAP—within the hour if possible. Since college students were notorious for having their cell phones glued to their ears, Sloane crossed her fingers that she'd hear back from them before she had to take off.

She used the waiting time to call the other three New Yorkers. Two were NYU roommates, one of whom answered the phone, and, as soon as Sloane mentioned last

April's lecture at Richard Stockton, said that she and her friend had registered, but ultimately blown off the lecture.

The third New Yorker, Deanna Frost, worked in the communications department of the New York Public Library in midtown Manhattan. Sloane got her voice mail as well, and left an equally urgent message.

Frustrated, she punched off her phone. Her growling stomach reminded her that all the people she was trying to reach were probably at lunch. She bought herself a grilled chicken panini and a Diet Coke, and ate them in the car. The weather was still too nippy to sit outside, and her hand was feeling the chill.

That reminded her she had an appointment with her hand therapist at four-thirty. It was already after one. She'd better get some results here soon, or she'd have to cut the information gathering short and do the rest long distance.

Two more Richard Stockton students called in the next half hour, both to say they'd gotten Sloane's message, checked out the e-mail, but were drawing a blank when it came to the woman in the photo.

Disappointed and time-stressed, Sloane was just thanking the last guy for his promptness and cooperation when the beep that signified her call waiting sounded.

It was Deanna Frost.

"Your message said you needed information about a particular woman who attended the seminar at Richard Stockton last April, that her safety could be at stake." Deanna was frank and to the point. "How can I help?"

"You were registered for the seminar," Sloane replied. "Did you attend?"

"Yes. I took an express bus from the Port Authority."

It was a long shot. Express buses ran from New York City to AC all the time. Still, Sloane had to try. "I see you registered using your personal Yahoo account. Are you at home now or at the library?"

"The library. Why?"

"Because Doris Hayden forwarded you an e-mail and a photo. Can you access your personal e-mail from there?"

"Of course. Just give me a minute." Some clicking sounds on a computer keyboard, then a pause. "Here's the e-mail from Richard Stockton. Let me open it."

A few more clicks. "Missing?" she murmured in distress. Clearly, she was reading Doris's e-mail. "How terrible. Was she kidnapped?"

"That's what we're trying to find out. Would you open the attachment and take a look at the photo?"

"Right now." A minute passed, then a slight gasp. "Penny."

Sloane's head snapped up. "You know her?"

"Only her name and that she works in fashion. We met the day of the seminar, at the Atlantic City bus terminal. It turned out we'd caught the same bus out of the Port Authority. When we realized we were both heading for the Richard Stockton campus, we shared a cab."

"So Penny did attend the lecture."

"That was the odd part. She didn't. She seemed so enthused about it during our taxi drive. But she never showed up."

"I don't understand. If you rode to campus together . . ."

"We got there an hour early. I dashed off to grab a cup of coffee. Penny wanted to take a walk. We agreed to meet up at the lecture hall in forty-five minutes. She never came. I assumed she had an unexpected change in plans. Even though we were barely acquainted, I was surprised enough to want to contact her, and make sure everything was all right. But I had no idea how to reach her. I didn't even know her last name."

"Truman," Sloane said woodenly. "Her last name is Truman. And it's possible you were the last person to have seen her before she disappeared."

"I don't understand," Deanna responded, clearly upset. "That seminar was almost a full year ago. Are you telling me she's been missing for that long?"

"That's what I'm telling you. The police and the FBI have been trying to determine her whereabouts. I have investigative experience, and I'm also a close childhood friend of Penny's. Her parents hired me to see what I could find out. You just helped me narrow down where she vanished from."

"But not why, or by whose hand."

"No. Not yet. Deanna, I'm going to contact the FBI, and let them know about this development. Their resources are obviously far more vast than mine. I'm sure the agent who's handling Penny's case will want to contact you. Please tell him everything you remember, down to the slightest detail. His name is Special Agent Derek Parker."

"Of course. Anything I can do. Anything at all."

"You have my contact information in that e-mail Doris Hayden sent you. Use it. Anytime, day or night. If you have a question, or if you recall even a tidbit of related information, please call me. Penny is very dear to me. I plan to find out what happened to her."

FBI New York Field Office
3:45 P.M.

Derek was in a foul mood.

He'd done a thorough job of prepping John Lee for tonight's stakeout. The listening device he'd given Lee was concealed in a pen, so tiny and unobtrusive that no one would spot it. Lee was edgy but under control. He'd do what he had to, since the alternative was jail. The entire squad was prepared for a long night, and Tony had made up the surveillance schedule.

With luck, they'd not only find out if Lo Ma really was responsible for the brutal killings of Xiao Long's girls, but they'd get some solid evidence on both Dai Los to pass along to the U.S. Attorney's Office.

So everything was in place. And Derek was wound up and ready to go.

Back in his Ranger days, he'd learned to eat when he

could, since the next opportunity to do so might not come for a while. With that in mind, he wolfed down a sandwich, grabbed some bottled water and a bag of chips, and headed back to his desk, intending to type up his interviews and return his e-mails.

That's when his mood had gone south.

At his desk, he'd found Sloane's voice mail waiting for him.

The message itself was pretty cryptic, saying only that she had a lead on the Penny Truman case, and she needed to talk to him as soon as possible.

Its vagueness was irritating enough.

But the fact that her voice still had the power to get to him the way it did—now, *that* really pissed him off.

He leaned back in his chair, linked his arms behind his head, and grudgingly let his mind go where he'd avoided letting it go since Monday.

When he'd walked into that conference room and she'd been standing there—it was like a punch in the gut. He'd written his reaction off as the result of being blindsided. After all, she'd been the last person he expected to see when he stepped through that door.

But now there was no excuse. He knew she was working for the Trumans, and he knew she had a personal stake in the case, since she and Penelope Truman were childhood friends. He was the agent of record. It was natural she'd be calling him with any information she stumbled on.

Derek was a hard, fast realist. He didn't delude himself—not then, and not now. He wasn't over Sloane. What they'd shared had been much more than an affair. Everything about it had been intense—the attraction, the connection, the sex. It had started—and ended—like an explosion, knocking them both on their asses, going up in fireworks and down in flames.

There'd never been any closure. There hadn't even been good-byes.

She'd been a stubborn, stoic coward, who'd shut him out and then walked away when the going got tough.

And he? He'd been a hotheaded, judgmental ass, who'd been too pissed off by her decision to see things rationally.

Abruptly, it was over.

That didn't stop him from thinking about her. He did. A lot more often than he liked. That was bad enough. But his reaction to seeing her again, hearing her voice, that wasn't just remembering. That was vulnerability. And vulnerability was *not* something he could accept in himself.

As if to challenge that weakness head-on, he picked up the phone and punched in her number.

She answered on the second ring. "Sloane Burbank." The road noise told him she was in the car.

"It's Derek."

"Oh, good." Her relief was genuine. "Thanks for getting back to me so fast. I was afraid I'd miss you, and I'll be out of town for the next two days working twenty-four/seven. Phone tag's not an option. We need to jump on this right away."

"What is it we're jumping on?" Derek asked drily.

Sloane filled him in on what Doug Waters had told her, about her trip to Richard Stockton, and about her conversation with Deanna Frost.

"So Penelope did buy that ticket to Atlantic City. It just wasn't her final destination." Derek scribbled down some notes.

"She meant to attend that seminar. We know she got to the college campus. So she disappeared on or near there, sometime between eleven-fifteen and noon. We need to figure out who else she might have talked to, where the common walking paths are, if any other suspicious activities were reported during that time period. We need to interview campus security, local police—"

"Hey, drill sergeant, stop." Derek snapped out the interruption. "I don't need an education in how to conduct a missing persons investigation. What I do need is some clarification. By *we,* I assume you mean *me.* And that's not going to fly."

"Don't tell me you still think Penny disappeared voluntarily," Sloane responded in a tight voice.

"I never thought that. But you're not the only one working twenty-four/seven. I'm in the middle of a case that's just escalated to front burner. I can't divert my resources, not now. What I can do is call—"

"Don't turn the case over to someone else." It was Sloane's turn to interrupt. "It'll take you just as much time to bring the new agent up to speed as it would for you to handle this on your own." A pause, as if Sloane were forcing out her next words. "You're the best there is, Derek. I need that for Penny."

"I wasn't going to suggest turning it over to another agent. I was going to suggest I call Newark and get Anderson involved. He was the agent who worked your friend's case in the Newark field office. Richard Stockton is in his jurisdiction, not mine. He'll call the Atlantic City RA. When we first ran down the AC lead, he worked with a good agent down there. Tom McGraw. He's smart and he's thorough. I'll call Anderson now, see if McGraw can get started on the legwork right away."

"Makes sense." Sloane's wheels were still turning. "One favor. I told Deanna Frost you'd be contacting her as the agent in charge. I'd appreciate if you'd meet with her, just for a cup of coffee. She works at the New York Public Library, so it's your jurisdiction. It would take maybe an hour of your time. But I think you'd have the best shot of getting her to remember something."

Derek's brows rose. "Better than you? That's one I never thought I'd hear."

"It's a question of chemistry, not skill. I only spoke with Deanna briefly. She's inherently decent and cooperative. But my instincts tell me she's also a reserved, intellectual loner. You'll be bigger than life to her. Between your FBI status, your whole former Army Ranger macho aura, and that classic charm of yours—trust me, she'll do handsprings to come through for you."

Despite his best intentions, Derek found himself grinning. "Can I hear my résumé again?"

"No. Just tell me you'll do it."

"Consider it done."

Sloane's exhale of relief was audible. "Thank you."

"I aim to please."

A taut endless silence.

Derek broke it first. "You said you'd be out of town. Will you be reachable by cell?"

"I'll make myself reachable. I'll be in Boston conducting a two-day workshop. I'm leaving at the crack of dawn tomorrow and I'll be back Friday night. During that time, I'll be on pretty much every minute. But I'll keep checking my cell for messages. Tonight I'll be home. Right now I'm heading into Manhattan for a session with my hand therapist, and I'm already running late. But I'll leave my phone on vibrate."

"Good enough. I've got an hour or two before people start heading home. I'll make some calls and give you a status report as soon as I have it."

"And since I'm sitting in the car fighting traffic, I'll call Hope Truman now and let her know where things stand."

"It's a plan. Talk to you later."

"Derek?" Sloane caught him just before he hung up. "I realize I'm the last person you want to work with. I'm no happier than you. Frankly, the whole situation sucks. But regardless of my personal feelings, or yours—or maybe because of them—I want you to know I really appreciate this. Penny was a big part of my childhood."

For a long moment, Derek stared down at his desk, contemplating her words. He knew how much they'd cost her to say. His reaction to them was a mixed bag—one he didn't care to analyze.

"No problem. Just doing my job."

CHAPTER SEVEN

Four-ten. It was 4:10.

Who ever thought that the simple act of telling time would matter so much?

And yet it gives me a tremendous sense of comfort. In my present world, day and night cease to matter. Time passes in a vague sense of nonreality. So when he paused outside the bathroom door, setting down the pail of toiletries and readying the key to lock me in, I'd looked around and spotted the wall clock for the first time.

A huge wave of relief swept through me. The tiniest awareness of something, anything, that related to life as I'd known it, was a gift.

What a fool I've been to take those gifts for granted.

Not anymore.

When he came to my room, announcing that I could have my bath, I almost wept with joy. Even the sight of the combat knife he was clutching didn't make me flinch, nor did the pressure of it at my throat as he led me outside my prison. I was too focused on the items in the bucket he was carrying.

Soap. Shampoo. Lotion. Common, everyday products that were so familiar and yet so precious.

He withdrew the knife when I was safely inside the bathroom. Twenty minutes, he said. That's all I have

It's enough.

With the door shut and locked behind me, I reached into the old ceramic bathtub and turned on the water, waiting for it to heat up. I'd decided on a shower rather than a bath. In part, that's because I don't want to waste an instant of my freedom waiting for the tub to fill, and, in part, because I want to wash away every drop of filth, not sit in it.

I glanced in the mirror just before turning on the shower spray and stepping in. God, I barely recognize myself. My face is gaunt. My eyes are huge, with big, dark circles underneath, and my pupils are dilated from the drugs. My hair is tangled, sticky with sweat. I'd lost my hair band when I struggled with him on campus. So my hair was loose, hanging down, limp and lifeless. I reached up, and my fingers touched the gash on my neck left by his combat knife. It wasn't being treated, so it wasn't healing. And it was far from the only mark on my body.

My gaze shifted to my arms. Needle marks. So many of them. And bruises, everywhere. From my capture. From those visits when the madness filled his eyes.

I shuddered and turned away, stepping into the wall of water that was my illusory reprieve.

Hospital for Special Surgery
New York Weill Cornell Medical Center
East Seventieth Street, New York City
4:50 P.M.

Constance Griggs was a forty-one-year-old divorcée with loans up the wazoo, an ex-husband who was as reliable as the rhythm method, and two small kids to raise on her own. She was a natural blonde with a trim figure, a healthy enjoyment of the opposite sex, and no time for a social life. Still, she was a born optimist who believed in happily-ever-afters and had a natural affinity for helping people. She was also fascinated with orthopedic medicine and the intricacies of the fine bones and blood vessels that composed the human hand.

Maybe that's why she was the best occupational hand therapist in all of Manhattan.

Sloane had been with Constance ever since Dr. Charles Houghton had referred her eight months ago, just after her second surgery. Dr. Houghton was a bona fide genius. He'd operated on Sloane twice—once to reverse the damage done by her initial surgery, conducted under emergency circumstances in a rural Ohio hospital. The surgeons there had done their best, but their focus had been on stopping the bleeding.

They'd patched her up, but their lack of expertise in treating such a complex injury left Sloane with major scarring around the tendons of her index finger, ultimately leaving it so stiff it could scarcely bend. Thankfully, she'd already moved back east and was being treated by Dr. Houghton, who immediately diagnosed the tendon as being stuck in flexion. He operated, removing the scar tissue and freeing the tendon to heal. Then he sent her to Constance for physical therapy. That was the good part. The bad part was that the healing process had to start from scratch. And Sloane was a lousy patient.

When the splint was finally removed, she began resistance exercises, and despite Constance's warnings to take it easy, Sloane had pushed herself too hard, too fast. As a result, the tendons in her index finger ruptured, and she'd been back in the operating room again. Dr. Houghton had done a brilliant job of grafting her tendon, the only negative being some residual nerve damage—and more rehab.

The process was grueling, painful, and frustrating as hell. But thanks to Constance, she could now bend her finger about two-thirds of the way to her hand. That was good—but not good enough.

Unless she regained full use of her trigger finger and was able to pass the pistol qualification test, reapplication to the FBI was out.

Sloane wouldn't give up. And Constance wouldn't let her. That was the other perk that had come out of this life altering nightmare. Sloane and Constance had become friends.

Constance worked directly with Dr. Houghton at the Hospital for Special Surgery. She also had a small private practice near her home in Morristown, New Jersey, where she worked two days a week. That kept her child-care expenses down and accommodated both her New York and New Jersey clients. It was also ideal for Sloane, who lived about forty-five minutes away from Morristown. So twice a week she went there and once a week she went to the hospital.

Today was hospital day.

"Hi, Connie," she said, greeting her therapist as she walked into the occupational-therapy room. "Sorry I'm late."

"It happens. Thanks for calling, though. I returned a few phone calls from patients while I waited." Connie glanced up from the various sensory reeducation tools she'd been laying out for Sloane's session, frowning as she saw the expression on her friend's face. "Bad day?"

"Weird day." Sloane sat down on the padded patient's chair at the examination table and flexed her fingers. The action didn't make her wince the way it once had, but the ache was still there and the lack of full sensation in her index finger was still glaringly apparent.

"You look stressed out," Connie observed. "How's the hand?"

"Depends on when you ask. Some days good, some days not so good. Also depends on who you ask."

"I'm asking you."

"Okay then, the throbbing's been keeping me up at night. That part I can handle. Now for the parts I can't. The feeling in my index finger still isn't back. Neither are my small motor skills, even though I do my exercises every day. And I'm still not hitting the damned bull's-eye on my archery course, even though I've reconditioned myself to drawing back the bowstring with my ring and middle fingers."

Connie rolled her eyes. "And I bet you haven't walked on water yet, either."

"I haven't tried." Sloane sighed. "Okay, I get it. You think I'm expecting miracles. But I'm not. Connie, it's been forever. I just want my life back."

"I know you do." Connie walked around to the opposite side of the examining table and pulled over her stool. Seated, she took Sloane's hand in hers, palm up. "I could give you a lecture on how far you've come. I could reiterate that it would take the digital nerve six months to regenerate under *ideal* circumstances, which yours clearly are not. I could remind you that with complicated hand injuries, there are no guarantees, especially when you're talking about the fine motor skills needed to shoot a pistol and rejoin the FBI. I could say a lot of things. But you know every one of them already, and it doesn't make your situation any easier to bear. So why don't we do some passive bending exercises and scar massage first. I'll do the work, you do the talking. Then we'll switch. You'll do active extensions and gripping exercises, and I'll talk. So start. Tell me what's going on in your high-powered life."

"Nothing cheerful." Sloane watched Connie put lotion on the scar-tissue massage tool, then begin a gentle motion with its roller ball, softening Sloane's skin and soothing the scars around her incision. "I'm involved in two missing persons cases. One of the subjects is an old childhood friend. The other's a college kid. Neither case looks too promising in the way of a positive outcome."

"That's terrible. No wonder you look so upset." Connie continued her work. "Are there ransom notes?"

"Nope."

"Is it possible that either or both of them took off on their own?"

"Possible. Not likely."

"Well, you never know what's going on in someone's life. Remember Lydia Halas?"

"Hmm?" Sloane's mind had drifted off for an instant as

she pondered the unlikely prospect that Penny was alive. She switched her attention back to Connie. "You mean Lydia Halas—my nurse?"

"Yup."

"Of course I remember her. She took care of me after both my surgeries. She was superefficient, but always compassionate. She gave me daily pep talks about how I'd recover and be myself again. Once she even sneaked me up a pint of Ben & Jerry's when I was losing my mind from the hospital food."

"That's Lydia." Connie smiled, bending Sloane's fingers to check her range of motion. "Anyway, she left here right before Christmas."

"She moved to a different hospital?" Sloane asked in surprise.

A shrug. "No clue. One day she just didn't come in. It turned out she didn't just leave HSS, she left Manhattan. The police checked it out, and apparently she and her husband had separated a few months earlier. There were rumors of abuse, but I never saw a mark on her. I know the separation was difficult for her. Apparently, she went to start over. I have no idea where. The point is, maybe your friend just wanted a new life. And a college student? They're the ultimate free spirits. Maybe this kid got bored and ran off to find some excitement. That sounds reasonable to me. So don't assume the worst. You could be surprised."

Sloane smiled fondly. "Connie, you'd find something positive to say if I told you I was having a tooth extraction without novocaine. I wish I had your nature."

"We can't all be that lucky." Connie's eyes twinkled, and she placed a wad of medium-resistance therapy putty in Sloane's palm. "Squeeze that for me with your entire hand. Then shift it to the space between your index and middle finger and squeeze again. And, while you're doing that, tell me about the guy."

"Guy?" Sloane complied, curving her fingers around the putty and exerting as much pressure as she could. After a minute, she placed it between her middle and index fingers and repeated the process. "What guy?"

"The one who's been on your mind all week. I recognize the signs, although they're new with you. I haven't seen you distracted by a man since—*him*."

Sloane grimaced. She'd told Connie about Derek months ago, during one of her weaker moments.

"Is there pain?" Connie asked.

"What?"

"Pain. You're wrinkling your face up. Is the pressure too much for your finger?"

"No." Sloane glanced down at the putty. "It's fine. That's not the problem."

"Ah, the guy. Who is he?"

"He's *him*," Sloane replied with a sigh. "In the flesh."

"Derek?" Connie's brows shot up. "What do you mean in the flesh? He's here in New York?"

"Yup."

"How do you know? Has he called you?"

"Worse. I saw him in person. He's assigned to the New York field office. And lucky me—he's the agent of record on my missing friend's case. So guess who has to work together?"

"You're kidding." Connie stared for a moment, then sucked in her breath and resumed treating Sloane's hand. She took away the putty and handed Sloane a spring-loaded hand-and-finger exerciser. "That's the usual pound-and-a-half resistance. I'm hoping we can move to the three-pound resistance sometime this month. Now grasp and squeeze." She watched as Sloane complied. "Did you know he'd been transferred to New York?"

"I knew he wanted to be. I haven't exactly followed his career. It's not the best way to forget someone."

"Not that you've managed to do that anyway. When did you see him?"

"Monday." Sloane rested her arm on the examining table and gripped the exerciser's palm bar, tensing her fingers and squeezing against the springs. She frowned, irked by the distance differential between what her trigger finger could accomplish and what the rest of her fingers could do. "And before you ask, he looks good. Better than good. My chest literally clenched when he walked in. Butterflies in my stomach. Roaring in my ears. The works. Just like when we were together. Except for the anger. That wasn't there until the end, when all hell broke loose. But it's there now, and it's as strong as ever. So's the resentment. I can't get past them. I doubt I ever will."

"Never's a long time," Connie noted. "Not to mention that there are two sides to every story. And that things aren't always what they seem."

Sloane gave a half groan, half sigh, and put down the exercise tool. "What is this—platitude hour? If so, it's not working."

"Fine. Then I'll just point out the obvious. You might not be able to get over the anger, but you sure as hell can't get over him. I call that a major snag, and an official catch-22."

"Maybe. Maybe not. I might get over him faster now that I have to deal with him again. Maybe the fantasies will be drowned out by the glaring reminder of what an insensitive, judgmental bastard he is."

At that moment, there was a brief knock on the door.

Connie looked surprised. "Yes?" she called out.

The door opened and Dr. Houghton stepped inside. He was a tall, lanky man, with salt-and-pepper hair, angular features, and dark eyes that bore right through you. He carried himself with an air of self-confidence that bordered on arrogance but stopped just short of it.

"Constance, before you go home, I need that file on—" He stopped, visibly surprised to see Sloane there, and glanced down at his watch. "I didn't mean to intrude. I thought Constance's last appointment was at four."

"It was," Sloane replied drily. "Unfortunately, I held her up. I was running late, and I hit tons of city-bound traffic." She resumed her work with the spring loaded exerciser, intent on regaining her fine motor skills. "How are you, Dr. Houghton?"

He glanced at her for a moment, then stared at the exercise she was performing, eyes narrowed, clearly making a quantitative assessment of her progress. He might just as well have come out and said that her question was superfluous and not worth addressing. His one and only interest was her hand.

Sloane wasn't offended. During one of their follow-up visits, Dr. Houghton had bluntly said that after all these years, he often didn't remember a patient's face, but he never forgot a hand. It wasn't rudeness; it was professional dedication.

She responded by providing him with what he wanted to know. "The healing process is coming along," she reported. "Connie's a miracle worker. I feel some definite improvement in my grip and strength in my index finger. I'm waiting for my radial nerve to catch on and catch up."

"It will—in time." Connie turned to Dr. Houghton. "Sloane is determined to rejoin the FBI."

Connie's gentle reminder found its mark, and Dr. Houghton's attention expanded to a more holistic view of Sloane. "You'll need the coordination and fine motor skills to qualify with your weapon. That's a tall order. Plus, the scars from your three surgeries will have to heal enough for you to manage the grip, and you'll need to be able to exert enough pressure to pull the trigger. When is our next follow-up appointment?"

"In three weeks," Sloane supplied.

"Good. We'll see the extent of your recuperation then." He turned back to Connie. "Call my office when you're finished. I have a few quick notes to pass on to you for tomorrow's patients. I have an evening engagement, so I'll be leaving within the hour."

"As will I," Connie replied. "My babysitter has a date and needs me home by seven. So Sloane and I will be wrapping up soon. I'll check in with you before I head off to catch the train."

"Fine. I'll be expecting your call shortly." His gaze flickered over to Sloane. "Good night."

"Good night, Dr. Houghton." Once the door shut behind him, Sloane released the exerciser and gave her hand a rest. "He's tough."

"The toughest," Connie agreed. "And the most brilliant."

"Meanwhile, tough or not, he has evening plans." Sloane blew out her breath. "My surgeon, your babysitter—it's date night in the tristate area."

"Not for me. It's time-to-be-mom night at my place."

"Yes, but Saturday you're having dinner with Ken the lawyer. That relationship seems to be heating up." Sloane's eyes twinkled. "So your date night could be a scorcher." A mock sigh. "While you're having the time of your life, think of me recouping from a two-day seminar by working round the clock."

"If you're looking for pity, forget it," Connie retorted. "You've passed up more dates than I care to count. You're married to your work." A pause. "And maybe to the past."

"I'll cop to the former, but not the latter. If anything, what happened between me and Derek is what made me swear off relationships. They're more trouble than they're worth."

Connie shot her a who-are-you-kidding look. "If you say so."

"I do."

Sloane's cell phone vibrated.

"Go ahead and answer," Connie said. "All we have left is the sensory reeducation wand and the Peg-Board. I'll set them up."

"And I'll make this quick." Sloane punched on the phone. "Sloane Burbank."

"It's me." Derek's familiar baritone grazed her ear. "Just

wanted to bring you up to speed. Both the Newark field office and the Atlantic City RA are cooperating. They'll cover the Stockton campus while you're away. And I'll be meeting Deanna Frost for coffee tomorrow morning. I'll get ahold of you in Boston if any new information materializes on any front."

"Call me either way," Sloane qualified.

"Fine. Gotta go now. My squad's waiting."

"Understood." Sloane swallowed, grateful for the news, wishing it didn't make her feel so damned indebted to him. "Thanks for the quick work. I hope something pans out from it."

"Me, too. So long."

"Bye." Sloane was about to punch off when her call-waiting beep sounded. "Sloane Burbank."

"Sloane, it's Bob Erwin. I just wanted to let you know that we found a blue hair band on the John Jay campus. We found it behind the building where the pool is. Two members of the swim team said that Cynthia Alexander has one just like it."

"Does it look like she accidentally dropped it?"

"No way. The bushes in the area indicate signs of a struggle. Plus, there are spots of blood on the ground and on the hair band. Everything's being tested for DNA. But if the report comes back the way I think it will, we've got an official crime scene."

CHAPTER
EIGHT

DATE: 27 March
TIME: 0100 hours

I saw her today. She's a true goddess, the epitome of all the word conveys. I wish it were time. But it's not.

It's *them*. I can feel their anger pulsing. They're unrelenting tonight. I have no choice but to answer their call.

Nom Wo Club
1:55 A.M.

The beat-up white van was parked on Mott Street, half a block from the target. Inside the van, the electronic surveillance was picking up every word being said around the table where John Lee was sitting. So far, there'd been an interesting exchange about pickup arrangements for a shipment arriving at the Canadian border next Tuesday night. That "shipment" would be another installment in Lo Ma's human trafficking enterprise. Helpful advance notice for C-6. With the assistance of ICE, the transaction would help the Bureau build their case against Lo Ma and his international criminal activities.

Other than that, it was a typical night at the gambling parlor. But if the information Lee had gotten was correct, all that was about to change.

Derek sat in the rear of the van, legs sprawled out in front of him, listening intently and eating the last of his shrimp chow fun out of the carton.

"This stuff is great, even cold," he commented.

"Yeah, one of the fine perks of the job," Derek's partner, Jeff Chiu, returned drily. "Great food and an imminent gang war. Who could ask for more?"

"Can't imagine." Derek finished off the quart of food, and sat up straight as he heard the tone inside the gambling parlor change, become tense. "What are they saying?"

"They're making preparations." Jeff was one of the few agents who was fluent in the complex Fukienese dialect. "Positioning themselves with their weapons. It sounds defensive, not offensive. They're waiting to see what Xiao Long's enforcer plans to do."

"Trash the place, or trash them," Derek muttered. He peered out the window as two dark sedans pulled up to the curb outside the club. "It's showtime. Let's see how far things go before the NYPD has to go in and break up the fighting."

"What did they say when you clued them in?"

"They sent over a couple of unmarked cars that are parked around the corner. The plan is to keep our presence here under wraps, and to give us as much time as possible to get something on the Dai Los. But as soon as violence or gunfire erupts, the cops will move in. At which point, they'll put the fear of God in both gangs. Maybe that'll make them think twice before they start an all-out turf war."

"Hope so."

Both agents fell silent as three men exited each car and strode purposefully into the club. Judging from his thick build, one of the men was definitely Jin Huang, Xiao Long's enforcer.

A staccato of angry voices immediately ensued, followed by crashing sounds.

"What's going on?" Derek demanded.

"The Red Dragons are tearing up the place and making

threats. 'Stay away from our girls.' 'Our turf . . . hands off . . .' That's the gist of what I can hear over the uproar." A pause. "The Black Tigers are denying any involvement. They're accusing the Red Dragons of stirring up trouble to start a turf war."

"Any mention of the Dai Los? The local businesses being extorted? The illegal import of the electronic devices or the women?"

"Nope. Nothing remotely coherent, much less specific. Just escalating threats, overturned tables, smashing plates and glasses."

In the midst of the turmoil, there was a loud thud and a cry of pain, followed by another.

"Okay, things are getting dicey now. They're throwing punches."

"Yeah, that much I figured out." Derek frowned as he heard a sharp warning shout, followed by a burst of light that illuminated the first-floor window. Forceful words, then a gunshot. "What the . . . ?"

"A warning shot at the ceiling," Jeff clarified. "And some torched drapes. Jin Huang is promising that next time, it will be the whole place."

As Jeff spoke, all six of Xiao Long's men burst out of the club and jumped into their cars, where the drivers were waiting. They screeched off into the night. An instant later, a bunch of people who'd been gambling at the club—John Lee included—flew out the door, together with the girls who'd been serving them, probably in more ways than one.

Derek flipped open his cell and made a call to one of the unmarked NYPD cars. "Gleason? It was a warning shot. No one's down. And the fire's restricted to a pair of drapes. So it's all yours. Have fun making their lives miserable. Keep me posted."

He flipped off the phone. "Anything going on?"

"Lee took off, so I can't hear anything inside the club," Jeff reported. "But the last sounds I heard were Lo Ma's gang members cursing the Red Dragons and putting out the fire." He sat back. "My opinion? If any of the Black Tigers is killing Xiao Long's girls, he's doing it on his own. Lo Ma's guys are pissed as hell. But they seem totally baffled."

"Maybe it's a rival gang trying to stir up trouble between the Red Dragons and the Black Tigers to strengthen their own position?"

"That's what I was thinking." Jeff watched as a couple of uniformed cops rushed into the club, weapons raised. "Let's check it out when we get into the office tomorrow."

"Agreed." Derek glanced at his watch. "It's three A.M. I doubt anything more's going to happen tonight. So why don't we eat the rest of the food I bought?"

Jeff arched a dubious brow. "It was cold before. By now, it's probably freezing."

"So? It's still the best in Chinatown. I'll take that over starving anytime."

"You've got a point."

A few blocks away, in an area devoid of streetlights, he sat in his car, waiting and sharpening his combat knife. He studied the girls as they scattered and headed in different directions.

It took him less than a minute to make his choice.

When she was isolated and far enough away from the others, he zipped up his jacket and pulled the thick down hood over his head, tugging it forward until his face was concealed. He fingered the coin in his pocket, made sure it was there. Then he seized his combat knife and stepped out into the night.

CHAPTER NINE

DATE: 27 March
TIME: 0900 hours

Peace. After last night, I deserve it.

This one was messier than the others. The drugs took longer. And she was stronger than I expected for someone so delicate. She broke my choke hold long enough to bite me and scream.

One scream—that's all she managed to get out. I cut her after that. Painful and nasty, but not lethal. Three deep slices across her throat. I was careful to avoid the major arteries. That part would come later. Right at the moment, I just needed her to know I meant business.

She got the message, fast. Her body arched, then stiffened, and she opened her mouth to let out a shriek of agony. I anticipated that—and I stopped it. I clapped my hand over her mouth and told her to shut up or I'd chop her into little pieces. I meant it, too. I would have.

She knew it. I saw it in her eyes.

She choked back her scream, although she retched a few times. Then big tears started sliding down her cheeks.

That didn't matter. She didn't matter. The real nuisance was the blood streaming down her neck and soaking into her jacket. The flow was intensifying. Soon it would pool at her feet.

I was forced to change my plan. That infuriated me. I hate change. And I hated her for making me deal with it.

I needed a different location. The abandoned warehouse I'd chosen was two blocks away. I couldn't carry her that distance. There would be blood all over the streets. Worse, all over me. I never allowed their blood to touch me. They were filth. Disease carriers. I'd brought my cleaning and disinfecting supplies, of course, but they were set up— along with everything else—at the warehouse.

I acted efficiently. Right down the street, I found an empty tenement. The basement door was open, the lock broken. Inside were a couple of rats and a rusted boiler. The place would do just fine.

I dragged her inside and tied her to a pole. Then I duct-taped her mouth, and injected her with enough Nembutal to keep her unconscious while I ran down to the warehouse and retrieved my equipment. She was still out cold when I got back. It took a lot of work on my part to wake her up. She really was more trouble than she was worth. That got me angry all over again. I was tired and impatient, so I set up the tripod and video camera, and started taping without my usual precision and fine-tuning. She didn't deserve the effort anyway.

The demons were roaring to life. I turned my full attention to silencing them. It took a long time before they were sated. I didn't mind. I liked hurting her. It appeased my anger. But it also felt good. Too good. That was wrong and dirty. I felt ashamed.

It was her fault. Her and the others like her. They were the reason the demons wouldn't go away.

She needed to be punished. She needed to feel every ounce of pain before I let her die.

I lingered until the shame faded and the triumph surged. Then I arranged her and the room as always, placed the coin beside her, and scoured away the evidence.

I couldn't wait to get home. I needed to scrub her off of me. I needed to cleanse the night from my body, and the demons from my mind. And I needed to sleep.

March 28
8:36 P.M.

Sloane's plane touched down in Newark Airport twenty minutes late. Then came the endless taxiing to the gate. Like Sloane, most of the passengers were business travelers. So they were used to delays. They glanced up, then continued scanning their newspapers or leaning back to relax against the headrests.

That wasn't going to cut it for Sloane.

Given the nonstop pace of the past two days, she was way too pumped up to relax. Between the intensive, two-day seminar she'd just conducted, Derek's phone call yesterday filling her in on the new leads that had resulted from his meeting with Deanna on Penny's case, and the news from Bob Erwin that the DNA on the hair band found at the John Jay crime scene matched Cynthia's, Sloane's brain was racing on overdrive.

She was ready to hit the ground running.

She'd promised Bob Erwin she'd drop by Mrs. Alexander's hotel tomorrow. Her goal there was to talk to the woman, to forge some emotional trust, and then maybe to glean a piece of information that Cynthia's mother didn't know she possessed.

As for Penny's case, Sloane planned to pay Hope Truman a visit. She wanted to be there when she provided Penny's mother with the latest update. That way, she could help channel her expectations in a realistic direction, while offering her the comfort of her presence.

Sloane frowned, surrendering to the realization that there'd be no sleep again tonight. She'd pick up the hounds, smother them with the attention she'd stored up for them all week long, then get on the computer and start doing some research into last year's Richard Stockton graduating classes—both undergrad and grad—and departing faculty members. She'd coordinate her efforts with Derek's and those of the Newark field office. There was more than enough work for all of them. Hundreds of the people who'd lived or worked at Stockton last year had since moved on to other endeavors. Any one of them could be a potential witness.

On that thought, Sloane felt the Boeing 737 slow down and ease around to the terminal, where it stopped. A minute later, the "Fasten Your Seat Belts" sign chirped and went off. That was all the permission Sloane needed. She grabbed her suitcase from the overhead bin, and by the time the cabin door opened, she was making her way to the front of the plane.

Before the other passengers had even stretched their legs and collected their things, Sloane was off the plane, down the ramp, and sprinting through Newark Airport.

9:15 P.M.

Derek was hoping for a quiet night.

He was pretty wiped out from the week. He could count the number of hours he'd slept since Monday on two hands. And, since he wasn't assigned to tonight's surveillance, he'd spent an entire day gathering information on rival gangs who might want to stir up trouble between the Red Dragons and the Black Tigers. He felt perfectly justified accepting Tony's offer when his boss had told him to go home and have a weekend.

He'd left about seven o'clock, picked up a couple of groceries, and driven home to his midtown east apartment. The high-rise he lived in was on Second Avenue, close enough to the noise of the Midtown Tunnel to make it affordable. That wasn't a problem; Derek could sleep through anything—or stay awake through anything, whichever was required. As for the apartment itself, it was tiny—not even five hundred square feet including the bedroom, kitchenette, and bathroom.

On the other hand, it had its perks. The place had just been renovated, there was a doorman around most of the time, and Derek had secured a parking space in the underground garage. And since he drove his Bureau car back and forth to work each day, that meant one less headache. Parking spaces in Manhattan were on the endangered species list. So, all in all, he had a good living arrangement, at least for the time being.

He let himself in, changed his clothes, and cooked his dinner. He was sitting at the kitchen table, enjoying his pepper steak and scanning the local sports section to see when the Yanks' opening game would be, when the phone rang.

He groped for his cordless phone, and answered. "Hello."

"Hey," Jeff greeted him.

Derek made a grunting sound. "Aren't you sick of me yet? We spend more nights together than a married couple."

"Actually, yeah, I'm very sick of you. So's my wife. She's glaring at me as I speak. But Gleason called right before I left. I wanted you to hear this ASAP."

"I can hardly wait."

"The NYPD found another one of Xiao Long's girls, this time in an abandoned Chinatown tenement just a couple of blocks from the Nom Wo Club. Same MO—she was drugged, raped, throat slit with a combat knife, and one of those python coins left at the scene. Although evidently, this time the sexual assault and the murder were more graphic and more violent. I don't have all the details. But Gleason's description wasn't pretty."

"How long ago was she killed?"

"That's the kicker. According to the medical examiner, the time of death was between five and six A.M.—yesterday."

"Yesterday."

"Today?" Derek's fork struck the table with a thud. He'd assumed the body had been there longer, and had only just been discovered. "We're talking right after our stake-out."

"Gleason said she lived near the Nom Wo Club. He figures she was on her way to Xiao Long's brothel to work around the same time everything went down at the club. Gleason's guess is she saw the cops and steered clear."

"Obviously, not clear enough." Derek's brows knit. "Either someone in Lo Ma's gang has a death wish, or whoever did this isn't one of his. Because no one in his right mind would provoke Xiao Long right after his enforcer was in their face, threatening their lives."

"My thoughts exactly. I expected Lo Ma's guys to retaliate by smashing up one of Xiao Long's gambling parlors. But to blatantly spit in his face by taking out another one of his girls—butchering her, no less—right after the fight at the club? Doubtful."

"It seems to me we're back to a third gang trying to start up a war for their own purposes."

"Gleason said the same thing. His team is already investigating that angle."

"Are they going to be able to minimize the collateral damage? Or do we have to get involved?"

Jeff sighed. "Not sure. The NYPD's up to their asses in the murders. We might have to back them up to make sure Xiao Long gets the message before he orders any killings. So I wouldn't make any hot plans if I were you."

"Not a problem. The only hot plans I had were a shower and bed. I'll be on standby all weekend."

"Yeah; me, too. Which means I'm in the doghouse here."

A corner of Derek's mouth lifted. "It's times like this I'm glad I'm single. Good luck wriggling your way out of the doghouse."

Hunterdon County, New Jersey
9:40 P.M.

Sloane dropped her bag off at home, then drove directly to the Wagners' house to relieve Elsa and Burt of their three frolicking charges. She called ahead, although she knew

Elsa would be awake for her evening ritual of ten o'clock tea and biscuits.

It took her several minutes, door-to-door, to get to the Wagners' house, a fact that Sloane always found amusing. The term next-door neighbors was a misnomer in their case. In truth, the two houses were set far back from the road and separated by six wooded acres.

Elsa greeted Sloane at the door, drying her hands on a dish towel. She was a round woman with white hair, black eyes, and a sharp nose who looked a lot like Frosty the Snowman, except when she smiled. Her smile was warm, as was her heart. She'd been a widow for decades, and the strain of running the house alone, not to mention the loneliness, was starting to take its toll. She was aging. She looked weary, the lines around her eyes and mouth more prominent than ever before, her step more unsteady. Which was why having her son around was a blessing, despite Elsa's sadness over his failed marriage.

Now she beckoned for Sloane to come inside. "You didn't have to rush over here tonight," she scolded. "Like I said on the phone, the hounds are playing tug-of-war with Princess Di and Burt in the rec room. You could have gotten a good night's sleep and dropped by in the morning."

"I know, but I missed my little troublemakers," Sloane replied, stepping inside with a rueful grin. "And as long as you were still awake . . ."

"I was making our tea. Now you can join us." She gave a little shiver as a blast of night air whisked through the front hall. Hastily, she shut the door, rubbing warmth back into her arms. "Brrr. I'm getting old. The calendar says it's spring. But to me, it's still winter."

"Age has nothing to do with it," Sloane assured her, wincing as she pulled off her gloves. "My hand is killing me. If March plans to go out like a lamb, it better hurry up and do a one-eighty."

At that moment, an outbreak of barking erupted from the rear of the house, followed by the skidding and scuffing of padded paws as the dogs raced across hardwood floors.

"I think your trio knows you're here," Elsa said with a chuckle. "You say your hellos. I'll get the tea and biscuits ready—for us, *and* for the dogs. They get special treats, too. My ten o'clock ritual has become quite the event." On that note, she headed off to the kitchen.

An instant later, Moe, Larry, and Curly hurled themselves into the room, tripping and shoving one another in an attempt to be the first to reach Sloane. She squatted down in time for the onslaught, starting with a group hug, then giving each one special attention. Her face was licked so many times that the chill in her cheeks dissipated.

"Hey, guys, I missed you, too—so much," she told them fervently.

Moe yipped a protest.

Sloane recognized the tone and stroked Moe's silky head. "I keep telling you *guys* is a generic term," she murmured. "It's a loving reference that's not gender specific." She kissed the top of Mona's head. "So it includes gals. I promise. You know I adore you all equally. You're just better at slathering on the guilt."

"She's female. What did you expect?" Burt strolled out, Princess Di in his arms. "By the way, no need to worry about Moe's ego. She and Di have won the last three rounds of tug-of-war. Larry and Curly are starting to feel the pressure."

Sloane laughed. "What can I say? Women have killer instincts when it comes to competition."

"Right." Burt fell silent, his lids hooded as he watched Sloane romping on the floor with her dogs.

She took no offense. Burt was a moody guy—friendly one minute, quiet the next. The divorce had hit him hard, which probably explained the way he tensed up around Sloane. Actually, around all women, Elsa had once confided. It seemed that Burt's wife had been carrying on with another man. Burt had walked in on them in his house, his bed. And it had all unraveled from there.

The divorce had been ugly, and Burt had walked away with the Classic Pages—the literary bookstore he owned and ran, the cabin in the Catskills he lived in, and a very bitter taste in his mouth.

He was a nice-looking guy in his early forties—lean, with short brown hair, scholarly features, and probing dark eyes. These days, he spent most of his time at his bookstore or here at his mother's. Partly to help her out. Partly because they each filled a void for the other.

"I think Di is jealous," he remarked now as the frisky Pomeranian struggled out of his arms and ran over to join in the lovefest.

"No reason for that. Let's fix it." Sloane leaned forward, scratching Princess Di's ears and pressing a kiss to the top of her head. "Thank you for sharing your home with Moe, Larry, and Curly," she told Di. "You're a beautiful, gracious hostess."

"And an active one," Burt added. "Believe me, she more than keeps up with your three."

"That's quite a feat."

Elsa poked her head out of the kitchen. "Our tea is ready," she announced. "Everyone join me in the kitchen."

The cherrywood kitchen was warm and inviting. The table was set up for a formal tea, complete with china, a silver tea service, and a perfectly arranged tray of shortbread cookies. On the floor beside the table was the canine corner—four water bowls, and a chinette plate with four biscuits on it.

"This looks lovely, Elsa," Sloane told her. "A real treat after the week I've had." She cocked her head in the direction of the drumming paws. "Assuming we'll have peace to enjoy it."

"They're usually polite," Elsa said, supervising as the four dogs sprinted in and went straight for the biscuit plate. "One each," she reminded them. "If you share, you each get seconds."

Sure enough, each dog snatched up a biscuit, then went to a separate spot to chomp on it.

Sloane blinked. "Could you teach me how to do that? Clearly, I'm lacking something in the etiquette training area."

Elsa smiled. "They're just like children. Better behaved at someone else's house, and far more enthusiastic about the snacks they're offered. When Burt was in grade school, he always came home telling me about the great snacks he'd had at his friends' houses. I'd call their mothers to find out what these amazing new treats were, only to learn we already had them. Then the other mother would inevitably rave about how well behaved Burt was, how neat and polite. I wondered if it was the same boy who scribbled on the walls with black crayon and chased down squirrels on our property—"

"Mother, I think you've made your point," Burt interrupted. "Sloane doesn't need a biography of my childhood."

"Of course, dear." Elsa gave him an apologetic look. "Let's enjoy our tea while the pups are busy."

They all sat down, and Elsa poured the tea and passed around the shortbread. "Tell us all about your trip," she urged Sloane as they ate. "Was it successful?"

"Yes," Sloane replied. "Exhausting, but successful."

Elsa gave a slight shudder. "The world has become such a frightening place. It's no wonder companies have to protect themselves against workplace violence."

"Is that what your seminar was about?" Burt asked, looking mildly surprised. "I thought you trained people in crisis management."

"I do. That includes companies as well. Your mother's right. The pressures of today's world have resulted in an increase in workplace violence. Employees need to be prepared to deal with the possibility."

"Right." Burt digested that. "How can you spot a potential loose cannon? Are there signs?"

"Usually, yes. Emotional withdrawal, mood swings, uncharacteristic tension, displays of temper. The tricky part is for the right people to pick up on those signs, and their severity, before it's too late." Sloane set down her cup. "Those closest to the subject often don't recognize how serious the situation is until it's too late. On the flip side, casual acquaintances— which, unfortunately, usually include coworkers—don't know the subject well enough to spot the telltale signs."

"So the psychos go undetected."

"Frequently, yes. But *psychos* is a pretty extreme term. Not everyone who takes hostages falls into that category. Every human being has a breaking point. The challenge is to realize when someone has reached his or hers— before it's too late."

"That's a charitable assessment." Burt rose to give the dogs their seconds.

"Just an objective one," Sloane returned factually. "That's not to say that subjects who take hostages are stable. They're not. But the point is moot. Full psychological evaluations are done by the experts—*after* the crisis is over. While it's ongoing, assessing the subject's mental health is essential only as it pertains to ending the crisis quickly and nonviolently."

"And how do you manage that? If a guy is barricaded in his office with hostages and a weapon, how do you talk him out?"

"By listening and tailoring my responses to what I hear. The subject has emotions, frustrations, and usually demands he wants to express. My job is to listen, and to establish a line of communication."

"How?" Elsa asked, turning up her palms in puzzlement. "If you tell him you understand what he's done, won't he realize you're just humoring him?"

"That's why I don't. Rather than emotional support, I offer emotional observation. I don't say, 'I understand'; I say, 'You sound frustrated.' It conveys my awareness that he's going through something, without saying that the way he's chosen to display it is okay. It's called emotional labeling. It's one of what the FBI's Crisis Negotiation Unit refers to as 'active listening skills.' I learned it when I trained."

"And you teach that to laypeople?" Burt inquired.

"Both in theory and in practice," Sloane confirmed. "It's like a lab course. There are classroom lectures and simulated barricades. It's a total process. When I finish up and head home, I'm confident that my clients are educated in how to react to a workplace hostage situation—both before the authorities arrive and after, should their assistance be required. They'll do what they can to control the situation, and when the pros do arrive, they'll work with them to achieve a happy ending."

"All that sounds so impressive." Elsa's sincerity was evident. But so was her exhaustion. Her lids had begun drooping as Sloane finished up her explanation, and now her voice had grown weaker. She looked and sounded as if she were fading.

It was late. And, despite her best intentions, Elsa was tired.

Sloane feigned a yawn. "The Bureau trained me well. Even so, intensive seminars like these take their toll. I'm wiped."

A faint, knowing smile touched Elsa's lips. "I doubt that."

"Don't. Between working round the clock since yesterday at dawn, and two shuttle flights, I'm not only beat, I'm dying for a hot shower." Sloane hoped she sounded convincing.

As it turned out, Curly came to her rescue.

Having polished off his second biscuit, he scrambled over, gripped her pant leg tightly between his teeth, and began tugging with all his might.

The perfect out.

"I think I'm being summoned," Sloane noted, freeing her pant leg and standing up. "The doggy treats are gone, along with their patience. I'll clear the table and do the dishes. After that, I'd better take these three home."

"Nonsense." Elsa rose, waving away Sloane's offer. "It'll take me ten minutes to finish up in the kitchen. You go collect the hounds' things. They're in the rec room."

"No, I insist." Sloane was already carrying china over to the sink. "You're a wonderful hostess. But you've done more than enough. Please go up to bed. I'll take care of everything and be out of here in twenty minutes."

"But you've worked nonstop," Elsa protested. "You just said you were exhausted. You need to get some sleep."

"I need to, yes. But it won't be happening." Sloane was efficiently washing and drying the cups and saucers. "I've got a pile of work waiting for me on my desk. So I'll get that hot shower, but sleep's relegated to the back burner, at least for tonight."

"Well, if you're sure . . ." Elsa's eyelids were at half-mast as she scooped up Princess Di.

"I'm sure. Thank you so much for taking care of my little terrors." Sloane leaned forward to scratch Princess Di's ears. "And thank you, too, Your Highness."

"You're very welcome from all of us." Elsa smiled faintly. "The hounds are welcome anytime. Burt?" She turned to her son questioningly.

"I'll be leaving, too," he supplied, carrying the empty tray over to the sink. "I'm opening the bookstore an hour early tomorrow to do inventory. So I'll lock up the house, then walk Sloane to her car, and head for home. I'll check in with you tomorrow."

"All right, dear." Elsa was already making her way slowly out of the kitchen. "Good night."

"Good night, Elsa." Sloane watched her disappear around the corner. "Your mother's not herself," she said quietly.

"No, she's not. I've taken her to the doctor. He's prescribed some vitamins. And he wants her to drink one of those nutritional supplement shakes every day." Burt's jaw tightened. "None of it seems to be doing much good. I guess life's just taken its toll on her after all these years."

"You're coming by and spending so much time with her must help. It gives her an incentive."

"Yes and no. She'd rather have grandchildren. That didn't work out." He cleared his throat. "At least not yet."

Feeling a little uncomfortable with the turn the conversation had taken, Sloane resumed her cleanup.

Burt stayed where he was, watching Sloane thoughtfully. "You're quite the dynamo," he observed at last.

"Not always." She didn't look up. "When my adrenaline drops, I'll collapse."

"Nice to hear you're not completely superhuman." Finally, Burt turned away. "I'll lock up and get Moe, Larry, and Curly's things."

"Thank you. By that time, I'll be ready to leave."

Ten minutes later, Burt walked Sloane to her car. He waited until she had settled the hounds in the backseat, and had buckled herself in and turned on the ignition.

"I enjoyed our conversation," he said. "Maybe we can continue it sometime over dinner."

Now Sloane was *really* uncomfortable. "These days, my life is crazy. I'm pretty much on overload. Dinner for me is a can of tuna."

"Then maybe when things quiet down."

"Maybe."

Burt hovered beside her car for another minute, his hands shoved in his pockets, his expression unreadable.

"I appreciate the escort," Sloane prompted, hoping to fill the void and end the conversation all at once. "And I'm grateful for your help with Moe, Larry, and Curly." A quick glance in her rearview mirror. "But I'd better get going. They're shivering."

"So I see." He acknowledged her claim with a nod. Then he stepped away from her car. "Good night."

"Good night." Sloane shifted the car into drive and veered around the top section of the driveway in a full circle so she was facing the road. This way, she could negotiate the twists and turns of the Wagners' endless driveway in forward rather than reverse.

She gave Burt a quick wave, relieved when he waved back and headed for his own car. He was obviously in a vulnerable state right now, and the last thing she wanted was for him to make more of their neighborly friendship than it was.

With the hounds yipping and standing up against the windows, Sloane put on her brights and headed back to the main road.

Her gaze fell on the digital clock.

Eleven-ten. Too late to make phone calls.

She was itching to know if the Atlantic City agents had turned up anything at the Richard Stockton campus.

She knew one person who'd still be awake.

Derek never went to bed before one.

That knowledge was irrelevant. There was no way she'd call him. Not at home. And not on a Friday night. He was probably working. Or out with a woman. Derek was way too hot to be spending his weekends alone.

Sloane felt that familiar knot tighten her gut, the knot that occurred every time she visualized Derek with another woman.

And she hated the fact that, despite what a bastard he'd been, despite the thirteen months that had passed since the two of them were over, that knot was still there.

CHAPTER TEN

DATE: 31 March
TIME: 0500 hours

I'm losing.

Time. Control. The culmination of everything I've planned.

All being threatened.

The demons are screaming. They won't be silenced. Satisfying them takes more time and energy each day. I must stave them off, devote my efforts to the preparations—for those already here, and those who have yet to arrive.

Especially for *her*. When her time finally comes, everything has to be perfect. She's my counterpart, my other half.

The epitome of all goddesses.

Most of the goddesses are in place—Aphrodite, Hera, Astraeus, Hestia—situated in the wings as they await their ultimate passage.

Gaia is not following the timetable. I can't allow that. She must be regulated until all the others are acquired and ready. Anything less is unfathomable.

I'll expedite my plan. Cut corners. I loathe that. Haste spawns regret. But my options are nil.

And Gaia isn't the only obstacle. A new one is presenting itself.

Athena.

She's still a warrior with a will of iron. She refuses to submit to the inevitable, and to accept her fate. With the others, acceptance came more easily. And the few times they resisted, I silenced them with drugs. That doesn't work with Athena. She can't tolerate any of the sedatives. Every time I administer them, she vomits profusely. She's lost so much weight and looks so ill that it worries me. I increased her meal portions and stopped sedating her, while at the same time taking great care to lock her up in case she had any thoughts of escape.

She still didn't eat. When I visited her room, she was just sitting on her bed, staring off into space. She looked dazed and weak. I went to her, and asked if she needed anything. She requested a cool cloth. I was happy to oblige.

I should have realized she was just trying to lull me into a false sense of security. When I returned with the cloth, she flew at me and tried to knock me down and run away. Of course I stopped her. But that wasn't enough. She had to be punished. I had to make sure she didn't try something like that again. So I had no choice but to hurt her. I know I was justified. Still, it upset me to hear her sobs. It upset me more to see her blood.

I bandaged her wounds. But I still had to make it up to her. So I brought her one of my lemon squares at dinnertime— a token of apology. She called me horrible names and flung the lemon square in my face. When I took out my handkerchief and began wiping my face, she overturned the dinner tray—dumping plates, plastic silverware, cups, and food— all on the floor. Then she swung the tray wildly, trying to strike me as hard as she could. I stopped her just in time. Then I sedated her and left her to lie in her own vomit. Even a gracious man can take so much.

Killing her is not an option. Not now. Not in anger.

That would be blasphemous. It has to be for a higher purpose.

I needed to be reminded of that higher purpose.

I needed to see *her.*

Hunterdon County, New Jersey
5 A.M.

The rest of the world might be just waking up, but for Sloane the day was well under way. She'd nodded off for an hour or two after devising a preliminary plan for the next phase of Penny's case, then leaped up at 4:30 A.M. and finished mapping out the details.

The FBI might already have started the ball rolling. She had to know where things stood at their end before she did anything. The last thing she wanted was to step on their toes, or bungle their investigation by doubling up on interviews they'd already conducted.

She had to speak to Derek. She'd wait until seven-thirty to call. He'd be at his desk by then. But for now, she needed a three-mile run to clear her head.

6:15 A.M.

Upon returning from their run, she'd unleashed the hounds in her backyard and romped all over the grounds with them until they were exhausted. The whole bunch of them, herself included, went inside and drank tons of water, after which the hounds plopped on the sofa and fell fast asleep.

With a loving smile, Sloane left them to their nap. She collected her archery gear and went out back, trudging over to the far side of her property where her archery course was set up.

She loved the bow and arrow. She always had, since she'd learned to shoot them as a kid. Being a target archer cleared her mind, sharpened her focus—and, these days, strengthened her grip. In her gut, she believed that one day her relentless target practice would play a major role in getting her back into the Bureau.

For now, she still anchored the bowstring with her middle and ring fingers. But one day that would change. Her trigger finger would heal. And the scars on her palm would toughen up enough to withstand the tight grip needed to anchor a Glock 22.

It was up to her to make that happen.

She reached her destination, and put down her gear long enough to set everything up. That done, she pulled on her leather glove with the reinforced finger pads to protect her injury. She checked to make sure her bowstring was adjusted to just the right tension, then pulled the first arrow out of its quiver and placed it across the bow. Planting her feet, she straightened, pulling back the bowstring as she took careful aim at the target. She gritted her teeth against the twinges of pain in her wrist and fingers, keeping her arm as steady as possible.

When her focus was dead-on and her breath was suspended, she let the arrow fly.

It cut through the air and struck the target in the red circle, a solid inch and a half away from the bull's-eye.

"Dammit," Sloane muttered. She lowered the bow, wiping her arm across her forehead and doing a few shoulder rotations to release the tension in her upper body. Patience. She had to have patience. At least she was hitting the red and the blue now. There was a time when black was a reach, with most of her arrows hitting the outer white ring, and a few of them flying off into the woods.

Even so, she wanted that bull's-eye so much she could taste it.

Her quiver held nine more arrows and she shot them all. Only one surpassed her first shot, lodging closer to the inside line of the red, just outside the coveted yellow circle.

Close but no cigar.

She put down her gear and went to collect the arrows.

Her cell phone rang.

Startled, she pulled it out of her pocket. It wasn't even 7 A.M. The caller ID read *restricted,* which gave her no clue. So she punched it on.

"Hello?"

The only response was some crackling noise and a prolonged silence.

"Who's there?" she demanded.

More crackling sounds and then the *beep-beep-beep* that told her the connection had been broken.

Before she snapped her phone shut, Sloane glanced down to see the number of bars registering. Four. Great reception at her end.

So the problem was with the caller, who probably had lousy cell reception and had, no doubt, punched in a wrong number. On that thought, she resumed her task of retrieving the arrows.

Her phone rang again.

With an exasperated sigh, she abandoned her task and whipped out her phone again. "Yes?"

There were those damned crackling noises, interspersed with silence.

"Is someone there?" Sloane asked in a strong voice.

There was a definite breath or two, another prolonged silence, and then the connection was broken.

Weird.

Just for the hell of it, Sloane accessed her log of received calls, zeroed in on the most recent entry, and made a callback attempt. But, as she suspected, the connection failed, and her display read *unavailable,* since the number was clearly blocked.

There wasn't a damn thing she could do about it.

With that, Sloane dismissed the entire incident and finished pulling the arrows out of the target. She packed everything up, collected her gear, and turned to head back to the house.

She'd barely taken three steps when the phone rang again.

This time the crackling was minimal and the breathing was audible.

"Who is this?" she demanded again.

Nothing. Just an awareness that someone was there and that whoever it was had no desire to hang up.

Abruptly, the phone call took on a whole new meaning. Violating. Personal.

The slow, raspy breathing continued, scraping Sloane's ear like chalk against a blackboard.

She stopped in her tracks. Gut instinct made her head snap up, and she looked around, although she had no idea what she was looking for. The woods were quiet. The trees were drizzled with snow. And the sun was slowly rising in the east. No one was around except a few deer. Then why did she suddenly feel as if she were being watched?

The caller was still on the other end of the line, breathing and waiting.

"Tell me who you are or I'm hanging up," Sloane stated in a hard, no-BS tone.

Silence.

She disconnected the call and turned off her cell phone.

She continued to scrutinize the yard, plagued by the nagging feeling that her anonymous caller was more than a phone presence. He was somewhere nearby. She could sense it.

The hair on the back of her neck stood up. She wasn't scared. She was poised to strike. Derek used to say that between her agility, her training, and her watchfulness, she was like a cat. And like a cat, her instincts were keen.

Whoever her intruder was, he didn't want to be seen—at least not this time.

She acted on autopilot. No display of apprehension. No slowing her pace. She just retraced her steps to the house, went inside, and locked the door. The last was a mere precaution, since she didn't believe she was in imminent danger. Whoever was toying with her had an agenda, and it didn't involve grabbing her right now, if at all. He'd had ample opportunity, and he hadn't availed himself of it. So he'd either been going for a scare tactic or playing games with her.

She didn't know which, why, or who.

But she intended to find out.

FBI New York Field Office
26 Federal Plaza, New York City
7:24 A.M.

Derek was drinking coffee at his desk, reading over what he and Jeff had dug up over the weekend, together with what the cops had found out. It was a long shot that whoever was torturing and killing those prostitutes was one of Lo Ma's guys—unless he had a death wish. It had to be some sick rival gang member who was desperate to start a war between the Red Dragons and the Black Tigers. Either that, or a psycho client of Xiao Long's brothels who had a thing for screwing and killing his prostitutes. Regardless, it wasn't one of the Black Tigers.

C-6 believed that. The NYPD believed that. Now the trick was to make sure Xiao Long believed it.

Late last night, Derek had met with John Lee, who promised to get word out on the streets. The problem was that Lee's connection was with Lo Ma's gang members, so his credibility stopped there. Leaving damage control to him alone was a mistake. So Derek had contacted Eric Chang, another of his confidential informants, who had an in with the Red Dragons, and who was tight with someone who was tight with Jin Huang. Chang had promised to get the message to Xiao Long's enforcer that they should be watching their backs for offenders other than Lo Ma's people, and also checking their brothel client lists for potential suspects. Not starting a gang war that had no basis.

Now Derek was poised and waiting for the outcome.

His phone rang. He snapped it up. "Parker."

"Hi, Derek, it's me."

"Sloane." He sank back into his chair. "What can I do for you?"

"Good morning to you, too," she answered drily. "I'm calling to follow up on our new leads."

"Which leads?" Derek asked brusquely.

An icy silence. "The Deanna Frost leads. The ones that surfaced when you interviewed her the other day. Like what Penny was wearing—her bright red pant suit with the red-and-black-print scoop-neck shell. And the fact that she walked past Alton Auditorium, and was heading for Lake Fred for her stroll. Not to mention her upbeat frame of mind, and excitement over the upcoming seminar, both of which scream *abduction*, not suicide or vanishing act. *Those* leads. Did the Newark field office turn up anything?"

"Not to my knowledge."

Again, Sloane got quiet, and Derek could actually feel her reining in her temper. "Has anyone done a friggin' thing since our last conversation?" she blurted out at last. "Did the Atlantic City RA send agents over to the Stockton campus or not?"

"Yes and yes. I followed up with Anderson, and the AC office sent Tom McGraw and one other agent over to Richard Stockton—"

"Good," Sloane interrupted. "Did anyone at Richard Stockton recognize Penny's photo yet? Did the Bureau turn up any witnesses who might have spotted her around Lake Fred the day she disappeared?"

"It's been just two working days since we gave them Deanna Frost's information. Expecting something solid to have materialized by now is unrealistic, even for you."

"You think? They could have worked over the weekend."

Derek rolled his eyes. "Give it up, Sloane. It's seven-thirty Monday morning. Most agents aren't even at their desks yet."

"You are."

"I'm me. Not everyone keeps my insane hours. Besides, even if I pressured the agents who are assigned to this to go straight over to the campus, the administration offices don't open till eight-thirty or nine. And the students don't wake up until noon. So there aren't a lot of people to talk to yet."

"There's the campus police. Last I heard they were open twenty-four/seven. They have incident records from last April. Maybe some of those dovetail with Penny's disappearance. There also might be video surveillance from the security cameras—"

"I've considered every one of those possibilities. So has McGraw. The situation's being handled. Give it time."

"*Time?* Penny's parents have been without her for a year. They're not sure what horrible acts of violence she's endured, or if she's alive or dead. They have no body, no answers, and no closure. I think that constitutes special circumstances." A pause. "Or am I barking up the wrong tree? Is this more about your ego than about this being low priority? Is this your petty way of shutting me out of the process? Because if it is, it's not going to fly."

"Now, why doesn't that surprise me?"

"That's not an answer." Sloane sucked in an impatient breath. "Never mind. I'm heading into the city now. One of my stops is Mount Sinai. As you know, Penny's father's a cardiologist there, I'm meeting with both him and Penny's mother to bring them up to speed. Unfortunately, the rest of my day's spoken for. But tomorrow I'll be driving back down to Richard Stockton and doing my thing—which includes lighting fires under the right asses."

"Sloane—"

"See you around, Derek."

John Jay College of Criminal Justice
Office of Professor Elliot Lyman
8:45 A.M.

Elliot tried for the third time to concentrate on the data he was inputting into his "loaner" computer, but to no avail. The machine was archaic, it was inferior, and it wasn't his.

With a sound of disgust, he pushed his chair away from

his desk and slumped back in it, raking both hands through his hair.

He hadn't expected everything to snowball like this.

The cops had been in here and confiscated everything. His entire professional life had been carried out the door as nonchalantly as if they were carrying out the trash.

And they just kept asking him questions.

He practiced his answers every night, anticipating what else they could question him about. But they always seemed to find something unanticipated to throw at him. Which made him so nervous that he fell all over himself when he spoke, and he could barely meet the gazes of whichever cops were asking the questions. He knew he came across as if he were hiding something. Charm and easy verbal expression had never been his strengths.

Meanwhile, things just kept getting worse and worse. Since Cynthia's parents had reported her missing, it was like he was caught in the middle of a bad crime drama. The latest rumor was that Cynthia's bloody hair band had been found by the NYPD in a wooded area behind the building that housed the swimming pool. It had been sent off to the DNA lab for confirmation.

The press was everywhere. He couldn't even go out for a sandwich without being attacked like a piece of steak in a lion's cage.

He couldn't breathe. He was about to implode.

There was a light knock on his semi-opened door. He swung his chair around to see who was invading his space now.

"Hey, stranger." Sloane stepped in, glancing around to see if they were alone. "Can you spare a few minutes for a pal? I know your next class doesn't start for an hour." She waved a brown bag in the air. "Fresh bagels with cream cheese."

Elliot's relief at seeing her was blatant. "Sloane. Thank God." He beckoned her in, then rose and walked over to shut the door behind her. "I'd be thrilled to see you even without the bagels. I'm not hungry."

"You have to eat." Sloane's practiced glance swept the office, noting the dust-free rectangular spots on Elliot's numerous tabletops that told her his PCs had been removed. Even his laptop was nowhere in sight. The only computer in the room was an outdated desktop. As for the file cabinet, it was half open and in disarray, files poking out here and there as if they'd been rifled.

The cops had clearly been here.

Picking up on her scrutiny, Elliot waved his arm agitatedly at the desktop that was clearly a substitute for his state-of-the-art workstation. "Look at that dinosaur. How can they expect me to work on it? It can't handle any of my programs. I can't run any of my software. And my confidential research is now public property."

"It's not public property," Sloane reassured him. "It's with the NYPD. Once they've checked it out for any leads in the Alexander case, they'll return it."

"Yeah, after their experts have either ripped off my work or trashed it. What ever happened to the First Amendment? They took everything, including all my servers, claiming they needed to look for artifacts of Cynthia's e-mails, forum postings, chat sessions, and assignments from Comp 201."

"They're not interested in violating your rights. They're interested in finding a kidnapper. And Cynthia's communications with other students and faculty may point them in the right direction. The NYPD had a warrant. That means they convinced a judge that seizure of your equipment was justified. In addition, the warrant only authorized them to extract material related to Cynthia and Comp 201. They weren't given carte blanche."

"I get it. But I could have extracted what they needed without exposing my life's work and my highly sophisticated equipment to some cretin they call a computer tech, or, worse, to one with enough brainpower to see my software's potential and rip it off. You may trust everyone in law enforcement, but I don't. My research is cutting-edge, and close to completion. But I haven't unveiled it to a soul. Now I might as well have auctioned it off on eBay."

Elliot might be overreacting, but Sloane understood why. From what she'd gleaned, he wasn't exaggerating the scope of his work. That was why John Jay's forensic computer department was funding his research big-time. Although modest in comparison to major universities, the budget they were giving him was large for a city college. The rest, Sloane suspected, was being subsidized by grants from law enforcement organizations, private security companies, and perhaps even the NSA. Elliot's software program had the potential to provide early warning of cybercrimes in progress by discerning unusual patterns in financial data—everything from credit-card purchases and banking transactions to sophisticated money-laundering practices employed by organized criminal enterprises and terrorists. His work was significant. And it was pretty damned sensitive.

To Elliot, that made the NYPD's actions the ultimate invasion.

Blowing out a breath, Sloane placed the bag of bagels on Elliot's desk and shrugged out of her coat. "I'm doing Sergeant Erwin a favor today. I'll see if, in return, he can expedite his analysis of your equipment and get it back to you ASAP." She turned, giving Elliot's forearm a gentle squeeze. "Trust me. Bob Erwin is a good man. All he's interested in is extracting information about Cynthia, her friends, and her potential enemies."

Sloane opened the bag and handed Elliot a bagel and cream cheese, neatly wrapped in wax paper. "Now sit down and eat."

Elliot stared at the bagel, then sank down in his chair. "I sound like a heartless bastard," he muttered. "The poor girl's been kidnapped. God only knows what the wack job who took her has in mind. And here I am worrying about my research. You must think I'm as shallow as they come."

"I think you're human." Sloane perched at the edge of

another chair, unwrapped her bagel, and began munching. "And I think you'd better eat that bagel before I do. I was up all night working, took a three-mile run with the hounds, and then did some serious damage on the archery course. I haven't eaten a solid meal in two days. So consider yourself forewarned."

A hint of a grin. "Yes, ma'am." Elliot unwrapped his breakfast and took a bite. "Thanks," he said quietly. "For the bagel, the pep talk, and the sensitivity. I realize you drove down here because of me. You're a good friend."

"I have my moments." Sloane reached over and grabbed a bottle of water from the small fridge against the office wall. "I assume you heard about Cynthia's hair band being found?"

"Yeah, with blood on it and near it. Is that true?"

A nod. "The DNA results came in. The blood on the hair band and on the grass where it was found is Cynthia's."

Elliot leaned forward. "What about prints? Were there any others besides Cynthia's?"

"Partials. They were smudged. The lab is seeing what they can come up with. But it doesn't look too promising."

"The poor kid."

"And her poor parents." Sloane wiped her mouth with a paper napkin. "I'm talking to Mrs. Alexander today. My fingers are crossed that she'll say something, anything, that I can give to Bob."

"Wouldn't she have told him everything she knows already?"

"Everything she *realizes* she knows," Sloane corrected. "You'd be surprised by the number of details we all store in our brains that never register in our consciousness without being prompted."

"Yeah. I guess I would." Elliot fiddled with the edge of the wax paper. "So it's your job to coax out some of those details?"

"One of my jobs, yes." Sloane resumed eating her bagel,

choosing her next words carefully. "Hang tough these next few days, Elliot. Everyone's working at maximum speed and efficiency. But until the investigation's wrapped up, life at John Jay won't return to normal. I saw the press converged at the edge of campus."

"They're vultures," he replied bitterly.

"You don't have to speak to them. If you're approached by a reporter, just keep walking and say nothing. Stay holed up in here as much as possible. Teach your classes. Do whatever research you can. I'll make sure you get your computers back quickly, so it'll be business as usual. Just keep it together."

Elliot was staring down at his desk. "Do you really think she's still alive?"

"I don't know. Time's not on her side. She's been missing for nine days. Statistically, that's way too long. On the other hand, we haven't found a body. Until we do, I've got to believe she's alive."

"Determined, optimistic Sloane." Elliot's expression was as dubious as it was grim. "You're one of a kind. But somehow I doubt the cops share your opinion."

CHAPTER ELEVEN

DATE: 31 March
TIME: 1130 hours

I had to leave work and come home to check on her.

She was lying on the floor in a pool of her own vomit. She was barely moving. And her color was bad—pale and greenish. This couldn't go on.

I got her up, gave her some water, and half carried her to the bathroom. She whispered a plea to shower, and I agreed. I'm not cruel. I couldn't deny her that shred of dignity. I gave her a fresh chiton to change into and made sure she was strong enough to stand on her own. Then I gave her a pail of toiletries and left the bathroom. I locked her in, waiting outside as always.

She still looked sickly when she came out. Her eyes were huge and dazed, and her skin was clean but chalk white.

I brought her back to her room and gave her a tray of food, which she ate without incident. As a reward, I mopped and disinfected her room, and put a fresh blanket on the bed, along with a newly printed copy of the chapter on Athena. No one could live in that stench of vomit.

She murmured something that sounded like thank you, and then she asked if she could lie down. She curled up like a child, covered herself, and fell fast asleep.

As I was leaving the room, I heard her call out for her mother.

That's when the voices told me what to do.

Mount Sinai Hospital
100th Street and Madison Avenue
New York City

Sloane wondered whether the meeting with Penny's parents would be as difficult as the one she'd just had with Carole Alexander.

Walking out of the parking garage onto East Ninety-ninth Street, Sloane headed toward Madison Avenue and Mount Sinai, replaying the conversation she and Cynthia's mother had just shared. It had started with, "I just wish they'd find my baby" and ended with, "All I care about is getting Cynthia home safe and sound."

In between, Sloane had heard the story of an all-around camper who loved sports, reading, cultural studies, and family. The den in the Alexander house had an entire shelf of swimming trophies Cynthia had won, both in high school and college. She was quiet, but strong-willed, and refused to give up when she wanted something badly enough. She dated, but not heavily, and there was no one special guy in her life. Between her studies and her athletics, there hadn't been time. But she had lots of male friends, and all those relationships were normal and healthy.

Carole went on to explain that Cynthia worked hard to perfect her skills. But the only person she was fiercely competitive with was herself.

Sloane had more than understood. In fact, listening to Carole Alexander speak, she'd gotten a déjà vu feeling. It was as if she were hearing her own mother talking about *her* high school and college years, rather than Cynthia's. There was no doubt that Carole and Cynthia Alexander shared the same unique mother-daughter bond that Sloane's mother shared with her—a bond that couldn't be explained or denied.

That thought brought a rueful smile to Sloane's lips. She'd been so crazy busy this week that she hadn't had a chance to give her folks a call. At this particular time, that was probably a good thing. Her mother could read her like a book, even over the phone, sometimes perceiving things about her even before Sloane did. And since crossing paths with Derek had thrown a monkey wrench into her life— one she wasn't ready to get into with her mother, or with herself, for that matter—it was best that she deferred calling Florida until she'd gotten a better grip on her emotions.

As she entered the teaching hospital's atrium, her thoughts were interrupted by a security guard asking where she was going.

She gave him Dr. Truman's name, then headed for the elevators, mentally switching gears from Cynthia's case to Penny's.

Dr. Ronald Truman had aged a lifetime since Sloane had last seen him, although she suspected that much of that aging had occurred since Penny's disappearance.

"Sloane." Hope Truman rose from her chair, gesturing for Sloane to take the seat next to her. "Thank you so much for coming to the hospital. Ronald couldn't get away, and he wanted to be here for this meeting."

"Of course." Sloane sank down into the leather chair that Dr. Truman held out for her, and waited until he and his wife were seated.

Sloane proceeded to tell the Trumans what they didn't know—the specifics of what Derek had learned from Deanna and the absence of details on the FBI's investigative plan going forward. And, most of all, the fact that Penny's state of mind had been upbeat.

"So we know almost the precise spot on campus where Penny vanished." Hope Truman sat up straight, her fingers tightly clasping her purse as a fresh surge of optimism coursed through her. "Surely that's enough of a lead to act on."

"It is," Sloane agreed. "I spoke to Special Agent Parker this morning. Based on this new information, agents will be visiting the campus to investigate."

"Why are there no details on this investigation?" Ronald demanded before Sloane could finish her answer. "Who are they interviewing? And when?"

"I'm not sure."

"You're not sure?" Ronald leaned forward, his eyes blazing. "In other words, more smoke and mirrors, courtesy of the FBI."

"That's not what I'm saying, Dr. Truman." Sloane chose her words carefully. "Just because the Bureau isn't comfortable sharing procedural details with me doesn't mean they don't have a plan. I'm sure they do."

"The decision of whether to share case details with you isn't the Bureau's. It's ours. We hired you."

"I understand your feelings. Unfortunately, it doesn't work that way." Sloane had to bite her tongue to keep from elaborating and letting Dr. Truman know just how livid she was about the approach Derek was taking.

It was bizarre to find herself in this position. Derek was always the cowboy, the one who made quick evaluations and then charged into the fray, the one who placed getting results over playing by the rules. She was the diplomat, the one who applied psychology and careful planning before she acted. He was the first-strike force. She was the crisis negotiator.

This time the roles were totally reversed. Worse, she had to be PC about her reaction to that, since to do otherwise would bash the Bureau. Which meant she had to defend Derek for his abrupt one-eighty, and swallow the fact that he might be doing this just to make her life difficult.

Maybe she was being completely irrational. Either way,

it didn't matter. She wouldn't dis the Bureau, and she wouldn't dis Derek. The former was out of loyalty and training, and the latter was out of respect. Whatever else he was, Derek was an outstanding agent.

She had to handle this just right to achieve the desired results.

"When I spoke to Special Agent Parker, I brought up several ideas," she informed the Trumans. "How quickly and how thoroughly they'll pursue them, I just don't know. In all fairness, Special Agent Parker is working on a different squad now, with a new pile of high-priority cases. So he has a lot to juggle. Compounding that problem is the fact that so many Bureau resources have been reallocated to counterterrorism."

"In other words, they don't have the resources for what they consider to be, at best, a long shot, and at worst, a cold case that will never be solved," Ronald interrupted.

"It's not that black-and-white. I'm just not sure where in the gray zone it falls." Sloane paused, then went for the gold. "Officially, the Bureau has the final say about how they handle things. Being an outsider, I have only so much latitude when it comes to making demands. I can't order them to provide me with full disclosure, or to include me in their planning."

"But I can." Ronald Truman responded just as Sloane had hoped. "The assistant director in charge of the New York field office is an old friend of mine. We attended Hopkins together. Plus, I have a former golf buddy who's now at FBI Headquarters in D.C. He's a supervisor in the Criminal Investigative Division. His father is one of my patients. When Penelope first disappeared, I made phone calls to both New York and D.C. Those conversations resulted in Penelope's case remaining visible, active, and being assigned to Special Agent Parker, who I was told was the best."

"He is." That much Sloane could say without hesitation.

"Then I don't give a damn what squad he's working on now. He's in charge of Penelope's case. We have new information to act on. I want him driving this hard and fast, with you brought up to speed and in the loop. I'll make sure of it."

"I appreciate that." Dr. Truman's Bureau connections were even better than Sloane had guessed. "Support like that will make a huge difference."

"Consider it done." Ronald Truman was already reaching for the phone. "Expect to hear from the New York field office later today," he announced, punching in a phone number. "When I'm finished twisting the right arms, you'll be getting an urgent call from Special Agent Parker."

Sloane gritted her teeth as she envisioned that call. "I'm sure I will."

FBI New York Field Office
26 Federal Plaza, New York City

"You've got to be kidding."

Derek stared across the desk at his squad leader, his jaw working furiously as the significance of Tony's words sank in. When he'd answered his boss's summons, walked into the corner office, and taken a seat, he'd assumed he was being summoned for an update on whether C-6's attempts to prevent a gang war had been successful. Or maybe some information on whether the cops had tracked down the psycho who was butchering Xiao Long's girls.

But this? Never.

"No, Derek, I'm not kidding. I'm dead serious." Tony leaned forward, fingers interlaced, wearing that Supervisory Special Agent Antonio Sanchez look that said there was no give in this situation. "Until further notice, the Truman case is your number one priority. Everything else is back burner. My orders came from the ADIC himself. My hands are tied. And so are yours."

Derek's fist struck the arm of his chair. "This is insane. Penelope Truman's been missing for a year. We got a few new leads, enough to warrant some follow-up from the Atlantic City RA. They're working those leads. There's not a damn thing I can add to the process, certainly not enough to yank me away from C-6 when we're sitting on a potential time bomb."

Tony didn't avert his gaze. "Time bomb defused," he supplied. "Your informants did their jobs. Xiao Long is turning his attention away from Lo Ma and toward other rival gangs, and the patrons who frequent his brothels."

"For now. We both know that unless Xiao Long finds his psycho, and fast, détente will be a thing of the past."

"If that happens, I'll have you back here with us in a heartbeat." Tony paused a moment. "Look, if this were only about Dr. Truman's connections, and his demands were baseless, I'd fight this decision. But if you put aside your anger long enough to be objective, you'll have to admit that the Trumans have a point. We're not just talking about a new lead here. We're talking about confirmation that Penelope Truman didn't just take off. She vanished from a college campus in broad daylight. Which not only points to foul play, but pinpoints a location for her disappearance. You were, and are, the case agent of record. You were initially assigned at the Trumans' request, because they were told you were the best. For months, you were their lifeline. Do you blame them for insisting that you continue running things?"

"No. What's more, I intended to—from here. But to set up shop in AC? How do you think Tom McGraw's going to feel with me breathing down his neck?"

"He's fine with it. We spoke ten minutes ago. He gets it that the Trumans feel a sense of security with you at the helm. He said you should check in to the Best Western tomorrow morning, then meet him at Richard Stockton at nine-thirty. Oh, and dinner at that pricey seafood place you liked last time. Your treat."

"Great." Derek felt as irked as he sounded. But McGraw wasn't the reason. "I feel like a friggin' marionette, with my strings being pulled."

"I don't think that's how the Trumans see it."

One dark brow rose. "I actually wasn't referring to the Trumans. There's another puppeteer in all this—a real master manipulator."

Tony's lips twitched. "Yeah, I see Sloane's hand in this, too. Truthfully? If you two are in the middle of a battle of wits, I'd say this round goes to her. You must have really pissed her off."

"That's my MO."

"Someday you'll have to tell me the whole story behind you two."

"Maybe. But first, I have to figure it out myself." Derek rose.

"Going home to pack?"

"Nope. Going to make a phone call."

Sloane jumped when her cell phone rang. She'd had two more hang-ups since she got home, and it was beginning to grate on her nerves.

Glancing at the caller ID, she was relieved, but not relaxed. This was one call she'd been expecting. And dealing with it would be a challenge of a different kind.

Steeling herself, she leaned back on her sofa, plumped a pillow behind her, and took a break from scratching Larry's ears to punch on the phone.

"Hello, Special Agent Parker," she said, propping her legs on the ottoman. "What can I do for you?"

"Smooth work," Derek responded drily. "Fast, too. Not great for inspiring a positive working relationship between us, but hey, that wasn't your intent. The important thing is, you got the job done."

"I aim to please."

"Now *that,* you didn't. Then again, that's standard operating procedure when it comes to us—except in bed. So why change now?"

That one stung. Sloane had expected Derek's feathers to be ruffled, but she hadn't expected such blatant hostility.

"You're being a bastard," she informed him, all banter vanishing in the blink of an eye.

"That's how I get when I'm manipulated."

"I didn't manipulate you. I sidestepped the obstacles you were throwing in my path."

"And the difference is?"

"This wasn't a power play. Nor was it an attack. You were dodging my questions. I had no way of figuring out why. Whether it was to cut me out of the picture or to mini-mize your involvement in Penny's case, the end result was unacceptable. So I found a way to keep you in the forefront and me in the loop."

"You did more than that. I'm not only handling the case, I'm running the show from our RA in Atlantic City. I'll be leaving before dawn and checked in to the Best Western by eight. I'm on my way home to pack. Wanna pick out my clothes for me? I wouldn't want you to feel out of the loop."

Sloane sat straight up. "They're sending you down there? What about your other cases? You just finished your C-6 training."

"Life's a bitch. Until I solve this case, or Chinatown ex-plodes into gang warfare, I'll be handling my C-6 responsi-bilities long distance."

"Now, *that* wasn't my doing. I never meant for—"

"Don't flatter yourself. It never occurred to me that you had *that* much influence, not even with Tony. You just planted the seeds. The rest was an ADIC who goes way back with Ronald Truman. So what do you think? The navy Brioni suit and the striped Gucci tie you gave me for my birthday? Or the charcoal Lauren suit and the maroon Armani tie I left at your place in Cleveland and you mailed back to me?"

Sloane's anger was rapidly escalating. "First cruel, now childish. Cut it out, Derek. Look, I'm sorry you're being shipped off to the Jersey shore. It wasn't my idea. In fact,

I'm less than thrilled at having you in my face every step of this investigation. But we play the hand we're dealt. So get over yourself. I'm not trying to control you. I'm just determined to solve Penny's case. Which means you and I are going to have to find a way to work together—like it or not."

"Right." Derek snapped his briefcase shut. "I'll be at Richard Stockton tomorrow around nine-thirty. So will McGraw."

"Then I'll meet you both there."

"I assumed you would." A tight pause. "Sloane, do *not* come charging in and start running the show on your own. If we want to maximize our chances of getting information on Penelope's disappearance, we need to pool our resources and logically decide who'll be most effective at handling what. Once we've divvied up assignments, *then* we'll act."

"Agreed. I had no intention of jumping the gun. I planned on waiting for you to arrive *and* for us to devise a productive strategy. I'm aware that my consultant status gives me less influence with law enforcement than an SA has—at least where it comes to those agencies who've never worked with me. But it also gives me a better foundation for connecting with laypeople, who are intimidated by being questioned by the feds and who react better to an empathetic approach—which, in case you haven't noticed, is *not* your forte."

"That's not what you said when you asked me to meet with Deanna Frost."

"I said you had a certain macho charm. That's a far cry from being able to connect with people using psychology and compassion."

"Really? They sound a lot alike to me."

"They're not. As for your I'm-in-charge speech, don't worry. I may be gone from the Bureau, but I still remember the rules. You're the agent of record."

"Meaning you'll let me take the lead? I'll believe that when I see it."

"You will—tomorrow. Oh, and Derek?"

"What?"

"Wear the Gucci. I've got great taste in ties. Much better than I do in men."

TWELVE

DATE: 1 April
TIME: 0500 hours

My plan would make the gods proud.

Hera. She could accomplish what I could not. She could do it without compromising my time line. And she could do it in a way that was ideal for Athena.

Hera would be rewarded. Athena would be soothed.

And one problem would be resolved.

I should have thought of this sooner. From the moment I first seized Hera last June, she'd been the ideal acquisition. The initial fight she put up was minimal. Her acceptance was swift. And, all these months, she'd cooperated without incident.

Maybe it was because she was older and recognized her own limitations. Maybe it was because she was older and valued life more than youth was able to foresee. Or maybe it wasn't her age at all, but simply her character. It didn't matter. She was the perfect choice.

When I unlocked her room and entered, she looked surprised to see me. I don't usually visit the goddesses so early in the morning. But for me to be comfortable, my plan had to be carried out before dawn. After that, the risk would be too great. Caution has always been my ally; recklessness my foe. I believe in order. Without it, chaos ensues.

I shut the door behind me and walked in. I stood respectfully at the foot of Hera's bed. I never sit on a goddess's bed. When I do sit, it's always in a chair, and always keeping an appropriate distance. I only approach the goddesses to give them their food or to accompany them to the bathroom. I make sure never to touch them, except with the blade of my knife or when discipline is necessary, after which I make sure to cleanse myself and them. To touch them for any other reason would be blasphemous.

Hera looked startled and then enormously pleased when I asked if she'd like to enjoy some fresh air. I felt proud that I could make her happy. I do so with all the goddesses, each in their own right. In Hera's case, I'd predated her arrival by decorating her chamber with a plush velvet chair, as regal as any throne, and a crown with an attached veil on the table beside it. Of course I also made sure to neatly place the chapter on Hera at the edge of her mattress. I'd seen her reading it several times, and looking at the illustrations. That pleased me immensely.

As the goddess queen, Hera deserved extra consideration. Pleasing her was an honor unto itself. Therefore, to ensure her contentment, I'd purchased an exercise bicycle a month after her arrival, and placed it in her room. That would nourish her physically. To nourish her mentally, I bought her copies of the *New York Law Journal*—a small connection to her former life—and had frequent chats with her about current events. And to nourish her spirit, I brought her bowls of fresh fruit, which always made her face light up.

I didn't lie to her, not even now when she was so eager for fresh air. I explained that in order to give her her walk, I'd need something in return. That made lines of concern crease her forehead—until she heard my request, and the reasons behind it. Then, just as I expected, she agreed, with all the compassion intrinsic to the goddess of marriage and childbirth.

Even in the predawn hours, with the air still cold and touches of frost on the grass, the grounds were lovely. Hera and I strolled in the garden behind the house. I chose that particular spot because it's buried in a cluster of evergreen trees. Again, that was my caution prevailing. The rutted road was miles away, the main road even farther. No matter where on the grounds we walked, spotting us would be a virtual impossibility. The manor is so deep in the woods and so high up in the mountains that it's nearly invisible. A worthy Mount Olympus.

Hera sucked in the cold morning air as if it were the most precious gift in the world. I was touched by her reaction. I found myself offering to take her walking again, both as a kindness to her and as an incentive for her to succeed with the favor she owed me.

She thanked me with all the grace befitting her. And when I escorted her inside, she was eager to reach out to Athena.

I brought her directly to Athena's room and unlocked the door. I was decidedly uneasy about what I'd find inside.

She was lying on her back, an arm flung over her face, her hair a tangle that said she'd tossed and turned all night. Her chiton was clean, as was she, which brought me a great sense of relief. It meant that because I'd refrained from administering the drugs, she hadn't vomited. But she'd withdrawn into herself. I could sense that because a fine tension rippled through her when I walked in, and yet she made no overt move to acknowledge my presence.

That changed abruptly when I urged Hera forward.

"Athena?" she asked softly.

Athena's arm jerked away from her face, and her head turned toward the sound of a woman's voice.

"It's all right," Hera assured her in a soothing tone. "I'm . . . Hera. I'm a visitor here, just like you. I thought you might enjoy some company. I know I would."

"Oh my God." Athena sat up, her disoriented gaze scrutinizing the older woman. "Are you real? Or am I hallucinating?"

I decided to insert myself at that point. I assured Athena that she wasn't hallucinating, that I'd brought Hera to her as a source of comfort. I reminded her how she'd called out for her mother last night. She clearly didn't remember having done that, but she flinched with emotion when she heard that she had.

Hera took a tentative step in her direction. "May I come in?"

Athena looked like a bewildered child. "Are you the person I heard through the wall? Is he keeping you here, too?"

"My room is next door, yes."

"And it's not just you. There are others here as well?"

Hera glanced at me for direction, and I nodded. There was no point in keeping it a secret. Soon all the goddesses would be united at the sacrificial altar, each one representing a gift to be savored in the afterlife.

"Yes, there are others," Hera told her.

"How many? How long have you been here? Where is this place? Why is he keeping us locked up like prisoners? What does he plan to do to us?"

I wasn't pleased with the rapid fire of Athena's questions, nor with the direction they were taking. Hera must have sensed it, because she placed a silencing forefinger to her lips.

"Take a deep breath and calm down," she advised. "I want to help, to offer you the comfort of a mother. But I can't if you won't let me. Nothing is going to be accomplished by this kind of agitation."

Athena's eyes were still glazed, and she was shaking with suppressed emotion. I thought, at first, that my plan had failed, that even Hera couldn't get through to her.

Then, abruptly, things changed. Athena met Hera's soothing gaze, and she promptly fell silent. As Hera had directed, she inhaled slowly, then exhaled. Finally, she nodded.

"I'm sorry," she said in a small, quavery voice. "I'm just frightened, and I feel so alone. Please, please stay. I won't lose control again."

I'd been right. This was exactly what Athena had needed.

I was so exceedingly pleased, and yes, relieved by the results, that I made an immediate mental note to stop by the market later today and pick up a mango and some kiwi for Hera. Those were her favorites.

"Delphi?"

At first, I didn't hear Hera addressing me, her voice was so quiet. But when she repeated herself, I turned and responded at once. "Yes?"

"Athena needs to speak freely and to accept my comfort without censure. That's essential if you want me to establish the kind of bond that exists between mother and daughter. I realize this request is unprecedented, but may I speak with her alone? You can lock us in here and stand guard just outside the door. You have my word that I'll keep her in check. But if we want your plan to succeed, I must gain her trust. If you allow this, it's much more likely that you can gain hers."

She had a point. Athena already looked calmer, and her shaking had nearly stopped. She was just sitting in the middle of the bed, watching us and waiting to see what we were discussing.

The room was escape-proof. Hera was trustworthy. And I had a goal to accomplish.

"Very well." I gestured for Hera to join Athena. "I'll allow you to talk alone. You have thirty minutes."

I waited while Hera walked over, perched at the edge of the bed beside Athena. Then I reversed my steps to the door.

I'd made the right decision. I knew it the minute I heard Hera's soothing voice, saw her reach out her arms to Athena.

By the time I locked the door, Athena was holding on to Hera and sobbing on her shoulder.

Once he was gone, and she heard the sound of the key turning in the lock, Eve Calhoun didn't waste an instant. Gently, she gripped the arms of the young woman who was clinging to her, and eased her away.

"Shh," she whispered. "We have to talk quietly. And we have to talk fast. He won't leave us alone for long. He's cautious to the point of paranoia. So I'll explain as much as I can, and you can ask me whatever you want. Just watch the tone of your voice. He has to believe I'm comforting you."

The young woman nodded.

"What's your name?"

"Cynthia. Cynthia Alexander."

"I'm Eve Calhoun." Eve made sure to keep her tone soft, almost crooning—a direct contradiction to her words. "Tell me the bare essentials of your background, and everything you remember since you were kidnapped."

"He thinks I'm Athena. The Greek goddess," Cynthia managed.

"I know. He thinks I'm Hera. Now stay calm and talk to me. Maybe together we can figure out a means of escape."

That gave Cynthia the impetus she needed. Swiftly, she told Eve who she was, and relayed the details of her kidnapping—including how hard she'd been fighting to escape.

"Don't," Eve advised her. "Don't fight. It only makes things worse. Although I'm sure he expected you to. Athena is the warrior goddess, and the goddess of wisdom. You're intelligent, athletic, and strong-willed. The correlation made sense. Just as mine does."

"How?"

"Hera's the mature goddess of marriage and childbirth. I'm a matrimonial attorney. The rest of my story is just like yours. I was doing laps at the pool at NYU. I left via Washington Square Park. He grabbed me, pressed a combat knife to my throat, and injected me with something that knocked me out. When I came to, I was here."

"When was that?"

Eve swallowed. "June second."

Cynthia turned sheet white, and stifled a gasp. "That's ten months ago."

A nod. "And I'm not the first of his victims. He kidnapped another woman last April. She's his 'Aphrodite.' And there have been two more victims since then. My frame of reference is fuzzy, but I think one arrived in September, and the other at the beginning of December. I know nothing about either of them, nor have any of us met. After that, months passed. The holidays came and went. He seemed calmer, more grounded. He stopped muttering bizarre things to himself about the honor of sacrifice, the rage of the demons, and the glory of the gods. His conversations became almost normal. He seemed content, almost tranquil. No new captives arrived. I began to assume—or maybe to pray—that the December victim had been the last."

"Clearly, you were wrong."

Again, Eve nodded. "Everything changed the week before you arrived. It's like he made a one-eighty, became totally unhinged. I still don't know what caused him to snap the way he did. But whatever it was, it made him angrier, more embittered, more frenetic. His eyes were veiled in madness, and he was fueled by some new brutality that I didn't understand, nor could I get him to open up and talk about it.

"That's when he started raving about seizing more goddesses, bringing them here to complete the circle as soon as possible. Sometimes he mentions three, sometimes four. And there was a 'she' he kept talking about, and another 'she' he kept talking to. Whether they were among the women he planned to kidnap and turn into his goddesses, or whether they were just voices in his head, I had no idea. What I did know was that other victims were inevitable."

"So when I was kidnapped and locked in the room next to yours, it came as no shock."

"Unfortunately, no."

Cynthia raked both hands through her hair. "I have so many questions."

"Ask them quickly. Just realize that I know as little as you do about what his agenda is, or how he chose us."

"Does he hurt you?"

"At the beginning, he struck me. He called it discipline. I caught on quickly, and stopped resisting. From that moment on, the discipline ended. If it's rape you're worried about, don't. He's never touched me in a way that's even remotely sexual. To the contrary, he's as respectful as a well-bred young man on his first date. In his mind, we're goddesses, not prisoners."

"You called him Delphi—why?"

"Because that's how he introduced himself. I remember some of my Greek mythology. But my only recollection of Delphi is as a shrine, not a person. It was an ancient site of the high Greek oracle." Eve shrugged, gesturing toward Cynthia's mattress. "I see you have your Athena chapter. I have mine on Hera. I've read it a hundred times. Nothing in it explains why he's Delphi. So your guess is as good as mine."

"Does he ever let you out of your room other than to bathe?"

"Occasionally, I'm allowed out of my room. Today was my first walk outside. Till now, it's been to join him for a cup of tea in an empty room down the hall that he's set up like a parlor. He brings me in there on the days when he needs a conversation partner—or listener—when he wants to discuss philosophy or the degradation of society as it exists today. Most of all, when he needs someone to turn to for maternal advice and support. He needs that, desperately."

"Why?"

"He never reveals anything personal about himself, and he becomes enraged if I try to steer the conversation in that direction. So I don't. But if I were to speculate, I'd say that he's not just insane, he's still part child himself. He has three sides to him—the child, the gentleman, and the lunatic."

"It's the lunatic that terrifies me."

"I know." Eve's expression was grim. "When that side of

him comes out, I cringe. He vacillates between raving bouts of insanity and vacant-eyed introspection. When the raving starts, I pray for the moment he leaves the house—which he usually does, after yelling, cursing, and smashing things. There's always the fear that he'll burst through my door and vent his rage at me. But, believe it or not, it's the vacant-eyed introspection that creeps me out the most. That's when he's impossible to read. He's vibrating with repressed violence. He delivers my meals, escorts me to the bathroom, and never speaks. He just looks right through me. It frightens me even more than his uncontrolled rage."

"So what do you do?"

"Stay silent. Walk on eggshells so I don't provoke him. And wait for the 'gentleman' to return. When he does, he's eerily normal—polite, hospitable, friendly. Like a gentleman caller in the eighteen hundreds, visiting to converse and exchange pleasantries."

"Oh God." Cynthia covered her face with her hands. "How do you survive without losing your mind?"

"Two ways. By using those occasions when he wants to have a scholarly discussion to divert myself. He's insane, but he's also highly intelligent. So I use that intelligence to keep my own madness at bay. The rest of the time, I stay sane by planning my escape. Now I have an ally—you. Please, Cynthia, cooperate with him. Stop fighting. We needed him calm, trusting, and—hopefully—off guard. Thank him profusely for bringing me to you. Be grateful, humble. Then, when you ask to see me again, he'll permit it. We'll use those visits to combine our resources, and come up with an escape plan." Eve rubbed her forehead. "My instincts tell me we don't have much time."

Richard Stockton College
Pomona, New Jersey
9:20 A.M.

Sloane had arrived a little after nine. She parked her Outback in the first parking lot off College Drive, which was the location Deanna had said the taxi dropped her and Penny off. Sloane followed the road with her eyes. As one of Stockton's main streets, College Drive curled around the entire campus.

Getting out of her car, Sloane stretched. Richard Stockton College sprawled before her, sixteen hundred rural acres, most of them wooded. Even if law enforcement covered every inch of the grounds, it was unlikely they'd find any physical evidence—not after a year. They'd have to find witnesses, people who saw something, even if they didn't realize they had. Lake Fred was large and centrally located. And on a spring day, that meant students hanging out, jogging, even just walking to class. *Someone* had to have seen *something*.

A light wind blew by, and Sloane tucked a strand of chestnut-brown hair off her face. It was a sunny morning, with temperatures hovering around fifty. Spring was finally showing signs of arriving. Good for her hand. Good for her investigation. Less pain, more outdoor activity.

She was itching to get going. But, true to her word, she'd waited, leaning against her car and reading through her notes, forcibly resisting the urge to head directly over to Lake Fred and start questioning people.

Her patience was short-lived. She glanced at her watch: 9:23. She was antsy as hell. And it wasn't just investigating Penny's disappearance that was propelling her. It was a surge of nervous energy.

She'd received three more hang-ups on her cell phone this morning. One during her run with the hounds, one when she was loading her briefcase into the car, and one about ten minutes before she arrived at Stockton. Same MO each time—a restricted call, thirty seconds of slow, raspy breathing, then a hang-up. The whole thing was really starting to piss her off. One more day of this, and she was going to pull a few strings and initiate a trace.

The sound of crunching tires reached her ears, and she

turned to see Derek's midnight-blue Buick LaCrosse pull into the lot. He parked alongside her Outback and jumped out of his car, tossing his overcoat into the backseat and grabbing his briefcase.

That was Derek. High energy. Like an explosive about to detonate. Never needed a coat, not even in Cleveland in the dead of winter. He just generated his own heat. Anywhere and everywhere.

Sloane quickly dismissed that thought. Bad enough that seeing him still made her whole body react. She wasn't about to compound it by remembering.

"Good morning." He strode over to greet her, every bit the crisp professional. "You contained yourself. I'm impressed."

She blinked. "Excuse me?"

"You waited for me to get here. Wise decision."

"And you wore the Gucci. Equally wise decision."

A corner of Derek's mouth lifted. "Yeah, well, I didn't have a lot to choose from. These days, I'm a T-shirt-and-jeans guy. One of the perks of working the streets of Chinatown."

"Who are you kidding?" Sloane asked wryly. "You love the classic suit-and-tie look."

"My budget doesn't. The cost of living in Manhattan has gone through the roof."

"True. And since T-shirts don't need dry cleaning, you must save a bundle. On the other hand, you must lose a chunk of time ironing and folding." Sloane's eyes twinkled as she saw Derek's jaw tighten, telling her she was right. "Once an Army Ranger, always an Army Ranger. Neatly pressed shirts, folded socks, lined-up shoes—"

"You made your point."

"Don't worry. I won't tell. I wouldn't want your squad to have the ammo to shoot holes in that macho self-esteem."

"Not to worry. My self-esteem's solid."

"Of course it is. There's nothing soft about you."

The minute she said those words, Sloane wanted to kick herself. She'd meant them as they pertained to Derek's un- yielding nature. But that's not the way they came out.

She felt the heat of embarrassment warm her cheeks. "I didn't mean . . ."

"I know what you meant." Derek wasn't about to let her off the hook that easily. "But what you *didn't* mean is true, too."

"God, your arrogance is staggering." Sloane raked her fingers through her hair. "Only you—"

"Yup. Only me." He paused, let the words hang between them like an electric current.

In the sexually charged moment that followed, Derek's gaze slid over her, taking her in from head to toe. He started with her dark hair, now glinting with golden high- lights, then shifted to her delicate features and equally delicate frame. He paused at her open trench coat, linger- ing on her formfitting black pantsuit—especially where the blazer defined the curves of her breasts.

Abruptly, he raised his head, his gaze refocusing on her face. "Regardless of what you've been through, you look great. I didn't get the chance to tell you that at our last meeting. I like whatever you did with your hair."

Sloane gave him a tight smile. "New cut . . . and high- lights. I got tired of looking like a Girl Scout."

"Funny. I never thought of you as a Girl Scout."

Okay, this conversation was getting out of hand. And Sloane's insides were clenched so tightly, she could barely keep up the pretense.

"Why don't you tell me what you've scheduled for to- day?" she asked. "I assume we're meeting with the college president and the campus police?"

"Yup. Both. Also, I printed a campus map so we could navigate more expediently."

"Ditto."

They both pulled out their maps.

"Penelope took the most direct route to Lake Fred, past the Alton Auditorium, which is right here." Derek pointed. "The lake is flanked on its two long sides by academic buildings and housing. That's the good news."

"And the bad news is that the two short sides are heavily wooded, and one of those sides has two smaller lakes beside it. More area, more isolation." Sloane sighed. "Let's think positive. It was a busy time of day, a nice time of year, and Penny would definitely have stood out. With the way she dressed and carried herself, there's no way she'd be confused with a grad student."

"Agreed." Derek looked around. "I wonder what's keeping McGraw."

On cue, McGraw's black Pontiac G6 sedan turned the bend and pulled into the lot.

"Sorry I'm late," he said as he climbed out of the car and grabbed his file. "I got stuck behind a garbage truck."

"No problem. It's just nine thirty-five." Derek gestured from Sloane to Tom McGraw and back. "Sloane Burbank, Tom McGraw."

"Nice to meet you." Sloane shook Tom's hand—using the loose, pressure-off-the-palm-and-index-finger grip that Connie had taught her.

"Same here. I've heard your praises sung often enough. You've got a couple of good friends at the Newark field office."

Sloane smiled fondly. "Gary Lake and Lucy Mullen. We went through Quantico together."

Tom's glance flickered to the hand he'd just clasped. "Sorry about what happened. How're you doing?"

"Better every day. Busier, too." As always, Sloane steered the conversation away from her injury. She hated pity—almost as much as she hated talking about her exit from the Bureau. "I assume Derek filled you in on my role in this case and my relationship to the victim?"

"Yup."

Sloane relaxed. Clearly, Special Agent McGraw was an easygoing guy. She could use one of those right now, so there'd be less weirdness in divvying up responsibilities.

Just the same, she took the bull by the horns right up front.

"I appreciate your prioritizing this case on such short notice," she told Tom. "I promise to dovetail my role with yours and Derek's. I'll work *with* you, following your lead. I was hired to join the team, not run it."

Tom gave her a crooked grin. "I hear you. One favor— could you teach that to my wife?"

"Sorry." Sloane grinned back. "Those rules apply only in business. Personal relationships fall under a separate jurisdiction."

An exaggerated sigh. "I was afraid you'd say that." All humor vanished, and Tom's expression turned sober. "I appreciate your diplomacy, but don't worry about stepping on my toes. If the new leads you turned up can help us figure out what happened to your friend, and who took her, I'm all for pursuing them in whatever way gets the best and fastest results."

"On that note, here's today's agenda," Derek inserted. "As we know, the college has an official police department, not just campus security. That makes it easier, because we're dealing with pros—okay, maybe semipros given that this is Pomona, New Jersey. I called the chief of police yesterday and arranged a ten o'clock meeting for this morning. He agreed to assemble everything he could by that time, including any parking tickets, incident reports, or daily permits issued last April fourteenth. Stockton's also got a pretty sophisticated closed-circuit television system. There are a bunch of cameras placed around Lake Fred, leveraging their manpower in some of the denser, wooded areas."

"Did the police save the CCTV footage from a year ago?" Sloane asked.

"That's one of the things we'll be finding out. I think we should all attend this meeting so we know precisely what we're dealing with. After that, we can split up and do our respective things."

"Yeah, ours is going to be a lot of schmoozing with the powers that be," Tom noted. "The president of the college isn't going to like our marching in and causing negative publicity for the school."

"True. On the other hand, he wouldn't want to be unco-operative when it comes to solving a potentially violent crime." Derek's tone said he was ready for the administration's reticence, and would do what was necessary to eradicate it. "We'll make sure that he and the campus police get lots of positive press for their efforts. It'll be fine."

He turned to Sloane. "During this morning's meeting, we'll find out which apartments, dorms, and lecture halls have a view of the section of Lake Fred where Penelope disappeared. Then we'll arrange to get printouts of the rosters you mentioned the other day—the tenants who lived in those apartments, the kids who lived in those dorms, and the students and staff who had classes in those lecture halls. You can get started interviewing whoever's still here a year later. We'll start searching for the ones who've gone elsewhere."

"Great." Sloane was pleasantly surprised by how much thought Derek had given this. "I'm also going to take a stroll around the lake right after our meeting. That's the time Penny disappeared. I'll talk to the students, the Frisbee players, the joggers—whoever usually hangs out around Lake Fred late morning, early afternoon. Maybe some of the regulars were also regulars last year. If so, I might be able to dig up a clue."

"Good idea." Derek nodded. "So let's head over to the main building and hear what the campus police have to contribute to this investigation."

As they trudged off, Sloane automatically flipped her cell phone back on to check her messages.

Three missed calls. All *restricted*. She doubted they were from clients. Clients left messages.

Frowning, Sloane made a mental note for later today—to pull those strings she'd been considering.

She was about to turn off the phone, when it rang. She glanced at the display, knowing full well what it would say: *restricted caller.* Big surprise.

"Do you need to get that?" Derek asked, watching her expression as the phone continued to ring.

"Nope. Not necessary." Sloane turned off the cell, flipped it closed, and stuck it in her purse. "I know what it's about. I'll deal with it later."

DATE: 1 April
TIME: 1230 hours

I was elated with the breakthrough Hera had made with Athena. I served her lunch, inviting her to sit on her throne while she ate. Then I presented her with her surprises—a big bowl of fresh fruit, and a copy of today's newspaper. The latter was a first. It was a sign of my trust, the greatest reward I could give her.

She'd earned it.

Richard Stockton College
4:20 P.M.

The wind had picked up, and there was a cold rain falling in a steady stream as Sloane trudged back to her car. So much for the spring weather. The sun and fair skies had deteriorated as the day progressed.

The day itself had been long and intense. First the meeting with the campus police. Then hours stationed at Lake Fred questioning anyone and everyone—until the rain had sent them all scurrying inside. Last, interviewing faculty members and students. A few tentative leads. Nothing rock solid—yet.

All that was just the tip of the iceberg.

Derek and Tom had slashed their way through academic red tape. With just the right choice of words, they'd convinced the college president that it would be in his best interest to cooperate—and to exert influence on the campus police to do everything the FBI asked ASAP. Records and CCTV footage would be retrieved and produced swiftly. Flyers with pictures of Penny would be posted all over campus, and an e-mail blast would go out asking all those who were residents of housing overlooking Lake Fred last April to contact the campus police or the FBI. Ditto for those who'd attended classes in key lecture halls overlooking Lake Fred.

Sloane wasn't discouraged. She'd known this was going to be a tedious process. But she wasn't going away. Come hell or high water, she was going to find out what had happened to Penny.

She couldn't wait to get into her car and put on the heat. Not so much for the chill in her body, but for the throbbing in her hand. This kind of weather was the absolute worst for her injury.

That wasn't in the cards. Lady Luck had another surprise in store for her. The minute Sloane reached the parking lot, she saw that her car was leaning heavily to the right. A flat. She could spot it from yards away. The right front tire looked like a pancake.

Great. Just what she needed to complete her day.

She squatted beside the car to take a look. It took three seconds to zero in on the nail that had punctured her tire.

Okay, she thought, tossing her briefcase and purse into the car, then rising and going to the trunk to get the tools she needed. So much for her Tahari suit. Now it would be waterlogged, filthy, *and* torn.

Ruining her clothes turned out to be the least of her problems. She'd forgotten that it had been several years since she'd changed a flat. Which meant that the last time had predated her injury.

Jacking up the car wouldn't be too bad. She'd bought

one of those hydraulic floor jacks. But removing the tire was hell. Thanks to the chill of winter, the lug nuts weren't cooperating. The second one was tight—very tight. Twisting it took all Sloane's strength, and dug the wrench into her palm. And the third one was frozen solid, and wasn't budging. After ten minutes of battling it, Sloane was sweating and tears had filled her eyes from the intensity of the pain. Her scar tissue was throbbing, her index finger was numb, and the nerve pain in her hand was shooting all the way up her arm.

Swearing, she threw down the wrench and flipped open her phone. It was either call a gas station or flag down some students—who were nowhere to be found, thanks to the rain. And Derek and Tom were still in a meeting, so she wasn't about to interrupt them.

So a gas station it was.

She punched on the phone—and was greeted by the fact that she had eleven missed calls, all from a restricted caller.

She was still staring at the missed-call messages and fuming over the fact that she'd received them, when she got that feeling again—like someone was watching her. She raised her head slowly and looked around, pretending to scan the area for someone who could potentially assist her with the flat.

There was no one in plain sight. That meant nothing, since whoever was out there didn't want to be seen. But he was there. She could sense it.

It was the where and the why that was irking her.

At that precise moment, her cell phone rang again, flashing the *restricted call* in the caller-ID screen.

Livid about this invasion of her personal space, Sloane refused to give in to the jerk responsible. No way would she give him the satisfaction of answering his call, or appearing to be panicked by the realization that she was being harassed. In fact, she'd act as if his call, and its significance, hadn't even registered in her mind.

To that end, she made a loud exasperated sound and turned off her phone, flipping it closed as if opting to ignore any incoming calls in lieu of getting help to fix her car. She'd psych Mr. Restricted out by denying him the very reaction he sought.

Despite her bravado, Sloane wasn't a fool. She knew that her caller was more than just an obnoxious telephone harasser. Whoever he was, his actions were personal. He was, at the very least, watching her and trying to scare her with his nonstop phone calls. At worst, he was someone with a personal vendetta, and was acting out, maybe even going so far as to shove a nail in her tire to cause her flat.

The good news was that, just like the other morning in her backyard, he wasn't coming after her. It was the same scenario. He'd had ample time and opportunity. She was alone, the parking lot was deserted, and the area was thickly wooded. Yet he hadn't assaulted her.

No, this was a head game—for the time being. But she had no intention of letting it continue. Whoever this son of a bitch was, she'd find out—today—and get a new cellphone number in the process.

The hell with the gas station. She wasn't calling them while dodging this wack job. She'd take a walk in the rain and find a blue light phone to call campus security. They'd help change her tire. Then she'd get out of here, get in touch with the right someones, and initiate a trace on her mystery pest.

She threw her tools into the trunk of her car and locked it. What a fine way to end the day. She looked and felt like a drowned rat, her car was out of commission, her hand and arm were throbbing like hell, and she was being stalked by some weirdo. It couldn't get much worse.

Evidently, she was wrong.

She turned back toward campus, intending to hunt down a campus phone—and promptly collided with Derek.

"Car trouble?" he asked, his eyes twinkling as icy sheets of rain streamed through his dark hair.

Leave it to Derek to be unbothered by getting drenched.

"I have a flat," Sloane informed him. "There's a nail in my tire. And I can't get the damned lug nuts to give."

"Outdone by a couple of lug nuts? That doesn't sound like you. The Sloane I knew would have bludgeoned those lug nuts off the tire and flung them onto the ground, where they'd be begging for mercy."

"That was then. This is now. Things change. Now, if you'll excuse me, I'm going to get some help." Sloane dragged her left sleeve across her face to wipe away the rain so she could see. Then she sidestepped Derek and started to walk away.

"Wait a minute." He grabbed her right arm to stop her. "I'll help you change the—" He broke off as Sloane emitted a stifled whimper. "What's wrong?"

She didn't answer for a moment, gritting her teeth as a jolt of pain shot through her arm. She flexed her fingers and winced as the pain radiated down, slicing through her finger and palm.

"I'm fine," she managed. "I just need to get the damned flat fixed."

"No, you're not fine." Derek saw her wince again, his gaze shifting to the arm he was still gripping. Abruptly, he realized what was going on, and released his hold. Instead, he caught her wrist and drew it toward him, turning her hand palm up.

Sloane bit back a moan of pain.

"Your whole palm is inflamed," Derek announced, frowning. "What the hell did you do, wrestle with the lug-nut wrench for a half hour?"

"I didn't time myself." Sloane tried to tug her hand away, but Derek wasn't complying. He stared at her injury, seeing it—really seeing it—for the first time.

"Jesus Christ," he muttered, scrutinizing the sharp incision lines and patches of scar tissue, now swollen and red from Sloane's battle with the wrench. "Your hand's like a battlefield."

Something inside Sloane went very cold. "Give the man a cigar. He finally gets it."

For a long moment, Derek said nothing. He just stared at her hand. When he raised his head, his midnight gaze reflected some ambiguous emotion that Sloane couldn't quite place.

"You and I need to talk," he stated flatly. "I'm driving you over to the student health center so you can get whatever first aid you need for your hand. While you're there, I'll come back here and change your tire. Then we're getting out of here. You'll follow me in your car. We'll drive to my glamorous Best Western. We don't have to go inside. We can sit in the car. Or walk around the parking lot with an umbrella. I don't give a damn. But we're having a conversation—a real one. Alone and without interruptions."

Sloane didn't even blink. "With all due respect, it's a little late for that. Thirteen months too late. Plus, I'm not in the mood. I'm in horrible pain. I'm freezing cold. I'm wet and dirty. I've got three pissed-off dachshunds waiting for me to pick them up, and an exhausted, elderly woman taking care of them when she should be taking care of herself. Oh, and I've got a few favors to call in so I can get my hands on cell-phone records and figure out who's been screwing with me via heavy-breathing hang-ups and following me around. So how about if you just drop me off at the health center and change my flat. Then you can take off, and we can skip the conversation."

"Wait." Derek held up his palm. "Go back to that part about the hang-ups and the stalker."

"I don't know if he's a stalker. Maybe he just wants a date. If so, I'll either say yes or get a new cell-phone number, depending on how hot he is."

"I'm not laughing."

"Neither am I. But I *am* perfectly capable of taking care of myself."

"And *I'm* capable of pulling the strings you need to bypass the red tape of initiating a call trace. You'll have your caller's info and a call block ASAP."

Sloane inhaled slowly. "If you can make that happen, I'll owe you one. In the meantime, I've got to take care of my car and my hand."

"Like I said, I'll help you with both."

"I appreciate that. But just so we're clear, the payment for all this help you're offering doesn't include a heart-to-heart."

"Wrong. You said you owed me one, remember?"

"I remember. And I meant it—with one stipulation. No personal conversation. I'm not interested in reliving our good-byes—or lack thereof."

"Sorry, that stipulation doesn't work for me."

"Why not?" Bitterness laced Sloane's tone. "You suddenly need to talk things out? The silence worked fine for you for thirteen months."

"Oh, you mean since you quit the Bureau, cut me out of your life, and walked away?"

"*Walked away?*" Sloane felt her restraint snap. After the past half hour, that was the straw that broke the camel's back. "How could I *walk* when I was *shoved*? The minute I didn't handle things the way *you* would have, you wrote me off." She broke off, fought for control, and then gave it up.

Stored-up rage exploded through her like cannon fire, and she planted herself right in Derek's face, raised her head, and met his gaze with her own blazing stare. "That day in the alley when I was stabbed, my life changed forever. *Mine,* not *yours.* You had no idea what I was feeling. Not the pain. Not the fear. And not the isolation. All you knew was that my assailant was caught, the incident was over, and I should have found a way to be the person I was before. I should have risen above all adversity, overcome the trauma, and emerged as strong as before, unscathed by a near-death experience. When I couldn't manage that, you categorized me as a weakling and a deserter—both to the

Bureau and to you. Ever the Army Ranger, governed by an uncompromising set of rules and principles. You might be the family rebel who kissed off West Point and went the ROTC route while your brothers and sister followed in your father's footsteps, but in this case, General Parker would be proud. Like him, it's your way or the highway."

A muscle was working furiously at Derek's jaw. "Is that how you see it? That *I* pushed *you* away? Then how do you explain the two dozen unreturned phone calls? Or the five times I showed up at your apartment, knowing full well you were home, and stood outside pounding on your front door and bellowing for you to let me in, making such a racket that your neighbors had me thrown out of the building? Fine. I was hard on you—maybe way too hard. But *you* shut *me* down, and shut me out."

"I nearly bled to death."

"You think I didn't know that? You think I wasn't there? I showed up at that hospital the minute the call came in. I made a huge scene trying to get in and see you. But the doctors refused—not that I could blame them. They were busy trying to stop the bleeding and get you to the operating room. After the surgery, I was told you were really out of it, and visitors were discouraged. So I peeked in on you and left. When I called the next day, I was told you were wiped out and didn't want visitors."

"That wasn't personal; it was true. I needed time alone."

"Fine, well, afterward, I saw you twice—once at home and once at work. The first time you were so drugged up on painkillers, I'm not sure you even knew I was there. And the second time you were so emotionally distant, we barely connected."

"Oh, we connected all right. Enough for you to let me know that I was overreacting in my response to what had happened and copping out by leaving the Bureau."

Derek's jaw tightened another notch. "I thought you were making a huge mistake. I still do. You could have been placed on medical mandate until you healed. You were a damned good agent. You speak more languages than I can count, and you're the best hostage negotiator I've ever seen. You can talk a subject out of any situation, no matter how dire. There's no good reason why you left. You could have stayed on, giving your all to the Bureau—the only difference being you wouldn't be carrying your gun or making arrests."

"The *only* difference? That's all the difference in the world. Would *you* have settled for that? Never. Picture yourself watching your fellow Army Rangers deployed to the Middle East while you stayed behind and coached from the sidelines. You'd go nuts—and so would I. A medical mandate would mean I wouldn't be a real agent anymore; I'd be a glorified pencil-pushing member of the support staff. And in my case that medical mandate wouldn't have been for a few months. It would have been for at least a year—as it turns out, more. Did you ever stop to consider what that would have done to me?"

Derek didn't answer, but Sloane could see by his expression that her point had gotten through.

"What's more," she continued, "when you saw how I was acting, did it ever occur to you that I was suffering from post-traumatic stress, not to mention enduring more pain than I ever anticipated? Or were you too pissed off that I was leaving the Bureau?"

"It wasn't just the Bureau." This time Derek blasted back, and Sloane was stunned by the suppressed rage in his tone. "You were leaving *me,* leaving *us.* No argument. No discussion. Just good-bye. As for what you were going through, give me a little credit. I've seen enough post-traumatic stress *and* pain to last a lifetime. I knew you were suffering. But what would you have had me do? I couldn't get through that damned wall you'd put up. Let's face it, Sloane, you were already gone long before you packed and left Cleveland. So, yeah, I was a principled, opinionated jerk. But at least I was willing to fight for what we had—which was rare as hell, by the way. You just gave up on it, along with your career. You were a coward, Sloane. You turned your back on everything, hoping to erase the past—and the pain—by starting a new life. But it didn't work, did it? It's still there, eating away at you, just like it's eating away at me."

Derek's words cut through the wind and the rain, hovering like a dark, ponderous cloud.

There it was. Raw, exposed, and excruciating. Put out there for the first time.

Sloane pressed her lips together and swallowed. Rain was pouring down her face. She was shivering violently. And the pain in her hand was bordering on numbness.

This was more than she could handle.

"I can't do this now, Derek," she said quietly. "If you want to tear open old wounds and have it out, fine. But later. I need to get to health services. And I need to call my hand therapist. I can't afford another setback—not again."

Derek took one look at her white face, and nodded. "Come on." He pressed a palm to the small of her back, guiding her toward his car. "I'll run you over there now."

"Thanks."

"Don't thank me. By the time I return to pick you up, I'll have changed your flat, started a trace on your phone stalker, and canceled dinner with McGraw. When you get back in this car, and after you've consulted with your hand therapist and made sure your physical scars are okay, that's when we're tearing open the emotional ones. So steel yourself. We're putting all our cards on the table and finishing what we started—once and for all."

CHAPTER
FOURTEEN

DATE: 1 April
TIME: 2100 hours
OBJECTIVE: Tyche

There she was. The goddess of fortune, prosperity, and luck.

She'd stayed at work late tonight. Usually, her schedule was like clockwork. She'd leave the martial-arts academy at eight-thirty. She'd wait until after the last class was under way and her bookkeeping work was wrapped up. Then she'd head to her car, and drive back to campus.

Once there, she'd park and either go straight to her dorm to finish up her assignments or trek across campus to play a few hands of cards with her friends. On those days, she'd still be back in her room by two; it was only Fridays that she stayed out all night for her weekly poker marathon.

Tonight would be a dry run. I'd follow her back to her campus, and make sure every detail was just as I've recorded it. Any adjustments had to be made now.

I had only a few days left.

And so did she.

Best Western Garden State Inn
Absecon, New Jersey
9:20 P.M.

Sloane rolled over and opened her eyes.

She blinked, totally disoriented, wondering where the hell she was. Darkness shrouded the unfamiliar room, although a single lamp cast enough light to tell her she was on a king-size bed covered by a bright blue-and-orange-print bedspread.

She propped herself up on one elbow, stared blankly down at the institutional-blue carpet as she tried to clear the cobwebs from her head. She hated this feeling—nauseated, headachy, and like her brain was filled with cotton. It brought back unwelcome memories of coming to in a recovery room after surgery.

No way she was feeling that way again.

She raked a hand through her hair, wincing as a twinge of pain shot through her palm, together with an unnatural stiffness and limited tactile ability and freedom of motion. She glanced at her hand, saw that it was bandaged and taped.

Abruptly, she remembered.

She was in Derek's hotel room. He'd driven her here after the nurse practitioner at Stockton's health services had treated her hand and given her some heavy-duty painkillers.

Sitting up, Sloane examined herself, noting that she was wearing an oversize olive sweatshirt with the Colorado State insignia on it. Derek's alma mater. She vaguely remember changing into it, peeling off her wet Tahari suit—now fit for kitty litter—and pulling on the warm sweatshirt.

The clock on the night table said it was after nine. Sloane's scrutiny said she was alone in the hotel room.

Beside the clock was an uncapped but unused bottle of springwater, and she reached out to get it—this time with her left hand. She gulped down half a bottle, partly because she was thirsty and partly to rehydrate her muscles and kick-start her brain.

She'd put down the water and was trying to piece together the events of the last four hours, when the door opened and Derek stepped in. He'd changed into jeans and a royal-blue fleece sweatshirt.

"You're awake. Good." He went over to the desk and set down two Burger King bags and a cardboard tray with two sodas in it. Sloane's stomach growled at the aroma.

Derek chuckled. "Awake and hungry," he amended. "No problem." He carried the food over and set dinner up on the night table. "I got you your favorites—a Whopper with cheese, a large fries, and a Diet Coke with lemon. I assume that hasn't changed?"

"No." Sloane's voice sounded raspy, probably from all that time spent in the pouring rain. "That hasn't changed."

"Good. Then we're all set to eat." He frowned, seeing how green around the gills she looked. "Is the Whopper too heavy? Because I also got a salad and a roll if you want something lighter."

"No way. I never turn down a Whopper. I'm starving. My nausea's from the Vicodin. It'll disappear as soon as I eat."

"It says on the bottle that it should be taken with food. But you fell asleep before I could get anything substantial into you."

"Not a problem. I know the drill. Vicodin and I are old friends. I keep our reunions short, because it's a narcotic and because it knocks me out. But it's also a hell of a painkiller."

"The nurse practitioner said she got you to eat some crackers when you took it."

A mental flash, and Sloane nodded. "She did. I ate four saltines."

"You need a solid meal. Here."

"Wait." Sloane reached out to stop him, frowning as she felt the nerves in her palm tingle. If she'd undone any of Dr. Houghton or Connie's hard work, she didn't think she could bear it. Not again

"I've got to get home," she announced, shoving back the

bedspread. "I'm fuzzy about what the nurse practitioner said, and what she did. I need to see my hand therapist. And the hounds . . . I've got to pick them up."

"The hounds are fine." Derek halted Sloane's motion, easing her back onto the bed. "Mrs. Wagner's keeping them overnight. I found her number on your speed dial," he added, preempting Sloane's next question with an answer. "And you're not going anywhere. Not till tomorrow morning. The nurse practitioner emphasized that about twenty times when she prescribed the Vicodin."

"But I have some nerve tingling in my hand." Sloane was trying to stay calm. "That could mean I redamaged something."

"The nerves are inflamed. That's it. Other than the fact that you tore up the tissue around your scars pretty badly with that wrench. The ice pack took down the swelling. Anyway, they did some tests. You passed with flying colors. And you spoke to your hand therapist, as did the nurse practitioner. Constance—I think that was her name—was satisfied with all the procedures that were done, and with the results."

"Right." Memory filtered back in fragments. "I did talk to Connie. She said I should follow the instructions health services gave me, take the Vicodin, and see her at her New Jersey office tomorrow at three."

"Exactly."

Relief surged through Sloane with the force of a tidal wave. Her hand would be okay. And the hounds were safe and cared for. "What about my car?" she asked.

"It's at the local gas station. The mechanic is patching your tire. It'll be good as new tomorrow, just like you." Derek unwrapped Sloane's Whopper with cheese and handed it to her. "Now eat. But use your left hand."

"I intend to." Sloane took the burger, her brows still drawn together in question. "How did my car get to the gas station?"

"I drove it there after I changed the flat. Tom picked me

up and brought me back to my car. Then he took off and I swung by health services and got you."

"I remember the drive." Sloane was still sifting through filaments of memory. "I also remember us pulling into the hotel parking lot, and going inside the room. Oh, and I remember your giving me this to change into." She plucked at the sweatshirt, which fit her like an oversize dress. "I don't remember much else. I guess I was pretty out of it."

"Those painkillers are strong. Still, you were pretty coherent until we got into the hotel room." A corner of Derek's mouth lifted. "Coherent enough to slam the bathroom door in my face when I tried to come in and help you change out of your wet clothes. But after you got into bed, you conked out. You've been asleep since."

"Wow. That must be three and a half hours."

"Close. Now eat your Whopper. You're dripping sauce on my bed."

Sloane glanced down quickly, smiling as she saw the predictable napkins and outer wrapper Derek had placed on her lap. "Somehow I knew that was a lie. Did you think I'd forgotten, Mr. Clean?"

"Nope." Derek took a bite of his own Double Whopper. "Just checking to see how lucid you are."

"More lucid by the minute. And this meal should help." Sloane chowed down, devouring her Whopper and eating her french fries with gusto. In between bites, she gulped down her drink.

"I never did understand the whole Diet Coke thing." Derek took a swallow of his root beer. "If you decide to pig out and stuff your face with fat and calories, why not go the whole nine yards? I think I've seen you eat junk food maybe five times since I met you. So why dilute a great experience with a drink that tastes like watered-down Coke syrup with a vile aftertaste?"

"It's actually pretty good." Sloane grinned at his description. "Especially with the lemon. Besides, if I'm going to gorge myself, why waste calories on soda? I'd rather use them on some extra fries."

"I say, go for both."

"Be the ultimate hedonist."

"Exactly. Pleasure's not something to enjoy half measure. Throw yourself into it, full force."

"Like you do everything."

"So do you."

Sloane's chewing slowed down. "I guess I can't deny that one. I'm pretty much an all-or-nothing girl."

"Which leads to our talk."

"Or not." Sloane gave him a hopeful look. "Can't I plead weakness from my injury? Being spaced out from my meds? Or appeal to your logic by saying we've been getting along so well, why ruin it now by getting into things that are going to start a war?"

"You could try them all. But none of them would work. This conversation is thirteen months overdue. And we're having it."

Sloane moved her take-out wrappers aside, then pulled up her knees and wrapped her arms around them. "If you review things rationally, we already had this conversation, right in the Stockton parking lot this afternoon."

"We got out some of our anger and emotion. But we didn't really get into the fundamentals. There's a reason we couldn't see each other's point of view a year ago, a reason why you walked away, and a reason why we never reconnected."

"Yes, there is. We're very different people. We have different coping mechanisms, different ways of thinking, different priorities. To make things worse, we have several things in common, none of which bode well for a lasting relationship. We're both stubborn. We're both proud. We're both strong-willed. And we're both intense about whatever it is we're into."

"Including each other," Derek noted drily.

"Fair enough. We're not just intense, we're passionate—

and, yes, that includes about each other and what we had. But that's moot. Because the bigger issues aren't going away. We'll never agree about who let whom down after I got stabbed. Neither of us will ever back down. And we'll never forgive or trust each other. So we're at a stalemate. Effectively, nothing's changed. Given that, what's there to talk about?"

"You're right."

Sloane was totally unprepared for what happened next.

In one swift motion, Derek shoved aside his Burger King wrappers and slid over onto the bed. He caught Sloane's shoulders and pulled her toward him, until she could feel the warmth of his body through their sweatshirts.

"There *is* nothing to talk about," he said in a husky voice. "Not now. Maybe never." He tilted back her head so their gazes locked. His eyes were blazing with midnight fire. Hers were startled, growing smoky with awareness. His thumbs trailed up the sides of her neck, felt her pulse beating faster. Then they shifted up to trace her lips, her cheekbones.

And suddenly the past was the present.

"I don't know if we'll ever fix things," Derek muttered, his breath grazing her mouth. "But you're right about nothing having changed, at least where it comes to how much I want you. Since you left, I've woken up more nights in a cold sweat than I can count. And from the moment I walked into that surprise meeting you arranged two weeks ago, from the second I saw you again, all I've been able to think about is getting inside you. My gut tells me you feel the same way. Am I right?"

Sloane didn't—couldn't—answer. The wall of Derek's chest pressing against her breasts, the woodsy, ambery scent of his Burberry cologne, the heated look in his eyes—it was all too wildly erotic and familiar.

She was stunned, not by her reaction, but by its magnitude. Hers and Derek's sexual attraction had always been off the charts. Their lovemaking had surpassed even that.

She knew that passion as overpowering as theirs didn't vanish just because the relationship didn't work out. But this? It was like a dam had burst open, and they were being sucked up by the rushing waters.

"Sloane," Derek repeated, his voice rough with restraint. "Answer me. Am I right?"

"Yes." She exhaled the word in a rush.

Derek's eyes darkened to near black. "Then screw our differences. Screw our similarities. Screw everything except this." His hands worked their way under her sweatshirt, cupping her breasts, rubbing her nipples until they hardened.

Sloane's entire body began thrumming, alive in a way it hadn't been since Cleveland. Breathing became difficult, thinking impossible.

Her hands, of their own volition, slid under Derek's shirt and up the hair-roughened planes of his chest. Even the bandages couldn't dull the sensation of touching him again, nor did they stifle the rough sound he made in his throat.

"This is a big mistake," Sloane announced, leaning up to brush her lips across his—first in one direction, then the other. "A *really* big mistake."

Derek shoved his hands into her hair, anchored her head so he could deepen the kiss. "I don't give a damn." He devoured her mouth, his tongue probing deep, rubbing against hers in a hungry, rhythmic motion. "Do you?"

"No." Sloane was right there with him. The taste of him, the sensation of his tongue taking hers in a blatant imitation of what was to come, was enough to drive away all coherent thought. She shifted onto her knees, wrapped her arms around his neck, and threw herself into the kiss.

"Your hand," he muttered, hesitating long enough to cover her right hand with his. "We have to be careful."

She tugged it free. "We will be. But only of that. Everything else is fair game."

"You're on."

There were no more words spoken.

Derek pulled the sweatshirt over Sloane's head, taking care to ease the right sleeve past her hand, and tossed the shirt to the floor. He then turned his efforts to getting rid of his own clothes, unzipping his jeans and tugging them down, while Sloane peeled off his shirt. Derek vaulted to his feet, shedding everything, his gaze locked on Sloane as she lay back on the bed, waiting.

She didn't have long to wait.

He lowered himself on top of her, pressing her into the mattress. They both shuddered at the contact. The idea of prolonging the moment, savoring the preliminaries—it definitely wasn't in the cards this time. Derek's knees wedged Sloane's apart, and she spread her legs wider, lifting them until she could hug his flanks. He propped himself on his elbows so he could watch her expression as his erection probed her, and pushed—deep—until he was all the way inside her.

Sloane's back arched and she cried out, her arms going around his back, her legs tightening, lifting higher around his hips. Derek made a low, guttural sound, sweat breaking out on his forehead as her body closed around him. He began moving, penetrating her in fast, uncompromising strokes. Their gazes held until neither of them could take it anymore. Giving in to their bodies' demands, he lowered himself fully onto her, his hands gripping her bottom so he could lift her into each forceful thrust.

The unraveling was fast, furious, and simultaneous.

Sloane's climax boiled up inside her and erupted. Hot, gripping spasms racked her body, radiating from her core, milking Derek even as his own orgasm slammed through him. He came in a rush, spurting into her and grinding their bodies together. He rasped out her name, and Sloane gave a wild little cry—the only sound she could muster— her nails scoring Derek's back.

When it was over, he collapsed on top of her. Their

harsh breaths were the only sound in the silent hotel room, and even those began to lessen, growing slow and steady as their bodies returned to normal.

"It's true," Derek managed finally, his lips near her ear. "Nothing's changed. The world could blow up when I'm inside you, and I'd never even notice."

Sloane's soft wisp of breath grazed his shoulder. "The world *does* blow up when you're inside me. That's the problem."

"I don't call it a problem. I call it a reprieve."

There was a heartbeat of silence.

"Maybe you're right," Sloane acknowledged at last. "Maybe it is is a reprieve. It's honest. It's uncomplicated."

"And it feels so damned good."

"That, too."

"Oh, you forgot to mention that it's also a great stress reliever," Derek teased. "With the way we combust, think about the record number of endorphins we must release."

"Good point."

Derek kissed the hollow at the base of her throat. "Angel," he murmured, inhaling deeply.

"Hmmm?"

"Your perfume. You still wear it. And it still drives me crazy."

Sloane's insides clenched. Yes, she remembered how crazy it drove him. She also remembered some of the spots on her body she'd dab the perfume to do just that.

"I have a small bottle in my purse." Her fingertips traced his spine. "I can go get it."

"Later." His voice was muffled against her skin. "Right now I want you to stay right where you are."

She could feel him hardening inside her. "I can tell."

"Busted." He kissed her, a slow, thorough exploration of her mouth. "Objections?"

"None." She was already breathless.

"Is your hand okay?"

"What hand?"

Derek gave a low chuckle. "Am I as good as Vicodin?"

"Better. But just as addictive. Maybe more—at least in bed."

"Bed is all we're talking about. Nothing more. Deal?"

"Deal." Sloane's hands and lips were doing their own exploration, relearning his body by touch and taste.

A hard shudder racked his body, and Derek pulled her more fully under him, thrusting all the way in. "I hope you didn't plan on getting much sleep tonight."

"Much? How about none?"

"None works."

CHAPTER FIFTEEN

DATE: 2 April
TIME: 0530 hours
OBJECTIVE: Tyche

Spring. The season of birth and new beginnings.

The world turning green. The trees starting to bud. And the college campus bathed in a golden glow as the sun rises. Lake Ceva is brilliant. Equally brilliant is the next goddess-to-be as she enjoys her morning jog.

Tyche.

Like the waters of Lake Ceva, she glistens as the sun sheds its first light on her. She's young, and her gait is smooth and even as she circles the path around the lake.

She has no idea of the glorious fate that awaits her. How could she? Right now she's still just a mere mortal. Soon she'll be a goddess.

Church bells. A reminder of the hour. I'd better go. I have a long drive ahead. I'm worried about Gaia. She can't be left alone. And I must prepare for Tyche's arrival. Disposing of the cell phones will have to wait. For now, they'll remain in my pocket. After I have Tyche, I'll dump them near a crack house in Irvington on my way back to New Olympus.

Even as I force myself to retreat, I can't help pausing for one last look.

Yes. Perfect. The choice. The timing. The spot.

Soon I'll have her—her and all the others.

After that, it will finally be time for my ultimate prize. My other half, the part of me that I've known was missing since I first read the inscription in my book: *To my little Apollo.*

Back then, I was too young to understand what that meant. But I understand now. Just as I understand what the gods have in store.

How long I've waited to bring *her* home. To show *her* the room I've built in her honor. To save her virtue by taking her with me.

To leave this mortal world and join the deities on Mount Olympus.

Gaia would determine when.

Eickhoff Hall, The College of New Jersey
Trenton, New Jersey
7:10 A.M.

Tina Carroll felt edgy.

She tossed onto her other side, dragged a pillow under her head, and made another attempt to fall sleep.

It didn't work.

She sat up in bed, raked her fingers through her hair, irked that her sleep time was ticking away.

She'd followed this same routine every morning since last year when she'd moved into upperclass housing. Along with that came the luxury of a single dorm room. Her rules. Her way. No roommate to compromise with or work around. That meant she could become the night owl that her bio clock naturally urged her to be. She could hang out with her friends—either partying or playing cards—do her schoolwork until dawn, then go out for her jog at sunrise.

Unlike other people, Tina found that exercising relaxed her and helped her sleep. When she got back to her dorm room, she'd take a quick shower, climb between the sheets, and zone out for a solid five hours. She'd scheduled all her classes for afternoons, and none on Fridays—benefits of being a senior. All of which dovetailed perfectly with her Friday all-night poker game. So the pieces of her schedule all fell nicely into place, and her life was just the way she wanted it to be.

Until now.

This past week she'd felt creeped out wherever she went, like she was being watched. She felt it when she came or left the academy, when she walked around campus, even during her morning jog. She never spotted anyone, nor had she seen even the slightest rustle from the trees. But her guard was up at all times. Just to be on the safe side, she also locked her dorm-room door when she was inside, and she kept her blinds shut when she showered or changed clothes. Plus, she slept in a T-shirt now, rather than in the nude.

Those precautions gave her an additional sense of security. But she was still edgy and alert, ready to defend herself if need be.

And after three years of Krav Maga classes, she could do that no problem.

Best Western Garden State Inn
Absecon, New Jersey
10:05 A.M.

Sloane was in the bathroom, gingerly towel-drying her hair with one hand, when Derek returned to the hotel room.

"Breakfast," he announced, placing a box of Dunkin' Donuts on the dresser. "Sorry it's junk food again, but my choices were limited."

"So's our breakfast break," Sloane reminded him, tossing aside her towel and emerging from the bathroom. "We've got to get back to work. As for the cuisine, I'm starving. I'll eat anything, fat and carbs included. So here I am." She gave an appreciative sniff. "Dunkin' makes the best coffee. I can't wait."

"No need to." Derek placed one steaming take-out cup into her left hand, his lips twitching as he eyed her. "Very stylish. I wish I had a camera."

"What?" Sloane glanced down at herself, swallowed up by Derek's black sweatpants and Colorado State sweatshirt, both of which she'd belted at the waist to keep them in place. "I'm not an ad for *Vogue*?"

"Uh . . . no. Then again, enveloped by my sweats, you're invisible. No one could find you to take your picture."

"Speaking of which, the Bureau should pay for my suit. It was a Tahari—one of my favorites. And it cost an arm and a leg."

"Don't hold your breath. Reimbursement for designer clothes isn't in the FBI budget."

"I remember." Sloane took a gulp of coffee, then sat down and helped herself to a jelly donut. "Pigging out has its advantages—especially when you're wearing clothes that are three sizes too big for you. No sucking in your gut. No struggling with zippers. Just eat as you wish. Then, when reality sets in, add a few extra miles onto your next morning's jog, and an extra hour of strength training and target shooting on the archery course."

"I wouldn't worry." Derek polished off his first donut and started on his second. "You haven't gained an ounce since Cleveland. After last night, I can attest to that."

A taut silence followed that declaration.

"Should we talk about what happened?" Derek finally asked.

"Not necessary." Sloane shook her head. "It was what it was."

"Very cryptic. Care to clarify?"

"There's nothing to clarify. You said it yourself—we have amazing chemistry in bed. If you're asking if I'm going to pretend it never happened, the answer's no. It did happen. We both wanted it to. It was incredible. It lasted all night. And now it's morning."

Derek took a careful swallow of coffee. "Is that your way of saying it was a one-shot deal?"

"That's my way of saying we shouldn't overthink this. No decisions are necessary. If we force ourselves to make them, it'll only complicate things and create all sorts of weirdness between us. We can't afford that, not personally or professionally."

"So the door's not closed."

"Not unless you want it to be."

"Uh-uh," Derek returned adamantly. "Not only don't I want it closed, I don't even want it ajar. I want it wide open. That way, we can walk through it whenever we both want to. Which I already do."

Sloane's eyes twinkled. "I'm that good, huh?"

"Better."

"So are you. But don't let it go to your head."

"I'll try." Derek grinned. "Although it's tough, given how many times you begged me to—"

"Enough," Sloane commanded, holding up a silencing palm—although she was openly smiling, relaxed in a way she hadn't been for ages. "If you start a game of one-upmanship, you'll lose. I'll be forced to show you the marks you left on my body—*everywhere* on my body—when you lost control. I'll probably have bruises for a week."

"But I get points for being gentle with your hand," Derek reminded her. His smile faded, and his brows drew together. "I was gentle with it, wasn't I?"

"That you were." Sloane glanced down at the bandages. "Are you still in a lot of pain?"

"Actually, no. My hand feels much better. I haven't taken a Vicodin since just after midnight. I'll be calmer once Connie's taken a look at it, but my guess is, it's on the mend."

"I'm glad."

The ringing of Derek's cell phone interrupted their conversation.

He put down his coffee, snapped open the phone, and answered. "Parker." A pause. "You have something for me?" Derek looked at Sloane and mouthed the words *campus police*. "Right. In the data-storage archives." A nod. "Makes sense. You're sure they include the surveillance footage from *that* section of Lake Fred? April fourteenth of last year? Perfect." He gave Sloane a thumbs-up. "Burn me a copy, starting a week before Penelope Truman's disappearance right up to the day she vanished."

"Two," Sloane ordered in a whisper, holding up two fingers. "Burn two copies."

"I'll need two sets of DVDs," Derek amended. "One for the FBI and one for Ms. Burbank." A quick glance at his watch. "I'll pick them up the minute they're ready. *How long?*" Derek's jaw tightened. "Four or five days? That's not going to cut it. Yes, I'm aware of how much footage we're talking about, *and* that it spans a full week. I'm also aware that we're talking about a potential homicide investigation. I'll get the college president to approve whatever overtime, equipment, and manpower you need to get the job done ASAP."

Another pause. "How's this for a compromise? Copy all the footage from April fourteenth and have that set of DVDs ready for me first thing tomorrow. The rest you can feed me in batches, as they're completed. I'll need the whole week's worth in three days max. Beg, borrow, and steal equipment, and work it round the clock if need be. Great. So we understand each other. I'll swing by at nine A.M. tomorrow."

Derek disconnected the call and turned to Sloane. "I guess we lit a fire under the right asses. They found that footage even faster than I expected."

"Even if it's taking them a millennium to copy it. What's the holdup?"

"They need extra disk drives, more techs—evidently, we're talking about producing quite a hefty DVD collection, somewhere around twenty-five disks."

"I suppose that makes sense. Well, at least you twisted their arms enough to get us the footage from the day of the abduction by tomorrow." Sloane sighed. "Part of this is me, and my impatience. Nothing about this case is moving fast enough for me. Or for the Trumans. I'm praying there's something on that damned footage that will lead to the answers they so desperately need."

"What they need is closure," Derek qualified pointedly.

Sloane shot him a glare. "You're about as subtle as an avalanche."

"Just making sure we're on the same page."

"Then I'll say it in plain English so you can stop worrying." Sloane neither flinched nor looked away. "Like I told you when I took on this case, I'm as aware of the odds as you are. It's been a year. Short of a miracle, Penny's dead. I'm not counting on handing the Trumans a happy ending. Just a modicum of peace and an end to the horror of not knowing."

"The knowing could be worse."

"I doubt that. Not after the scenarios they've imagined all these months."

"Maybe. But the problem with knowing is that any hope they've held out, however irrational, will be gone."

"I get it, Derek. And we'll talk about counseling when the time comes. Right now we're getting way ahead of ourselves. First we have to solve the case. Then we'll deal with the aftermath. So back to the video surveillance. Can you messenger my copies to me tomorrow? I want them hot off the disk drives."

"Are you footing the bill for messenger service? Because the Bureau sure won't."

"I realize that. I'll take care of the expense."

"Then consider it done."

"What about your copies? Will you be sending them straight down to Quantico?"

"Pretty much. First, I'll scan each of them to see if anything obvious jumps out at me. Then I'll overnight them down to the FBI lab. They can pick up subtleties I can't."

"My thoughts exactly." Sloane caught her lower lip between her teeth as her mind organized the task into a logical sequence. "You have the manpower and the technical sophistication of the FBI backing you up. I have the personal investment and the luxury of being my own boss—which means no time accountability. So I can watch and rewatch DVDs round the clock. With all that going for us, something will turn up. It has to."

Derek was just opening his mouth to reply, when his cell phone rang again. He punched it on. "Parker." He was quiet for a while, his forehead creased in concentration. "The dates and times match up? What about today? Nothing? You're sure?" A harsh exhale. "Okay, e-mail me your whole analysis. In the meantime, just give me the phone numbers." He grabbed a hotel pad and pen, and scribbled something down. "Thanks, Chuck. I owe you one."

Sloane eyed Derek as he disconnected the call and stared at the piece of hotel stationery. "Does this relate to our case?" she asked. "Or should I butt out?"

"No, you shouldn't butt out. It's about you." Derek raised his head to meet her gaze. He didn't look or sound happy. "That was the analyst I had checking out your phone records to figure out where your 'unavailable' calls were coming from, and who your mystery caller is. Seems the calls are being made from two separate cell phones. Both disposable. Both currently turned off. Clearly, your stalker doesn't want to be traced."

"Not a shock. What else?"

"The timing and the escalation of the calls. They started at dawn on Monday, along with your sense of being watched. They've been increasing in number ever since. Yesterday afternoon took the prize. Nineteen calls. Most of which were made while you were at Stockton."

"This isn't the first time I've been harassed. It's happened a couple of times, usually while I was consulting on a high-profile case. Remember, the Bureau protects you by keeping your name out of the media. That doesn't work with me. I'm a private consultant."

"What high-profile cases are you consulting on?"

"Several. Some ongoing, some recently completed. Some involving law enforcement, some not. That's all I can tell you. My client list is confidential."

"Which ones have you taken on most recently—like in the past week or two?" Derek demanded. "Cases that have resulted in your name showing up in the newspapers, which makes them public record?"

Sloane inclined her head thoughtfully. "I'm helping the NYPD in their search for Cynthia Alexander, the missing John Jay student. The whole campus is crawling with media because of her disappearance. I've been mentioned in the papers because of that. Oh, and I was also mentioned because I spoke at a Crimes Against Women seminar at John Jay the day before Cynthia went missing. Then, of course, there's the Truman case, cold as it is. Ronald Truman is a renowned cardiologist and author. He's been pretty vocal about the fact that we've uncovered new leads on Penny's disappearance, and about the fact that he's hired me and elicited the full cooperation of the FBI."

"Let's see." Derek counted off on his fingers. "A seminar about women and crime. Two missing persons cases—both involving women. Both unsolved. Both with lots of media attention. And both with you right in the middle of them. Not a coincidence in my book."

Sloane paused. "Nor mine. Not when you sum it up that way. So maybe my harasser spotted my name in print. Maybe whatever he read either turned him on or pissed him off. Probably the latter. There are still lots of chauvinists out there."

"You're assuming this guy is just some media hound or a wack job who gets his thrills out of scaring the shit out of notable women he finds in the newspaper by following them around and barraging them with crank calls?"

"I'm not an idiot, Derek. I realize this is personal. And that this guy is probably unstable and could be gearing up to go after me physically, not just call or watch me from a distance. That's why I wanted to nip his calls in the bud.

But, as I said, I have a lot of clients. So I didn't connect the dots the same way you did."

"You're still not connecting them. You're classifying this guy as some warped outsider. Did it ever occur to you that he's an insider—one who's personally involved in a case you're working on? That he's targeted you as a threat that needs to be eliminated, either by scaring you off, or worse? Remember, you're a lot more vulnerable to an attack than the police or the FBI."

"Good point." Rather than worry, a glint of hope lit Sloane's eyes. "If we follow your theory, that opens up a whole new realm of possibilities—particularly since most of the missed calls came yesterday while I was at Richard Stockton. My anonymous caller must have spent the better part of the day focused on me and what I was doing—which was investigating Penny's case. What if *that's* the case he's connected to? What if he's following me because the Trumans brought me in to work with you to solve it? It would fit your theory. If this jerk's done his homework, he knows I'm good at what I do. He also knows that Penny and I were close friends. Close enough that I might figure out something before the authorities do. His increased activity yesterday means he feels threatened—which could work in our favor."

"Except for one small detail. Your safety." Derek was scowling. "You just said it yourself. He's probably not going to limit himself to telephone calls and random drop-bys to freak you out. He's already stalking you, maybe even leaving you little warning messages—like the nail in your tire. He's getting bolder, more aggressive."

"And, hopefully in the process, more careless."

"His next step will be direct contact."

"Good. Maybe we can jump the gun and lure him out."

"Forget it. We're not using you as bait."

Sloane said nothing. And *that* said everything.

"Sloane." Derek's voice held a warning note.

She blew out a breath. "Let's save the knock down,

drag-out fight for when, and if, it's necessary. Right now it's not. Changing the topic, what time is our meeting with Tom McGraw? And when will my car be ready?"

"We're meeting Tom at eleven-thirty at the diner down the road. He's at Stockton now, picking up whatever they've pulled together so far. And your car should be ready by now. We can give the gas station a call to confirm, then drive down to pick it up. That'll still give us enough time before the meeting with Tom to call Verizon and arrange for a call block on those two phone numbers."

"Nice try," Sloane returned drily. "But forget it. Change in plans, thanks to your astute theory. I don't want to shut this guy down. Or, more importantly, tip him off. If we do, he might go back into hiding before we can find out who he is and what he knows. No way I'm letting that happen. Not when he might be connected to Penny's disappearance. Her case has been cold for almost a year. This might be our best shot at solving it."

"Maybe. But it's not our *only* shot. Plus, we're not even sure if this is the case your stalker is involved in."

"The odds are good. The case might be old, but my involvement is new. An ex–FBI agent, a childhood friend of the victim, a personal agenda to get the guilty party—I raise quite a red flag. More like a banner."

"Fine." Derek was visibly pissed. "All the more reason for you to be careful. Who knows what this guy's planning for you—and when? I repeat what I said earlier—we're not using you as bait."

"I can take care of myself, Derek."

"I'm well aware of that." He folded his arms across his chest in that military stance he reserved for times like this. "But circumstances are different now. You can't carry a gun."

"I don't need a gun to annihilate someone. You've seen me in action."

"Yeah, I have. You're lethal. But Krav Maga only goes so far. It can't stop a bullet that's fired from a distance."

"Then I'll have to make sure it doesn't come to that."

"How?"

"I'll use my bow and arrow." Sloane knew that particular tone of Derek's only too well. And she wasn't buying. "Don't you dare snap into macho protective mode. I won't put up with it. I have three dachshunds. If I wanted a Doberman, I'd buy one."

"What you've got is a bodyguard—gratis. Which is lucky for you. Because you couldn't afford my services if I charged you. Army Ranger, remember?"

"I remember." Sloane bristled. "I also remember you're a pain in the ass."

"Yeah, well, it's a package deal. Cope with it."

"Not a chance. Look, Derek. We slept together last night. We'll probably sleep together again. But that's where it ends. Sex isn't a relationship. You're not back in my life, and I won't tolerate your inserting yourself in it. So cut the knight-in-shining-armor routine. I didn't need it then, and I neither want nor need it now." She snatched up her purse and marched across the hotel room, where she began rummaging through the front closet. "Lend me a jacket. We're picking up my car and meeting Tom. This subject is closed."

CHAPTER SIXTEEN

DATE: 3 April
TIME: 2100 hours

How fitting that my most coveted prize is turning out to be my most worthy opponent.

Artemis. My twin.

Smart and resourceful as she is beautiful, she didn't miss a beat when she discovered the flat tire I'd arranged to keep her near me—something I never would have done if I'd known the skies were about to open up, and that no one on campus would offer her help. She'd injured herself. That was my fault. I'll have to make it up to her.

She's also every bit the cunning huntress. If circumstances were different, she might even dig up enough suspicious information, connect enough dots, to point the investigation in my direction.

But circumstances aren't different.

And there won't be enough time.

Hunterdon County, New Jersey
10:30 P.M.

Sloane was fighting a losing battle.

For the past half hour, she'd been battling out a full-scale tug-of-war. She was tired, breathless, and losing big-time.

The only thing that was in worse shape than she, was the item being tugged—which, in this case, was her sweat sock. Moe had already chewed three holes in it, Larry had stretched it beyond recognition, and Curly was yanking on it so hard, he was making little grunting sounds with each rhythmic pull.

"I give up." Sloane let go of the sock and rolled over onto her back on the living-room rug, laughing as the three victorious hounds abandoned the sock to leap on her, licking her face and nibbling on her hair. "You're way too strong for me. Although, for the record, three against one isn't a fair fight."

She sat up, frowning at the clock on the wall. It was almost ten-thirty at night, and still the messenger hadn't arrived with the DVDs. She'd checked outside at least five times to see if the messenger had done a dump-and-run. Nothing. And to make matters worse, she couldn't reach Derek to find out what was going on. She'd been trying him since ten o'clock this morning, and his cell phone was going straight to voice mail.

She was torn between being royally pissed and a little worried. Derek was on-the-dot punctual. He would have been at Stockton, in the campus police's faces, at nine o'clock sharp. If they'd been running late, he'd have planted himself in their office like a drill sergeant. And if they'd been *this* late, he would have called to alert her.

Unless he was knee-deep in balancing the demands of the Bureau with the need to apply pressure on the college administrators to get what he wanted.

Any way you sliced it, Sloane wasn't happy.

Moe barked in her face to protest the lack of attention she was receiving, and Sloane responded by scratching her ears and giving each pup a kiss on the snout. "Thanks for being the only dependable ones in my life," she told them.

At that moment the doorbell rang.

"And thanks for being my good-luck charms," she added, scrambling to her feet.

All three hounds were oblivious to the compliment.

They were off on a single-minded mission—to find out who the visitor was.

They were delighted with who they found.

Sloane was not.

"Burt." Her brows rose in surprise when she saw her next-door neighbor's son standing on her doorstep, a covered casserole dish in his hands.

It was hard to miss the obvious disappointment in Sloane's tone, and Burt gave her an inquisitive look. "Bad time? I realize it's late, but you're usually a night owl. I'm sorry. I should have called first."

"Don't be silly." Sloane felt terrible. Burt had been a lifesaver these past weeks, taking care of the hounds, checking on the house for her. And here she was being rude to him for a reason that had nothing to do with him.

"Please, come in," she said, opening the door and trying to keep the hounds from leaping all over him in greeting. "I'm the one who should apologize. I was waiting for an important package that's being messengered over. It relates to a case I'm consulting on—an urgent one. I thought you were the messenger." She smiled. "But a friendly face is welcome, too. And not just by me." Sloane gestured toward the hounds, who were battling one another for center stage with Burt. "You have quite a fan base in this house."

"That's good to know." Burt squatted down to greet each dachshund individually. Simultaneously, he reached out and handed Sloane the casserole dish he was holding. "My mother made this. A tuna casserole. She was afraid you weren't eating."

"No worries there. I polished off a quart of beef with scallions a little while ago. But Elsa is a sweetheart." Sloane took the casserole dish. "*This* will be tomorrow night's dinner." She beckoned Burt inside and shut the door behind him. "I'll pop this in the fridge. Can I get you something— soda, beer, wine?"

"Are you having something?"

"Root beer." She gave him a rueful look. "But don't go by me. I'm on painkillers, so alcohol is off-limits."

"Actually, root beer would be great, thanks. I want to stay alert. I might have some more driving to do tonight."

Sloane heard a strained note in Burt's voice, and she studied him as he rose from tussling with the hounds. Something was bothering him. It was written all over his face. She was on the verge of asking, then checked herself. First, it was none of her business. And last, she didn't want to mislead Burt into thinking there was anything more than friendship between them. She hadn't forgotten the vibes he'd exuded when she'd had dinner at Elsa's.

"I'll be back in a sec," she said instead. "Make yourself comfortable."

She went into the kitchen, slid the casserole into the fridge, and grabbed two bottles of root beer. When she returned, Burt was perched at the edge of a barrel chair in the cozy den just opposite the front door. He was stroking Curly's head absently, but his mind was a million miles away.

"Here you go." Sloane offered him the bottle, then sat down on her favorite old sofa, settling onto the thick cushion and facing her guest. "You and Elsa have been amazing," she began. "I don't know what the hounds and I would do without you."

"That's what neighbors are for. I'm glad we could help." Burt raised his head. "How's your hand doing? It's still bandaged. Is the wound raw?"

"A little. Although it's much better than it was yesterday. I think my occupational therapist will remove the bandages tomorrow. She's just playing it safe. I did a pretty good number on the area surrounding the scar tissue. Between that, and the nerves and tendons I aggravated—my therapist was pretty pissed. And my surgeon's going to kill me when I meet with him in two weeks. He's like an artiste; he doesn't like his work tampered with."

"I can relate to that. Art of any kind, including that of a

surgeon, is a gift. It should be recognized and respected. I'm probably more fervent about that because I own a book-store. Talent like that awes me." Burt took a swallow of soda, then rolled the bottle pensively between his palms. "Beauty itself awes me. It's rare. Innocence is rarer still. And decency, respect . . ." He gave a bewildered shake of his head. "Those are practically nonexistent. So when I see them devalued, it maddens me."

Sloane was getting that uncomfortable feeling again. "Life has its ups and downs," she said simply. "But there's still plenty of goodness and beauty in the world. Some-times they're just hard to see."

Burt's head came up, and he grimaced at the expression on Sloane's face. "I'm really sorry. I dropped by to cheer you up, and instead I'm a walking poster for depression." He cleared his throat. "Today was a rough day. I had to meet with my ex-wife. We had some remaining personal items to divvy up. It was difficult, to say the least. Then I dropped by my mother's, and found her slumped over the kitchen table, white as a sheet."

Sloane started. "Is Elsa all right?"

"For now." Burt took another swig of root beer. "Besides her usual cooking and cleaning, she'd spent the rest of the day gardening, trimming bushes, and pruning hedges. She pushed herself way too hard. She was weak, exhausted, de-pleted, and dehydrated. I called the doctor. He was kind enough to come over, rather than putting my mother through a trip to the emergency room."

"And?"

"Her blood pressure had dropped way down. She needed potassium, a vitamin-B shot, and a dose of IV fluids."

"Where is she now?"

"Sleeping. I hired a nurse's aid to stay with her over-night. But that solution's just temporary. It's not feasible for the long term."

"If the problem is financial, I'd be more than happy to help out," Sloane offered instantly. "I've known your mother since I was a kid. She's not only a neighbor, she's a friend."

"Thank you, but no." Burt shook his head. "That's incredibly kind of you. And, believe me, I'm not refusing out of some misplaced sense of pride. If money was the answer, I'd take you up on your generous offer without hesitation. But it's not. The fact is, my mother's getting weaker. I can see her deteriorating before my eyes. And there's not a damn thing I can do about it."

A spark of realization struck Sloane. "That's why you didn't want a beer. And what you meant when you said you might need to do some more driving tonight. You're afraid Elsa will need to be hospitalized."

"I want to be prepared . . . just in case. If all is well and she's stable in the morning, I'll leave, make arrangements at the bookstore, and pack some things. That way I can move in and take care of her until that's not enough."

"When is the nurse's aid leaving?"

"Tomorrow at one. That'll give me enough time to take care of everything and get back here. I'm taking Princess Di with me so the nurse's aid can concentrate on my mother."

Sloane's mind was racing. "My appointment with my hand therapist is at ten. I'll be back here by early afternoon. If you run into any complications—traffic, getting someone to handle the bookstore—anything, give me a call. I'll stay with Elsa until you get back. If necessary, I'll bring the hounds and spend the night."

"You've got enough on your plate."

"Yes, and all of it is transportable. I can work just as easily at Elsa's house as I can here. So, please, don't hesitate to turn to me for help."

Before Burt could reply, the telephone rang.

"Excuse me for just a minute," Sloane requested. She picked up the phone. "Hello?"

"How's the hand?"

"Connie." Sloane was touched by her friend's concern. But her reaction was tempered, given that her thoughts were still preoccupied with Elsa's failing health. "My hand is doing much better. I'm following all your instructions. You'll see that for yourself when you take a look at it tomorrow." A quick glance at Burt's troubled expression. "Listen, you're a sweetheart for calling. But it's a bad time to talk. I've got company. So I'll see you tomorrow at ten, okay? Thanks for checking up on me."

"Not so fast," Connie interrupted. "Who's your company? It's Derek, right? I knew it. The other night wasn't a fluke. And it wasn't a one-night rekindling either. It was a new beginning. I could see it written all over your face."

"Like I said, this is a bad time." Sloane ground her teeth to keep from saying more than she wanted to right now. "We'll get into this tomorrow. Right now my neighbor's here. He was kind enough to drop by to see how I feel and to bring me a delicious casserole his mother made. I'm being spoiled by all of you."

As she spoke, the doorbell rang again.

"Sounds like you're even more popular than you thought," Connie commented at the other end of the phone.

"Not really." Sloane waved away Burt's gesture of offering to answer the door, and mouthed the words: *That's okay; I'll get it.* "That doorbell means that the messenger I've been waiting for with the material I need for my case has finally showed up," she informed Connie. "I'd better run, before he decides no one's home and I have to wait another day for my package."

"Okay. But we *will* talk about this tomorrow. And this time I want every juicy detail."

"Good night, Connie." Sloane hung up and hurried to the door. "Finally," she muttered to Burt, who was managing to keep the hounds from attacking the front door. "I was beginning to think he'd never get here."

She pulled open the door, simultaneously reaching into her pocket for a few dollars to tip the messenger—and froze.

Derek was standing on the doorstep.

"Hey," he greeted her, waving a padded pouch in the air. "Special delivery."

"*You* brought it—why?" she asked bluntly. "Also, where have you been all day? What happened to your cell phone? And what took so long for the DVDs to be burned?"

"I've been breathing down people's necks and playing political Ping-Pong all day. It turns out that four separate cameras cover the full section of campus between the parking lot and Lake Fred, which is the route we assume Penelope walked—and I wanted the surveillance footage from all of them. That caused a bit of an uproar, and added a shitload of time to the process. As for my cell—dead battery, forgot my charger. And I couldn't get a messenger who'd drive up here this late, so I brought the DVDs myself. Anything else?"

Sloane drew a slow breath. "Come on in." She stepped aside so he could comply. "How did you find this place? It doesn't show up on any GPS I've ever seen."

"I'm smart. And I've got a good sense of direction. Hey, fellas—and lady." He squatted down and greeted the hounds as they broke free and raced over to jump all over him. A broad smile spread across his face as he scruffled and tussled with each of them. "Looks like you haven't forgotten your old pal Derek. Well, I haven't forgotten you either." He pulled three little kongs filled with peanut butter out of his jacket pocket. "Still your favorites?" He chuckled as the dogs tripped over one another to get to the kongs. "Is it okay?" He tilted back his head, glancing quizzically up at Sloane.

"By all means." She made a wide sweep with her arm. "They'd never forgive me if I said no."

"Hear that, gang? They're yours." He distributed the kongs, and each dachshund snatched his or hers, then hurried off to a separate corner of the den to enjoy the treat in private.

"I think they call that bribery," Sloane commented, shutting the door behind Derek.

"Not in this case, In this case it was long-time-no-see

gifts." Derek came to a halt as he spotted Burt for the first time. "Am I intruding?"

Burt rose. "Actually, I'm the one who intruded. Sloane was expecting the package. She wasn't expecting me."

"Derek, this is Burt Wagner, my next-door neighbor Elsa's son," Sloane said. "Elsa and Burt are the lifesavers who took the hounds when I got hurt yesterday, and who care for them whenever I travel or when my work keeps me away for insane hours. I'd be lost without them. Burt, this is Special Agent Derek Parker of the FBI. He's a colleague and, in this case, the messenger who brought me the package I've been waiting for."

The two men shook hands.

"An FBI agent. That's pretty exciting," Burt said. "Do you work in the Newark office?"

"No. New York," Derek replied. "But the New York and Newark field offices often work together, if it becomes necessary."

"Clearly, this is one of those times." Burt turned to Sloane. "I'll get going now. I want to check and see how my mother's doing."

Nodding, Sloane walked him to the door. "Remember what I said. If Elsa needs me, I'm there. Just call. Either way, I'll check on her tomorrow. In the meantime, tell her to rest and get her strength back. And please, thank her for the casserole."

"I will. And, Sloane—I appreciate your support." Burt touched her arm lightly. "At times like this, it's good to know someone cares." He raised his head and met Derek's gaze. "Nice to meet you, Agent Parker."

"Derek," he corrected. "And same here."

Sloane had barely shut the door behind Burt and turned around, when Derek—who'd already plopped down on the sofa, crossed his ankles on the hassock in front of him, and folded his arms behind his head—commented, "That guy's dying to hook up with you."

"Excuse me?" Sloane's brows rose.

"You heard me. He might as well be wearing a sign that says 'I want to get into Sloane Burbank's pants.'"

"His mother's not well. He thinks she's slipping away. I doubt he's thinking about sex."

"I'm sorry to hear about his mother, but he's definitely thinking about sex—specifically with you."

Sloane made an exasperated sound. "Fine. He wants to have sex with me. I appreciate the tip."

"What about you?"

"What about me what?"

"Do you want to have sex with him?"

"Oh, for God's sake, first you assume the role of my bodyguard, and now you're monitoring my sex life? I thought I made it clear that—"

"Good," Derek interrupted with a look of smug satisfaction. "You don't want to sleep with the guy. Wise choice. He's not your type. Too needy. Too ordinary. And a little weird; lots of questionable baggage beneath the surface."

"Thank you, Dr. Ruth. You're pretty impressive—you got all that from a two-minute introduction?"

"Am I wrong?"

Silence.

"I rest my case." His teeth gleamed as he gave her that sexy, lopsided grin.

"You are *so* arrogant, it's astounding," Sloane muttered. "I'm surprised no one in C-6 has killed you yet."

"They're a tolerant bunch."

"Obviously." Sloane glanced thoughtfully toward the door. "I feel sorry for Burt. He's alone, making life-altering decisions about his mother with no guidance whatsoever."

"I hope you're not suggesting that you'll be providing that guidance."

"No, I don't think that would be wise. Besides, I'm not qualified. I'm thinking of a friend of mine. He might be able to help. He's the steady, calm type. He also has a medical background, and he's going through something similar to what Burt is."

"He?" Derek's brows rose. "Does this *he* want to sleep with you, too?"

Sloane rolled her eyes. "Hardly. I've mentioned him to you in the past. Luke Doyle. He's a medical assistant at Bellevue Hospital."

"He's the guy you went through 9/11 with, isn't he?"

Sloane nodded soberly. "There's something binding about sharing an experience like that. We touch base every so often. He's a good, decent person. The more I think about it, the more I think that talking to Luke would be good for Burt."

"Doyle," Derek repeated, his eyes narrowed as he searched his memory. "Why does that name ring a bell?"

"Because Luke's mother is Dr. Lillian Doyle—the John Jay sociology professor who spoke at the Crimes Against Women seminar with me. We've done quite a few panels together." Sloane sighed. "Unfortunately, she has cancer, and, from what I gather, not a lot of time. Luke is caring for her. I think it would be very cathartic if he spoke to Burt."

"It sounds like a good idea," Derek agreed. "Give him a call—*tomorrow*."

It was impossible to miss Derek's implication. Sloane folded her arms across her breasts and eyed the hassock where Derek had propped his feet. "You seem to have made yourself comfortable. I take it you're planning to watch the DVDs with me? Or have you already watched them?"

Derek shook his head. "I barely had time to get them, much less watch them. I saw enough to make sure the footage covered the right date and the right part of campus. Then I grabbed the DVDs and took off. We can go through the first batch of footage together."

"That works. I'll grab a couple of sodas—unless you'd rather have a beer?" She paused, knowing full well what his answer would be.

"Not when I'm working," he confirmed. "That hasn't changed."

"Okay, then I'll get the drinks. You set things up. The TV and the DVD player are over there." She pointed.

"Done. Sloane—wait." He halted her in her tracks. "Any more phone calls?"

"No," she replied in as casual a tone as she could muster. "Not a one."

Derek's eyes narrowed on her face. "But something's bothering you. What is it? And don't bother telling me nothing. I know otherwise."

Sloane gave up. Whether it pissed her off or not, he read her too well. "No phone calls, but a prolonged surveillance—I think. I don't have any proof to support that. Just gut instinct. I didn't see or hear him, not inside the house or on the grounds. And I've been in and out a bunch of times. I was looking for the messenger, but I was also scouting the area for my stalker. He was out there, watching me. I could feel it."

"He's studying your routine, figuring out the right time to act. No problem. He won't be getting it. I'll make sure of that." Sloane opened her mouth to protest, but Derek shut her down fast. "Don't waste time arguing. I'm not backing off, and we have hours of footage to watch. And, by the way, take a Vicodin. You've been rubbing your wrist since I walked in, and you wince every time you do. You're also white as a sheet, and you've got that drawn, pinched look between your eyes. That means you're in pain."

Sloane wasn't sure whether to tell him he was way off base, or to tell him to butt out. In the end, she opted for neither, and went for the truth.

"You're right, I am in pain. But if I take a Vicodin, I'll conk out."

"So? You'll watch the footage as long as you can. If you doze off, I'll pause the DVD until you wake up. I'll make myself a sandwich and take the hounds out for their late-night constitutional. If I remember right, they'll do an excellent job of waking you up when they burst back in here like three attention starved toddlers."

"That's true." Sloane couldn't argue with that. Still, she hated the idea of relinquishing even a teeny fragment of control over her life, especially to Derek.

"It's a nap, Sloane." He addressed her ambivalence as clearly as if she'd spoken it aloud. "It doesn't mean you're leaning on me, or that you're letting me back in. You drew the line. I get it. But there's nothing acquiescent or emotionally binding about what I'm describing. We're partners, supporting each other in order to solve a case."

"Nice explanation," she returned drily. "But you forgot one thing in your textbook description—the amazing sex part. Most partners don't sleep together."

"Okay, partners with benefits." He grinned. "Does that description work better for you?"

Despite her best intentions, a smile curved Sloane's lips. "Yes," she said, acknowledging the fact that she was going to need that Vicodin-induced nap for more than just the all-night DVD watching. "That works just fine."

Eickhoff Hall, the College of New Jersey
Trenton, New Jersey
April 4, 12 P.M.

Tina was psyched.

She'd finished her philosophy paper earlier than expected and delivered it to her professor's office. The rest of her work could be done over the weekend.

Which meant she wouldn't miss her all-night poker game after all.

She was feeling very lucky. She'd been on a winning streak these past few weeks. If it continued, she'd be able to pay for the Krav Maga fight gear she'd had her eye on at the academy. As things stood, she got her classes free, in exchange for being a part-time office manager. But, as her skills increased, she found herself loving the adrenaline rush and aggression release that came with the accelerated training. She wanted to increase the number of classes she took. She also wanted to start participating in the one-on-one fight sessions that were offered several times a week to expose the students to real-life street fighting. For the latter, she had to buy fight gear. And that meant big bucks.

What better way to earn them than at the poker table?

Pulling on some comfortable sweats, Tina snapped open her cell phone and pressed a number on speed dial. "Hey," she said, greeting one of her poker friends. "The game's at your apartment tonight, right? Good. I'll pick up some munchies and a six-pack on my way over. Prepare to take a huge beating."

Bellevue Park South
New York City
April 4, 12:15 P.M.

"Thanks for meeting me." Sloane took a bite of her hot dog and settled herself on the park bench overlooking the playground, and directly across the street from the medical center.

"No problem," Luke replied, removing his white medical coat so he wouldn't drip mustard on it. "I'm sorry for the one-star food. But I could only get away for an hour."

"Hey, don't knock one of New York's great traditions," Sloane said with a grin, taking another bite of her frank. "What respectable New Yorker hasn't dined alfresco with one of these babies? It's a rite of passage. Besides," she added in a more serious tone, "I appreciate your meeting me on such short notice."

"It was no big deal for me. I walked across the street. But you drove all the way from New Jersey, which means this is important. Is everything okay?"

Sloane nodded. "It wasn't that much out of my way. I had to see my hand therapist for a follow-up visit. She's at Cornell Medical Center today—and, as a result, so was I."

Luke gestured toward her hand. "I was going to comment on the bandage. What happened? I hope not a setback."

"A minor one. Would you believe I aggravated the scar

tissue by trying to change a flat tire on my own, and had a huge battle with a lug-nut wrench?"

He chuckled. "Knowing you? Yes. How is it healing?"

She sighed. "I've got some inflammation and tenderness. But I'm fighting the good fight, following doctor's orders and all that. So I'm on my way to recovery. Someday, when I stop being an impulsive idiot, I'll be as good as new."

"It'll happen sooner than you think. Have patience."

"Me? That's a lost cause." Sloane inclined her head in Luke's direction. "How's your mother? I've been at John Jay several times in the past week, and I haven't run into her. That's unusual."

An expression of sad resignation flashed across Luke's face. "She goes in to work more sporadically these days. She's tired. As for the pain, some days are better than others. I try to make her as comfortable as possible. She's a trouper; never complains. But it's difficult to watch."

"I'm so sorry," Sloane replied softly. Instinctively, she continued. "How are you doing?"

"Not well. She's all I have—" Luke broke off, fighting to keep his emotions under control. "Nothing in life prepares you for this. Not even 9/11." He exhaled sharply. "Let's talk about something else. What did you want to see me about?"

Sloane hesitated. "I had a personal favor to ask. But seeing how much you're hurting—maybe it isn't such a good idea."

"Why don't you let me be the judge of that?"

Sloane nodded, then proceeded to tell Luke all about Burt and Elsa, and the idea she'd had for Luke to reach out to Burt. "Having said that, I don't want to put you in the position of having to cope with your own trauma firsthand *and* make it worse by helping a stranger through a similar experience. Not to mention the fact that Elsa's condition pales in comparison to Lillian's. So why don't we shelve this?"

"No." Luke gave an adamant shake of his head. "I'd like to help. Focusing on other people's pain helps me put my own in perspective."

"You're sure?"

"Absolutely. Sitting around describing the loss I'm about to endure is one thing. Applying my experience to get someone through a similar crisis is another matter entirely."

Sloane squeezed his arm. "You haven't changed a bit. You're still one of the most calming and empathetic people I know."

"Right back at you." Luke took a bite of his hot dog. "Tell me about your neighbor. I take it his father is out of the picture."

"He passed away a number of years ago. Again, the situation wasn't as traumatic as yours—at least not from Burt's perspective. He was a grown man when his father died. You were a child. Elsa, though, was another story. She was pretty dependent on her husband. She's transferred a lot of that dependence to Burt."

"That's not an unusual scenario. And, for the record, you're giving me way too much credit. My father's death wasn't that big a blow. Truthfully, he wasn't around much."

"Traveling?"

"No, cheating."

Sloane winced. "Sorry. I didn't mean to put my foot in my mouth."

"No problem." Luke gave an offhand shrug. "It was a long time ago. My point was that Burt might have been more affected by losing his father than I was. And that definitely applies to Elsa. My mother's a survivor. Until now, with her cancer taking over, she's always been strong and independent. But for a traditional woman like Elsa, she probably felt lost when her husband died. So she turned to her son. Is Burt her only child?"

"Yes." Sloane nodded.

"Does he have a family of his own—a wife, kids?"

"Neither. He just went through an ugly divorce. That compounds the problem. He's angry and brooding. Not to mention alone way too much. He definitely needs someone to talk to."

Luke's gaze was steady but intuitive. "And you've been elected for the job. Which worries you because he's starting to get attached."

A half smile. "Like I said, you're the same Luke. You pick up on everything. Yes, I'm a little concerned that he's misinterpreting our friendship. Plus, you have medical training and a more intrinsic understanding on your side. I'm hoping that if you speak to him, make a few suggestions about concrete steps he can take, he'll feel more useful and less at loose ends."

"Give me his phone number." Luke took out a scrap of paper and a pen, and jotted down the information Sloane recited. "I'll give him a call. It'll do me some good to concentrate on someone else's problems for a change. Besides, there's a lot I can suggest, things he can do to make a positive difference. I know from my own ordeal that it makes you feel a hell of a lot better to *do* something productive, rather than to sit around waiting for the inevitable. Especially since, from what you're describing about Elsa's condition, the inevitable could be a long way off."

"I hope so. Elsa is a wonderful woman. She's always been so strong. It's creepy how she went downhill so fast."

"What type of illness does she have?"

"That's another thing. I don't know. Burt never actually told me what's wrong with her. All I know is that she's weak, she's on medication, and she needs to have someone with her. He had a nurse's aid there yesterday, and I pitched in when she left, but I think she's going to require a regular health-care worker. And Burt won't take money from me, not even as a loan."

"I could look into some insurance angles," Luke replied. "Sometimes it's not *what* you say, but *how* you say it that can make a difference between covered and not covered. Give me a few days. Let me see what I can do on that front. In the meantime, I'll give Burt a call, see if he wants to meet me for a beer. For obvious reasons, I don't have much free time. But a beer and a talk, including some suggestions about how he can get more extensive in-house nursing care should do it. By then, I'll have some referrals to pass along to him. I think we can get Burt in a better place."

"That's very generous of you. Thanks so much, Luke."

"You're very welcome." He glanced at his watch. "I'd better get going. The hospital's short-staffed." He rose, exchanging a quick hug with Sloane. "Take care of that hand. And I'll keep you posted."

After Luke dashed off, Sloane tossed her napkin into the trash, then started the three-block walk to her car. She was lucky to have found a lot with some space. Parking in Manhattan was a pain.

She was half a block away when she got that feeling again.

Stopping in her tracks, she ignored the pissed-off pedestrians who strode around her, muttering four-letter words and glaring in her direction. She plucked her sunglasses off her nose and scrutinized the area, feeling the presence of her stalker as vividly as if she could see him.

Unfortunately, she couldn't.

But she knew damned well he was there.

CHAPTER SEVENTEEN

DATE: 5 April
TIME: 0530 hours
OBJECTIVE: Tyche

She's rounding the southern corner of Lake Ceva. I can hear her familiar gait, coming closer with each rhythmic tread.

Soon she'll come into view—right on schedule.

My anticipation is growing.

I can sense my grip on the combat knife tightening. It feels so natural in my hand. Adrenaline thrumming through my veins. My heart pounding. My entire body taut and ready to strike.

One quick scan of the area, just to be sure.

Thankfully, deserted.

I'd had an unexpected close call when a new, unknown jogger decided to take this route at this time—today of all days. It had thrown me, and compromised my plan. Pre-dawn on a college campus meant most students were first turning in for the night. This kid was an anomaly.

I was devising the best plan to get rid of him, when he eliminated the problem for me. He stopped, glared at his iPod, and began tinkering with it. Apparently, it wasn't functioning correctly, because he abandoned his jog and headed back to his dorm, shaking the iPod in annoyance as he left.

He shouldn't be so angry. That broken iPod had saved his life.

Now Tyche was alone.

She came into view, ponytail swinging, her breath coming quickly as she neared her spot.

Closer.

Closer.

Now.

As always, Tina stopped beside the same knotted oak tree, and took a swig of water. Ten seconds to rehydrate and catch her breath, and she'd be off again.

He came out of nowhere, an ominous dark blur lunging out of the woods. He was pressed up behind her in a heartbeat, his right arm wrapped around her throat, a large blade glinting in his hand. She winced as the blade grazed her left shoulder.

"Don't make a sound, Tai Kee," he ordered in a low voice. "Just come with me. And don't try to fight me. If you do, I'll slit your throat."

No thought was necessary. Her Krav training took over.

Tina reached up with both hands and grabbed her assailant's right wrist, pulling his arm out and away from her throat. She then flipped his knife-wielding hand palm side up. Gripping it with her left hand, she jammed down with her right, snapping his wrist. She heard the audible crack, followed by a sharp cry of pain, and a hiss of something that sounded like "Bow Za" followed by "Chao Ji Bei."

The combat knife fell from his hand and dropped to the grass.

Tina was far from finished.

Still holding her assailant's injured right wrist with her left hand, she whipped around to face him, striking him in the face with her elbow as she did. Her hair tumbled free as her hair clip flew off and fell to the ground. She ignored it. A split second's view of her attacker told her he was tall. Broad-shouldered. Dressed all in black. Wearing a black ski mask.

Her right hand wrapped around the back of his neck and she used her forearm to twist his face to the side. In one motion, she released his right arm, grabbed his right shoulder with her left hand, and jerked him down to deliver a knee strike to his groin. Along with his agonized groan, she heard a jangle, saw two silver tags topple out of his shirt, dangling from a chain she'd felt when she'd anchored his neck.

Before he could recover from the first knee strike, she yanked him down again, this time delivering a knee strike to his face. She connected squarely, and blood spurted from his nose, oozing through the ski mask. He folded over in pain, and she followed up with a right elbow strike to the back of his neck. He bent farther forward, and she used that to her advantage, standing up and delivering a round kick to the back of his right knee as she pushed him away.

He lost his balance and fell to the ground. Two items flew out of his pocket. One landed beside him. The other sailed off into the woods.

The item beside him was a hypodermic needle.

"Ta Ma De," he screamed, clutching his groin and rolling around in agony.

That was Tina's cue. She turned and broke into a dead run, getting as far away as fast as she could. She didn't stop until she reached her room.

When the door was safely locked behind her, she called 911.

Delphi slammed the front door behind him—so hard that the entire house vibrated from the impact.

Downstairs in their respective rooms, all the women leaped to their feet, fearful over what was happening, more fearful over what would happen next.

He tore through the house on a wild rampage, alternately smashing things, groaning in pain, and shouting English and Chinese profanities.

An hour passed. The intensity of his rage did not.

The goddesses cringed in their rooms, panicked over the outcome of this tirade. They understood that no new goddess would be joining them. Something major had gone wrong. And, whatever it was, Delphi would be taking it out on them.

But who? When? And how?

Waiting it out, and the apprehension that accompanied it, were unendurable.

Finally, they heard the stomping of his footsteps heading downstairs. Each of them froze and waited.

The metallic clink of keys. The moment or two until he found the one he wanted. And then the fumbling that indicated he was beyond fury and into psychosis.

Surprisingly, it was Hestia's door he unlocked.

"I need your help," he commanded, shutting the door behind him.

Hestia flinched. She was calm by nature, but Delphi had terrified her from day one. She compensated by obeying all his rules, and asking for as little as possible. Her goal was to remain almost invisible, a plan that seemed to be working, based on the fact that Delphi rarely spent any time with her. And it was unprecedented for him to single her out.

Until now.

She forced herself to rise, knowing he expected a response, and unsure what response would provoke him least. Before she could decide, he stepped out of the shadows and into the light, limping painfully toward her. As he approached, she could see that his nose was bloody, there was an ice pack strapped to his pants in the groin area, and his right arm was twisted at an unnatural angle.

Now she understood why he'd chosen her to come to.

"You're badly hurt," she confirmed quietly. "What can I do?"

"Hestia, the goddess of home and hearth," he muttered. He was half out of it from whatever narcotics he'd taken for the pain, and from the sheer exhaustion resulting from his rampage.

"Yes," she replied, keeping him calm by agreeing with him. "Now I'm Hestia. But before that, I was a nurse. Which is why you're here. Describe your injuries to me, and how you got them."

"Tyche, that bitch." He was rambling, yet the pieces were easy enough to put together. "She launched a counter-strike. Against me of all people. I was her savior."

Bravo, she thought silently. *Whoever you are, Tyche, you got away. And you caused him pain in the process. I pray you take this to the police. If you do, maybe there can still be hope for us.*

Aloud, she said only, "Show me."

In answer, he rolled up his sleeve, and she could see that his wrist was badly swollen and discolored. With his left hand, he reached into his jacket pocket, and pulled out some first-aid supplies. "I used ice on the drive back," he told her. "I stopped at a pharmacy and bought an Ace bandage. I need you to wrap my wrist. I can't do it one-handed."

Hestia examined the wound. "The swelling is bad. The wrist could be fractured. You need to have it X-rayed."

"I can't and it isn't," he retorted. "I'll continue to ice it. I'll also elevate it and rest it. Now help me with the Ace bandage."

She summoned all her courage and tried one last time. "It's at least a grade-two sprain, if not a grade three. Which means, at best, the ligaments are partially torn, and, at worst, they're completely torn. The joint will be impacted. You need to get to a hospital."

"I said no!" he shouted. *"Whatever treatment I need, you'll provide. You're a nurse. You worked in a hospital. Now fix it!"*

"All right." Alarmed by his outburst and the crazed, drugged look in his eyes, she took the Ace bandage, and with trembling fingers, she wrapped his injured wrist from the base of his fingers all the way to the top of his forearm, overlapping the wrap so it was as snug and supportive as possible without cutting off the circulation. "That should help," she said. "Apply ice for twenty minutes at a time, every three to four hours. Do that for two days. Use the wrist as little as possible; it needs rest. Also, keep it elevated as much as possible. Prop a pillow under it when you sleep."

He glanced over her handiwork. "A skillful job. I knew you were Hestia. I was right when it came to you. I was right when it came to all my goddesses. Tyche was a gross error in judgment. I don't allow myself those."

"Of course not. Nor do you make them." Hestia prayed she was choosing the right words. "This Tyche who hurt you isn't destined to be a goddess. That's *her* flaw, not yours."

Some of the wild rage left his eyes. "You're right. She's the deficient one, not I."

"Exactly." Hestia felt a surge of relief. "As for your nose, clean it up and apply an ice pack. That'll take down the swelling. But the injury to your groin could be serious. I strongly urge you to see a doctor."

His gaze hardened again. "I know what signs to look for. I'll handle it."

"What about painkillers?"

"I have what I need."

"Of course you do." He clearly had a drug connection. Hestia well remembered the hypodermic needle he'd had the day he kidnapped her at knifepoint. She'd cooperated so he didn't have to use it. Needles didn't frighten her; she administered them every day. But she knew that if she'd had any chance of getting away when he first grabbed her, that chance would have evaporated if she were unconscious.

As it turned out, it hadn't mattered.

There'd been no chance. No escape.

Delphi was turning away from her, limping painfully toward the door. "I'll be back when the bandage needs to be reapplied."

"That's fine. But don't neglect the other wounds. And be sure to get some rest."

He paused, glanced back at her. "You'll be rewarded for your loyalty and compassion."

With that, he left. As he was shutting the door behind him, Hestia heard him mutter: "As for that little bitch—Mount Olympus is lost to her. She's a whore like all the others. She'll rot in hell. I'll make sure of that."

Martial Arts Academy
Flemington, Hunterdon County, New Jersey
April 6, 8:15 P.M.

Sloane pulled into the parking lot, relieved that the academy had called and asked her to teach tonight's Krav Maga class. She needed a distraction. She'd spent days watching the video footage, until her eyes were bleary and her head was filled with cobwebs. And still she hadn't spotted Penny.

At least three times, she'd had a surge of hope, paused the DVD segment she'd been watching, rewound it, and leaned forward, rechecking it in slow motion only to have her heart sink when she realized it wasn't Penny.

By tonight, every frame was starting to look alike.

She'd known there was a lot of footage to go through, but she never imagined it would be this intricate and difficult. The sheer number of DVDs was daunting enough. But between the glare of the midday sun, the indistinct features of the people walking by, and the wooded sections blocking certain angles from view, Sloane was frustrated. She had assumed that Penny's red business suit would have jumped right out, especially in a sea of T-shirts, dark sweatpants, and jeans. Evidently, that wasn't the case—at least not yet.

But Sloane refused to give up.

Derek had already sent every DVD the Stockton campus police had fed him down to Quantico for more sophisticated analysis. There was one more day of outstanding footage yet to be burned, but the FBI and Sloane were concentrating on the day of Penny's disappearance, and the day or two before it, when the kidnapper would most likely have visited the campus to finalize his strategy.

Eventually, *something* had to turn up.

Sloane turned off the car, gathered up her Krav gear, and headed into the academy. She expected to have some time to set up before the students arrived.

That idea was forgotten the minute she stepped through the door.

The entire reception area and front office were jammed with people, including two local newspaper reporters and a photographer. It looked like a political press conference and—judging from the phrases being thrown around, like "physical assault" and "attempted abduction"—it sounded like the set of a TV crime drama.

"What's going on?" Sloane called out, although she had no idea who was going to answer her.

Mark Donaldson, one of her more avid and early-arriving students, took on that role, walking over and raising his voice so Sloane could hear him above the crowd. "I guess you haven't been watching the news. Tina was attacked at knife-point yesterday. The local press is all over her. So are all the students who just finished up their seven o'clock Krav Maga and tae kwon do classes."

"Is Tina all right?" Sloane asked instantly. "When you say attacked, do you mean robbed? Raped?"

"Neither. She used her Krav to beat the crap out of the guy. Pretty cool, huh?" He jerked his thumb in the direction of the office. "Talk to her yourself. She's in there."

Sloane shoved her way through the two dozen people until she reached the office. Spying Tina's overwhelmed expression, she switched into take-charge mode. "Interviews are over," she announced, holding up both hands and glaring pointedly at the press. "Leave your business cards on the table by the door. If Ms. Carroll wants to get in touch with you, she will. Everyone else—if you're not here to take a class, please say your good-nights."

"Just a few more shots," the photographer cajoled.

"*No.*" Sloane's tone was adamant. "I won't be saying this nicely again. I want everyone to clear out *immediately.* Starting with members of the press." A penetrating stare at one tenacious reporter. "If you need encouragement, be aware that I have the cops on speed dial. I also have two of them as students in my class."

"Better listen to her," Mark Donaldson chimed in. "She's ex-FBI. And if you think Tina's tough, Ms. Burbank will body-slam you out the door."

With grimaces and under-the-breath comments, the press filed out, followed by the stream of curious students.

Sloane waited until the crowd had dissipated. She then gestured to Mark that she'd be out in a minute, and retreated into the office, where she and Tina were now alone. Shutting the door behind her, she walked over to Tina, who was sitting stiffly at her desk, and placed a gentle hand on her shoulder. "How are you holding up?"

"Okay, I guess." Tina forced a smile, but Sloane could see right through it. The poor girl was still shaky. "I'm a little overwhelmed by all this craziness. And I still feel like the whole thing was an out-of-body experience."

"What about physically?"

"Physically, I'm fine, other than a minor flesh wound on my left shoulder. It happened when he first grabbed me and put that mega-knife across my throat. The cut stings like hell, but it's not serious. The college medical center treated it, bandaged it up, and sent me home with some painkillers."

"Mark said this happened yesterday." Sloane stuck with the basics, until she could decide if Tina was ready to supply details. "Were you at your dorm?"

"No. I was out running. I do laps around Lake Ceva every morning at five-thirty. The guy came out of nowhere. He put that serious-looking blade across my throat, muttered something I couldn't understand, then told me to shut up and come with him or he'd slit my throat."

Tina proceeded to fill Sloane in on the next thirty seconds of self-defense, a spark of pride flashing in her eyes when she described the Krav Maga techniques she'd used to disarm her attacker and put him out of commission.

"Nice job," Sloane commended. "I couldn't have done it better."

"Thanks. Anyway, I took off as soon as I knocked him off his feet," Tina concluded. "I never knew I could run that fast."

"Adrenaline. It's a powerful tool when your life's at stake." Sloane was pleased to see Tina's color coming back. "So you got back to your room and called the campus police?"

"The second I locked my door. Two armed cops came ASAP. So did three campus security officers—and half the students who live in my hall. My room was like a three-ring circus. I had my parents on the phone, pretty hysterical, and wall-to-wall people asking me for details. One of the security officers took me to the medical center so my wound could be treated, and so I could set up a counseling appointment for this morning. I was pretty freaked out. Then the security guy took me back to my dorm, where I answered as many of their questions as I could. Half of what I said is a blur. The whole day seemed surreal. Honestly? I just wanted the whole thing to go away."

"That's perfectly natural," Sloane murmured. "You'd just gone through a traumatic experience."

"Yeah, well, it didn't help when the news spread all over campus and suddenly reporters appeared and students I didn't even know started coming up to me to get the gory details. I tried to duck everyone, but it was impossible. I came to the academy tonight hoping to get away from the mass pandemonium, and to have some normalcy and peace. Guess that wasn't in the cards." Tina dragged her fingers through her hair. "It's weird. When I drove away from campus tonight, I looked over at Lake Ceva. The area where I was attacked is roped off. It looks more like an official crime scene on *CSI* than like real life.

"It *is* an official crime scene," Sloane reminded her. "Just because you were smart enough and skilled enough to get away doesn't make the attack any less of a crime." A careful pause. "Did you see the man who attacked you?"

Tina shook her head. "Not really. He was wearing a ski mask. I saw his build, his height, even a slit of his eyes. But not enough to identify him. And he only said a handful of words, all of them in a low, raspy voice. I couldn't even make out a few of them."

"Do you think he might have been another student?" Sloane asked.

"I don't think so. He seemed older. His physique, his voice, even the way he moved. It wasn't like he was a young guy. I could be wrong. But that was the impression I got."

"You said you delivered a knee strike to his face, and that you connected with his nose. Was it bleeding badly?"

"Yeah, all over the place. It soaked through his mask and dripped onto the ground."

"Good. Then there'll be DNA evidence."

"I can't imagine otherwise." Tina blew out a slow, calming breath. "The police did one of those mouth swabs on me for a DNA sample. This way, they'll be able to differentiate his blood from mine. Although most of the blood was his. I only had blood on my shirt from where the cut oozed through, and a little bit on my hair clip."

"Your hair clip?"

Tina nodded. "It came loose when we were struggling. It slid out of my hair, and bounced across my shirt as it fell. I remember noticing the bloodstain on it when it was lying on the grass."

Sloane went very still as the commonalities clicked into place.

Two attempted kidnappings—one successful, one not. Both on college campuses. Both leaving behind either a bloodstained hair band or hair clip at the crime scenes. Both within a few weeks of each other. Both in the New York/New Jersey area.

Coincidence?

No way.

"He planned on drugging me," Tina was continuing. "A hypodermic needle fell out of his pocket when I knocked him down. That and something else. I saw it go flying off into the woods."

"Tina, did the campus police say when they'd be getting back to you?" she asked.

"In a day or two." Tina rubbed her sore shoulder anxiously. "I'm sure the college is trying to spin this so that panic won't erupt, in spite of the media coverage. After all, this was an atypical, isolated incident. It's not like TCNJ has a high crime rate. So the school's probably urging the police to take a responsible but low-key approach. Not that it's done any good. The story's in all the papers. It's spread across the campus like wildfire. All the girls are freaking out, just knowing this guy's out there somewhere. I don't blame them; he's clearly a wack job." A hint of a smile. "Although I think I put him out of commission for a while."

"No doubt he's got some serious wounds to deal with," Sloane agreed.

As satisfying as that knowledge was, it wasn't comforting. Tina had kicked this guy's ass. Wherever he was holed up, nursing his wounds, it had to be close by. He was badly hurt, and ripping mad. None of which bode well for what came next.

"The police were trying to figure out if there was a motive specific to me," Tina was saying, "but I think I was just in the wrong place at the wrong time. Forget ransom; I can barely pay my tuition. My only assets are my poker winnings, which are just enough to buy my fighting gear. And, to my knowledge, I don't have any enemies, certainly not psychotic ones."

"Of course not." Sloane's wheels were still turning—fast. She had to choose her words cautiously, approach this in a way that wouldn't frighten Tina. The poor girl had been through enough. But the truth was, potential victims weren't the only ones Sloane was concerned about. She was worried about Tina. If the attack on her and the attack on Cynthia Alexander were related, then they might be dealing with a serial rapist or a serial killer. And that changed everything.

Not only would the manhunt become bigger and more widespread, but if Tina was the first girl to have gotten away from this psycho, *and* to physically overpower and humiliate him in the process, there was a good chance his rage would compel him to return and do God knows what to her.

Sloane wasn't going to let that happen. She'd pull whatever strings she had to. But Tina would have police protection.

Speaking of police, Sloane would call Bob Erwin the minute she finished teaching tonight's Krav class. The College of New Jersey Police Department wouldn't have reason to make the connection to the John Jay kidnapping. But Bob would, once Sloane filled him in. He needed to know *everything* about Tina's assault. Her ordeal, and whatever details of it she could recall, could be the break he'd been looking for to solve Cynthia's case.

He'd need to interview Tina.

"Tina," Sloane continued, setting the stage. "You know I have quite a few contacts in law enforcement. I want to run this incident by them, just to get their take on it. Obviously, I'll keep the campus police in the loop. But the more professional views we elicit, the better chance we have of catching this guy before anyone else gets hurt."

"That makes sense."

"My NYPD contacts will want to ask you a couple of questions, just to expedite nailing this guy. Would that be all right?"

Tina's eyes narrowed. "NYPD? This isn't just about what happened to me, is it? It's about that girl who was kidnapped at John Jay College. I read about her in the newspaper. Is there a pattern between what happened to her and what happened—or almost happened—to me?"

"There are some definite similarities," Sloane replied candidly. "Except that the other girl, Cynthia Alexander, is still missing. Sergeant Erwin of Midtown North is working round the clock to find her."

"Then call him. Tell him I'll talk to him right away. If anything I say can help him find her, I'll take him through my assault step-by-step."

Sloane gave Tina a grateful smile. "Thanks. I will."

As it turned out, Sloane didn't call Sergeant Erwin—at least not the minute she stepped out of class the way she'd planned.

When she left the martial-arts academy and flipped on her cell phone, she found two terse, urgent messages from Derek.

"What's up?" she asked the minute he answered his phone.

"You tell me. An hour ago I got a call about one of your stalker's disposable cell phones."

"He used it?" Sloane stopped in her tracks, car key in her hand. "Where was he calling from?"

"The College of New Jersey. And *he* wasn't the one at the other end of the phone. The campus police were. Seems they just found the phone in a cluster of trees near Lake Ceva, where one of their students was attacked yesterday. Tina Carroll. But something tells me you know more about that than I do."

CHAPTER EIGHTEEN

DATE: 7 April
TIME: 0130 hours

The demons have been howling all night.

I can't hear or think above their tirade. My head is about to explode. They've crept inside it. They're relentless. Pounding away like a jackhammer. Coupled with my other injuries, the agony is unbearable.

I can't stand it any longer.

And I can't escape it.

I'm waiting for the extra syringe of morphine I injected to work. The seconds have ticked by so slowly—it feels like an eternity. This throbbing must stop.

I did as the demons commanded. I watched the most recent videotapes. I could see for myself the power I wield, the enormity of the purification process with which I've been entrusted.

I know what I'm capable of doing to a filthy *Ji Nv* like Tyche.

The demons have ordered me to wait. Disinfection first. Revenge later.

But Tyche won't get away with her intolerable desecration. She'll suffer.

And she'll suffer by my hand.

Till then, let the whore parade around campus, boasting of her physical prowess, feeling utterly victorious and safe. On the other hand, if she's smart, she'll lock herself in her dorm room and tremble in a corner, knowing full well she's not.

Soon. The demons will demand it. There will be no shame in the pleasure I take. Not with her. I'll revel in the terror in her eyes when I have her. When she realizes it's me. When she finally comprehends that there's no escape. That my violation of her unworthy body is only the nightmarish beginning. That she's going to die. That her death will be prolonged, and preceded by unendurable suffering.

I'll describe to her what might have been. She'll hear my voice every second as I slowly cut her flesh. No drugs. Not with her. I want her to be wide-awake and alert. To hear every word. Feel every slice. Watch every rivulet of her blood seep away. By the time death comes, she'll welcome it. Scream for it. Beg for it.

That image alone will have to suffice for now—until the demons decree otherwise.

Right now they condemn another *Ji Nv* to die.

I *must* regain full use of my body—now. The pain is inconsequential. I'll manage it with the morphine. But the rest . . . how can I accomplish everything I have to in my current condition?

Weakness is unacceptable. One more day. That's all I'll allow for my injuries. Tomorrow night, I'll silence the demons.

The morphine is starting to work. Good. Because tonight I have a different, more important task to attend to—choosing an alternate goddess. I must study my Ancient Greek literature. The goddess I select will be far more deserving than the original. So will the woman I choose to embody her.

And, in the end, she'll join the others.

Starbucks
120 West Fifty-sixth Street, New York City
9:20 A.M.

Derek carried a tray with two tall steaming Starbucks cups and two blueberry scones over to the corner table.

"One venti cappuccino with skimmed milk and one venti café americano, black," he announced, setting the cappuccino down in front of Sloane and passing her a blueberry scone.

"Thanks. I only ordered a grande."

"I know. But I owe you. Not only did you battle rush-hour traffic so we could talk before you headed over to Midtown North, but you convinced Erwin to include me in your meeting. I normally avoid stepping on the NYPD's toes, especially in situations like this where I technically have no connection to the case. My connection here is you, and the fact that your stalker's cell phone was found at the crime scene. On the other hand, after Tina Carroll's attempted abduction, we're no longer talking about the single John Jay disappearance Erwin's investigating. We're talking about at least two related attacks, with the possibility of others. And with the two attacks we know of occurring in two different states, FBI involvement might be imminent anyway."

"I agree. So based on all of the above, I accept the extra-large cappuccino. I need a hefty jolt of caffeine. As for the blueberry scone . . ." She eyed the one in front of her. "We had a very recent conversation about how seldom I eat junk food."

"Yeah, but you love Starbucks' blueberry scones."

A half smile. "You always bought two for yourself, because I pretended I didn't want one."

"I remember. And you took 'just one bite' of my extra scone until it was three-quarters gone."

"Half," Sloane said in defense.

"If you say so." Derek sat down across from her and

took a belt of coffee. "Either way, feel free. I'll polish off whatever you leave over." He leaned forward, interlacing his fingers in front of him and meeting her gaze. "I know we discussed this ad nauseam on the phone last night. But I want to try to make some sense of it before we head over to Midtown North—and I can't. That cell phone the TCNJ cops found in the woods on campus means that the bastard who's been stalking you is the same guy who attacked Tina Carroll."

"Unless her assailant stole my stalker's phone, which I doubt, yes. And I don't get it either." Sloane sipped at her cappuccino, as unsettled by all this as Derek was. "The parallels between Cynthia's disappearance and Tina's near abduction are straightforward. They're both college students. They're both athletes. They were both attacked on their respective campuses when the grounds were virtually deserted. The timing of the two attacks is only several weeks apart. And now the blood on both their hair fasteners—it all fits the pattern of a repeat performance by the same criminal. But why would he be stalking me? When we thought the harassment was tied to Penny's case, it made sense. I grew up with Penny, and I knew a lot about her. That made me a potential threat. But now—where do I fit into the equation?"

"You also knew Tina," Derek pointed out.

"Casually, yes. We both worked at the same martial-arts academy. She took a few of my Krav classes. Oh, and we planned a few tae kwon do parties for the kids together. But I don't know the first thing about her private life, her friends, her family—anything that would make me a threat to whoever attacked her."

"What if he's not viewing you as a threat? What if he's viewing you as a target?"

Sloane grimaced. "Derek, I know you think this guy is after me in some way, and I admit his weird behavior has me on edge. But Tina's attack makes your theory weaker, not stronger. This assailant grabs his victims when they're isolated. If he wanted me, he's had tons of opportunity to attack me. I might not go to college, but I do go for a several-mile run with the hounds every morning. Most of my route is all woods and no civilization. I *know* he's been watching me at home. I sense it. Which means he's well aware of when I go out running. So why hasn't he acted?"

"Maybe he's waiting."

"For what—a formal invitation?"

Derek's grip on his coffee cup tightened. "I don't know. That's what's driving me crazy. My gut tells me there's something we're missing." The crease between Derek's brows deepened. "Even without considering where you fit into all this, we've got to face the prospect that we're dealing with a serial killer."

"I agree. Either a serial rapist *and* killer, or a serial killer—one who's done a hell of a job of getting rid of his victims' bodies so they're never found."

"There are a bunch of ways to make that happen. Some we've come up against, some we haven't. I hope Erwin will let me join him when he interviews Tina. The details she remembers may help us establish a profile on this guy." Derek clearly had thought this through. "If Tina delivers, I'm putting a call in to one of my colleagues at the Behavioral Analysis Unit in Quantico. He and I have worked together in the past. He'll do me the favor of putting this at the top of his list."

"Good. And I'll call Larry Clark. He's retired now, but he was an SSA at the BAU. He's served on panels with me at John Jay. He's sharp as a tack, and he's got twenty-five years of Bureau experience. I'm sure he can help us."

"Works for me. Between your contacts and mine, we'll get our criminal profile." Derek took a bite of his scone, chewed it with a vengeance. "Now let's get back to you. Finding that cell phone in the woods clinches it. I'm arranging for you to have round-the-clock protection. So pick your poison—FBI, the police, or a PI. I've got lots of friends who owe me favors. So don't bother arguing. It won't work."

"I wasn't going to argue. And I'll let you decide who the lucky candidates are. But under one condition. Get that same level of protection for Tina, too. You know as well as I do that this sicko is going to come back for her. She outsmarted him, beat the crap out of him, and got away. He's not going to be satisfied until he's gotten even *and* gotten rid of her."

"Agreed. And already taken care of. When I met with The College of New Jersey campus police, they were more than happy to assign several rotating officers to Tina. They'll watch her twenty-four/seven. The only stipulation is that she's got to stay on or around campus. No drives to the academy, not till her assailant is caught."

Sloane blew out a sigh of relief. "Thank you. Tina's a really great girl. She shouldn't have had to go through this trauma at all, much less prolong it by walking around campus glancing over her shoulder in fear."

"Police protection only goes so far. Tina won't be safe until we've caught this psycho." Derek glanced at his watch. "Time for our meeting. Let's see what Sergeant Erwin can tell us."

Midtown North Precinct
308 West Fifty-fourth Street
New York City

Bob Erwin carried a file folder and three bottles of springwater into the large interrogation room—now doubling as a conference room—and shoved the door closed behind him.

"Here you go." He distributed the bottles to Sloane and Derek, then took a seat at the table, placing the file in front of him. "Trust me, you're better off with the springwater than with the coffee," he pronounced. "I had a cup this morning. It tastes like sludge—as usual."

"Thanks for the warning." Sloane uncapped her bottle and took a swig. "It's just as well. I'm flying on caffeine as it is."

"Ditto." Derek settled himself in the chair beside Sloane and across the table from Erwin. "I lost count of how many cups of coffee I've downed since five A.M." He put the bottle of water down, rolling it between his palms. "I appreciate your including me in this meeting and bypassing all the bureaucratic crap."

"No arguments there," Bob agreed. "Although I am curious about your interest in this. You're with C-6, not violent crimes. I'm aware that you and Sloane worked in the Bureau's Cleveland field office at the same time, but you worked two different units. Is this all about your friendship with her, or does the FBI have other reasons for assigning you to this case?"

It was a fair question, one that Derek answered as honestly as possible.

"The Bureau knows I'm here, although I'm not here at their request. And you're right; I am with C-6. But before that I was with Violent Crimes. I'm still the agent of record on a few of those cases, one of which I'm heavily involved in bringing to closure. I'm actually temporarily stationed in the Atlantic City area in order to make this case top priority. Sloane happens to be consulting on that case. I'm sure you're familiar with it; it's been in all the newspapers."

"The Truman case." Sergeant Erwin nodded. "I remember when Penelope Truman first disappeared. It was a high-profile kidnapping. Bizarre that a year later, her body hasn't been found." A questioning look at Sloane. "Any reason the Trumans called you in?"

"Penny and I were friends since kindergarten. The Trumans are grasping at straws, and they saw me as their last hope," Sloane supplied simply. "So I started working that case a few days before Cynthia was kidnapped from John Jay. To further complicate things, I started getting harassing phone calls at the same time as I got involved with both cases. I had no idea which one was prompting the calls. We traced the cell number of my caller. It was a disposable cell phone. No way to know who or where he was, until he used the phone again. The next call that was made from that number came from the campus police at TCNJ."

"The cell phone that was found at the crime scene where Tina Carroll was attacked." Bob steepled his fingers, resting his chin on top of them. "This is a strange can of worms. The connection between that attack and the physical evidence and circumstances surrounding Cynthia Alexander's disappearance are too close to be circumstantial."

"Yet there are still so many outstanding questions." Sloane leaned forward. "Were Cynthia and Tina this guy's only victims? How did he choose them? If there were others, how many? Over what period of time? And what has he done with his victims, given that no bodies have turned up?"

"You forgot one question. Was Penelope Truman also one of his victims?"

Sloane went very still. "What are you basing that supposition on? I know Penny disappeared from a college campus, but we're talking about a crime that happened a full year ago. In addition, she wasn't a college student anywhere, much less at Richard Stockton, she disappeared in broad daylight when the campus was in full swing, and there was no physical evidence left behind. Plus, there's no way her assailant could have planned that kidnapping, since Penny was a onetime visitor on the Stockton campus."

"I realize there are inconsistencies between the Truman case and the other two we're discussing. But that's just it; we're limiting our analysis to just a few cases. We might have to expand our thinking. You yourself just said that we have no idea how long these kidnappings have been going on, or if any or all his other victims are college age. This guy might just have a thing for college campuses. He also must have a thing for water, because he grabbed one girl right after she finished swim practice and the other girl at a lake on campus."

"And Penny disappeared from a campus lake as well," Sloane murmured. "Lake Fred. Which fits your water theory." She spread her hands, palms up, in a baffled gesture. "But I still can't get past the recklessness factor. This guy is clever. He's also a planner. He knows when to make his move and get away with it. Penny wasn't kidnapped during predawn hours, or spring break, or any other time when the Stockton campus would be deserted. Even if the kidnapper happened to be at Stockton, scoping out women when Penny was there; even if he spotted her, and liked what he saw, why would he grab her at midday in front of a potential sea of witnesses? Why take such a stupid, impulsive risk?"

"I don't know," Bob answered candidly. "I'm not an expert on the mind of a serial killer. But we can't ignore the aspects that do fit the profile—an attractive young woman, a college campus, and a proximity to water."

"Motive," Derek supplied.

"Huh?" Sloane inclined her head quizzically in his direction.

"He'd take the risk if it suited his motive. Maybe he wasn't scoping out just any woman. Maybe he was targeting Penelope."

"Why?"

"Because of her relationship to you."

"Derek . . ."

"Start with the basics Bob just laid out," Derek instructed, cutting off Sloane's protest. "Add to them the personal connections that link one case to another. Your longtime friendship with Penelope. Your casual friendship with Tina. The fact that the cell phone used to harass you belonged to the guy who attacked Tina. Everything ties back to you. And, on a separate note, if Bob's supposition is right and Penelope's disappearance is linked to the others, then our theory that the Truman case is the one our Unsub is worried about your stepping into is back on the table."

"What theory?" Bob asked.

"That Sloane's inside knowledge of Penelope Truman could result in a lead that the police and FBI missed, and that the Unsub is freaked out about that. Let's say he kid-napped Penelope a year ago. He feels safe at this point, like he's gotten away with it. Then suddenly, out of nowhere, the victim's family retains Sloane—an ex–FBI agent, and a close childhood friend of the victim's—to investigate their daughter's disappearance. That would explain his harass-ing Sloane and sticking to her like glue. And that's just part of the motive—the impersonal part. There's more. There's a pattern here, with Sloane at the center."

"Before we go there, tell me one thing," Sloane inter-ceded. "Where does Cynthia Alexander fit into this idea you have that all these kidnappings tie back to me? I never even met the girl."

"True." Sergeant Erwin slid the file toward her. "But if Derek's right, you wouldn't have to. There's more than one way for a perp to see a link between his victim and the person he's linking her to. In the case of Cynthia Alexan-der, I'd say it's a likeness to you rather than a relationship. You yourself noticed it. Cynthia sounds a lot like you must have been as a college kid. Same interests, same varsity athlete, same captain of the swim team, same wholesome, hardworking student. Plus, she's from Cleveland, where you just left, and she's enrolled at John Jay, where you just lectured."

"That's quite a reach."

"Not if this wacko is fixated on you, it's not," Derek stated flatly. He turned to Bob. "I think Sloane represents more than a threat to this guy. I think he's obsessed with her. I'm just not sure if it's an idealization obsession or a homicidal obsession. That's why we need to establish a profile on him. The BAU will help. But the more informa-tion we can give them, the better. We have to delve into every disappearance in the tristate area over the past few years that shares a common pattern, however vague, with these three cases. And we have to get as many details as possible from the one person we know has had contact with the Unsub." He met Bob's gaze head-on. "Which brings me to my other request."

"You want to be present when I interview Tina Carroll."

"Yes."

"I anticipated that one." Bob pushed back his chair. "I had a police escort drive her into the city. She should be in the waiting room by now. I'll show her in."

CHAPTER NINETEEN

I thought I had Gaia under control. I don't.

It's snowballing way too fast.

I can't call on Hera. I can't call on any of my goddesses. And I can't turn to my mother as I did when I was a child. God, I miss those days. She made everything right. When I was frightened or confused, she read me stories of the great Greek gods and their heroic feats. Apollo the sun god. Artemis the moon goddess. Their world was my escape.

I miss my youth. It was just the two of us back then. Life had yet to intrude. She taught me so wisely and so well.

She no longer can. I'm being squeezed into a corner from which there's no escape.

Worse, the demons won't relent. Each day their shouting grows louder, stronger.

I feel the walls closing in. Sweat is pouring down my face, my body. The morphine can dull the pain, but not the panic.

I'm being crushed on all sides.

Midtown North
New York City
11:05 A.M.

Tina looked like a bewildered kid when Sergeant Erwin showed her in. Her eyes were wide, her stance was rigid, and her gaze was darting everywhere. It reminded Sloane, once again, how young twenty-one really was, and how much Tina had been through.

"Come in and take a seat, Tina." Bob spoke very gently and kindly to her. "I can offer you water, soda, or coffee. Which would you like?"

"A Coke would be great. Thank you," she said in a small voice.

Bob nodded, and headed off to get the soda. At that moment, Tina spied Sloane and the relief that swept over her was palpable. "Sloane," she acknowledged, leaning over the table to greet her. "I'm so glad you're here."

Sloane rose, reached over, and squeezed Tina's arm. "That's why I waited. I want to be here for you. But I want you to understand that, technically, you can ask me to leave. This is a law enforcement investigation, and I no longer officially fall into that category. It's up to you. Just tell me if you'd prefer I go."

"No. Please stay." A shaky swallow. "I thought I was pretty strong, but I'm on the verge of losing it."

"I will stay, and you won't lose it. You're strong. Just sit down and take a few deep breaths. I promise, Sergeant Erwin is a great guy. He just wants to catch the scum who attacked you and potentially others—women who weren't as well trained as you are, and couldn't escape." Sloane gestured toward Derek, who'd risen to his feet and was waiting quietly. "This is Special Agent Derek Parker of the FBI. He's a major part of this investigation, too. I can personally guarantee he won't bite. He and I worked in the same field office when I was with the Bureau."

Tina managed a small smile. "Hello, Agent Parker."

"Nice to meet you, Tina." Derek shook her hand. "I'm sorry for what you went through. But from what Sloane tells me, your attacker is sorrier. You did some serious damage to his body."

"Not serious enough." Tina grimaced. "The cops have checked all the local hospitals. No one with the kinds of injuries I inflicted on him admitted himself."

"That doesn't mean he didn't need medical attention. It just means he didn't get it anywhere that would have kept a record of his visit."

"I didn't think of that."

Bob returned with the soda, and they all sat down.

"I know you've been through this a dozen times with the local police, but just once more, tell us what happened early Saturday morning," Bob began.

Tina recounted the entire incident, from when she stopped at the oak tree for her water break, to when her assailant attacked her, to the steps she took to extinguish him as a threat.

"I'm impressed," Bob said, smiling faintly. "I know some cops that couldn't retaliate that quickly, at least not without drawing their weapons." He jotted down a few notes, then continued. "Can you describe the knife he held to your throat? Clearly, it was large enough to injure your shoulder."

"It was big and intimidating. The blade was at least half a foot long, and broad, too, a couple of inches wide. It was made of thick steel, with a curved edge near the top. The handle was dark, with ridges for the grip. Oh, and it had a narrow vertical piece dividing the handle and the blade. Kind of like a guard to prevent the user from cutting himself when he held it."

"Sounds like a Bowie," Derek concluded. "It's powerful and versatile. The big ones can be as long as swords. And the ones with saw teeth machined into the back side of the blade have been used in the military for decades. A good choice for this Unsub, and an easy knife to come by."

Tina's head came up. "That reminds me. I think he was in the military at some time."

"What makes you say that?"

"When I grabbed his shoulder, I felt a chain around his neck. And when he jerked forward in response to my blows, dog tags fell out of his shirt, dangling from the chain."

Bob was scribbling notes again. "Could you make out anything on the dog tags?"

"No. It all happened too fast. The whole thing lasted about thirty seconds."

Derek's wheels were turning again. "You said he told you to come with him or he'd slit your throat. You also said he muttered some things you couldn't make out. Was it because he spoke too quietly or because his words were muffled by the mask?"

"Neither. The words he used didn't sound like English. I don't know what language they were. The first phrase was something like 'tai kee.' He used it when he first came at me. If he weren't holding me at knifepoint, I would have assumed he was calling me by someone else's name."

"'Tai kee.'" Bob glanced at Sloane. "You speak Mandarin. Does that mean anything to you?"

Sloane frowned. "*Tai ji* means 'birthmark,' but that makes no sense in this context. If it's a Chinese dialect, I wouldn't recognize it."

"What else did he say?" Bob asked Tina.

"When I attacked him, he shouted a couple of things. He was probably swearing at me." She squinched up her face, trying to remember. "*Bow za* was one. And *chao ji bei*. Oh, and at the end he yelled out, *ta ma de*."

"Oh, he was definitely cursing at you," Derek assured her. "Even I know *ta ma de*. It means 'fuck.' As for *bow za,* you're pronouncing it phonetically. It's *biao zhi*." He spelled the English transliteration. "That means 'bitch.' *Chao ji bei* must mean something equally flattering, but I don't know what. I'll check with my squad or one of our language analysts on both *chao ji bei* and *tai kee*."

"Since when do you speak Chinese?" Sloane asked in surprise.

"I don't. I just know how to curse in it." Derek gave Sloane a half smile, then turned back to Tina. "You said you caught a glimpse of your attacker's eyes through the holes in his mask. Would you say he looked Asian? And what about his voice—did he sound Asian?"

"No and no." She shook her head again. "His eyes were round, not almond-shaped. And they were light. So was his skin. I saw his wrist when I broke his knife hold. He was Caucasian. As for his English, it was unaccented. It was also the primary language he used, with the exception of those curses."

"He could be second- or third-generation American," Sloane pointed out. "His family could originally be from the Far East."

"Or he could have been stationed there." Derek took another belt of water. "The dog tags imply that he served. He'd certainly master curse words that way. What I don't understand is why was he resorting to using them when his victim—all his victims so far, for that matter—were clearly American."

"Something else to ask whoever develops a profile on this guy."

At that moment, Derek's cell phone rang. He glanced at the display, then rose. "Excuse me for a second," he said, heading into the far corner of the room.

He punched on the phone, turned his back to the table, and spoke as quietly as possible. "What have you got for me?" he demanded.

At the other end of the phone, Joe Barbados, one of the FBI's top forensic engineers down in Quantico, hunched forward in his chair. "I've been going through all the DVDs, one by one," he replied. "But I'm primarily concentrating on the footage we have of the exact date and approximate time that Penelope Truman vanished. I'm examining the footage from every angle captured by the four different cameras in that area of Lake Fred."

"And?"

"And in one of the segments that's focused on the woods behind the lake, I spotted some lens flare. It seemed out of place because it was coming from the lower half of the frame. So I isolated it and did some tweaking to see what it was or where it was coming from. I can't be a hundred percent sure, but to me, it looks like a knife. And a large one, at that."

"Yes," Derek hissed under his breath. Aloud, he said, "Nice work, Joe. Can you e-mail me a picture or two ASAP?"

"Sure. I'm not completely done with my analysis, but I'll send you a jpeg of what I have so far, and a final when I'm finished. You'll have the rough within the hour, and the final by tomorrow morning."

"Great. Oh, and include the time stamp on it."

"Done."

"Thanks." Derek punched off the phone and rejoined the group. "Sorry about that. What did I miss?"

Sloane edged him a sideways glance. He'd gotten a lead. She could feel it, even though his expression remained unchanged. His adrenaline was pumping. Whoever had called him had given him something solid. But whatever that lead was, she'd have to pry the details out of him later. Clearly, it wasn't for sharing with everyone in the room—at least not yet.

She turned her attention back to the interview.

Southern New Jersey Medical Center
Trenton, New Jersey
2:30 P.M.

The high school across the street is letting out, students trampling one another on their way to athletic practice or the nearest mall.

No one noticed as I walked in through the emergency room entrance of the hospital. Nurses from the morning shift are finishing up their paperwork and preparing to brief the afternoon shifts when they arrive in a half hour. Everyone is either busily working or champing at the bit to get out. The admitting desk is crowded and the staff looks frantic as they try to process the new patients and direct people to the right areas.

Blend. Be invisible. Act natural. Avoid the security cameras. Push beyond the physical agony and the deafening voices of the demons. Stay focused. Between the maintenance cart and uniform I "borrowed," I can easily get lost in the crowd.

I catch a glimpse of my reflection in the window. I look like hell. It's the pain. It's making me crazy. Sweat is matting my hair and beading up on my forehead. I look like a junkie or a lunatic. I'm anything but. I'm one of the few sane people left—sane and decent. A man who knows right from wrong.

That's why I've been chosen.

I need that morphine.

Deep breaths. Slow, deep breaths. I can do this.

I pluck out my sweatshirt and make sure nothing's fallen out of the pockets. Reassured, I abandon the cart at the base of the stairwell, and start climbing. I've done my homework. So I know where I'm going.

I have to pause at the landing of each floor to gather my strength. Plus, the noise of the demons is so loud, my skull is about to cave in.

Somehow I make it to the fourth floor. The nurses' station at this low-key wing would have only a few RNs at the desk. Less people, less chance of being discovered.

I had to pick a hospital near the TCNJ campus. I want them to think that what's about to happen was committed by the same person who attacked Tyche. That I'm nearby, crippled with pain and hiding out as I self-administer my morphine.

By the time the cops get the call, I'll be miles away, preparing to satisfy the demons, planning the capture of my alternate goddess.

I have enough ketamine. If necessary, I can always get more on the street. But the other drugs . . . I need more.

Seizing a new cleaning cart from the closet, I shuffle my way down the corridor until I have a view of the nurses' station. Good. Just as I thought. Two nurses. Both on their computers. Both on the far side of the desk. I can head in the opposite direction without being noticed.

Halfway down the corridor, I spot my victim. An elderly man, either heavily sedated or in a coma, with a respirator by the head of his bed, and no visitors in his room. I leave my cart, walk noiselessly into the room, and calmly disconnect the respirator tube. My action triggers the alarm, and I'm out of the room in a heartbeat.

By the time my cart and I are headed back in the direction from which I started, nurses are yelling "Code Blue" over the sound of the wailing alarm, and every available staff member is racing into the old man's room. All except one, who's hurrying toward the nurses' station.

A medication nurse. She's wearing an ID tag, and around her neck is the necessary key to the medical cabinet. From the bold-lettered words on the ID tag, I can read that she's a supervisory RN. I can't make out her name, nor do I care. She looks like a wrinkled old bulldog, from her stout build and crabby scowl to her arrogant, short-legged waddle. Her patients will be better off without her. So will the staff. Once she's gone, the chief of staff can promote a worthy, compassionate type to take her place. Someone maternal to protect and care for those in need. As it should be.

I pull on my latex gloves, and watch Nurse Bulldog disappear around back. There's no doubt where she's going, or what she's going for.

I have only one goal, and nothing is going to interfere with it. I feel no remorse for what I'm about to do. It's for survival, not for the gods, and not for the demons.

Five minutes, and I'll be finished and gone.

So will Nurse Bulldog.

I move quickly and silently. An instant later I'm standing a few feet away from the medicine cabinet. Nurse Bulldog is concentrating on unlocking and opening it. I let her. The handle turns, and she pulls open the door. She reaches inside. I glance around. No one's in sight.

I reach inside my multipocketed sweatshirt and retrieve my trusted knife. In one long stride I cross over to her.

She never hears me. I'm on her before she knows what's happening. I grab her from behind, slitting her throat and slashing through the carotid artery. She drops to the floor like a thick sack of grain, blood spurting from her neck and pouring around her. The thud of her body is barely audible over the din of the Code Blue alarm.

Upon fleeting inspection, I'm pleased to see that my sweatshirt and custodial uniform look to be spared. Only my gloves and knife are bloody. And no one will be finding those.

I put away my knife and step over her body. It's quite a challenge to avoid the growing pool of blood now spreading across the floor. But I'm careful to leave no footprints. I retrieve the black plastic bag from my pocket and load it with what I need. Morphine, Demerol, Nembutal, fentanyl, and OxyContin, plus a handful of syringes. Then I step over her body once again. I peel off my gloves as I peek around the corner.

I toss the bag onto my cart, and walk calmly toward the stairwell. The halls are now silent. Obviously, the staff did whatever they could without the medication Nurse Bulldog went to get. That disturbs me. Did the old man die? He didn't deserve to. As I pass by, I hear snatches of conversation from the staff members exiting his room. They're upset, but it's because the respirator was tampered with. The old man is alive. I'm greatly relieved.

Reaching the stairwell, I abandon the cart, grab my bag, and force myself to hustle down the steps, cursing Tyche for the agony in my groin. Finally, I reach the ground floor and reclaim my original cart. I push it to the back of the hospital and out the quieter rear entrance. I unbutton my uniform, stuff it in the cart, and take off with my black plastic bag.

As I drive away, I wonder what the reaction will be when Nurse Bulldog is discovered. If her personality matches her demeanor, the cheers will outnumber the sobs.

For some reason, that strikes me as amusing.

2:45 P.M.

Nurse Kate Reilly was more than ready to go off duty. That unexpected Code Blue had really thrown her. When she last checked, Mr. Remis had been doing just fine. He was recovering from a head injury sustained in a car accident. His vitals were stable. The respirator had been functioning perfectly—every connection checked and double-checked.

It hadn't been hard to restore the situation to normal. But the fact that someone had unplugged him from his respirator? That was beyond chilling. Who would do such a thing? Especially to Mr. Remis, who was a sweetheart, with a loving family, very little money, and a kind heart. The whole incident had been a nightmare.

To top that off, she was getting a little worried about her supervising nurse, Gertrude Flyer. Gertrude was a stickler for punctuality and responsibility. She never missed a day, never neglected a patient, and never gave less than her all. The instant the Code Blue had sounded, she'd rushed off to get potentially needed medication for Mr. Remis. But she'd never come back. That was unprecedented.

Bothered, Kate went looking for Gertrude. As she passed the front of the nurses' station, something on the floor toward the back of the station caught her eye.

Abruptly, she stopped, all the color draining from her face.

She never heard herself scream. She just stood there, her hands covering her mouth, staring at the gruesome sight before her.

A river of blood was flowing out from the back of the nurses' station. And crumpled in front of the open medication cabinet was Gertrude Flyer's butchered body.

FBI New York Field Office
26 Federal Plaza, New York City
3:45 P.M.

Sloane paced back and forth in Derek's cubicle.

"Okay, you ordered me to accompany you to your office straight from our interview with Tina. I've been here for hours while you tried to hunt down your language analyst and then your partner. Are you going to tell me what they said or what I'm doing here?"

"I bought you lunch," Derek reminded her, settling himself at his computer and calling up his e-mails. "That's two meals in one day. One for each hour you had to wait. To my way of thinking, that makes us even."

"Derek." Sloane marched up to his desk, folding her arms across her breasts and staring him down. "I'm not amused. I'm pissed. And not only about this afternoon's runaround. About this morning's, too. What was that phone call you took during the interview about? I know it had something to do with this case. I could feel it when you came back. You were practically vibrating."

"Such an astute woman," Derek taunted under his breath. "Can't pull the wool over your eyes." He concentrated on his computer screen as he ran through the new e-mails in his in-box. "No, no, no . . . yes. There we go." Double-clicking, he opened the e-mail from Joe.

Here's the rough photo, it read. *Let me know what you think. Final version in the* A.M.

Derek glanced around impatiently, then spotted a chair. He dragged it over and set it behind his desk, then gestured for Sloane to walk around and view the screen with him.

"First, I couldn't find either Jeff or my language analyst, Yan Dié," he replied. "I have calls in to both of them. We'll have our dialect answers soon. Second, that call I got during the meeting was from Quantico. It was the forensic engineer who's enhancing the video footage for me. He found something." Derek went on to detail what Joe had told him. "So let's take a look and see what we've got."

Sloane leaned forward, watching intently as Derek opened the jpeg. The image appeared slowly, and it was definitely rough and gravelly looking. But the glint of light was unmistakable, as was the shadow around it. And they each had a definite shape.

"That light is a knife," Sloane stated decisively. "A long, thick knife, just like the one Tina described. And the shadow around it could definitely be a man."

"I agree. So does Joe, at least about the knife. He's fine-tuning the image for us just to be sure. I'll have his final jpeg first thing tomorrow. If it turns out we're right about the knife *and* the man—which I think we are—I'm going to ask Joe to check out the corresponding footage from the path around the lake. Maybe we'll get lucky. Maybe we'll not only get a good fix on the Unsub, but we'll be able to spot Penelope from one of the camera angles."

"Look at the time stamp," Sloane said, pointing. "Eleven twenty-nine. It coincides perfectly with the time line Deanna Frost gave us for Penny's walk around Lake Fred."

"Yup. So if Joe's final product comes in as I suspect it will, we've got our Unsub placed at Penelope Truman's crime scene. We've also got more than enough connections between the three woman—and you—to establish a pattern. It's time to get the BAU involved."

"I agree." Sloane looked pensive as she raked a hand through her hair. "The only thing that's still bugging me is how the Unsub knew Penny would be at Stockton that day, taking a walk around Lake Fred at that specific hour. Tina and Cynthia had routines that he could easily have kept track of. But Penny's routine was to catch a subway to work. So how did he know—" Sloane broke off as a possibility occurred to her.

"What?" Derek asked, reading her expression.

"Give me a minute to follow up on a lead. It's a long shot, but it might give us our answer." She opened up her file folder and flipped through her notes. "Here we go," she murmured. She held the spot she'd found by placing her index finger on it, then flipped open her cell phone and punched in the relevant number.

"Doug Waters's office," a professional female voice announced.

"This is Sloane Burbank. I need to speak with Mr. Waters immediately."

"He's in a meeting, Ms. Burbank. If you'll leave me a phone number where you can be reached—"

"Is his meeting in the building?" Sloane interrupted.

"Well . . . yes, but—"

"Page him," Sloane instructed. "Tell him I only need three minutes of his time. He can excuse himself to go to the bathroom and be back before everyone's refilled their coffee cups. I apologize for the inconvenience. But this is an FBI matter. So there's really no choice."

"Of course." The poor girl sounded like she was going to faint. "Can you hold for just a minute? I'll track him down."

"Certainly. And thank you."

"Boy, you're an even bigger bulldozer than you used to be," Derek muttered. "That girl's probably popping a Xanax as we speak."

"Very funny." Sloane shot him a look. "We're talking about catching a serial killer. That trumps whatever's going on at Merrill Lynch."

"It's good you never had dreams of joining corporate America. You'd suck at the politics."

"So would you." Sloane's mouth snapped back down to the receiver as she heard the click that indicated someone had picked up.

"This is Doug Waters."

"Doug, hi, it's Sloane Burbank."

"So my secretary said when she dragged me out of an important client meeting."

"I'm sorry for that. But the FBI and I have acquired new information on Penny's disappearance. I'm assuming that finding out what happened to her is more important to you than three minutes of a meeting, no matter how high-powered the client and how many millions your firm will pocket in the process."

"You know it is." Doug's tone changed entirely, the edge gone from his voice. "Have you found her?"

"No. But we believe we're getting closer. I have one or two questions for you, and then I'll let you get back to making your next million."

"Shoot."

"When you and I last talked, we discussed the Classical Humanities lecture-series seminars given at Richard Stockton College. I know they were held one Saturday afternoon a month. You mentioned that Penny really got into the academic scene and attended the seminars with some regularity. You also mentioned that she'd written the date of that last seminar—April fourteenth—on the calendar months beforehand. Did she normally do that? And last, since she went to a bunch of these lectures, can you elaborate, give me an idea of her routine—from registration to attendance? Any procedure she usually followed, predominantly on the days of the seminars themselves?"

"Sure. First of all, yes to your first question. Penny was organized. And since she registered in advance, the dates went on our calendar in advance. As for the rest . . ." Doug was quiet for a moment, obviously gathering his thoughts to give Sloane the most comprehensive answer possible. "I told you when we first talked about this that humanities seminars aren't my thing. But they definitely were Penny's. She kept the seminar brochure in her purse so she could juggle other commitments around those dates, if possible. She missed a few of them because of work or other plans, but on the whole, she went to the majority of them." He paused, blew out a breath. "On those days, she had a distinct routine. She took the same early bus out of the Port Authority. She knew she'd get to Stockton early, but that was her plan. She was a city girl through-and-through. You know that; you grew up with her."

"You're right. She was."

"But every once in a while she liked the fresh air and open spaces of a rural town."

"Yes. She did," Sloane replied quietly, memories rushing through her. She and Penny had spent many happy weekends at the cottage in Hunterdon that Sloane now called home. Penny loved apple picking, nature hikes, and marveling at the wildlife that didn't exist in the city.

"I get bored in the country," Doug was saying. "So that became part of Penny's alone time. She used the extra time before the seminar started to take a long walk on campus. She enjoyed the birds, the scenery—that sort of thing. She especially liked that big lake. I don't recall its name."

"Fred," Sloane supplied. "Lake Fred."

"Right, that was it. She'd either walk around it, or hang out and feed the ducks."

Sloane squeezed her eyes shut for a second to shake off the nostalgia. Besides, she had her answer. Keeping track of Penny's routine at Richard Stockton was as easy as keeping track of Cynthia's or Tina's. So it was no accident that the Unsub had been lurking in the woods at the same time that Penny was walking around Lake Fred. He knew she'd be there. And he was lying in wait.

"Thank you, Doug," Sloane said. "You've been a big help."

"I'm glad." He cleared his throat. "I might not have any right to ask, but would you let me know when the case is solved? Relationships are complicated. Even though Penny's and mine ended, I still care about her. I want to know what happened—and by whose hand."

"I understand. I'll call you personally as soon as I have answers I can share.

"I appreciate that."

Sloane punched off her phone and glanced over at Derek. "Penny had a routine every time she went to Stockton, which was nearly every time there was a Classical Humanities seminar. The lecture schedule was published well in advance, and each lecture was on a specific Saturday a month. Her ritual was to show up early and take a walk around Lake Fred. So even though it was broad daylight, even though the area was crowded with students, the Unsub knew it was his best chance to grab Penny. It wasn't spontaneous. It was planned. And he pulled it off."

"I'm not an expert on the minds of serial killers," Derek replied. "But I do know they're usually smart, methodical, and single-minded. Penelope was clearly the Unsub's target. He wasn't going to stop until he had her."

"To do what with? Kill her? Rape and torture her beforehand? And where's her body? We've got to find her. And we've got to find *him*—the vile animal who did this." Sloane lowered her head, fighting the quaver in her voice. "If I'm the common link here, then it's my fault that Penny was taken."

"You know that's irrational." Derek's response was quiet but definitive. "We're dealing with an unbalanced offender. You represent something pivotal in his abnormal mind. That makes you a victim, not a catalyst. None of this is your fault."

A long silent moment passed.

Then Sloane inhaled sharply and raised her head, her composure restored. "You're right. I apologize for losing it. As we both know, I'm neither immune nor objective when it comes to Penny's case."

"Don't apologize. You're human. You and Penelope grew up together. For you, this is personal as well as professional." Derek hesitated, then reached out, taking Sloane's uninjured hand in his. "We'll get him. I promise."

Sloane's gaze shifted to their joined hands, but instead of pulling away as Derek had expected, she gave him a grateful smile. "I know we will. But thanks for the promise. Thanks also for . . ."—she paused, searching for the right words—". . . for your commitment and support."

That clearly was not the entirety of what she wanted to say. Derek knew it, and so did Sloane. But before Derek could explore the issue, his cell phone rang, interrupting the moment.

Visibly irked, he snapped open the phone. "Parker." His tone was curt, his jaw tight.

A minute later, his entire demeanor transformed from annoyance to frustration and anger. "Goddammit," he ground out. After that, he fell silent again, listening intently. His expression grew grimmer by the minute. "Yeah, I heard you. Southern Jersey Medical Center on Hamilton Road. I'm on my way." He punched off the phone, shoved it in his pocket, and rose.

"What happened?" Sloane asked.

He angled his head toward her. "It seems that Tina did more physical damage to her attacker than she realized. A shitload of narcotics were just stolen from a pharmaceutical closet in a Trenton hospital not ten miles away from TCNJ. Whoever stole them created a Code Blue by disconnecting a patient's respirator tube and diverting the entire staff to his room. The supervising nurse went to get the necessary meds. She unlocked the narcotics cabinet, and was promptly killed for her efforts."

"How?"

"Her throat was slashed. The bastard severed her carotid artery. It looks like the weapon used was a small Bowie-type knife." Derek grabbed his jacket. "I'm heading down to Trenton now."

Sloane had already jumped to her feet and was gathering her things. "I'm going with you."

CHAPTER
TWENTY

DATE: 8 April
TIME: 0830 hours

Nightmares. Sweat. Flashes of Tyche, dying by my hand. Glimpses of hell. Hallucinations or realities. No longer sure. Can't resume my other life. All my strength must go to serving the demons, and finalizing my arrangements. Then the goddesses and I will all move on to Mount Olympus.

I used to want only the eternal beauty of the afterlife for her. Now I crave peace for me. And Artemis. I need Artemis. She'll heal my pain, join me in my splendor. I missed her yesterday. I drove by her house. Need to see her. Worth everything. But she's not home. *Where is she?*

What if something happened? She could be hurt . . . violated . . . No. She can defend herself against anything. FBI agent. Too much time with him. Can't let him try to corrupt her.

There's no place on earth worthy of a goddess like Artemis. Her strength, her beauty, and her purity are lost on this world.

They'll be embraced on Mount Olympus.

Must warn her.

Couldn't do it yesterday. Tried to wait, but the morphine

was making me sick. Gagging. Sweating. If I didn't get home soon, I'd black out.

Tyche. It's her fault. All of it. Filthy slut. Unworthy whore.

Men are pawns. Captives to the sluts who share their beds. Gone are decency, chivalry, protectiveness. Destroyed by society's immorality and degradation. Destroyed by the whores who rule it.

Biao zhi. Infected me with her black soul. Kept me from Artemis, from my mission. Rage and hatred eat at me. Need vengeance. But the howling of the demons cripples me. Need to appease their rage . . . silence them . . . only one way to do that.

I'll leave early . . . satisfy the demons. Then they'll release me long enough to destroy Tyche. I can purge, move on. All accounts must be settled. All goddesses must stand at the sacrificial altar. As must I.

It's *her* will. And the will of the gods.

Hunterdon County, New Jersey
9:15 A.M.

Yesterday's crime scene had left both Derek and Sloane quiet and grim. The murder of that poor head nurse had been horrifying. Even after the body was removed, the memory lingered—Gertrude Flyer, in pools of her own blood, her throat sliced open, not to mention the image of the weapon that must have done this to her—all that had thrown Sloane more than she'd expected.

It had taken a glass or two of Merlot and a long, hot shower—one she'd intended to take solo, but wound up otherwise—to start Sloane's unwinding process.

The process had been furthered by the massage Derek had given her afterward.

And brought to a successful conclusion by a long night of marathon lovemaking.

Now Derek's fingers were biting into Sloane's hips, his grip anchoring her as he drove them both toward orgasm.

Sloane sat astride him, her thighs clamped against his sides. She was trembling from exertion, her body rising and falling, moving faster and faster as the urgency to climax increased.

She was so close . . . so close.

"Now," she managed, her nails digging into Derek's shoulders as she reached the limit of what she could bear. *"Now!"*

His grasp tightened to just short of painful, and his lower body thrust upward so fiercely that he lifted Sloane off the bed. It was exactly what she needed, his penis lodged so deep inside her, stretching and filling her until it pushed her over the edge. She exploded into orgasm. It wasn't gentle, tender, or shivery. It was hot and wild and primitive, boiling up from the very core of her being, then erupting, storming through every pore of her body.

She cried out, but her cries were drowned out by Derek's shout as he came in a convulsive rush, his hips pistoning back and forth as he spurted into her.

For one brief instant during that maelstrom of sensation, their gazes met, each one seeing the intensity—and the raw vulnerability—in the other's eyes.

The instant passed.

Sloane collapsed on Derek's chest, shaking with the aftermath of her physical efforts, feeling like she'd run a marathon. Her muscles felt watery, and she let every part of her go limp. She could hear Derek's heart racing against her ear. His breath was coming in short, raspy pants. The two of them were both drenched in sweat and Sloane shut her eyes, wondering if she'd ever have the strength to move again.

"Did I succeed?" Derek's voice was hoarse, his fingers combing through her damp hair.

"That depends. What was your goal?"

"To take your mind off the phones that haven't rung yet, the DNA results that aren't in yet, and the jpeg that hasn't arrived yet."

"In that case, yes. You definitely succeeded." Sloane

propped her chin on his chest. "Then again, you've succeeded four times already since last night."

"Give me fifteen minutes and a protein bar. I'll make it
five."

Sloane laughed. "I'll give you a half hour. It'll take me
that long to get my muscles to work, and to eat my own
protein bar."

"We'll compromise. Twenty minutes, a protein bar each,
and this time I'll do most of the work. You just have to lie
back and enjoy."

"Now, *that* I can manage." Sloane blew out a contented
breath. "We are pretty amazing together . . . in bed," she
hastily qualified.

He got her implication, and ignored it. "Just *pretty* amazing? In that case, we definitely need round five. I'm going
for *very* amazing."

He drew her mouth down to his. Their lips brushed,
parted, then fused in a slow, heated kiss. Derek was just
about to deepen the kiss and say "screw it" to the twenty
minutes and protein bars, when the bed dipped in a rolling
wave motion. Sloane's mouth was nudged aside, replaced
by a cold, wet nose. Derek lurched back, startled, and found
himself staring into Moe's soulful brown eyes.

Seeing that she'd captured his attention, she nudged him
with her snout, and barked.

One bark. That was all the other two hounds needed.
Racing paws tore through the house, and an instant later,
all three dachshunds were on the bed, bounding from blanket to pillows, and barking to be heard over one another as
they squirmed their way in between Sloane and Derek.

Larry leaped off the bed first, rushing to the bedroom
door, then turning to glare pointedly at Sloane.

"They need to go out," Sloane said, biting back laughter
as she saw the douse-of-cold-water expression on Derek's
face. "I usually jog with them at dawn. It's way past that.
Larry's letting us know that they've been more than tolerant, but that they've reached their limit. FYI, they won't be

holding it in much longer. Soon they'll be donating puddles for me to clean up. Larry's the most direct. He's issuing an ultimatum. Curly's going for a more subtle approach. He's prancing on my back, pausing now and then to scratch me like a bone he's digging up. And Mona's feigning patience and holding it in so she can flirt with you."

"I see." Derek scratched Moe's ears and was rewarded with a two-minute cheek-licking session. "I'd almost forgotten what mornings are like with these three."

Sloane felt an unwelcome twinge as a memory popped into her head. The hounds were just puppies. It was a particularly cold, winter morning in Cleveland, and snow was falling in a blanket of thick flakes.

That was the day she and Derek had introduced the hounds to their first snow experience.

They'd taken them outside, enjoying their sheer delight as, one by one, the exuberant dachshunds discovered the miracle of snow. Sloane and Derek had romped around with them, laughing until their sides hurt as they watched Moe, Larry, and Curly shove their snouts into the accumulating inches, then come up with white noses. After that, they'd alternately tried catching snowflakes on their tongues and racing around. Their stubby little legs had sunk into the cold white powder, and it hadn't slowed them down a bit.

It seemed like a lifetime ago.

"A penny for your thoughts," Derek interrupted her reflections.

"Hmm?" Sloane's head snapped up. "Oh, I was just thinking that I'd better meet their demands ASAP. I don't want a major cleanup job on my hands." She knew Derek didn't believe her, but she didn't modify her statement. "Rain check on round five?"

"Definitely. With many more rounds to follow." Derek didn't press her. But he did stop her as she started to climb out of bed. "I'll take the hounds for their run. You put up a pot of coffee."

"Okay. I also picked up a few blueberry muffins the other

day. I'll put them out with the coffee." Sloane eyed Derek speculatively as he pulled on his clothes. "I know why you're doing this. You don't want me out in the woods alone."

"Right." He didn't deny it. "I promised you round-the-clock protection. Well, today I'm it."

"Ah. Well, you're doing a great job. Remind me to put in a good word with the Bureau."

Derek paused in the doorway, looking back over his shoulder at Sloane as the hounds rushed passed him, heading off to fetch their leashes. "I'll do that." A quick wink. "One suggestion. When you put in that good word, leave out the *really* steamy perks of my bodyguarding."

A half hour later, Sloane and Derek were sitting at the breakfast nook, sipping on coffee and munching on muffins. The hounds, having gobbled up their breakfast and lapped up their water, were sprawled on the kitchen floor, snoozing.

"It's after ten. Why haven't we heard from anyone?" Sloane asked impatiently.

Derek glanced at his watch. "I called Joe while I was jogging with the hounds. He's a perfectionist, so it's taking him a few extra minutes. But we'll have our final within the hour. As for the rest, Yan Dié, my language analyst, is coming in around noon. She'll decipher our curse words ASAP. Bill Mann, my colleague at the BAU, had meetings scheduled all morning, so we'll hear from him after lunch. And the DNA found at the crime scene is being analyzed as we speak."

"I know." Sloane grimaced. "I wish I'd at least get a return call from Larry Clark. Then I could run some of this by him. He's got years of experience with the BAU."

"He's also retired and living on a ranch in Virginia. He might be out riding. Or napping in a hammock."

"Fine, you made your point." Sloane went back to eating her muffin. "I'll try to take it down a notch."

"Good idea." Derek gazed pensively into his coffee mug, that familiar furrow between his brows

"Something else on your mind?" Sloane asked.

"Actually, yes." He raised his head, looked at her. "You asked me not to revisit the past, and I intend to respect your wishes—for the most part. But there are some things I do need to know, if for no other reason than because we're working together and I have to understand the full extent of your physical and psychological limitations."

"Such as?"

"Such as yesterday. You think I didn't notice your reaction to the crime scene at the hospital. You're wrong. I did. You're a strong, self-sufficient woman. You're also a pro at hiding your vulnerabilities. But I saw how white-faced you became when you looked at that bloody floor, listened to the police describe the details of the homicide. At one point, you actually flinched. Knives still freak you out. I'm not judging you," Derek quickly clarified. "But I need you to tell me exactly what happened the night you were injured, and whatever permanent damage it resulted in—not just to your hand, but to your psyche."

Sloane considered his request, saw its merit, and slowly nodded. "God knows, I've told this story often enough. Reliving it shouldn't upset me. But it does—on many levels. I also have to warn you, it's not exactly appetizing breakfast conversation."

"Not to worry. They have yet to invent the subject that kills my appetite."

"True." Sloane pushed away her food, and interlaced her fingers on the counter in front of her as she thought back to that life-altering day. "I don't know how much you're already familiar with. At the time, your squad was working with three other field offices trying to solve that string of family homicides."

"All I know is that there was a bank robbery gone bad in some small town in Ohio, that a bunch of innocent people were being held at gunpoint by the robbers, and that a crisis negotiation team was called in."

"Ten," Sloane qualified. "There were ten innocent people

being held hostage—the guard, the bank manager, two tellers, and six customers. Yes, the bank was in the sticks. But we were the closest field office with a CNT. So the team of us—Laurie, Jake, Andy, and I—went to the scene, along with SWAT, and the local sheriff and police. The gunmen were armed to the hilt, panicking, and headed up by a ringleader who was *not* the negotiating type. He and his two sidekicks had already successfully held up several banks in Ohio, Kentucky, and Tennessee—and he'd killed one guard in the process. I wasn't about to let that happen again, not on my watch."

Sloane paused, reaching past the coffee for a bottle of water and twisting off the cap. "I was the primary negotiator on the case," she continued after gulping down some water. "I was on the phone with that SOB ringleader for five and a half hours. My team was engaged every second of that time. They gathered intel, liaised with all the field offices that had dealt with these subjects, and worked with SWAT and the locals to get me what I needed. Because of their hard work, and mine, we defused the ticking bomb. The hostages were safely released, every agent and local went home alive, and all three subjects were taken into custody—eventually."

"I'm guessing that the 'eventually' you're referring to is what resulted in your getting your hand carved up."

"Yes." This was the tough part, because Sloane would forever blame herself for underestimating her attacker. "At the end of the standoff, SWAT went in. They handcuffed two of the subjects, including the obnoxious ringleader. The youngest subject, who was barely eighteen and built like a wiry monkey, tried to escape. He squirmed his way out the bathroom window and took off. Based on my position outside the bank, I was the first one to see him running. So I took off after him. I was way ahead of backup. I cornered him in an alley a few blocks from the bank. When I yelled for him to drop his weapon and get down on his knees, he did. I walked over to him. It wasn't until I was handcuffing him that I holstered my gun."

She didn't excuse herself or make light of her actions. "I should have waited for Jake, so he could cover me. But I didn't. I thought I had things under control. I was wrong. The wiry monkey was quick. He reached down and whipped out a switchblade from inside his boot. He pivoted around on his knees, and went at me. He sliced up my right hand until I dropped the handcuffs. And even then he didn't stop. He slashed my hand a few more times for good measure. I knew he'd severed some serious blood vessels. The pain was excruciating, my palm was gushing blood, and I was so weak I couldn't stand up. I saw him running past me, heading back up the alley to escape."

Pausing, Sloane took another swallow of water, then studied her scarred palm as she finished up the story. "I acted on instinct. I grabbed my weapon with my left hand. I fired three shots. The last one hit that little SOB in the back. I saw him jerk from the impact and collapse to the ground. An instant later, Jake came tearing around the corner of the alley. That's when I passed out."

"And?"

"And the wiry monkey came through surgery just fine. Better than I did." Sloane's jaw tightened. "They removed the bullet from his lung. He's healed—and behind bars. I testified at his trial. But Jake—if he'd gotten there one second sooner, he might have caught one of my stray bullets. If anything had happened to him, I'd never have forgiven myself. I can't believe how stupid and reckless I was. That will *never* happen again."

Derek frowned. "You're being way too hard on yourself. The kid still had a knife in his hands. He could have stabbed Jake as he rounded the corner. As for the little shit himself, if I'd been in your shoes, he'd be dead."

"No, he wouldn't be." Sloane managed a small smile. "I'm better with my weak hand than you are. You'd have missed him altogether."

"You're probably right." Derek was watching her expression. "So after you passed out, that's when they rushed you to the closest hospital, where you had the emergency surgery."

"Mm-hmm. And you know the rest of the story."

"Not really. I know where the hospital was, since I tried to visit you there. And I know the snatches of information you blurted out to me in the Stockton parking lot the other day."

"That's enough. There's no point in going over an entire year of surgeries and physical therapy. I think I answered your question about why knives freak me out. Whether you choose to understand it or dismiss it is up to you."

"And whether you choose to stop blaming yourself for what happened is up to you."

Sloane gave him a hard stare. "I was a good agent, *and* a good hostage negotiator. I've got great instincts. And I'm smart. But not that time. That time I royally fucked up. I should have waited for backup. Because I didn't, my whole life changed. An agent's life was put at risk. And me . . . let's leave it at that."

Before Derek could answer, a resonating *bing* sounded from his laptop.

"E-mail." Derek was already on his feet, heading to the coffee table, where he'd set up his computer.

"Is it from your forensic engineer?" Sloane asked, following close behind.

"Yup. And there's an attachment. That'll be the finalized jpeg." Derek waited until Sloane was perched on the arm of his chair before opening Joe's e-mail.

It read:

Derek — This is the best I could come up with. The lens flare is definitely a knife. From the size and shape of it, I'd guess it to be a Bowie type. And, based on body mass and physique, the shadow is a man. You can't tell from the still, but when I watch it in motion, it looks like he's drawing the knife out of its sheath. So you've got a subject and a weapon.

Hope that helps. Let me know if you need anything else. — Joe

"Open the jpeg," Sloane urged.

Derek clicked on the attachment, and he and Sloane watched the jpeg appear on the screen.

"He's right," Derek stated. "There's no doubt about it. That's the kidnapper and the weapon."

"Absolutely." Sloane squinted, peering at the details of the photo.

"Let's go for broke." Derek leaned forward, and punched the reply button.

Quickly, he typed:

Great work, Joe. This is spot-on. One more favor. Can you switch your analysis to the cameras that face the lake, and do an in-depth search from ten minutes before through ten minutes after the time stamp on this jpeg? With our Unsub taking out his knife, there's a pretty good chance he'd spotted his prey. I'm hoping you can do the same.

FYI, Penelope Truman is medium height, with black shoulder-length hair. She'll look more styled and sophisticated than the college girls. And she was wearing a red pant suit, which should make it easier to pick her out of the crowd. If you find her, follow the footage. Maybe we can pinpoint the location where the Unsub grabbed her. It's a wooded area. Check clusters of trees and less populated sections of the lake path. Let me know if you find anything. Thanks — Derek.

"Good thinking." Sloane rose from the arm chair. "But even without that added bonus, we have three definable victims. Which means the BAU can classify two of the victims as no-body homicides, and our Unsub as a serial killer."

Sloane's phone rang. She picked it up, hoping it was Larry. "Hello?"

"Sloane? This is Burt. Is it a bad time?"

"Burt." He was the last person she'd been expecting. "No, of course not. I'm just buried in work. Is there a problem with your mother?"

A brief hesitation. "Sort of. Her vitals aren't great, and the doctor's not happy with her deterioration. I took her to see him today, and he ran some tests. Hopefully, the results will tell us what's going on. In the meantime, she's on strict bedrest. I'm stuck at the bookstore tonight doing inventory. I won't be back until around ten-thirty. The visiting nurse will only be at my mother's place until seven. She's leaving a casserole in the refrigerator, but my mother's not up to warming it up, much less sitting down at the kitchen table and eating it. And then there's Princess Di, who needs to be walked and fed. I was wondering if I could impose—"

"Say no more," Sloane interrupted. "I'll go over to Elsa's a little before seven while the nurse is still there. I'll pretend I'm just dropping by to say hi so she won't feel like a burden. I'll feed and walk Princess Di while the nurse is still with your mother. After she leaves, I'll heat up the casserole and we'll have a lovely dinner in the upstairs sitting room. Stay at the bookstore as late as you need to. I'll be with Elsa until you get here."

Burt's sigh of relief was audible. "Thanks, Sloane. I can't tell you how much I appreciate it."

"There's nothing to appreciate. You've come to my rescue on more occasions than I can count. I'm delighted to help. So, do your inventory. I'll see you when I see you."

She hung up the phone.

"What was that all about?" Derek asked.

Sloane explained the situation to him.

"I'm sorry about Elsa. I know how fond of her you are. As for Burt . . ." Derek frowned. "That guy's a little out there. I'm not thrilled about your being alone with him, even with his sick mother upstairs, and the security assigned to you parked right outside."

Sloane waved off Derek's concerns. "You're right, he is odd. But he just went through a messy divorce, his mother's all he's got, and she's slipping away. I think he's scared."

"He's got the hots for you, you know."

"I noticed."

"To my way of thinking, a recently divorced, vulnerable guy who's odd and wants to hook up with you doesn't sound like the ideal companion."

"I'll keep that in mind." Sloane smiled. "But I wouldn't worry. Burt's seen my Krav Maga skills firsthand. I gave him and Elsa a demonstration once when I picked up the hounds. He's also seen me shoot. I'm pretty intimidating with my bow and arrow. I'm also getting more accurate every day. At this point, my arrows consistently strike the red, in a tight cluster around the bull's-eye. Truthfully, I think Burt's fascinated by me, and at the same time, half afraid. He's not exactly the macho type. He wouldn't try anything for fear of his well-being."

Derek looked amused. "When you put it that way, maybe I should be scared, too."

"Maybe you should."

The phone rang again. This time it was Derek's cell. He punched it on.

"Parker," he answered. "Mrs. Truman." He shot Sloane a how-do-you-want-to-handle-this look. "Actually, I was going to get in touch with you either later today or tomorrow. Yes, we have some new information. But it's only part of the whole picture. I was waiting until I had all the facts before I called you."

Tell her we'll call her together on speakerphone. Sloane mouthed the words.

Derek nodded. "I understand. You're both anxious. Well, I'm reviewing the update with Sloane Burbank as we speak. Why don't the two of us call you back on a landline using a speakerphone. That way, we can all take part in the discussion. Fine. Give us five minutes." He punched off the phone. "Dr. Truman is with her," he informed Sloane. "So this will be a four-way talk, complete with a castigation and interrogation session. Do you still want to take the lead? Because I assume that's why you were signaling me."

"Yes, but only because I know them. It might take the tension down a notch or two." Sloane's pause was grim. "Not that my news is comforting. It implies the very worst of outcomes. This whole thing sucks." She made a deferential gesture. "But this is your case. I told you I wouldn't step on your toes, and I won't. If you'd prefer to tell them what we found—"

"No, I think it should come from you," Derek replied emphatically. "I'll fill in the official details, emphasizing the role the FBI lab at Quantico is playing, and the fact that our forensic engineer's analysis is still in the works. I want the Trumans to feel reassured that all the FBI's resources are being utilized for the purpose of solving Penelope's disappearance."

"And I get to confirm their greatest fear. Because no matter how I spin it or cushion it, they're going to draw the same conclusion we have—that Penny is dead."

TWENTY-ONE

DATE: 8 April
TIME: 1530 hours

She walked right by me, eyes glazed, pupils as wide as saucers, oblivious to everything except the plastic bag stuffed in her pocket. *That* she fingered nervously, anxious to shoot up what she'd just scored.

She weaved her way into the four-story tenement, so unsteady on her feet that she could barely make it. No surprise given the number of needles she'd probably stuck in her arm this past week.

She looked strung out. Which meant she wasn't as high as she needed to be. That was good news. She'd be more susceptible to pain.

That was mandatory. She *had* to feel every life-draining slice of my knife.

For the third time, I vomited in the street. I'd overdone it on the morphine. I knew it would make me sick, but I had no choice. How else could I dull the pain enough so I could drive down here and satisfy the demons?

I never do this during the day. And never right out in the open. But I'm desperate. The demons won't let me sleep until I give them what they want. *Now.*

I know she's alone. Her two "roommates" left to go

shopping. They'll be gone for a while. Not that anyone will notice. No one gives a damn who walks in or out of this dump they call a "resting house." A lovely euphemism for the basement where whores live when they're not at work. Late night is when their "careers" soar, when they go to that garish brothel on East Broadway and service the men.

Not this *ji nv.* Not tonight. She won't be alive to service anyone.

I don't know why the demons chose her, nor do I care. I've seen her come and go from the brothel a dozen times, even followed her here on two separate occasions. She's been doing her job the longest. The demons must know that and have deemed her the one to punish. And made me their messenger.

Even so, I'm furious that she's forced me into this vulnerable position. My hands are starting to shake. The rage is beginning to pound through my body. Damn, I hate her, more every second. I can't wait to carve her away, bit by bit.

One more minute—enough time to sit down, get her fix ready, maybe even tie the tourniquet around her arm. But not enough time to inject the heroin. I want her alive, awake, aware, and terrified.

And then I'll send her to hell.

It's time.

I walk down Eldridge Street, past a bunch of punks who look as seedy as the block we're walking on. There's garbage strewn everywhere. The sleazy teenagers are darting into doorways, probably picking up their Xstasy to sell tonight. They're high as kites themselves, and wouldn't remember my hooded sweatshirt or black gym bag if they fell over me.

The stench of the tenement is vile—a combination of sex, filth, and drugs. I retch, but there's nothing left to vomit up except bile. The staircase to the basement is cluttered with needles. I expected that, having followed her here before. The demons must have been preparing me.

As assumed, I find her in the basement, crouched down

on the concrete floor. Her back is propped against the wall as she concentrates on arranging what she needs for her next fix. The rest of the place is as still as death.

I pull on my latex gloves. Then I shut the front door behind me and turn the lock.

She looks up. Not surprised. Not anything. No emotion at all in those dark, almond-shaped eyes.

"No," she informs me. Her words are slurred, and the rest she mutters in Fukienese. But I understand enough. She's instructing me to come to the brothel and make an appointment with "Susie." She has the additional audacity to tell me she's very busy and that she takes cash only.

My hatred and revulsion escalate.

"I'm not a client," I respond in her dialect. Calmly, I unzip my bag and take out the photo equipment. I extend the tripod legs, set it in place, and anchor the video camera. I arrange it at the perfect angle so I can capture everything on tape.

She looks vaguely puzzled, and asks who wants a picture of her.

"I do." I press record, finishing up that part of the ritual. Then I cross over to her, whisk out my prefilled hypodermic, and inject the ketamine in one quick stab to her thigh.

She opens her mouth to yell in pain. I stuff a rag in it. Then I press her against the wall and hold her there, waiting for the ketamine to do its job.

She fights like a wild animal. I restrain myself, knowing I'll have all the time in the world to vent my fury—until she reaches up and slashes her nails across my neck. *My* neck. None of them has ever touched me before. I've been too strong, too focused. It's the morphine doing this—and the slut.

She does it again. That pushes me over the edge. Rage courses through me, stronger than my will. I don't care that the ketamine hasn't taken full effect. She touched me. She dared to lay one of her filthy hands on my body. I'm sickened.

I backhand her across the face, calling her what she is. *"Chao ji bei,"* I snarl, backhanding her again. She lunges like a tigress, clawing at me and trying to lurch up and escape.

I take out my combat knife, slash across her chest, up her neck, and down her arms.

She screams silently, the rag absorbing the sound. She stares at the blood oozing down her body, and then stares at my knife.

This time I see fear. Fear and pain.

Her muscles begin to tense up as the ketamine does its job. She's stiff. And she's scared. Even though her eyes are glazed, she knows. She feels.

That's what I want. It's what I need.

I grab her legs and drag her onto the filthy floor, where she belongs. Flat on her back, like a trapped cockroach about to be crushed. Then I begin the second part of the ritual. I cut off her clothes, piece by piece, throwing them aside. I'm determined not to allow myself to experience that profane surge of pleasure. I spread her legs wide, tying one ankle to a radiator, and the other to a water pipe. She's delicately formed, her body firm, her curves gently rounded.

Like Artemis.

The very thought sends me into a tirade. How dare I compare a whore like this to my pure and precious Artemis? It must be the morphine. Nothing else would do this to me.

I unzip my fly. I never take off my clothes, not with any of them. That would demean me. I flinch as I touch myself. The pain in my groin is still bad, even with the morphine. As always, I extract a condom from my pocket—another absolute necessity. She's a harborer of germs, of disease, of everything evil.

I can't get the image of Artemis out of my head. It's wrong, so wrong. I hate myself for it. But I can't make it go away. Not until I make this whore go away.

I rip open the condom wrapper. I can't harden my body enough to slide the damn thing on. It's the injury. No, it's the demons. They know I'm thinking impure thoughts about the purest of women. That terrifies and infuriates me. I rub myself fiercely. But to no avail. The pain in my testicles is too severe. And the demons are cursing me, threatening me, mocking me.

I go wild. I shove the condom over my flaccid penis. It's her fault. Hers and Tyche's. Two *biao zhis*.

I force my weight on top of hers, crushing her into the concrete floor with all my might. I lift up only to guide, shove, cram myself into her. It won't happen. I begin pounding myself against her, desperate to penetrate. I *can't*. I *can't*.

Sweat is pouring off of me. Pain lances through me with each unsuccessful thrust. Her blood is on my sweatshirt. I don't care. I'm gripping her hair, pulling at it to gain leverage. It won't work. Nothing will work.

I launch myself off of her, seize my combat knife.

I'll conquer her one way or another, give the demons what they demand.

The first slices are deep, cutting through muscle and tissue, severing blood vessels and puncturing organs. The feeling is euphoric, obliterating the rage, replacing it with a hunger for more.

Excitement and power surge through me—the kind I get when I violate them. I'm shaking as I respond. I cut her again, and again, and again—each cut deeper, more frenzied. Time and place cease to exist. I'm blind to everything except the escalating pleasure taking possession of my senses. Building. Building.

I stifle a shout as my body shudders, culmination shaking me to the core. I close my eyes, a prisoner to the feeling, my body lurching repeatedly as I fill the condom that hangs loosely from my aching member.

My muscles go slack, and I roll onto my back, letting my eyes close and my head relax, loll to one side. I suck air into my lungs.

I open my eyes and see her, or what's left of her. Bloody. Mutilated. Butchered into nonexistence.

I spit into her mangled face. Then I find the coin I brought, and place it beside her, in the stickiness of her spilled blood.

The pain in my wrist, my nose, my testicles—none of it matters.

The exhilaration is far greater. Because now I understand what the demons have been throbbing for.

It's the purest form of pleasure. Savoring evil, rather than festering over its temptation.

A true victory. One I must revel in. And learn from.

Hunterdon County, New Jersey
4:15 P.M.

As it turned out, Sloane and Derek had another four-way conference call, this time with FBI SSA William Mann and former SSA Lawrence Clark. The two men had worked closely together at the BAU for fifteen years before Larry's retirement, so they were pleased to be doing so again. They listened carefully to the details Sloane and Derek provided.

"How are we handling this?" Bill asked afterward in his customary blunt style. "If you want the BAU on board in an official capacity, then this phone call and request for our help has to technically be initiated either by Derek in his SA capacity, or by Sergeant Erwin at Midtown North. But if you want to skip the red tape and let Larry handle this alone, as an independent consultant, that's fine. You'll get the best there is and any of you can request his help."

"With one exception," Larry taunted good-naturedly. "Now that I'm a consultant, I actually get paid. You know, real money, not like the Bureau salaries."

At his end of the phone, Bill chuckled.

"We'd really like you both on board," Sloane answered. "That's why I reached out to you, and Derek reached out to Bill. This case is getting broader in scope. We could use both your expertise and the resources of the Bureau. Larry, the Trumans have offered to pay whatever fee you quote them, plus all your expenses. Their only stipulation is that you make this top priority."

"Meaning they want me up there yesterday."

"Exactly."

He drew a thoughtful breath. "I've got another urgent case to wrap up. That should happen tomorrow. I'll drive up there as soon as I'm done. In the meantime, I can get started down here. If you either e-mail or fax me any case-file data, I'll review it. Then we won't lose any time. I'd need a day to familiarize myself with every detail of the case anyway."

"Consider it done." Sloane was relieved and grateful. "I really appreciate it."

"It's faster than I could get started," Bill said truthfully. "We've got a couple of sensitive cases in the works right now, and I'm pretty much up against a wall. So Larry driving up there to do the investigative work would be ideal. He can check out the crime scenes, work up the victimology with you, and get the ball rolling. In the meantime, now that I have Derek's official request, you have the full cooperation of the BAU. If I'm tied up, you can speak to my partner, who's an excellent profiler. I'll e-mail you her contact information. Then I'll brief her, and our major-case specialists. You'll be in good hands. And I'll make myself available to you as often as possible. Let's schedule our first video conference for the seventeenth."

"Fine with me," Larry agreed. "Does ten o'clock work?"

"It works and it's now on my calendar."

"I'll reserve the video conference room in New York, and we'll make ourselves available," Derek said, after receiving Sloane's nod.

"Before we hang up," she jumped in quickly. "Is there anything you can suggest that would make us more productive at our end, at least until Larry gets here?"

"Send Larry everything you've got ASAP. Do preliminary searches in VICAP and CODIS based on what you know so far. Derek, ask one of the task-force detectives on

C-6 to get you access to the NYPD database, and do the same kind of preliminary search in RTCC. When Larry gets to New York, share all the results with him and let him do his investigative work. We'll review everything on the seventeenth and see if we can derive additional patterns in either the crimes or the offender, which will allow us to further detail the profile."

Sloane didn't look heartened, and Derek understood why. All the databases Bill had mentioned were only as useful as the data law enforcement officers provided. If pertinent violent crimes hadn't been entered, VICAP wouldn't have them. If their Unsub didn't have a police record, there'd likely be no record of his DNA in CODIS. As for RTCC—the NYPD's data warehouse to stop emerging crime by establishing patterns—it might shed a few insights. Could it benefit them? Maybe. But was it even close to a panacea? No way.

"Was there anything we gave you that would lead you to think in any one particular direction?" Sloane tried.

Bill blew out a breath. "I understand how frustrated you feel. Honestly, I'm not giving you the runaround. But that's a tough question to answer, since we have very little to go on and every case is different. Based upon the pattern and the targets—all attractive women on college campuses taken at knifepoint—plus the fact that none of them have resurfaced alive, I'd say we have two no-body homicides and an attempted third one, committed by a serial sexual killer."

"What about the fact that all the victims knew or were connected in some way to Sloane?" Derek asked. "Isn't that an anomaly in your basic profile?"

"It's specific to this case, yes," Larry explained. "But we can't give you a full analysis on its significance until I've done my investigative work. In general, serial killers who commit sexual homicide—including no-body homicides—have no direct connection to the victims. They choose them based upon availability, vulnerability, and/or desirability. If there's a variation to that profile—namely the victims' ties to Sloane—we'll probe it fully. What we do know about this offender is that he's organized. His attacks have been planned, and his victims were targeted. Thanks to his third victim's escape, we have a basic physical build and body type, a suspicion that he served in the military, a knowledge that he's Caucasian yet speaks some Chinese dialects—"

"Fukienese," Derek interrupted. "All the phrases our C-6 language analyst came back to us with were either Mandarin or Fukienese. They're still working on the first phrase. It's possible Tina misunderstood it."

"Good. We know Fukienese is a much rarer dialect than, say, Cantonese. All these things will factor into our analysis. Till then, all we can give you are the generalities you already know. Our Unsub is a white male, uses a combat knife as his weapon, probably has vivid sexual fantasies, some of them violent, and kills for sexual gratification. Offenders that fall into this category have a different assault site, murder site, and disposal site. We know that our Unsub's assault sites are college campuses, but we don't know his murder or disposal sites."

"We also don't know his motivation," Sloane murmured.

"Or his trigger," Bill added. "Something incited him to act at this particular time, something emotionally impacting. But until we know more about him, it's impossible to guess what that might be. Again, once Larry gets there, we'll start filling in the blanks."

"Well, here's another blank we can fill in," Derek announced, leaning over his laptop to read an e-mail that had just arrived in his in-box. "It's no great shocker, but it is an important piece of information. The DNA results from the sweat stains and strands of hair found on that custodial uniform at the hospital just came in. They match the unknown blood splatter found at Tina Carroll's crime scene. And the drops of blood found on the custodial uniform belong to the murdered nurse. So we can add a few more crimes to our Unsub's résumé—homicide and drug theft.

He ripped off morphine, Nembutal, fentanyl, and OxyContin plus a bunch of syringes."

"The morphine must be for his pain," Bill mused. "Nembutal is a pretty strong, fast-acting barbiturate, probably what he's injecting into the women he grabs to knock them out."

"Bill . . . five o'clock meeting." Somewhere in the background at the BAU, Bill was being summoned.

"Listen, we've got more than enough to get started with." Derek brought the conversation to a close. "We really appreciate both your time and what you're doing to help us. Larry, I'll get you everything we've got on the case. See you soon."

"I'll start reading as soon as I get your case file. I look forward to meeting you, Derek. And, as always, to seeing you, Sloane," Larry replied.

They hung up, and Sloane turned to Derek. "That went well. I wish we could do more now, but at least I feel as if we're *finally* making some headway."

"We are. And that e-mail I just got confirms it."

"I never got the chance to ask you—what translations did your language analyst come up with?"

Derek grimaced. "She verified the phrases we already knew. As for the other two, *chao ji bei* is, shall we say, a degrading Fukienese term used for certain types of women. It translates into 'stinky bitch.' But let's just say that *ji bei* is a crude reference to a female reproductive organ, and leave it at that."

"Lovely." Sloane's tone was dry. "And nothing on *tai kee*?"

"Just on close-sounding substitutes. She verified the phrase you came up with that means 'birthmark' in Mandarin. The only phrase that came closer was *tai chee*, which means 'too late' in Cantonese."

"I guess 'too late' can be ominous. Maybe he meant it was too late for Tina." Sloane frowned. "Although the context is off. Tina said he used it like a proper noun."

"There's no point in beating our heads against the wall," Derek concluded. "If there's something to find, Yan Dié will find it." He stood up and stretched. "It's almost five o'clock. I want to check in with Joe, see if he found anything on that video footage. After that, I'm going to head back to the city, get the case file to Larry, and see if I can start on those preliminary searches."

"Don't you have to be in Atlantic City?"

"Not if I'm running down a lead in the Truman case that requires my being in New York. I need to get one of my former NYPD detectives who's now part of the C-6 task force to get me into Puzzle Palace so I can access RTCC." He glanced at his watch. "Why don't you make photocopies of your notes on the case, so I can include them in the material I send Larry. Also write down any specifics you want included in my database searches. I'll combine your specs with mine, and compile a list of criteria to run against the databases. Right now I want to call Joe. I got the sense he has something for me. His last e-mail came in twenty minutes ago, and it sounded optimistic."

"Then call him," Sloane urged. "I'll photocopy my notes and make that list. You get Joe's update, and head back to the city to get started."

"You do know that a relief security detail is on its way to your house," Derek reminded her. "Manny Gomez. He's a great guy. Went from retired NYPD sergeant, to semi-retired and going crazy, to running a small security company. He's got a top-notch team working for him. You'll be in good hands. He's due here at six. I'll wait till he gets here, introduce you, and then hit the road. Manny will drive you over to Elsa's house when you're ready to go."

"Okay." Somehow, Sloane didn't feel like arguing. In fact, she welcomed the knowledge that a detective would be keeping an eye on her. Until her trigger finger was up to par, she wasn't in a position to shoot down an armed killer, no matter how good her reflexes were. She was fast, but a bullet was faster.

She went to get her file, and Derek went to the phone.

"Joe," she heard him say. "Did you isolate that red flash you spotted?" A pause. "Sure I'll wait a minute—if you send me something worthwhile." A long silence. "Yeah, I'm at my laptop. Fire away."

A minute later, the *bing* of the incoming e-mail sounded. The *click-click* Sloane heard was Derek, opening the jpeg attachment.

"Damn, you're good," were his next words. "Let me get Sloane in here to see if she can identify the woman."

"Here I am." Sloane dashed back into the room, leaning over to study the screen. It was a woman, dressed in red, standing behind a tree and sipping a bottle of water. The picture wasn't crisp or full face, but Sloane could clearly make out the profile.

The years melted away, and the knot in her stomach tightened. "That's Penny," she confirmed without hesitation.

"You're sure?"

"Positive."

"Okay, we have confirmation of the victim's identity. Now let's see what else we've got." Derek opened the next jpeg.

In this photo, Penny had put away her water and was about to take a step toward the path. At the same time, her head was angled slightly toward the camera, and she looked puzzled, as if someone in the woods had called her name.

Sloane must have made a pained sound, because Derek looked up at her. "You all right?"

"I'm fine."

"Ready for the last one?"

"No. But open it anyway." Sloane clenched her teeth as Derek complied.

The third photo appeared on his screen.

A dark, hooded figure had his right arm across Penny's throat, and his left hand over her mouth. Their faces were angled away from the camera, and the lighting in that area was poor—no surprise, given that he was restraining her in a thick cluster of trees—so it was hard to make out the details.

But from the seclusion of the spot he'd picked, it was no wonder none of the students strolling along the lake path had noticed anything or were even glancing their way. The two of them were practically invisible.

Sloane strained to make out what was happening. The man was behind Penny, but there was no missing the silver glint of the weapon protruding across the left side of Penny's throat.

It was a long, Bowie-type combat knife.

Bile rose in Sloane's throat. Suspecting what had happened to her childhood friend, and seeing it unfold before her very eyes, were two different things.

"You okay?" Derek asked quietly.

Sloane gave a tight nod. "We're going to get this son of a bitch," she said in a hard, no-bullshit tone. "And when we do, he's going to wish he was never born."

TWENTY-TWO

DATE: 10 April
TIME: 1600 hours

I wasn't going to make the same mistake as last time. This time I'd use my tranquilizer gun. No direct contact. No threats at knifepoint. I'd render her unconscious from a distance, firing one simple tranq dart. Then I'd drag her body into the woods, tie her up, and bind each leg to a tree. I'd wait until she came to, then make her feel the pain of her betrayal.

I raised my weapon—and stopped.

She was stretching before she got started on her usual jog around Lake Ceva. Two solidly built guys arrived simultaneously, one settling himself at the far end of the lake with a textbook, the other strolling the perimeter, drinking in the fresh air. Then a third guy showed up in shorts and a T-shirt. He joined Tyche in her run, keeping a comfortable pace beside her.

Their disguises were pathetic. Even a moron could tell they were cops.

So I went away, returning now, with my tranquilizer gun, when classes are over and she's back in her dorm.

Biao zhi.

Campus police pretending to be college students, sitting in the archway outside each building entrance.

I watch the *real* students exiting the building, complaining as they walk. Having campus security posted outside Tyche's door, 24/7, is screwing up their social lives. Their parties are all on hold. No one wants to risk sneaking alcohol past the cops. So they've been going to other dorms to party. And it's really starting to piss them off.

I almost laugh aloud at the absurdity of their concerns.

I'm surprised by my own reaction. I should be enraged over wasting my time, and furiously planning how to outwit the cops and get into her room.

But I'm not.

She's simply not worth it. My knowledge is greater now, my understanding deeper.

It isn't true evil that courses through Tyche's blood. It's ignorance and unworthiness. She isn't the same kind of filth as the *ji nv* I eliminated the other night. She's just a stupid *biao zhi*, who will never know what she just sacrificed.

The loss is hers. Let her remain in this ugly world, full of diseased and soulless people. While I and the true goddesses soar to Mount Olympus.

That's the greatest punishment I can impose upon her, after all.

FBI New York Field Office
26 Federal Plaza, New York City
5:15 P.M.

Jeff rounded the corner and strode into Derek's cubicle, ignoring the fact that his partner was hunched over the keyboard.

"I just got a call from the Fifth Precinct," he announced. "Another prostitute's been murdered. Butchered, from what they said. Details are sketchy right now. But it sounds like the same MO. Naked, tied up, throat slashed, coin placed right beside the body. The M.E. put the time of death on Tuesday, sometime between two and five in the afternoon. The body was in a tenement on Eldridge—not a warehouse this time, a resting house. The NYPD got an anonymous tip about the body. The caller was female and could barely speak English."

"One of the victim's friends, coworkers, or roommates," Derek said grimly. "And if the cops found her in a resting house on Eldridge, you know she's one of Xiao Long's girls." He threw down his pen in frustration. "Shit. This is the last thing we need. Xiao Long was on the verge of having his gang declare all-out warfare on the Black Tigers. Last time, we narrowly avoided a war. This time, we're going to have to do major damage control. And I mean *major.*"

"I know." Jeff gave a sober nod. "The M.E. said he'd move as quickly as possible on the autopsy. They're doing a drug screen to see if she's got ketamine in her system, like the others. And they'll check to see if the Unsub abused her sexually—and, if so, if it was as vicious as the slashing. Because, like I said, this one was really brutal."

"Our psycho's had too much time between prostitutes," Derek said in a dark, sardonic tone. "He stored up his hatred and his swimmers." A disgusted sound. "These days all I do is deal with psychos. And I'm not getting any closer to tracking them down." He glanced at the database he'd been accessing, then logged out, mentally putting the Truman case on hold. "This is going to be an all-weekend deal," he informed Jeff.

"I expected as much. When I spoke to the Fifth, I asked for their help. Until we can convince the Red Dragons and the Black Tigers that neither of their gangs is involved in these murders, we're going to have to turn Chinatown into a police state."

"And deal with the fallout from that, too." Derek reached for the phone. "I'd better call Sloane and tell her that I won't be seeing the light of day—or her—this weekend."

"Yeah. I'd better make a similar call." Jeff headed off. "I'll be back in ten."

"Mm-hmm." Derek was already punching in Sloane's speed-dial number.

He frowned when her phone went directly to voice mail. Then he remembered she had an appointment with Connie before meeting Larry at John Jay. "Hey, it's me," he said after the beep. "Listen, I'm going to have to cancel our weekend plans. A Bureau emergency just landed in my lap. I'll be stuck in the office all day tomorrow and the entire weekend as well taking care of it. I'll give you a call as soon as I can."

Hospital for Special Surgery
New York Weill Cornell Medical Center
East Seventieth Street, New York City
5:30 P.M.

"Thanks for taking me so late, Connie." Sloane slid into the padded chair across from Connie at her physical-therapy table. "I'm meeting a colleague at John Jay around eight o'clock. The hounds are troupers, but do have their limits, and my neighbor who usually watches them is ill. So I combined all my Manhattan appointments into the latter part of the business day."

"Actually, it worked out well for me, too." Connie sat down on her stool, moved the sensory reeducation tools off to the side, and checked Sloane's palm. Before they began any aggressive steps, she wanted to make sure it was healing on schedule, with no internal complications. "I'm meeting my date at a restaurant in midtown at seven-thirty. So the timing's ideal. You and I can have an hour together, and I'll still have an hour to make myself gorgeous and catch a cab to the restaurant."

"A hot date, huh? Ken the lawyer?" Sloane's eyes twinkled.

"Yes." Connie grinned. "He's turning out to be a keeper—at least for now. Let's see how he handles the probation period."

"You're tough."

"And you're sleeping with Derek again." Connie propped

her elbow on the table and studied Sloane intently. "It's
written all over your glowing face. Wow. That happened
even faster than I thought."

"You and me both." Sloane didn't even bother trying to
deny Connie's shrewd assessment. "Our chemistry—it's
like something you read in a novel and say, 'Yeah, right,
like that could ever happen in real life.' But there it is, and
neither one of us can fight it."

"Why would you?" Connie tucked a strand of blond hair
behind her ear. "It sounds like sexual heaven. Have you
talked?"

"Every day," Sloane replied, with a casual shrug. "We're
working on a case together."

"Who cares? Have you discussed the *breakup*? Who
said what, felt what, did what, and why? It's the only way
you're going to get past this."

"I told him the details of the knife attack. We exchanged
a few angry words about feelings we've been harboring. It
was more than enough. I don't want to delve too deeply into
this. Frankly, what we have now is wonderfully uncomplicated. If we start dredging up the past, it's going to get
messy, angry, and accusatory—all of which will destroy a
great thing."

"So your new relationship is just sex?"

"Not just sex," Sloane assured her. "Amazing, addictive
sex." A quizzical look. "Since when has that offended you?"

"It doesn't offend me. I'm all for amazing, addictive sex.
But in this case, it won't work."

"Why not?"

"Because you're in love with the guy." Connie flattened
her palms on the table, looked Sloane straight in the eye.
"You've been in love with him since Cleveland. And no
matter how pissed off you feel, no matter how much of a
grudge you hold, you're not going to be able to bury those
feelings or make them go away."

Sloane's jaw tightened. "Maybe not. But I can damn

well try. I never intend to be that vulnerable to another human being again. The fallout is too much for me to handle."

"What fallout?" Connie demanded. "This is the part I don't get. I know he disagreed with your decision to leave the Bureau. I know his reaction hurt you deeply. But he didn't break your trust. He didn't desert you when you were in the hospital practically bleeding to death from the wounds to your hand. He didn't ask you to ignore his phone calls. And he didn't ask you to pack and leave without saying good-bye. So where is this sea of resentment coming from?"

"My job at the Bureau meant the world to me," Sloane replied in curt, clipped tones. "I wanted to be a special agent for as long as I can remember. Derek knew that. He respected it—or at least I thought he did. The fact that he expected—and still does, for that matter—me to accept being placed on medical mandate, turn over my weapon, and become a Bureau pencil pusher—stunned me. And the more I explained, the less he understood. He effectively labeled me a coward and a quitter. My pain, my emotional meltdown, none of it got through that thick skull of his."

"Maybe he just needed time to—"

"Maybe nothing. Underneath that charismatic exterior is an Army Ranger, a soldier to the core. You know the motto—'Rangers lead the way.'"

"DNA. That's hard to overcome when your whole family are West Point grads," Connie reminded her.

"Actually, it should be easier. Yes, Derek's father and siblings all went the West Point route. But Derek didn't. He went the ROTC route. He wanted to have other options. And he's been the black sheep of the family ever since. His father *still* hasn't forgiven him, not really. I know that, on some level, that bothers Derek, even after all these years. He made a choice, one his father didn't understand or agree with. But he still should have supported it. That's what love is about. Given his own experience, Derek should have been the first one to accept *my* choice and support *me*. But somehow, when it came to my decision to leave the Bureau, all that support went right out the window. He couldn't or wouldn't put himself in my shoes. He was an obstinate, unfeeling SOB. So yes, I walked away. Or, to be more precise, he drove me away."

Sloane pressed her lips together, then finished in a less composed tone: "I don't fall easily. But when it came to Derek, I fell hard. The forever kind of hard. I believed in him, and I trusted him with my heart. He let me down big-time. So that's why my loving him can never amount to anything. We're just too different."

"Or too much alike."

"In some ways, yes. And neither of us is going to back down. So the affair is spectacular, but anything more is out."

"If you say so." Connie sounded decidedly unconvinced.

"I do. And now I'd like to drop the subject." Sloane extended her hand to Connie, palm up. "We have a hand to fix."

Connie gripped Sloane's wrist and examined the palm. "The inflammation is significantly improved and the swelling has gone down. I think we can resume some of our less strenuous exercises. But I'm going to start with some scar massage." With that, she put lotion on the scar-tissue massage tool and began a light, gentle motion with the roller ball. "Any pain?"

"So far, so good," Sloane replied, trying not to recoil instinctively or tense up. She hated that she was doing that again. Right after the stabbing, it had been a reflexive action the instant her palm was touched. But over the months she'd worked with Connie, trust had begun to build, until finally the defensive reactions had subsided. Until now. Now she was regressing, and all because she'd been stupid enough to wrestle with a lug-nut wrench and inflame her palm all over again.

"It's okay," Connie said, reading Sloane's expression.

"The trust is still there. Self-protection is a natural instinct in situations like this. So relax. We'll regain the ground we lost."

The door flew open, and Dr. Houghton barged in, wearing his surgical scrubs, totally oblivious to anything except his own agenda. "I just finished that emergency surgery," he informed Connie. "It was even more complicated and intricate than I originally anticipated. The damage is extensive. On the plus side, I was able to control the bleeding and save all his fingers. But he has extensive nerve, bone, and tendon damage. That's what you get when you stick your hand in a running lawn mower. He's in recovery now. I need to review the preliminary occupational-therapy plan with you. Since you're working late, now is as good a time as any."

Connie cleared her throat, and tipped her head in Sloane's direction.

Dr. Houghton's brows drew together, then arched in surprise as he got Connie's message, and became aware that someone else was in the room with them. His probing stare flickered to Sloane. "Oh. I didn't realize you were here." His tone was icy. "Speaking of reckless actions, it's lucky for you that Constance is as skilled as she is. Otherwise, you might be back in surgery yourself."

Sloane blinked, uncertain what to say.

Connie took care of it for her. "Fortunately, it won't come to that. Sloane's been following your instructions to the letter. Her palm is healing nicely. We've resumed using the medium-resistance therapy putty. So it's a moot point."

"Not if she continues to risk her well-being by doing careless things like trying to change flat tires." Dr. Houghton approached the table and glared down at Sloane's palm. He gave a tight nod, clearly pleased with what he saw. "Try to remember you haven't rejoined the FBI yet. And if you want to heal to the point where that's possible, you'll have to use some common sense." He turned away, fired a look at Connie. "I'll need a half hour of your time before you leave tonight."

"Not a problem." Connie stayed calm and patient. "Sloane and I will be wrapping up by six-thirty. I'll come directly to your office."

"If I'm not there, I'll be in post-op. Page me."

"I will."

Without so much as a good-bye, Dr. Houghton left, shutting the door firmly behind him.

Sloane looked at Connie, totally bewildered. "What was *that* all about? Dr. Houghton isn't known for his charm, but he's never blatantly rude either. Is he that furious about my aggravating the injury?"

"It isn't that." Connie sighed, resumed her work on Sloane's hand. "He's just on overload. He's a brilliant surgeon, and he won't do anything half measure. That man he just operated on, by all rights, should have lost at least two of his fingers, that's how mangled his hand was when he was rushed in. Dr. Houghton spent hours in the operating room, saving those fingers. He's a one-of-a-kind surgeon. His personality is another story. And he's particularly on edge these days. He's really short-staffed, and that's requiring him to take on more than a surgical role. Recovery-room procedures, IV drips, and the administration of antibiotics are usually handled by the nursing staff. Well, there are very few nurses left that he trusts enough to delegate responsibility to. So he's feeling—and showing—the stress. As you pointed out, he's not exactly a people person."

Sloane digested that. "Is he impossible to work with? Is that why so many nurses have quit?"

"Nope." Connie shook her head. "His nurses and hand therapists have been with him for years. Like I said, he's tough, but he's brilliant. Watching him work is like watching a master sculptor. It's just been a big relocation year for HSS in general, and our department in particular. In the past six months, Dr. Houghton has lost two of his most experienced nurses. Marsha Brown, who'd been with him for a decade, left this week. Her husband got an amazing promotion in California. So they moved to Palo Alto. Marsha accepted a position at Stanford University Hospital—thanks to a glowing reference from Dr. Houghton. So Marsha's gone. And you know about Lydia. She left in December. So we're now down two top-notch nurses."

"Aren't they interviewing potential candidates?"

"Yes, but the problem is, any potential candidate has to get Dr. Houghton's seal of approval. And his standards are beyond high. He still hasn't been impressed by any of the nurses interviewing for Lydia's position, and we've been interviewing for four months. So I'm not holding my breath that we'll be seeing a substitute for Marsha anytime soon."

Sloane considered the situation and nodded. "As a fellow perfectionist, I can understand Dr. Houghton's frustration. I didn't know Marsha, but Lydia was the best nurse I ever had. By the way, how is she doing?"

"Not a clue." Connie's forehead creased as she did some passive resistance exercises with Sloane's fingers. "None of us has heard from her. Which is so unlike Lydia. She's such a warm person, and our department is like a family. Especially Lydia and me. We both worked so closely with Dr. Houghton that our jobs overlapped. So we saw a lot of each other. We might not have socialized outside of work, but I considered her a friend. Marital problems or not, I'm pretty upset that she still hasn't contacted me, or anyone else, for that matter. I even checked with the hospital administrator. He said Lydia never gave notice or left a forwarding address for her final paycheck. He seemed as surprised by her departure as we were. Her husband must have done quite a number on her to make her take off like that."

"Even so, that's a pretty drastic step. Lydia never struck me as being rash. Just the opposite, in fact." The investigator in Sloane kicked in. "What about her husband? Did any of you talk to him?"

"Michael, one of our male nurses, did, just recently as a matter of fact. Lydia's husband, Nick, is a very traditional guy. So we figured it would be easier to approach him man-to-man, rather than via what he'd perceive as a nosy broad. It didn't matter. Michael got nowhere. Nick became very defensive. He insisted that he and Lydia were resolving their marital problems. He claimed that one day she just went to work and never came home. According to him, he was worried, so he drove around the hospital looking for her. He even checked around Rockefeller University, where she liked to watch the East River ferries come in and dock at the Sixty-third Street ferry landing. So he was either lying, or the rumors of spousal abuse that were floating around the hospital were true, and things were bad enough for Lydia to take off without telling Nick she was leaving."

The details of this story were beginning to sound way too familiar, and Sloane's stomach knotted. She wasn't going to jump to any hasty conclusions. On the other hand, she wasn't going to overlook anything either. "Rockefeller University? Lydia liked to hang out there?"

"Not hang out." Connie shot her a strange look. "She just went there for a closer view of the ferry landing. The university's right at Sixty-third Street. She probably went to an upper floor to peer out a window, or walked over to one of the nearby parks."

"Right. To see the East River."

"No, to watch the ferries. And *I* didn't supply this information, Nick did." Connie put down Sloane's hand and inclined her head quizzically. "Why are you acting so weird? And why are you asking such strange questions?"

It's a coincidence, Sloane reassured herself. *It has to be.*

"What else did Nick say?" she asked.

"Nothing of significance, at least not according to Michael. Then again, Michael had some trouble understanding Nick's English. He's got a pretty thick Greek accent. Oh, he said he'd called the cops, which we already knew, but that they didn't turn up anything."

"I want to talk to Michael," Sloane announced, coming to her feet. "Is he in the hospital now?"

"He's down the hall." Connie rose as well, putting aside her therapy tools. "But you're not talking to him until you tell me what's going on, and why we're cutting your therapy session in half."

"One last question, since you and Lydia were friends." Sloane blew right by Connie's demand. "Does Lydia have any family here? Not just in New York, but in the States?"

"No. She has two sisters and both her parents, but they're all living in Greece."

"What about friends outside the hospital? Who did she stay with during the separation?"

"That one I can answer. Lydia's family is very religious. She was afraid they might call and find out that she and Nick were separated. So she moved into the spare bedroom."

"So she never left. And there's no one who can account for her whereabouts." Sloane raked a hand through her hair, forcing herself to stay calm. "Connie, I promise I'll explain everything to you. But first, I have to speak to Michael. In the meantime, I need you to get me Nick Halas's contact information."

Twenty minutes later, Sloane left the hospital. Making this phone call was essential before she met with Larry. Because it was possible she'd have even more to discuss with him than she'd had an hour ago.

She checked her cell phone. Good—three bars. She finally had the reception she needed.

She punched in Bob's direct number at Midtown North.

"Sergeant Erwin," he answered.

"Bob, it's Sloane Burbank. I'm so glad you're at your desk."

"Yeah, well, my wife's not. But since the media got hold of the information that Cynthia Alexander's disappearance could be part of serial kidnappings, I practically sleep here."

"I'm afraid I'm not about to help cut back on your hours," Sloane said ruefully. "I need you to do me a favor. Check out a missing persons report that was called into your precinct on December fifth of last year. The woman's name is

Lydia Halas. The call would have been initiated by her husband, Nick Halas." She gave Bob their address and telephone number as well as the facts Connie and Michael had just provided.

"I don't think I like where you're going with this."

"Neither do I. Look, this could be a total waste of time. I don't want to press the panic button—yet. On the other hand, the profile fits. In which case, Lydia Halas could be another victim of our serial killer."

CHAPTER
TWENTY-THREE

DATE: 14 April
TIME: 1600 hours

At last. Her bedroom.

I cross the threshold with all the respect due a goddess, especially this most significant one. I inhale deeply. I can smell her fragrance. Not perfume, just the pure, natural scent of her skin.

The room is simple, tasteful. Exactly as I expected. The only objects on display are the very personal things that make her Artemis.

I need to be part of those things. The gloves allow me to immerse myself in her life without worrying about leaving fingerprints in a room I should never enter, on items I should never touch.

I pick up a photo from her dresser, smile as I see her standing between two people who are obviously her parents. She's petite like her mother—has the same smile, delicate features, and bone structure. Her coloring she inherited from her father—the chestnut hair and golden-brown eyes. And the stubborn chin as well. Yet she emanates a strength and fire that's hers and hers alone.

The three of them are holding up an archery trophy she won in college. How fitting for my Artemis. Her parents are beaming with pride. They'll be even prouder when they realize where their daughter has been chosen to spend eternity.

I put down the picture frame and walk over to her night table. There are several rubberlike balls and a few hard plastic implements. I recognize the healing tools for her hand.

With a wave of compassion, I pick up each tool, study it. There have been so many times I've wanted to reach out to her, let her know that on Mount Olympus, her injury will be nonexistent. She'll feel only reverence and joy—no pain, no suffering. Only the sanctity of eternal life.

I replace the tools and stare at her neatly made bed.

The urge to be close to her is too great. I can't deny myself this one earthly pleasure.

My shoes are already off. I'd removed them as soon as I'd stepped into the house. This way there'd be no footprints, and no dirt tracked in from the outside to soil her personal space.

I gingerly lower myself onto the bed, inch over to the center. The mattress is soft, and I sink into it. The pillow beneath my head has the scent of her hair. I could lie here forever. It feels so right.

I indulge myself for a half hour. I might have stayed longer, but I can feel myself starting to doze off. I can't risk falling asleep. Discovery at this point would be a disaster. I haven't had the chance to show her the shrine I've built in her honor. Once I do that, she'll understand.

She's not coming home anytime soon. It doesn't take a psychic to predict that. Whenever she's home or almost home, either the black Ford Focus or the silver Toyota Corolla is parked nearby. Inside is one of her two bodyguards. They're like homing devices, going wherever she goes. The Corolla by day, the Focus by night: 8 A.M. to 8 P.M.; 8 P.M. to 8 A.M., like clockwork.

Still, I'm not taking any chances. Mr. Corolla could reappear at any time.

I climb off the bed. I'm ready to go now. I linger in the bedroom doorway for one moment longer, savoring every detail.

I leave the same way I came.

As I slip out, I can hear the hounds whining.

FBI New York Field Office
26 Federal Plaza, New York City
4:35 P.M.

Derek was convinced he now knew what the term *dead on your feet* meant.

Slumped over his desk, his stomach growling and his mouth parched, he tried to remember the last time he'd eaten. He couldn't. He also wondered if he had the strength to go get a bottle of water, since he knew how badly dehydrated he was. But the fatigue was winning the battle. It seemed he needed the rest more than he needed the fluids.

He and everyone at C-6 had lived at the field office all weekend. They'd needed every agent and every minute to defuse the time bomb that would go off if Xiao Long decided to ignore the information being strategically leaked that a psychopath, and not Lo Ma's gang, was responsible for killing his girls.

There was only so far he'd trust his informants. Especially since all they were giving him were words. There was nothing concrete to back up their claims. Derek was quite sure Xiao Long had his enforcer on speed dial. Somehow, some way, they had to give him solid proof. Thus far, none had been forthcoming.

The weekend had been a real joyride. C-6's entire squad had been out on the streets, meeting with their contacts, striving to keep the lid on this explosion. At the same time, precautions had been taken and safeguards initiated—just in case all their efforts failed.

The NYPD had posted cops on virtually every street corner in Chinatown. As a result, the streets were empty, and Chinatown was a ghost town. The restaurant owners were

screaming, the shop owners were screaming, the produce-
store owners were screaming. Everyone who owned a business in the district was screaming—*and* demanding answers,
first from the NYPD's Fifth Precinct, then from Puzzle
Palace and the mayor's office. All they got was the stock
phrase *orders from the top* from the precinct, and the infamous *no comment* from the NYPD higher-ups and the PR
folks at the mayor's office.

Derek felt like a rat racing through an endless maze that
kept leading him back to his starting point.

The phone on his desk rang. He was half tempted to ignore it. The last thing he needed was someone else blasting
his eardrum.

Responsibility took over, and Derek fumbled for the
phone, shoving it under his chin. "Parker."

A second later, his head popped up, his exhaustion forgotten. It was the M.E.'s office.

"You have something for me?"

"Yeah," the medical analyst at the other end replied.

"Tell me it's significant."

"Significant enough for you to send my wife and me on
vacation—and not to the Jersey shore; to a Caribbean is-
land."

Derek's pulse began to pick up. "Go on."

"Our offender is getting careless. Either that, or this
mangled woman put up a hell of a fight. We found his sa-
liva on what was left of her face, and skin and tissue underneath her nails."

"And it took you this long to—"

"Easy. We wanted to finish the autopsy and the lab analysis before we called you. The drug panel shows high levels
of ketamine in her blood, and the type of wounds inflicted
are identical to the other murdered prostitutes. The difference is, this one was far more brutal. He sliced her up almost beyond recognition."

"I knew that."

"But you didn't know why. All the previous victims were

repeatedly sexually violated. Obviously, he wore a condom and was very careful about it, so there was never any trace of semen. But there *was* extreme swelling and tissue tearing in the vaginal canal, sometimes even bleeding. He violently raped his previous victims, make no mistake about it."

"And this one?"

"This one shows none of that. No swelling, no tearing, not even any inflammation. In fact, I'd make an educated guess that he never even penetrated the woman."

"He couldn't perform," Derek concluded. "That must have infuriated him. So he took it out on the victim by butchering her."

"You got it." A pause. "Do you want to hear the rest?"

"What rest? There's more?"

"Oh yeah. I told you this was worth a Caribbean vacation. I meant it."

"Continue."

"The last test we were waiting to complete was the DNA test."

"You found something in CODIS. You know who this psycho is."

"Yes and no. We found something in CODIS. As for who it is, that's your job."

"You lost me."

"What we found, we found in the forensic index. Two separate hits. One in New York, the other in New Jersey."

By this time, Derek was sitting up stick straight, every vestige of fatigue having vanished. "I'm listening."

"I'm sure you are."

Three minutes later, Derek burst into Antonio Sanchez's office. "Tony, we have to talk. Now."

His drained SSA looked up from the pile of unanswered phone messages he'd been putting off returning. He was just about to tell Derek that whatever he wanted would have to wait, when he saw his expression.

"You got a lead?" Tony demanded.

"Better."

A wave of relief crossed his boss's face. "That's news I'd put anything aside for. Come in and shut the door."

Derek complied, remaining on his feet as he spoke. The adrenaline flowing through him was too powerful to allow him to sit. "Not only do I have a solid lead that will get Chinatown back to normal," he told Tony, "but it's possible I can use that same lead to solve the Truman case—and a handful of others. Good enough news for you?"

Tony just stared. "Explain," he ordered.

Derek did, supplying both fact and supposition, leaving out nothing in the process.

"Damn." Tony shook his head in amazement. "No one could ever accuse you of providing unimpressive leads." Even as he spoke, his wheels were turning. "The first thing I have to do is get the NYPD on the phone, secure their cooperation."

"Are you kidding? They'll celebrate. After the weekend they just had, they'll be popping open the six-packs before you say good-bye."

"Not before they issue a Crime Stoppers flyer, written in both Mandarin and English, announcing that a Fukienese woman was killed on Eldridge Street." Tony was scribbling down notes. "The flyer will clearly state that the police are searching for . . ." A questioning glance at Derek.

"A white male, light eyes, medium-to-tall in height, solid build, probably between his midthirties and forties," Derek supplied. "Armed and violent. Tell them to post the flyer all over Chinatown, outside restaurants and shops, on telephone poles, on people's asses if they have to."

Tony chuckled. "Once that's done, I'll deal with the community leaders, get all the bigwigs off our backs. Word will spread like wildfire. In the meantime, you and the squad talk to your informants. Get them to spread the news in the right places and to the right sources. You and I will handle the official route. We'll work with OPA to issue a formal press release. There won't be a human being in the tristate area that isn't aware of the physical description and psychological makeup of the Unsub we're looking for."

"Including Xiao Long. This should be more than enough to give him the proof he wants that the Black Tigers aren't responsible for his girls' deaths. Nor, for that matter, are any other rival gangs. He'll back down. Gang tensions will subside. And Chinatown can resume business as usual."

"So what are you waiting for?" Tony asked, grinning as he reached for the phone. "Go clue in the rest of the squad. You've got a lot to accomplish before you head back to Atlantic City to finish solving the Truman case."

John Jay College of Criminal Justice
New York City
4:55 P.M.

Larry rose from the patch of grass he'd been examining—a small but trampled section of the area cordoned off and designated as Cynthia Alexander's crime scene.

"The CSI team did a thorough job," he told Sloane. "The Unsub clearly grabbed Cynthia Alexander as she left the building. There was a struggle; you can see that from the flattened and pulled-up sections of grass. If this had been winter, CSI probably could have pulled a shoe or boot print from the snow. But there's nothing here to work with. Just the blood and the hair band they're already analyzing."

"No surprise there. The NYPD's team is the best there is." Sloane raked a weary hand through her hair. She and Larry had been retracing routes all weekend, examining crime scenes, reviewing victimology. They'd even reinterviewed Tina Carroll, whom Larry had asked some intuitive questions about the Unsub's demeanor, his level of anger, and his level of aggression.

He and Tina then went over every physical or body-type feature she could remember, and every word her attacker had said, both in Chinese and in English. Larry had lis tened intently as she took him through the entire encounter, just as she had for the police. But Larry didn't stop there. He took it a step further, pressing for more detailed answers from Tina.

Had her attacker said or implied anything that would indicate what kind of area he was taking her to —urban, rural, or suburban? When he was standing directly behind her with the knife to her throat, had she picked up on any smells that would provide a clue about that—the odor of hay or manure, the smoky, diesel-fuel smells of the city, the freshly cut grass of the suburbs? Had he used the plural anytime he spoke, indicating that she'd be joining others? Had she caught even a glimpse or a flash of his vehicle, which must have been stashed in the woods? Had there been any time during the days immediately preceding the attack that she'd sensed she was being watched or followed, not only on campus but anywhere else she'd gone?

That last question brought a reaction.

Tina had been repeatedly shaking her head in the negative. Abruptly, she stopped. "I told the police that I felt as if I were being watched every morning when I went out running. But I didn't think beyond the place where the attack occurred. Now that you phrase it that way, it wasn't just at Lake Ceva that I had that feeling, or even just at school. It was also at the martial-arts academy. When I walked to my car, when I stepped outside for some fresh air, I had this strange feeling that someone was watching me. Even on the drive back to school, I'd glance in my rearview mirror a bunch of times because I felt like someone was following me. I never saw anyone suspicious, so I figured I was being paranoid. But now that you bring it up, maybe he wasn't just watching me at school. Maybe he was stalking me, trying to figure out the best place to grab me."

"Maybe," Larry had quietly agreed.

That had confirmed what Sloane and Larry already suspected. The Unsub's victims weren't random. They were deliberately selected. And the only common threads thus far were the victims' gender, the settings in which they were attacked, and their connection to Sloane.

She and Larry had been going at this for days. And she had a sinking feeling that they were still stuck at square one.

"We've gone over the victimologies ad nauseam," she stated flatly as she and Larry headed back to their respective cars. "We've retraced every step the Unsub might have taken, reviewed every aspect of the kidnappings, revisited all the crime scenes, and reinterviewed every potential witness. Have we learned *anything*?"

"We've learned that this Unsub deviates from the typical serial sexual killer in several ways. His victims aren't random. He's not interested in gloating over his superior skill and intelligence, because he hasn't so much as contacted us. Nor has he flaunted his crimes by leading us to his victims' bodies. It's possible he's watching us and getting a charge out of seeing us flounder, but that's not enough to fuel his need for power and mastery. He's filled with the kind of leashed violence that has to have an outlet, or he'll implode."

"He could be torturing his victims before he kills them."

"True. But if that's the case, why not go for easy targets? Why pick such specific and risky ones? No, Sloane, this Unsub has an agenda. It's up to us to figure it out. Until we understand his specific motivation, we're not getting anywhere."

"How do we do that? Where do we start?"

"With you."

"Excuse me?"

"It's become increasingly obvious that you're central to this guy's actions. So instead of profiling *him*, let's profile *you*. Let's head over to my hotel, order some food so we don't faint, and examine the fine print of your life. Who might have an ax to grind with you? Who might have a thing for you, but hasn't acted on it? Who have you interacted with over the past year who's new and different from before? Who's been in your life for ages, but in some peripheral way that makes him invisible to you—your mailman, gardener, pizza delivery guy? That kind of thing."

"In other words, make a spreadsheet of my life."

"You got it." Larry shot her a questioning look. "Are you willing?"

"Absolutely." Sloane's hope surged at the prospect of doing something productive. "I'll compile a list of every human being I know, if I have to. I'll put asterisks next to the ones I think merit a second look. Any questions you come up with, I'll answer. And I won't eliminate the women, because the majority of them have husbands or significant others in their lives, most of whom I'm acquainted with. Hell, I'll even go through my college and high school yearbooks tonight, if you think that would help."

"You've got a natural affinity for this." A hint of a smile curved Larry's lips. "When you decide to rejoin the Bureau, maybe you should consider applying to the BAU."

"My rejoining the Bureau isn't up to me," Sloane reminded him. "It's up to them. And to this." She held up her hand.

"You'll get there. I have faith."

Sloane's cell phone rang, and she stopped to scoop it out of her purse. "It might be Bob Erwin," she told Larry. "He's trying to determine whether Lydia Halas was another of our Unsub's victims. More and more, it's looking like she was."

Larry made a sweeping gesture with his arm. "Go ahead. Take the call."

Sloane punched on her phone. "Sloane Burbank."

"It's me."

Her brows arched at the sound of Derek's voice. "I thought you were locked up in hell."

"I was. I'm not anymore. Is Larry with you?"

"Yes. We're finishing up at John Jay. Why?"

"Because the DNA from that butchered prostitute in Chinatown came back."

"Wait a minute. You're confusing me. I read about the murdered prostitute, and I assumed that was part of the emergency you mentioned when you canceled our weekend plans. But I had no idea there was DNA evidence, and I still have no idea why you want to share this information with Larry and me."

"Because the offender's DNA matched the DNA of the blood splatter found at Tina Carroll's crime scene, and the DNA of the sweat and hair found on the custodian uniform at Southern New Jersey Medical Center—worn by whoever stole all those drugs and slit the head nurse's throat."

Sloane stopped dead in her tracks and leaned against a tree. "Are you telling me we're talking about one killer for both sets of crimes?"

"Yup. We know for a fact that the same Unsub was responsible for the three crimes I just described to you. With regard to this last murder—which was the mutilation of a Fukienese prostitute—there've been a string of identical crimes in Chinatown these past few months, all with the same pattern. And with regard to the kidnappings, you know as well as I do that I have strong evidence indicating that the Unsub who attacked Tina is also responsible for the disappearances of Penelope Truman and Cynthia Alexander."

"And Lydia Halas," Sloane added woodenly.

"Who?"

"She was my nurse at Cornell Medical Center when I was recovering from my surgeries. She left four months ago, with no word to anyone and no notice to the hospital. And the pattern . . ." Sloane proceeded to describe the when and where to Derek. "Bob's looking into it now. But I don't have a good feeling."

"Shit." Derek made a frustrated sound. "It makes you wonder how many more victims he's grabbed that we don't know about." A pointed pause. "And how many more he plans to grab—including you."

"Larry and I are addressing that issue now," Sloane replied. "I'm obviously central to these kidnappings. So we're taking the opposite approach. Rather than profiling the Unsub, we're profiling me. We're heading over to his hotel now and putting my entire life down on paper, hopefully to figure out what's motivating this psycho." A thoughtful pause. "What you just told me is a big help. It answers one of the major questions Larry's been grappling with—where our Unsub is unleashing his violence."

"Yeah; well now you know."

Larry had heard enough of the conversation to figure out what was going on. He waved his hand, getting Sloane's attention.

"Derek, hang on a minute." A quizzical look at Larry.

"Ask Derek if he can get us case files on the murdered prostitutes. Whatever's not classified, right down to the smallest detail. It could be a huge help."

"I heard what Larry asked. Consider it done," Derek responded. "I'll have the files brought over to Larry's hotel ASAP. I'm doing the same with Bill down in Quantico. I just spoke to him. By the way, this new development changes things significantly, so Bill's putting off our conference call until he and Larry have each had the chance to review and discuss everything." Derek broke off as Jeff called out something to him in the background. "I've gotta run," he told Sloane. "I've got a shitload of things to tie up at this end. I'll call you as soon as things quiet down. Good luck with your profile."

Hunterdon County, New Jersey
10:15 P.M.

Sloane was so exhausted when she pulled into her driveway that she could hardly focus. She'd never delved as deeply into her own life as she had today. Her brain felt like it had turned to mush.

In addition, Bob Erwin had called to tell her that it looked like her instincts were right. Lydia Halas's "leaving home" was decidedly suspicious and fraught with holes. The police records did indeed indicate that Nick Halas had called in his wife's disappearance and filed a missing persons report. The cops had followed up by interviewing Nick, as well as the neighbors in their apartment. The couples who lived on either side of them had reported hearing several heated arguments between Nick and Lydia— accompanied by slamming and thudding sounds that could have been anything from Nick punching walls to striking his wife—adding that they had no proof he'd been abusing her, but they weren't surprised when she'd left. And since there was no evidence of foul play, and lots of signs that the Halases' marriage was rocky enough for her to take off, the investigation had been dropped.

But now Bob had probed deeper. It was true that Lydia, who'd been a conscientious employee for twenty years, had given no notice to the hospital, nor had she discussed the possibility of resigning with Dr. Houghton or anyone on his team. She'd also left behind all her clothes, jewelry, and personal items—which could signify a frightened woman running from her husband, or an average woman who'd been taken against her will. In addition, none of her credit cards had been used since her December disappearance— another detail that mirrored Penny's disappearance.

The parallels had been strong enough to persuade Bob to contact Lydia's relatives in Greece. Not a single one had heard from her.

Combining all that with the other links of Lydia's disappearance—the college campus, the body of water, and the connection to Sloane—Bob was ready to add Lydia to the list of potential victims.

Sloane climbed out of her car, gathered her purse and her files, and shoved the car door shut with her knee. She paused to wave good night to her nighttime security guard,

Hank Murphy, who'd been right on her tail and was now parked at the curb in his Ford Focus.

He flashed his headlights and waved back.

She headed up the front walk, fishing for her keys at the same time. She located them just as she reached the door. Jostling her files around, she fitted the key into the lock and elbowed open the door, simultaneously flicking on the hall light and plopping her files onto the hall table.

Instantly, she knew something was wrong.

Part of it was gut feeling. Part of it was the absence of the hounds rushing to the door to greet her.

Pure instinct took over.

Sloane inched her way over to the locked cabinet where she kept her personal weapon. Silently, she removed the key from its hiding place and slid open the cabinet drawer, pulling out the Glock 27. It was smaller and lighter than the 22 that was standard issue at the Bureau—but it did the job just fine.

By this time, she could hear the dogs whining, scratching to be released from whatever prison they'd been confined to. Gripping her pistol, she called out, "Moe, Larry, Curly—I'm home. Where are you?"

She was rewarded by a barrage of barking and scratching from the spare bedroom. Still holding her weapon poised and ready to fire, she eased over in that direction, twisted the doorknob, and pushed open the door.

The three dogs came flying out, jumping up and down, looking a little disoriented, but unharmed—and thrilled to see her.

She squatted down, hugged each of them fiercely, while never lowering her head or her gun. She was so relieved, she almost started to cry. The hounds were okay. That was the most important thing. Now she'd investigate who her visitor had been, and if he was still here.

The kitchen light was on, but she always left it on, so the hounds would never be in total darkness. Still, she started there. Slowly, room by room, she went through the house, gun raised, ready to fire if need be.

Nothing had been stolen, and nothing seemed to be disturbed.

Until she went into her bedroom.

He'd been here. She could sense it. Evidently, so could the hounds, because they shoved past her and began sniffing every square inch of the bedroom floor.

Flipping on the light, Sloane swept the room with her gaze and her pistol. No one was there—now.

But she quickly spotted that her picture frame was sitting at a different angle than it had been before, her hand-therapy tools had been rearranged, and one of the pillows on her bed was propped slightly higher than the other—not to mention that there was a faint, but distinct imprint of a person's body on her comforter.

Still scrutinizing the room, she picked up the phone and dialed 911. Clearly and concisely, she reported the break-in, then provided the operator with her name, address, and phone number, as well as with the facts that no one had been injured and there was no sign that the intruder was still on the premises.

That call complete, she punched in the home phone number of Gary Lake, a special agent who'd graduated from Quantico with her, and who now worked in the Newark field office. One of his ancillary responsibilities was being part of the Evidence Response Team.

He answered the phone on the second ring.

"Gary?" she began. "It's Sloane. I hope I didn't wake you."

"Hey." He sounded surprised. "Nope, I have some work to do before I turn in. Ironic you should call. I was just talking about you to Tom McGraw. I told him the Bureau needs you back; you're an awesome agent."

"He mentioned it. Thanks for the praise. Listen, Gary, I need a favor. Someone broke into my house."

"Are you okay?" All personal catch-up vanished as Gary immediately transformed into a hundred percent special agent and concerned colleague.

"I'm fine. Thankfully, no injuries, not to me or my dogs. I already called the local police. They're on their way. But there are mitigating circumstances to this break-in. I have reason to believe that the offender is wanted by the FBI and the NYPD—and not for robbery. For drug theft, kidnapping, and multiple murders. I realize you live about twenty minutes away. But I need you to come over and see if you can find even a shred of evidence—a fingerprint, footprint, anything—to prove that this is the same offender. Can you possibly swing it?"

"I'm on my way."

"Thanks, Gary." Sloane felt another wave of relief. "I owe you one. I'll leash up my dogs and take them outside so we don't further contaminate the crime scene. And I'll fill in the locals when they arrive."

"See you in twenty." Gary hung up.

The minute Sloane stepped out the front door with all three hounds in tow, Hank opened his car door to determine what was going on.

"I'm fine, Hank," Sloane called out to him. "Someone broke into my house while I was in the city."

He jumped out of the Focus, retrieved his weapon, and rushed up the driveway.

"The intruder's gone," Sloane assured him as he bounded up the front steps and reached the door. "I called the police. There's no cause for alarm. No one's hurt and almost nothing was touched."

Hank scowled. "Why didn't you come out and get me the minute you realized you'd had an intruder?"

A rueful smile. "It's the FBI agent in me. Trained to defuse a situation quickly and safely. I just grabbed my pistol

and checked out the place. And I saw right away that whoever had broken in here was gone. Besides, I had to make
sure my dogs were all right. Which they are."

"Next time, clue me in. That's what I'm here for." Hank
whipped out his cell phone. "I'll call Derek."

"No, don't." Sloane put her hand on his arm to stop him.
"There's nothing Derek can do, and no reason for him to
freak out. Like I said, the intruder's gone, and everything's
fine. Besides, look." She pointed toward the road as a local
police car sped up to her house and veered into the driveway. "The cops are here."

Simultaneous with her announcement, the hounds went
into a barking frenzy.

"Easy," Sloane soothed them. "It's okay." She turned
back to Hank. "I also called someone from the Newark field
office's ERT. Everything's under control. We've got more
than enough law enforcement here. Derek's in the middle of
a Bureau crisis. I'll fill him in when I actually have information to pass on."

Hank hesitated, clearly ambivalent about Sloane's request.

"I'll take full responsibility for this," she assured him
quietly. "Please, Hank. I'm a big girl. I'm also a trained FBI
agent, even if I'm not with the Bureau now. I know what I'm
doing. And you're welcome to stay for the police questioning. In fact, I'd welcome it. You can fill in anything pertinent I omit. I'm sure they'll want to talk to you anyway."

"All right." Hank relented as two uniformed police officers walked over, ready to take Sloane's statement.

At the same time, Gary's car swung into the driveway.

"That's an FBI agent," she explained to the cops. "I
called him. He's with the Bureau's ERT." She saw their
miffed expressions and hurried on. "It's possible that whoever broke into my house is wanted by the FBI and the
NYPD. So Special Agent Lake will be searching my house
for evidence. In the meantime, I'll give you a full report of
the break-in. And this is Hank Murphy, my security guard.

He's been with me all day, but he'll gladly answer any of your questions as well."

That seemed to appease them. She said hi and thank you to Gary, and then told him to go in and do his thing. She and the hounds stayed outside with Hank and the cops, where she filled them in on what she had—and hadn't— found upon arriving at her house tonight. There had been no sign of the intruder. He'd come and gone when no one was home except her dogs, whom he'd locked in the spare bedroom. No one was hurt. Nothing was stolen. And nothing was damaged.

Then the questioning had started. Sloane knew the rundown, and she responded as coherently as her dazed mind would allow. Hank filled in an occasional detail, which Sloane greatly appreciated. She felt like she was operating in slow motion, the adrenaline that had been pumping through her now plummeting and dropping her to earth with a thud. She had no idea how much time had passed, or how long she had stood outside answering the officers' questions.

No, she didn't believe this could have been a prank. Yes, she kept her front door locked. Yes, she definitely believed this was personal. And, yes, she was convinced that the break-in was linked to the other crimes in question.

Finally, after what seemed like an eternity, Gary stepped outside onto the front porch.

Sloane's head came up. "Did you find anything?"

"Yup." He held up a sealed Ziploc bag. "There were no fingerprints or footprints. But there were these few strands of hair on your pillow that weren't your color or texture. I'll have them analyzed as quickly as I can."

"Great. And after you do, run the DNA in CODIS and please be sure to cross-check against the forensic index."

Gary met her gaze and nodded. "I'll be in touch."

"And once you are, do we know who we're arresting?" one of the officers asked.

"Not yet," Sloane replied. "But we will."

One by one, the law enforcement crowd left her house.

Hank waited until she and the hounds were safely locked inside before he returned to keep vigil in his car.

Sloane sank down on the carpet and hugged and scruffled each hound. They tolerated it for a minute or two, then raced back to the bedroom to explore the strange, new smells.

It was only then, when Sloane was sitting alone on the floor, that she felt the throbbing in her palm and the pain in her index finger. She looked down and realized she was still clutching her pistol.

And she knew that, pain or no pain, she would have used it.

TWENTY-FOUR

DATE: 16 April
TIME: 0900 hours

I'd made a fine selection. The right goddess to replace Tyche.

Linda Crowley. Professor of East Asian Studies at Princeton. Artemis had audited her Advanced Mandarin class last fall. Professor Crowley, who took brisk evening walks around Carnegie Lake, who enjoyed the simple wonders of nature. She would have been an ideal Demeter.

But when I arrived, university cops were patrolling the streets and swarming the campus like ants on an anthill. Security was tight, and the entire community was on high alert.

The grounds were deserted. No one was walking around Carnegie Lake or anywhere else. Success had escaped me.

I left Princeton in a hurry, heading as fast as I could toward home.

That's when it struck me.

The extended involvement of the FBI and police departments throughout New York and New Jersey had squeezed me out of my home turf. Campuses in both states would be like high-security prisons. Fulfilling my mission would be impossible.

With that realization, I lost it entirely. I'm sure no one could blame me, not even the gods. I was trapped. Stuck in an immoral world, powerless to reach Mount Olympus.

Filled with rage, I drove so recklessly that I was lucky to make it home alive. Once inside, I smashed whatever was in my path—chairs, tables, the vases I'd bought for Demeter's flowers. I even put my fist through a wall, ignoring the cuts and lacerations. I actually considered going back to Queens and butchering every whore in the borough, just to spit in the cops' faces.

I pictured the whores. Their depraved bodies and faces after I slashed them to bits. I fell to my knees, dug my knife deep into the carpet, and tore it apart, visualizing their bleeding, severed bodies as I shouted obscenities. I grabbed the furniture that was in my way, hurled it against the walls. Pieces of wood shattered, like the bones and ribs of their bodies.

Abruptly, I couldn't breathe. The room started spinning, then fading, dark spots flashing before my eyes. I fell to the floor, gasping for air. For one horrifying minute, I thought I was dying, that this was the gods' punishment for my falling short of their expectations. Death, followed by hell. No. Please, no. This couldn't be what they intended.

Comprehension dawned. I had to prove my worthiness. They were testing me. I couldn't, *wouldn't*, fail them.

I crawled into the kitchen, grabbed a paper bag, and breathed into it until the hyperventilation subsided.

I wasn't going to die. I had to find another way to fulfill my mission.

Seeking inspiration, I went into the room I'd crafted for Artemis, stopping to collect my precious childhood book. I sat on the floor, slowly turning the pages, starting, as always, by reading and rereading the loving inscription. I read on, pausing on the story of Demeter, then focusing on the illustrations of Artemis and Apollo. The archer god and goddess, both depicted with their bows and arrows.

That's when I remembered the photo I'd seen on her dresser.

And suddenly there was hope.

Again, the gods are smiling down upon me. My alternate plan for a substitute for Tyche exceeds the original by far. Professor Crowley had been an excellent choice. But this is a windfall.

I smile as I think of the age-old sales pitch: "Buy one, get one free." I wish I could let its creator know how far I'd surpassed it. My slogan would read: "Buy none, get two free."

Hunterdon County, New Jersey
11 A.M.

Sloane was frustrated and edgy.

She and Larry still hadn't finished a comprehensive list of everyone who'd crossed paths with her in her lifetime. Analyzing and reviewing it at least a dozen times hadn't helped. She never realized how many people she knew. And the list just kept on growing. However, none of the individuals she'd come up with seemed to fit the profile of a serial killer.

Of course there had been some shady characters, along with violent ones, whom she'd helped convict when she'd worked at the D.A.'s office. Larry was checking into any of them that might have been recently paroled. As for her FBI career, it had been brief. Plus, she'd been working white-collar crimes, not violent ones. So unless one of the offenders she'd talked into surrendering during a hostage negotiation crisis was out of prison, that seemed like a dead end.

Her current life as a consultant was no more fruitful when it came to producing likely suspects. The clients who retained her services were either corporations or law enforcement—and, in the case of the latter, her assignments were in a teaching or investigative capacity. She was no longer a special agent, nor did she have the strength and dexterity to pull the trigger of her gun with enough speed and accuracy to suit her. So actively assisting in the apprehension of criminals was out.

From there, Larry had questioned her about her male friends, both long-standing and new, about guys she'd been involved with and dumped, as well as about the men enrolled in her Krav Maga class. They talked about colleagues, acquaintances, and neighbors from A to Z in New York, in Cleveland, and here. Everyone from Andy Zarelli her hairstylist to Luke Doyle, her friend from 9/11, had been added then crossed off the list.

That brought up the subject of Burt. Larry put an asterisk next to his name. He was single, a little eccentric, able to come and go with relative ease, and overtly interested in Sloane.

Sloane was so overwhelmed by the whole procedure, she didn't know what to believe.

What she did know was that, when they touched on Elliot, she realized how long it had been since they'd talked. She'd been at John Jay a host of times this past week, but she'd been totally focused on the investigation. So she hadn't thought to drop in on Elliot. He was doubtless at his desk—where he was a permanent fixture—working on the software program he was so diligently developing to help stop cybercrime. And in between, he was probably looking out his office window at the police presence on campus, cringing at the invasion of privacy, and fraught with anxiety over what had happened to Cynthia Alexander.

He might be a geek, but he was a kindhearted guy. Fine, so he wasn't James Bond. A violent crime like this— one that struck so close to home—threw him and, yes, scared him. He felt vulnerable to the attacker, and claustrophobic from the press. But, most of all, he was worried about Cynthia. Elliot truly cared about people, particularly his students.

TWISTED 287

Initially, it was that caring, coupled with Sloane's genuine affection for Elliot, that prompted her to pick up the phone and make an appointment to see him. But as she was about to dial his number, an interesting idea occurred to her.

Elliot was a genius at what he did. Always had been, always would be. He was committed to his work, with a fervent sense of responsibility to the financial institutions bankrolling his research. Add to that his great and long-standing aspirations to utilize his talents in ways that could truly benefit society.

The sum total of that thought process got Sloane wondering if the program Elliot was developing—albeit focused on subtle patterns in financial transactions—was robust enough to be utilized in other ways.

Eager to explore the possibility, Sloane had set up an appointment with Elliot for later that day. The plan was for her to come by his office around three, after which they'd catch a drink together.

Pacing around the kitchen, Sloane refilled the hounds' water bowls and—for the tenth time—looked out the window toward Elsa's house. She'd been hoping to see Burt's car so she could chat with him. He'd called her the night of the break-in, asked if everything was okay. Since then, nothing. Which was odd, since he was taking constant care of Elsa these days.

Maybe it was time to go over there and check things out.

She was just about to leave the house when her phone rang. She ran back in and picked it up. "Hello?"

"Sloane? It's Gary."

"Gary." She felt a surge of guilt. She'd been meaning to call her friend for the past two days to thank him for rushing over at the drop of a hat *and* at 11 P.M., no less. But she'd been so busy and preoccupied working with Larry that she'd literally forgotten.

"I'm so glad you called," she told him sincerely. "Although *I'm* the one who should be calling *you*. I'm so sorry.

I've been crazed by this case, and I let the time get away from me. But that's no excuse. I can't thank you enough for what you did the other night."

"No apology necessary. It's obvious you have your hands full. But the thanks I'll accept, especially since you're about to have even more to thank me for."

Sloane's ears perked up. "Go on."

"Your hounds are off the hook," Gary informed her lightly. "The strands of hair I plucked off your pillow were definitely human."

"What a relief." Sloane smiled. "Now I won't have to revoke their bedtime privileges."

Gary sobered, relaying the information Sloane had been waiting for. "I've got results from the DNA analysis. There was no match to existing offenders in CODIS. However, I ran it through the forensic index, as you requested. There were three hits. One NYPD case, and two local New Jersey cases."

Sloane bit her lip. A serial killer had been in her house, on her bed. That fact was more than a little unsettling. Still, on a purely professional level, this was a lucky break. The offender who was committing these heinous crimes was now officially identified—through DNA evidence—as the same man who was stalking her and who'd invaded her home. It provided another factual piece in this puzzle, one more link that could result in finding and convicting their Unsub.

"You're right, I do have more to thank you for," Sloane replied. "Originally, I planned to spring for drinks. Now it's dinner. Your choice of restaurants."

"Sounds great. Give me a day to check out *Zagat's* and pick the most expensive restaurant in New Jersey."

"Take all the time you need. Oh, and Gary? With regard to the matching profile you found on that NYPD case, I know it probably referenced the Fifth Precinct. But could you also send the results to Sergeant Bob Erwin at Midtown North, and Special Agent Derek Parker at the New

York field office's C-6 squad? These crimes are all tied to
their cases as well."

"Not a problem. I'll take care of it right away."

"After you e-mail everything to me first, of course."

"Of course." A dry chuckle. "I'm not pissing off the
Queen of Krav Maga."

Sloane waited long enough to print out Gary's attachment
and to forward the entire e-mail to Larry so he could have
a heads-up on the new information. Then she took the
hounds out to do their business. Once they were back inside, comfortably snoozing on the living-room sofa, she
gathered up all the material she needed to go over with
Larry, left the house, and hopped into her car. Across the
street and right on cue, Denny Sparks, her daytime security guard, started up his silver Toyota Corolla and waved
at Sloane, letting her know that all systems were go. Sloane
waved back.

First stop, Elsa's, she thought as she drove next door.
She wanted to check on her neighbor, and find out why Elsa
had been alone these past few days.

Pulling up to the top of the Wagner driveway, Sloane got
out and rang the doorbell.

A redheaded woman with a kind smile and a professional air answered the door, along with Princess Di, who
was barking protectively—until she saw Sloane. Then she
jumped up, front paws on Sloane's leg, and began wagging
her tail and pawing Sloane for attention.

"I can see you're not a stranger," the redheaded woman
said with a twinkle. "May I help you?"

"I'm Sloane Burbank." Sloane pointed toward her house
as she bent forward to stroke Princess Di's ears. "I live next
door. And you are . . . ?"

"Charlene DeSoto. I'm a registered nurse. Mr. Wagner
hired me to look after his mother part-time, while he's
working at his bookstore."

"I see." Well, that explained Burt's absence. "Is Mrs. Wagner worse?" Sloane asked. "Does she need anything? Because I was just going out, and I'd be happy to pick up groceries, or medication, or even food for Princess Di."

"That's not necessary, Sloane." Elsa's voice, weak but reassuring, echoed from the living room. "And, no, I'm not worse. If anything, I'm improving. The pain is better and I was able to come downstairs today. So stop sounding so anxious. Please come in."

Nurse DeSoto stepped aside and gestured for Sloane to comply. She did, going straight to the living room, Princess Di at her heels.

"As you can see, I'm feeling better. Just not at peak strength." Elsa was lying on the sofa, a crocheted afghan draped over her. She looked pale and tired, her face drawn. "Burt is just a worrywart. He doesn't like the idea of my being here alone. And your friend Luke was kind enough to help us find an excellent nurse whose services would be covered by our insurance."

Sloane relaxed. "I'm glad to see you're out of bed, and looking more like yourself. But I don't blame Burt for worrying. I do, too. Why didn't he call me to help out? I'd gladly have come over and kept you company."

"After what you've been through this week? We wouldn't hear of it. In fact, it's *you* I'm concerned about, not me." Stiffly, Elsa winced and struggled to ease herself into a half-sitting position.

Charlene hurried over, skillfully assisting Elsa, then propping a cushion behind her back. "Mrs. Wagner really is much better," she assured Sloane.

"Indeed I am," Elsa concurred. "I just need to be given different types of pain medication at specific times. Plus, I need to have my blood pressure checked regularly. That's why Burt thought a nurse would be beneficial."

"I understand," Sloane replied.

With a nod of thanks to Charlene, Elsa continued. "I heard the commotion outside your house on Monday night.

Burt said he saw at least one police car turn in to your driveway. He assured me that he'd called you, and that you'd said
you had a break-in, but that no one was hurt and nothing
was taken. Is that true?"

"Yes." Sloane was *not* going to upset Elsa with unnecessary details. "Some items were moved around, and the
hounds were confined to the spare bedroom behind a shut
door. So they were quite peeved. But that was the extent of
it. For all I know, it was a couple of teenagers, playing a not
very funny prank."

"Well, thank goodness that's all it was." Elsa sank back,
visibly relieved. "I was hoping Burt wasn't shielding me
from the truth. Obviously, he wasn't. By the way, I asked
both him and Charlene if they'd noticed anyone prowling
around on Monday, but they hadn't."

"Not a soul," Charlene confirmed. "And I was outside
several times, taking Princess Di for her walks. As was Mr.
Wagner, when he returned."

"I appreciate your vigilance," Sloane responded. "With
all the woods around here, it's easy to come and go without
being spotted."

"Burt has been keeping an eye on your property every
night," Elsa added. "He's at the bookstore now, but he
should be home by midafternoon. Fortunately, it's a quieter day. He needs a break, given the number of hours he's
been putting in." A questioning look. "You said you were
heading out. Will you be gone long? Because I know Burt
would be happy to look after the hounds. He can pick them
up and bring them over here. Princess Di would love the
company."

Sloane was about to decline the offer, when it occurred
to her that, given her commitments in the city, she might
not be home until late. Plus, it would give her a chance to
talk to Burt.

"Actually, I'd really appreciate that—*if* Burt wouldn't
mind."

"Of course he won't. You know how fond of your pups

he is. He'll take good care of them. And if you're running late, just call, and they can stay the night."

"Thank you, Elsa." Sloane rose. "I'll check in with Burt later. In the meantime, you take care of yourself."

"I am and I will." A resolved smile. "Those are my doctor's orders, not to mention my son's. Between the bunch of you, I'll be myself again in no time."

A few minutes later, Sloane said her good-byes and drove off. She was glad Elsa was in good hands.

She just wished that one of Lady Di's strolls had corresponded with the arrival of her intruder. Maybe then, either Charlene or Burt would have spotted him.

Holland Tunnel
1:45 P.M.

Sloane had been fighting traffic for a while now. She was very relieved to emerge from the other end of the tunnel and finally be in Manhattan. Now she just had to crawl her way up to John Jay.

Twenty minutes and two blocks later, her cell phone rang.

Using her hands-free, she answered. "Sloane Burbank."

"When were you planning on telling me that our serial killer had broken into your house and tried out your bed?" Derek demanded without preamble.

The last thing Sloane was up for was one of Derek's macho tirades.

"I didn't realize I was subject to house rules," she replied. "I handled the problem. I also made sure you got a copy of the report—which you obviously did. By the way, don't blast Hank. I told him not to contact you. I can take care of myself—as I always have. And it's not as if the DNA results are any great revelation. You're the one who's been suspicious of my stalker from the start, dead set on the fact that I'm at the heart of his crime spree. This proves you were right. I figured you'd be gloating, not biting my head off."

"Well, you figured wrong." Derek still sounded miffed. "Are you okay?"

"Except for the fact that I had to wash the comforter and the rug three times each so the hounds would stop their incessant sniffing, I'm unscathed."

"Good." Derek blew out a breath. "Sloane, I know we've beaten this conversation to death, but you don't seem to get the fact that this psycho's ultimate target is *you*. I want you out of that house. Move to a hotel or to a friend's place. Move in with me. Stop being so damned stubborn."

"Moving in with you would guarantee violence," Sloane returned drily. "The minute you started ironing my bras, we'd kill each other." She maneuvered her car around a BMW, simultaneously trying to put an end to this ongoing debate. "As for the rest, I told you, I'm not letting this Unsub scare me off. I won't turn my whole life *and* my dogs' lives upside down to move somewhere that's no safer than home. This psycho's not interested in my house; he's interested in me. Wherever I go, he'll find me. At least I know my own turf. I sensed someone had broken in the instant I opened the front door. I grabbed my pistol—and, yes, I would have used it."

"I believe you. But you don't carry your pistol when you go for your daily run. Don't you think the Unsub's memorized your route?"

"I'm sure he has. And, if I changed it, he'd memorize the new one. I have to keep things business as usual. He's fixated on me. We've already cut off his ability to reach me by phone—which I'm sure he's figured out. I don't want to do anything else to rock the boat and push him even further over the edge."

"Yeah, right. And if you happen to draw him out of hiding while you're keeping things business as usual, all the better."

"If it results in us capturing him, I'd be thrilled." Sloane rushed on, nipping the rest of Derek's argument in the bud. "Tell you what. From now on, I'll have Hank check out the house before I go inside. He already follows me with binoculars during my run. Now, do you have any news for me?"

Derek's grunt indicated he knew she was placating him, that he didn't like it a bit, and that this conversation was far from over. But he let it go—for now. "This Unsub of ours is a real Houdini. He diverts attention from himself so no one notices when he strikes. I headed down to Eldridge Street on the Lower East Side and questioned a few people. The victim's roommates barely speak a word of English. Hell, they wouldn't talk to me even if they were fluent. They're way too scared. After that, I ran into a couple of teenage junkies, who think they remember a guy in a hooded sweatshirt hanging around the resting house. Of course they never saw his face. Plus, they were high as a kite. So I took what they said with a grain of salt."

"Wise decision." Sloane honked her horn as a taxi driver cut her off. "I'm on my way over to John Jay. I've got an idea I want to pursue. Then I'm off to Larry's hotel for the next round of 'Sloane Burbank, this is your life.'"

"What's the idea you're pursuing?"

Sloane's lips curved. Trust Derek to never miss anything, no matter how casually it was mentioned. "I'll tell you if and when it becomes a reality. In fact, given this particular idea, you'll be the first one I call."

"Ah, I sense I'm being used."

"Maybe a little. Then again, if you come through for me, I could arrange to use you in ways you'll really, really like." Sloane could almost hear Derek's body react.

"Now, *that* got my attention," he announced. "Although you do know that you're blackmailing and sexually harassing a federal agent."

"True. But I'm also giving him an amazing fantasy to savor. And, trust me, the reality will far exceed it."

"Promise?"

"Scout's honor."

"Then I'm putty in your hands."

* * *

It was just before three when Sloane knocked on Elliot's office door.

"Come on in," he called in his usual distracted, working voice.

Sloane walked in. "Hey, stranger."

"Hey, Skippy." Elliot swiveled around in his chair, folding his hands behind his head.

Sloane made a face at the reference to her old high school nickname. Always on the run, always attuned to an athlete's need for protein and electrolytes, she'd been a big fan of peanut-butter-and-banana sandwiches. Elliot and his braniac friends had found this hilarious. They'd nicknamed her "Skippy" as a poke at her peanut butter of choice.

"Very funny," she retorted now. "News flash—maybe if you'd eaten more peanut butter and less Dunkin' Donuts, you wouldn't have been such a weenie at our Krav demonstration."

"Point taken—although, for the record, I've switched to Krispy Kremes. They're high in endorphins. I'm never happier than when I'm eating them." Elliot took her retaliatory barb right in stride. "Actually, I feel honored that Nancy Drew took off a few minutes to see me."

"I *like* seeing you—usually," Sloane added wryly, her lips twitching at the old familiar banter. "As for Nancy Drew, she had it easy. She handled one case at a time. I've been flung into a snake pit."

"Sounds appealing."

"It's exhausting. I wouldn't mind if I were seeing results. But each day seems to provoke new questions, and yield no answers." All humor having vanished, Sloane shot Elliot a quizzical look. "How are you holding up?"

"I'm fine," Elliot assured her. "Honestly. I've gotten used to reporters jabbering outside. As for Cynthia, I realize it looks bleak, but I'm not giving up. I've said a few prayers for her. I still believe in those, you know. Weird for a tech guy, huh?"

"Nope. I believe in them, too. And I'm an ex–FBI agent. Prayers are sometimes all we've got." Sloane shut the door behind her with a firm *click*, and sat down in the chair across from Elliot's desk.

"Uh-oh." A wary expression crossed his face. "We're not talking about prayers anymore. And you're not just here to say hi. What's up?"

"What does that mean? I told you the truth—I've been thinking about you, and worrying about how you were doing. Plus, I miss hanging out with you and trying to understand 'geek speak.' "

"I'm sure that's true. And, for the record, I missed you, too. But those aren't the only reasons you're here. You never shut my door so emphatically. Not unless you have something confidential to discuss—which usually involves a topic I'm not going to like."

Sloane began to laugh. "Nice observation," she said. "Ever think of writing a software program to analyze body language?"

"Nope." Elliot's gaze flickered briefly to his computer screen. "I'll leave the people reading to you. I've got my hands full. Between my classes and my research, I'm toast." He jiggled his mouse, and when the LCD monitor came to life, he clicked on the results window. Briefly, he glanced at it. "This project is turning out to be even more challenging than I expected. It's literally taking over my life. I doubt I'd be good for much else."

"How about expanding the scope of your project? Are you up for that? Because that's why I shut the door." Sloane grinned as she saw surprised interest glint in Elliot's eyes. "See? When I shut the door *emphatically,* it's not always to bring up a topic you don't like."

"You win. What kind of expansion are you talking about?"

Sloane inhaled sharply. "First, I need your word that this conversation is confidential. Everything that's said *must* stay between us."

"Done."

"Next, I want you to understand that this whole idea I'm about to broach is mine and mine alone. For now, it's also strictly hypothetical. I haven't mentioned it to a soul, and when and if I do, we'll need to get a lot of approvals to make it happen. *If* it's feasible for it *to* happen. That's the part only you can answer. Is my idea within the realm of possibility, or is it a great concept but a millennium away from becoming a reality?"

"I won't know till I hear it. And I'm listening." Elliot shifted in his seat, rife with surging adrenaline. He diffused it by getting up, grabbing two bottles of water from his minifridge, and handing one to Sloane as he sank back down.

"Thanks." She twisted open the cap and took a swig. "I'm not privy to the details of your research. Partly because they're sensitive and classified, and partly because I wouldn't understand what you were talking about if you told me. But I do remember the project involves identifying traits of cybercrime in a sea of financial transactions. Your program is designed to recognize hard-to-detect patterns in seemingly unrelated data. I also remember a particular high school buddy of mine who had grand dreams of using his remarkable talents to contribute to society in a major way. I think saving lives would fill that bill, wouldn't it?"

Sloane didn't need Elliot's response. It was written all over his face.

"So here's my hypothetical question," she concluded. "Could your system do the same thing for violent crimes that it's doing for cybercrime? If I provided you with a slew of unrelated facts, could your program find patterns that we human investigators might miss? Patterns that could, say, lead us to a serial killer?"

Elliot stared at her for a moment, his eyes blinking rapidly as his mind raced. "Wow. When you think big, you really think big." He rubbed his jaw. "In other words, you'd supply me with facts and hunches on all the cases, I'd feed them into my program, and we'd see what linkages emerge."

"That's the gist of it."

"Obviously, we're talking about the pig who kidnapped Cynthia Alexander." Elliot rolled his pen between his fingers. "According to the information being leaked by the press, the daughter of that big-time cardiologist, Dr. Ronald Truman, was kidnapped last April by the same wack job who kidnapped Cynthia. I figured it was all hype. But now that you're using terms like *serial killer*, I have to wonder. Is it true? Is Dr. Truman's daughter another one of this guy's victims?"

"I believe so, yes." Sloane nodded. "I'm very limited in what I can say—at least for now. But we do have circumstantial evidence linking the crimes."

"*We?*" Elliot echoed. "Are you involved in that investigation?"

"Penny Truman was my dearest childhood friend. You didn't know her because she went to a different high school than we did. But I've known her since grade school. So, yes, I'm privy to certain aspects of the ongoing investigation."

Elliot stopped rolling his pen. "In other words, you were hired by either her parents or the FBI to help find her."

"No comment."

"That's all the comment I need."

Sloane took another gulp of water, carefully weighing what she said. She was walking a fine line between relating what was publicly available and revealing privileged information.

"I'm sure you read about Tina Carroll," she continued.

"That student at The College of New Jersey who was attacked on campus, but who kicked her assailant's ass? You bet I did. Good the hell for her."

"I agree. Well, thanks to that ass kicking, the offender's DNA was found at the crime scene. It was recently matched to the DNA left at Southern New Jersey Medical Center by whoever killed the head nurse and stole drugs from her station."

"Shit." Elliot paled. "You weren't kidding when you said you were talking about a serial killer. Are there other victims?"

Another nod. "Some actual, some potential."

"Potential? You mean, you've identified women who could be next on his list?"

Sloane raised her hand. "Present and accounted for."

"You?" Elliot jolted upright.

"Me." Briefly, Sloane told him about her stalker, about the cell phone found at Tina's crime scene, and about the fact that someone had broken into her house—someone whose DNA matched the DNA found at the other crime scenes she'd just described.

"Shit," Elliot repeated, sinking back into his chair.

"That's about all I can ethically tell you—for now," Sloane concluded.

Elliot's jaw tightened, and he slid forward, elbows propped on the desk. Sloane could almost see the apprehensive geek transform into the determined scientist.

"What's your theory on how the cases are related?" he asked.

"For starters, all the victims we're trying to find or protect are somehow connected to me. And all in random ways—from a close friendship to a college junior whose interests and lifestyle up to this point closely mimic mine. How do you feed a piece of data like that into VICAP? You can't. It's too abstract. And here's another equally abstract reality that VICAP wouldn't know what to do with—all the victims were kidnapped in close proximity to bodies of water on or near college campuses. Whoopee. Seventy percent of the earth is water. So, real as that information is, it's totally useless. We don't have a way to take these obscure facts and do something with them. Do you?"

"Actually, yes." Elliot didn't miss a beat. "What you're describing is exactly what my program aims to accomplish.

In layperson's terms, it combines the ability of the brain to find patterns in seemingly unrelated data with a computer's ability to rapidly analyze mountains of data. The result is to uncover criminal activity long before its impact becomes devastating, either in monetary losses, damaged reputations, or empowerment of organized criminal enterprises—or, worst case scenario, terrorists."

"You said 'aims to accomplish,'" Sloane repeated. "Is your program capable of doing that yet? Have you developed it to the point where such results are attainable?"

"I've run a few tests on data sets with known outcomes. The results have been encouraging. I'm still fine-tuning the program so it can dynamically adapt to each specific set of data and yield the most precise outcome. But that's not what you're asking. What you're really asking is, can I adapt my program to analyze your particular set of information and find patterns in the victimology, maybe even links to the offender himself."

"Okay, fine." Sloane waved her hand impatiently. "That's what I'm asking."

"The answer is, I won't know until I try. My opinion? I think it's more than possible. I'll need to define new variables, get a complete, detailed rundown of every victim, and of the offender himself—including characteristics you either know or suspect about him, and their relative weightings. I'd also need every unrelated but significant bit of data you collected, and access to the major law enforcement databases—VICAP, CODIS, and RTCC, given the NYC crimes. Between all that, plus some additional programming on my part, we should have what we need. In many ways, both analyses are similar. We know there's a needle in the haystack. The question is, how fast can we find it? So, in a long-winded way, I'd have to say yes, I'm cautiously optimistic that we can do this."

Sloane knew Elliot. He was hard as hell on himself. So if he thought he could pull this off, that was good enough for her. "How long would it take to get results, and what kind of access would you need?" she pressed him.

He thought for a minute. "I'd say about ten days. Most of the work would involve building interfaces between VICAP, CODIS, RTCC, and my system." Elliot paused, a frown knitting his brows. "Hypothetically, I could start the process while you get the authorizations and the right people on board."

"Getting you those authorizations would be my job to accomplish." Sloane grimaced. "It isn't going to be fun."

"But I do have project contacts at the FBI, NYPD, and NSA, and the necessary security clearances for working cybercrime, for whatever that's worth. They know me and my work well. I can call in a few favors—prime the pump, so to speak. I'll give you the names of my contacts so you can work them along with the powers that be for access to the crime data I'll need. I'll call my contacts, too, and give them a heads-up to maximize the chances of getting the decision makers on board quickly."

"That would be great. Hey, every little bit helps."

"Doing this would be amazing." A note of pride crept into Elliot's voice. "I'd be using my program to help catch violent criminals early in their crime spree. We wouldn't have to wait for enough time and victims to pile up so that law enforcement could establish the investigative trail they'd need to find and convict bastards like this one. I could be directly saving lives, not just eliminating the money that enables the killers."

"Yes, you could." Sloane studied Elliot's expression, heard the conviction in his tone. "This isn't hypothetical anymore, is it?" she asked bluntly.

"Nope." His response was equally blunt. "Not if you can get the right people on board, it isn't."

Sloane shot him a wry look. "Have you ever known me not to get what I want?"

"Not even once."

"Well, I don't intend to start now." Sloane rose, reaching across Elliot's desk and extending her hand, ready to seal the deal. "I'll get started on my end right away. Are you in?"

Elliot didn't hesitate. He clasped Sloane's fingers in a firm handshake. "You bet your sweet ass I am."

TWENTY-FIVE

DATE: 21 April
TIME: 0700 hours
OBJECTIVE: Persephone and Demeter

The weekend was a total success. I was brilliant. The gods were with me. Their cheers drowned out the shouts of the demons. The demons can no longer stop me. Nor can the mortals. The gods won't permit it. They'll never again question my allegiance. And, in a matter of days, they'll guide me and the goddesses to Mount Olympus.

I have Demeter and Persephone. That was my major triumph.

I arrived at Penn State right on schedule. Professor Helen Daniels and her daughter, Abby, followed their customary Sunday routine. They attended church, then stopped at Stone Valley Recreation Area for a picnic, followed by an ambitious hike around Lake Perez.

I'd memorized the wooded, deserted section they'd pass and at what time they'd pass it. The rest was easy. Both women were slight, so it was easy to keep them quiet while the hypodermics did their job. Besides, they were so terrified by the combat knife that they scarcely made a sound.

I put them in a room together to accelerate their adjustment. It was the right thing to do. The proximity would give

Demeter a chance to calm her child. Persephone would reap the benefits that only a mother could provide, and Demeter would draw comfort from that fact. Together they would soothe each other, which would swiftly and ultimately help them accept their fate.

Everything was almost ready. I had only to settle Gaia and—at long last—claim my Artemis.

Office of Professor Elliot Lyman
John Jay College of Criminal Justice
New York City
8:10 A.M.

After a sleepless night, Elliot left his East Village apartment at dawn, hopped on the subway, and made his way to Columbus Circle, where he got out and walked the two blocks to John Jay.

The sun was still rising and the halls were deserted when he unlocked his office. Most people would probably think he was nuts for being so obsessed with this project. But with his initial work complete, and just a little more tweaking before he'd be ready to test his system, he was champing at the bit.

Sloane had come through, just as she'd said she would. Her FBI colleague, Special Agent Derek Parker, had kicked in, working hard and fast with some of Elliot's contacts at the Bureau to navigate the back channels of the Department of Justice so Elliot could gain access to VICAP and CODIS.

The NYPD had been a tougher sell. It had taken days of lobbying—not only by Elliot and by Sergeant Erwin—but by Erwin's captain at Midtown North, to pull off the coup of getting Elliot access to the Real Time Crime Center. Given that the RTCC was the NYPD's enormous data warehouse of criminals, arrest records, and public records, the top brass at Puzzle Palace was less than enthused about handing over full access to a computer professor.

Midtown North's lobbying had been a great help. Then

again, the groundswell of negative publicity surrounding Cynthia Alexander's disappearance from John Jay, and the mayor's daily calls to the police commissioner, pressuring him for answers, hadn't hurt either.

Now Elliot leaned back in the chair at his workstation with a sigh of relief. Just yesterday, with the help of a trusted grad student, he had digitized the last of the remaining police case files into crime description profiles—a detailed collection of facts, figures, and descriptions about each crime. Last night before heading home, Elliot had typed the cryptic command to run the load script and fill his system's database with years of violent crime data on rapes, murders, and assaults. The process had taken all night to complete on its own. Perfect timing. He'd walked in just after it finished. He'd then spent the past two hours double-checking and fine-tuning.

It was now time to test the latest refinement of his life's work.

With great anticipation, Elliot typed in three simple words: *find related crimes,* and then pressed the enter key. It would be hours before any results were displayed. And his meeting with Sloane, the FBI, and the NYPD wasn't happening until one o'clock. So, rather than sit here and drive himself crazy, he grabbed his jacket and decided to walk up to the Krispy Kreme on West Seventy-second Street. He'd buy a couple of dozen donuts for himself and his grad students, and then head up to Central Park, where he could sit at the lake, eat, and think.

Any way you sliced it, this was going to be a very long day.

Hunterdon County, New Jersey
10:15 A.M.

"Don't you *ever* need sleep?" Sloane mumbled, stuffing her face in the pillow.

Derek grinned, moving her hair aside so he could kiss her neck. "When you're in bed next to me? Not a chance."

Sloane cracked open one eye and glanced at the clock. "It's after ten. Weren't you supposed to go through your Army Ranger workout at the crack of dawn, or at least do some push-ups or something?"

"I did my whole workout at five when you were out cold. But I could definitely go for some more push-ups." His palm ran down her side, over her hip, and across her thigh, his fingertips making lazy circles toward his goal. "By the way," he muttered. "I gave the hounds a two-mile run. So if they complain, they're lying. Ignore them. I, on the other hand, am still enjoying being used. You did promise to outdo my fantasy with your reality. You made a nice dent last night. But then you conked out. Which means you still owe me. So pay up."

Laughter bubbled up in Sloane's throat, and she rolled onto her back, gazing up at him. "You're impossible."

"It's one of my best qualities."

"No, that would be your stamina." Sloane's palms glided over his biceps, then across his hair-roughened chest, and down to his six-pack abs. "Mmm. I can feel the burn. Good workout."

"Thanks." He caught her hand and dragged it down his torso, right to where he wanted it. "Now *I* can feel the burn."

"A mere spark," she assured him, her eyes glinting. "I'm just getting started. You'll go up in flames before I'm through. After all, I did say scout's honor."

"Yeah, you did." Derek gritted his teeth as she teased him with her fingertips, her touch feather light—and right on target.

"Were you a Girl Scout?" he managed.

"Mm-hmm." Sloane repeated the motion, this time intensifying the friction. "For years and years."

Derek arched, his entire body rigid. "Thank God."

The foreplay lasted as long as either of them could withstand it. Then Derek hooked his arms under her knees,

lifting and opening her as wide as possible, and pushed all
the way inside her—and then some.

He was going for amazing.

It was better.

Banter vanished. The only sounds in the room were
harsh groans, ragged breathing, and the creaks of the bed
frame, which kept getting louder and faster with each stroke,
until the headboard was slamming against the wall.

Neither of them heard it.

Derek pinned Sloane to the bed with the full weight of
his body, his thrusts deep and primal, his chest heaving
with each breath. Sloane wrapped her legs high around his
waist, meeting him thrust for thrust, as their climax roared
down on them.

A split second before he came, Derek grabbed Sloane's
hands, lifted them high over her head, and interlaced his
fingers with hers. She didn't fight it. She didn't pull away.

She didn't want to.

Her grip tightened in his as the first spasms of her orgasm wrenched through her. She cried out, convulsing
again and again as Derek spurted into her, coming as violently as if he hadn't done so just a handful of hours earlier.

The whole experience was overwhelming—far more
than Sloane had wanted it to be. Not just the sex, but what
went with it. Emotions were starting to get tangled up in
whatever was going on between them. Then again, maybe
those emotions had never gone away. Maybe the two of
them were playing out some elaborate charade that was
more avoidance than it was reality. If that was the case . . .
well, right now Sloane wasn't ready to think about it. And
she certainly wasn't ready to talk about it.

Obviously, neither was Derek. His muscles relaxed, and
he sank onto her and into her—blanketing her body with
his, and emitting a wiped-out groan that sounded as if he'd
survived a shipwreck.

Still trembling with aftershocks, Sloane managed a weak smile. "Can I take that groan to mean 'paid in full'?"

"You can take it to mean I think I'm dead."

"You're not. I can vouch for that."

"Good to know." Derek's voice was muffled, his face buried in the curve of her shoulder. Their fingers were still intertwined and neither of them made any attempt to change that. "You're so damn sexy," he announced drowsily. "I go crazy when I'm inside you."

"I noticed." A pause. "I go crazy, too."

"I know." He left it at that, then gave a huge yawn. "Nap time."

"No, get ready for meeting time," Sloane reminded him.

Another groan. "Let's send proxies instead."

Laughter rippled through Sloane. It felt good to laugh, and to feel so languid and vibrant all at once. The past few weeks had been one long, frustrating uphill battle. And now they had two more abductions thrown in the mix. A professor and her daughter. Kidnapped from Sloane's alma mater.

Today's meeting was going to be long, tough, and intense.

"Given all that's going on, I doubt proxies would work," Sloane informed Derek. "But you get points for trying." She wriggled a bit. "I need a shower. So, by the way, do you."

"Two minutes." His voice told her he was drifting off. "And, no, not paid in full. Paid for now."

"For now?" Sloane blinked in disbelief. "After an all-night marathon, you want more? Dear God, I'm dealing with a sex machine *and* a loan shark."

"Yeah, but a hot one."

"I can't argue that. You *are* hot. Arrogant, but hot."

"Damn right." Derek's words were slurred and sleepy. "And that's a good thing. Because you're way too much for any other man to handle—in bed and out. I'm the only one qualified for the job."

Before Sloane could reply, her cell phone rang.

"Ah, shit," Derek muttered. "Let it go to voice mail."

"I can't. It could be about our meeting today."

"You're right." Rousing himself from his half sleep, Derek released one of Sloane's hands, reached over, and groped for the phone on the night table. "Just make it quick." He resettled himself on top of her.

"I will." Sloane took the phone. "But not so I can enhance your afterglow. We've got to get to the city."

"Okay, okay, you made your point."

Grinning at Derek's grumpy tone, Sloane punched on the phone. "Sloane Burbank," she said into the mouthpiece.

"Sloane? Hi, it's Luke. Did I catch you at a bad time?"

"No, not at all. It's good to hear from you." Sloane felt her gut knot a bit. Hopefully, Luke was calling with an update on Burt. She didn't want to think what else this call could be about.

"Are you sure?" he was asking. "It sounds like I woke you up."

"Nope. I've got a meeting I'm preparing for." She asked the dreaded question, wishing she didn't have to. "Your mother . . ."

"She's stable," he assured her quickly. "Fighting every step of the way, in fact. She's right here with me. I'm sure she'll attest to what I've said loud and clear."

Sloane got the message. Lillian was far from fine. Her cancer was in its final stages. But Luke certainly wasn't going to say that in front of her. He wanted to sound as upbeat as possible.

"However, I am calling on her behalf," he continued. "She wanted to call you herself, but she's in a bit of pain today."

"Please apologize to Sloane," Lillian called out in the background. From the sound of her voice, Sloane could tell that her "bit of pain" was actually a fair amount of pain. "I just don't understand how that mix-up could have happened," Lillian managed. "I'm so upset about it."

"What mix-up?" Sloane asked

"Your name." Luke drew a slow breath. He sounded so exhausted that Sloane's heart went out to him. "I know you're aware that my mother is retiring a little earlier than expected. Well, the college is holding a small party in her honor, right at John Jay, on April twenty-eighth, at seven P.M."

"Yes, I know. And I—"

"You know?" Luke interrupted. Now even *he* sounded upset. "That makes this even more embarrassing. You've worked with my mother for several years, served on a number of panels together. She has a tremendous amount of respect and admiration for you."

"As I have for her." Sloane was totally at sea.

"To be blunt, your name was inadvertently deleted from the guest list. I have no idea how. It was on the original; I saw my mother enter it before she e-mailed the attachment to the department secretary at John Jay. There was obviously a screwup when the invitations were mailed out. Somehow your name was missing. So you never got the invite. As you heard for yourself, my mother is mortified. She hopes you'll accept her apology and come to the party. I'll give you whatever specifics you need now, and a new invitation is already on its way."

Sloane blinked in noncomprehension. By this time, Derek was propped on his elbows, gazing quizzically down at her.

"Luke, I have no idea what you're talking about," Sloane said. "If there was a screwup, they obviously fixed it. I received my invitation on Saturday, and RSVP'd right away. Please tell Lillian that the only mix-up is what she saw on that final guest list. Of course I'll be there. I wouldn't miss it."

"That's great, and my mother will be delighted." Luke sounded as puzzled as Sloane. "Although, frankly, I'm not sure how this happened. I saw the final guest list. And your name was definitely omitted."

"I'll never understand computers. The printer might have cut off a line. Who knows? The important thing is, neither you nor your mother has anything to apologize for. I feel very included, and I'm honored to have been invited."

"Thank you, Sloane." Luke sounded very, very relieved. And given that he wasn't the emotional type, this incident had obviously thrown Lillian badly—which was the last thing she needed at a time like this. "I'll tell her right now. She'll feel much better."

"Tell me what?" Sloane heard Lillian ask.

"Everything's fine, Mother," he called back. "Sloane got her invitation, and she'll be at the party. I'll fill you in in a minute."

"Luke, I realize now's not the best time to talk," Sloane inserted quickly. "So I won't keep you. But before we hang up, thank you for what you did for Elsa and Burt. It's made a big difference to Elsa's state of mind—not to mention her health."

"I hope it helped Burt, too, even if just to make him feel a little more informed about his options, and in control of the situation," Luke replied. "He's not the easiest guy to talk to, or to read."

"You tried. That's all that matters."

"Let's hope so. Sometimes trying is good enough. Sometimes it's not."

Sloane swallowed hard. "I take it things have deteriorated at your end."

"More quickly than I expected," he responded, keeping his voice low so as not to upset Lillian. "I'm just taking it a day at a time, managing my mother's pain, and keeping our spirits up. Oh, and I've taken a leave of absence from work," he added, his voice returning to normal. "All these years, my mother and I have both been so immersed in our careers, we've scarcely seen each other. Now we can finally enjoy spending time together."

"You're an amazing son. I'm sure that brings Lillian a great deal of peace." Tears burned behind Sloane's eyes. "Why don't we catch up at the retirement party? That way we don't have to talk in code. And in the meantime, you can get back to your mother."

"I think that would be best. Right now you're obviously in

a time crunch. So go finish preparing for your meeting. You can fill me in on Elsa's progress at the retirement party."

"I hear you," Sloane replied. And she did. Luke was making it seem like it was *she* who was pressured to hang up. "By the way, tell Lillian I'm making that strawberry cheesecake she loves, and bringing it to the party."

"I'll do that." There was a wealth of gratitude in Luke's voice. "I'm sure it'll make her day. See you on the twenty-eighth."

Derek sat up the minute Sloane ended the call. "What was that about?"

Briefly, she explained.

"I'm sorry," he said gently. "I know how fond you are of Lillian."

"What can I say? Sometimes life sucks." Sloane blinked away her tears.

"You didn't tell me about her retirement party. Or that you were attending."

"Things have been kind of hectic around here, with two new abductions. I guess it slipped my mind."

"Not a problem." Derek's wheels were turning. "I assume this party will be small and intimate, with just the significant people in Lillian's work life there."

"I assume so." Sloane's brows drew together. "Where are you going with this?"

"To the party."

"Excuse me?"

"I'll be your date. That way, I can meet the people you interact with at John Jay, and give Hank the night off."

"So you'll be going as my bodyguard," Sloane clarified.

"Bodyguard *and* date."

She shot him a dark look. "I don't need a bodyguard. As for a date, this might surprise you, but most guys *ask* a woman for one of those. They don't announce it as a fait accompli."

"I seem to remember hearing that rule of etiquette somewhere." Derek shrugged. "Oh, well. I'm not most guys."

"No kidding." Sloane slid out from between the sheets and headed for the shower. "It's a good thing you're dynamite in bed," she called over her shoulder. "Otherwise, you'd be out of here on your ass."

"Thanks for the warning." Derek followed her into the bathroom. "As luck would have it, I'm also dynamite in the shower." He leaned past her, reaching into the tiled stall shower and turning on the water. "I'll give you a quick demonstration while we get ready for our meeting."

Conference Room 531T
John Jay College of Criminal Justice
New York City
1 P.M.

"Let's not waste any time," Derek proposed, glancing around the oval table where Sloane, Elliot, Bob Erwin, and Larry Clark were gathered. "We've got a ton of ground to cover. Everyone's here. Everyone's been introduced. There are two urns of coffee on the credenza, and two dozen bottles of water in the minifridge next to it." He waved his arm in that general direction. "Bill, how about you?" he asked, turning his head so his voice was aimed at the speakerphone. "Are you set?"

"Ready to go," Bill confirmed, projecting loud and clear from the BAU in Quantico.

"Good. Then let's get started." Derek flipped through his notes. "To begin with, C-6 has set up surveillance all over Chinatown in the hopes of catching our serial sexual killer, now dubbed 'The Butcher of East Broadway.'"

"Catchy name," Bob noted drily.

"Yeah, well, that catchy name is all we've got so far," Derek continued, scowling. "We've succeeded in relieving the gang pressure in Chinatown. And there've been no more murdered prostitutes—yet. But the local residents are nervous. So are the local business owners. The situation's strung tight as a bowstring. We're really hoping that our surveillance will spot this guy. It's our best chance of catching him, since he's more careless with his prostitutes than he is with his kidnapping victims. Especially this last time. In addition to his usual python coin, he graced us with a DNA sample."

Whipping out a press release, Derek continued: "Obviously, you're all aware that two more abductions took place on Sunday, both of which carried our Unsub's signature style. Just so we're all on the same page, here are the details."

He picked up the printout and read directly from it. "Dr. Helen Daniels and her daughter, Abby, were kidnapped sometime between eleven-thirty A.M. and three o'clock P.M. at Stone Valley Recreational Center, which is located fourteen miles from Penn State's main campus at University Park. Dr. Daniels is a professor of horticulture at the College of Agricultural Sciences. Her daughter, Abby, is a junior at the College of Liberal Arts, working toward a B.A. in crime, law, and justice."

"That's the same degree that Sloane . . ." Elliot started to blurt out the obvious, then fell silent.

"Correct," Derek told him. "Penn State is Sloane's alma mater, and her undergraduate degree is exactly the same as the one Abby Daniels is a little over a year away from receiving."

"I'm sorry I interrupted." Elliot's face was flushed.

"No apology necessary," Derek assured him. "Your point is well taken, and supports our theory that the Unsub is intelligent and well versed in the entirety of Sloane's life."

Elliot shot a quick, concerned look at Sloane, who was sitting straight and alert, displaying positively no emotion.

"Back to the kidnappings," Derek continued. "Helen and Abby Daniels had a weekly ritual of going to church Sunday mornings, then stopping at Stone Valley for a picnic followed by a hike on the trails of Lake Perez, a seventy-two-acre body of water at the recreation center. Abby was supposed to meet her boyfriend at his apartment around three o'clock. Her mother was expected home around the same time by her husband. Neither woman showed. Based on the kidnappings in New York and New Jersey, the campus police jumped right on it, and contacted the FBI field office in Philly. Agents from the State College RA were dispatched, and started an investigation in concert with the state and local police. Their search dogs led them to a wooded area off the hiking trail where there were definite signs of a struggle. Plus, the cops found two discarded hypodermic needles at the scene. The investigation is ongoing, but it's evident that our Unsub has struck again, making these two cases officially part of our task force."

"He's starting to unravel," Bill asserted from the other end of the phone. "He's making mistakes, getting careless enough to leave evidence behind. Also, he's moving out of his comfort zone, which, up until now, has been the New York/New Jersey area. Hopefully, all this will work to our advantage. Careless leads to capture."

"Agreed." Derek nodded. "Any other updates?"

"I have two," Larry announced. "In my investigation of the circumstances surrounding Lydia Halas's disappearance, I discovered enough unexplained coincidental details to support Sloane's theory. I'm convinced that Ms. Halas, too, was a victim of our Unsub."

"Great," Derek muttered.

Larry passed copies of a stapled report around the table. "In the interest of time, I wrote up the particulars. If anyone has questions, I'm available to answer them." He turned to Sloane. "My second update relates to that voluminous list of people we came up with, including just about everyone you've ever known. In checking out the names, I uncovered something involving Lauren Majors."

"Who's Lauren Majors?" Bob asked.

"My mortgage broker," Sloane responded. "She handled the details of my mortgage when I bought the summerhouse from my parents." A wary look crossed Sloane's face as she met Larry's gaze. "I'm almost afraid to ask. What did you uncover?"

"Lauren Majors disappeared on September twelfth of last year, during a visit to her sister at Rutgers University.

She was last seen walking along the Raritan River. The cops were swamped with cases at the time, so her sister chose to hire a PI instead. He came up empty. I retraced his steps, and, in my opinion, this wasn't a random disappearance. It was an abduction—one that fits the profile of our Unsub."

"I don't believe this." Sloane's veneer cracked a bit, and she raked a hand through her hair. "It's like this bastard has invaded every aspect of my life, and helped himself to innocent women along the way, simply because we crossed paths. Why? It makes no sense. Lauren and I barely knew each other. We met four, maybe five times."

"Since we can't answer that—at least not yet—and since we all agree that until we do, you're in perpetual danger, we've elicited Professor Lyman's assistance." Derek's tone and expression were grim. "Everyone here has been briefed on the professor's artificial intelligence system. I'll let him supply us with the details." A nod in Elliot's direction. "The floor's yours, Professor."

Elliot had been furiously taking notes as everyone around him shared facts, observations, and gut reactions. More and more he realized the awesome responsibility he held in his hands. This was no longer about proving the merits of his system. It was about saving lives—Sloane's included. He had no intention of failing.

Tamping down his nerves, he began.

"I realize that what I'm about to describe to you is going to sound like a reach. But every technological advance once fell into that category. All I ask is that you listen with open minds, and an awareness that none of this is meant to diminish the contributions of law enforcement."

With that, he went on to describe the basics of his system in a succinct and compelling manner, omitting as much "geek speak," as Sloane called it, as possible.

He concluded by saying, "My computer model emulates the mind of a great detective. I spent countless hours working with New York's finest to distill their knowledge, experience, and talent into my artificial intelligence system." A faint smile. "Even with their instincts dulled by six rounds of beer at 'choir practice,' the cops I worked with are better than any computer could ever be at solving crimes. But, as I said, with their input, I think my program comes close."

There were a few chuckles, after which Sloane asked Elliot about his progress.

"The data structure is almost complete," he replied. "I'll format the last of the information from this meeting and enter it tonight. From there, I expect to have to fine-tune the system—respond to its questions for direction, provide more information as needed. I can't promise how long all this will take, and I can't promise where it will lead us. But my hope is that it will be in the direction of the killer."

Elliot paused, glancing from person to person. "And, should any of you still think is a bunch of crap, remember that it's only serving as an augmentation to your classic ongoing investigation. Therefore, we have nothing to lose."

"I can't argue with that one," Bill's voice resounded through the speaker phone. "I say go with it."

"I agree." Bob Erwin nodded. "I was one of the cops whose brain Elliot picked. He's a brilliant guy. And nothing he's doing is like a scene out of *Alien Encounters*."

Everyone chuckled at that one, and the light moment dissipated some of the tension in the room.

"Elliot's point is well taken. We do have nothing to lose," Larry said. "The rest of us will continue our investigation while Elliot runs his. It doesn't matter who comes out ahead. We all have the same goal—catching this serial killer."

"So we're in agreement," Derek concluded. "We have our marching orders. Let's schedule a follow-up meeting."

"Lillian's retirement party is the twenty-eighth," Sloane noted. "Let's avoid that date since several of us are attending."

"I'm off-site and unreachable all day on the twenty-ninth," Bill supplied. "Does the thirtieth work for everyone?"

"We'll make it work," Derek stated flatly. "Same time and place?" He looked around the room for reaction.

Everyone voiced their assent.

"Maybe the meeting will be unnecessary," Sloane murmured, not sure whether she was trying to convince everybody else in the room or herself. "Maybe by then, Elliot's system will have nailed the guy."

"Maybe." Derek's jaw was tight. "But until then, we're tightening security around you."

Office of Professor Elliot Lyman
John Jay College of Criminal Justice
New York City
9 P.M.

It had been a long day, punctuated by the sheer number of donut crumbs sprinkled around Elliot's computer, not to mention in between the keys on his keyboard.

The meeting had finished up around four o'clock, after which Elliot had stayed on to talk to Sloane about the Penn State kidnappings, and to thrash around ideas on a search strategy for his program.

It was close to 5:30 by the time he got back to his office. He was operating on overload from all he'd ingested and all he'd explained, not to mention that he was worried sick over Sloane's safety.

He needed time alone to recoup.

He'd shut his office door, taken two aspirin, and closed his eyes for a power nap. After that, his plan was to stuff a jelly donut down his throat for the energy boost he needed to get back to work.

He must have fallen into a deeper sleep than he'd intended.

He jumped up with the sense that too much time had passed. Sure enough, the clock on his desk said 8:40. Dammit. Three hours lost.

Automatically he checked his computer screen. Nothing yet.

Following his earlier plan, he made the rest of the Krispy Kremes his dinner. That did the trick. His mind jolted awake from the sugar high, and he was alert and ready to work.

Abruptly, the results window of his system popped up, displaying an early success using the test data he'd provided:

> *Strong linkage. Rapes reported March 13, June 23,*
> *September 3. Victims African-American women, ages*
> *20, 27, and 30. Locations: Cypress Hills Houses,*
> *Blake Avenue, East New York section of Brooklyn,*
> *New York. Edenwald Houses, East 229th Street,*
> *Bronx, New York. 143rd Street, Jamaica, Queens.*

These crimes were over three years old. The NYPD had arrested the perpetrator just six months ago. Imagine if they'd been able to solve the crime in three months rather than three years. How many women had that SOB raped in the intervening period? How many victims might have been spared the lifetime scars caused by this traumatic violation?

Elliot's thoughts were interrupted by words scrolling across the screen: *Press Y to continue, N to Start a New Operation.* He typed *N* and pressed the enter key.

The latest kidnappings had been entered into the database.

> *Professor Helen Daniels and her daughter Abby. Two*
> *simultaneous victims. Lake near a college campus.*
> *Hypodermic needle. State College, Pennsylvania.*

Carefully, Elliot checked his notes from the marathon debriefing this afternoon one last time, and circled the final key piece of information to enter. It was a tentative profile of the "Unsub"—as Sloane referred to him in FBI speak—that had been developed by the BAU. Carefully, Elliot added the target profile to his system.

White male. Mid-to-late thirties. Probably a loner. Can't establish normal sexual relationships with women. Aberrant behavior most likely rooted in warped sense of male/female relationships developed during childhood. Targets prostitutes as high risk, high-visibility victims. Either eldest son or only child. Strong belief that he is more intelligent than the masses and exempt from social restrictions. Possible military background, stationed in the Far East. Knowledge of Mandarin and Fukienese. Chosen homicide method—cutting/stabbing/slashing. Copper coin with python on one side and goddess on the other left at each crime scene.

Satisfied that all the information had been properly structured, Elliot typed in the phrase: *constrain results using Skippy as target.*

Despite his worry over Sloane's safety, he had to grin. She'd punch him out for using her nickname. Maybe that's why he'd done it. Maybe he was grasping for something comforting, a touch of humor to cling to as the only semblance of humanity in this nightmarish ordeal.

The system responded: *constraining results using Skippy as target.*

Elliot then entered the final command: *find relationships using victims.*

The status window displayed: *thinking . . .*

There was no point in sitting here, gaping at the screen in anticipation. The truth was, Elliot had no idea how long it would take his system to generate results. It could be hours, days, weeks before anything materialized. *If* anything materialized at all. He shoved that thought aside with a shudder. No way. He had to think positive.

The system's progress would need to be monitored 24/7. A schedule had been created and posted online, with Elliot and his two most trusted grad students taking turns watching. Elliot would have his cell phone on at all times. Anything that showed up was to be reported to him immediately. The process was complicated. Sometimes the system presented a single search path, other times it presented multiple ones. In the case of the latter, decisions would have to be made—one branch, another branch, or all branches. Sloane and the team would provide the investigative instincts. Elliot would be responsible for the rest.

Time was of the essence.

So was getting it right.

CHAPTER TWENTY-SIX

DATE: 28 April
TIME: 0800 hours

The anointment room has been scoured and readied.

The goddesses themselves feel the excitement in the air. They don't understand what its cause is, but they will. Each of them has so completely transformed into her namesake that all their passages will be peaceful and natural. That's as I intended it. I'm proud that I've done such a splendid job. I'd feared for Gaia. Now that fear is gone.

I'd also feared that Demeter and Persephone had arrived here too late to adapt to what was to come. Their progress astounds me, as does Demeter's knowledge of plants, fruits, and vegetables and how they make the spirit grow and thrive.

What a profound contribution she'll make to Mount Olympus as their new goddess of agriculture.

As for Persephone, she's like the onset of spring. Young, fresh, rife with promise. She reminds me so much of what Artemis must have been like at that age.

It pains me that I wasn't able to give Artemis this opportunity back then, when she was young and naive like Persephone is now. If things had been different, she wouldn't have had to waste her life in this ignoble wasteland. Like Persephone, she could have embarked on womanhood as a goddess, rather than battling her way through a mire of depraved mortals before arriving at her final destination.

I'll make it up to her. Here at New Olympus, I am Delphi. It's the perfect pseudonym. Delphi, Apollo's sanctuary, a shrine ultimately dedicated to him, but before that, to Gaia. Once I soar to the real Mount Olympus, I'll take my rightful place as Apollo himself. My first order of business will be to have an elaborate temple built for Artemis—one that far surpasses the Temple at Ephesus previously dedicated to her. Everyone will worship at her shrine, just as they'll worship Gaia at Delphi.

And I'll be joyful. Because no one could ever revere either of those two goddesses more than I.

Ascension is almost upon us.

New Olympus will be gone, having outlived its usefulness. Our souls will have long since separated from and risen above the vessels known as our bodies. Those vessels will have been consumed in a glorious funeral pyre, leaving nothing behind but ashes.

My temporary monument to the gods will be no more.

The dust—all that remains of each vessel—will be written up in law enforcement files, and, eventually, forgotten.

But the goddesses and I will live on throughout eternity.

Now all that's left is for me to bring Artemis here so she can take her rightful place among us.

Our enemies are still out there. Like the serpent Python, they're set on killing us, and preventing our passage into eternity.

They're fools. Nothing they do will matter. Artemis trusts me. She'll come willingly.

For now, we share our special connection in my dreams.

In mere days, we'll share it forever.

John Jay College of Criminal Justice
Multipurpose Room
New York City
7:05 P.M.

The austere, cafeteria-like room at John Jay College had been transformed into a warm party room. Dusk was just filtering in through the windows, creating a social aura rather than an academic one. Strains of classical music drifted through the room, which was filled with festive decorations, bowls of punch, platters of hors d'oeuvres, and trays of hot dishes. The setting seemed more like a private dining room at an exclusive club than an all-purpose room at a city college.

Twenty or so people—mostly faculty members, law enforcement colleagues who taught workshops at John Jay, and a few of Lillian's close friends—were milling around, chatting and helping themselves to the food.

"This is lovely," Sloane murmured as she and Derek hovered in the doorway. The party was business casual, so Sloane was dressed in a bright aqua silk blouse and black silk pants. And Derek was wearing a blue striped dress shirt, unbuttoned at the collar, and navy slacks.

"It certainly is." He voiced his agreement with a nod. But his penetrating midnight gaze was already scrutinizing the room's occupants. "The school did a great job. And this private room is very conducive to keeping a close eye on things."

"Derek, our Unsub isn't a moron," Sloane muttered drily. "He's not going to burst into a public place, club me over the head, and carry me off. So could you please stop looming in the doorway like a mountain lion about to tear someone's throat out?"

Derek relaxed, and his lips twitched at her analogy. "Point taken. I'll leave the mountain lion at the door." Another quick glance around, this time more relaxed and friendly. "Do you know everyone here?"

"Not even close." Sloane shook her head. "A few casual acquaintances from my visits and workshops here."

"There's Elliot." Derek tipped his chin in the direction of the buffet.

"Predictably standing next to the food," Sloane noted, following Derek's gaze. "The attractive redhead he's talking to is Lucy Andrews. She's a professor here in the sociology department, like Lillian. The two of them also coinstruct a Gender Studies course called Sex and Culture." A pause, filled with sad realization. "I'm not sure if she'll cancel the class now or run it alone."

"She looks like a take-charge kind of woman. My guess is she's perfectly capable of handling the course alone—if she chooses to."

Derek's frank remark caught Sloane off guard. She wasn't sure how to interpret it, and she angled her head to gauge his reaction. "Do you want to meet her?" she asked offhandedly. "She's smart, single, and just broke up with her boyfriend. Could be a match made in heaven. So what do you say? Shall I make the introductions?"

One dark brow arched. "Not amusing. And not interested."

"Too bad. She'll be impressed when I tell her you're an FBI agent. And she'll be *really* impressed if you show her your Glock."

"Tempting." Derek shrugged, with a glint of humor in his eyes. "I don't need to flaunt my assets. Any way you slice it, I'm an impressive guy. Women just can't keep their hands off of me. It's a curse. But I'm learning to live with it." He chuckled as Sloane jabbed him in the ribs with her elbow. "You asked for that one."

"Maybe. But that doesn't mean I have to like your answer."

"True." Derek pressed his palm into the small of her back, guiding her into the room. "You know," he commented. "That reaction of yours sounded a lot like jealousy.

Come to think of it, so did that whole speech about the redhead."

"Don't flatter yourself."

"I'm not. I'm just making an observation—one that happens to be a real turn-on, by the way." Lightly, he caressed her back, his fingers warm against the cool silk of her blouse.

Sloane couldn't help the inadvertent shiver that ran through her. She felt it, and so did Derek.

"Yup, this party is definitely looking up," he declared. He steered her toward the buffet table. "Let's get some food and something to drink." A quick wink. "Once I'm fortified, I can charm throngs of women into bed. Punch?"

"Don't tempt me."

He chuckled. "Not me. That mysterious liquid stuff in the bowl. Do you want some?"

"Sure." Sloane wished that Derek's cavalier attitude didn't make her feel so irked. She wished she didn't give a damn whom he slept with. She just wished she didn't give a damn, period.

Derek leaned past her, ladling out two cups of punch. "Stop fuming," he murmured near her ear. "You're all I want. If you don't know that by now, then you're not just high maintenance, you're dense."

Sloane felt his words down to her toes—which irked her even more.

"Still pissy, huh?" Derek grinned as he handed her the punch. "If I play by your rules, you're pissed. If I tell you I want you, you're pissed. What you *really* want is *not* to want *me*. Well, that ain't gonna happen. So just give in to the inevitable."

"No."

"Fine. Your choice." With another offhand shrug, Derek handed her his glass of punch so he could reach around her to fill two plates with food. "There's just no satisfying you, Sloane Burbank," he said in a low, husky voice, his breath grazing her hair. "Except in bed. Now, *there* I seem to be getting straight A's."

"Say that any louder, and I might choke you," Sloane warned, accepting her plate of food and taking a pointed step away from Derek.

"I appreciate the warning. I'll keep my intimate comments to a whisper."

"Hey, you two." Elliot strolled over, his plate piled high.

"What, no Krispy Kremes?" Sloane inquired. "Your stomach might go into shock."

"Nah. Krispy Kremes are for work. *Real* food is for parties."

"Where's Lillian?" Sloane asked, her gaze darting from person to person.

"In the ladies' room. Luke's waiting outside for her." Elliot saw Sloane's expression, and gave her shoulder a reassuring squeeze. "Actually, it's a good day. I haven't seen Lillian so energetic in weeks. I think being the guest of honor agrees with her."

On cue, Luke wheeled Lillian into the room.

Sloane couldn't deny Elliot's words. Despite her pallor and obvious loss of weight, Lillian looked pain-free and in good spirits. She had Luke stop the wheelchair several times so she could talk with her guests. Then she spotted Sloane, and twisted around to tell Luke.

He managed a smile as he pushed his mother's wheelchair over to where Sloane, Derek, and Elliot stood.

If it was possible to age in a matter of days, Luke had done so. He looked positively haggard, as if he hadn't slept in weeks, with deeply etched lines around his eyes and a tight furrow between his brows. It hadn't been that long since Sloane had seen him, yet his shoulders were stooped as if he were carrying the weight of the world on them. Then again, maybe he was.

"Hey," he greeted her. "It's good to see you."

"Same here." She leaned forward to kiss his cheek. Then she bent down to do the same for Lillian. "You, my dear lady, look fabulous," she declared. "I'm not sure you should be allowed to retire."

"And I'm not sure I'm ready to leave," Lillian replied with the air of someone who'd made peace with death. "But God has other ideas. So I'll trust in His decision."

Silently, Sloane marveled at her courage. "Derek," she said aloud. "This awe-inspiring woman is tonight's honored guest, Dr. Lillian Doyle. Her escort, who also happens to be a friend of mine and a great guy, is her son, Luke." She gestured from Luke and Lillian to Derek. "This is Special Agent Derek Parker. We were colleagues in the FBI field office in Cleveland, and we've been working together on special cases here in the Big Apple."

"Now, *that* sounds intriguing." Lillian's eyes twinkled as she shook Derek's hand. "I'd love to ask you questions about those cases, since I find criminal investigations fascinating. But I know better. As Sloane has taught me over the years, everything is either confidential or classified. Both those words mean 'butt out.' "

Derek chuckled, reaching over to meet Luke's firm handshake. "We try to say it more diplomatically than that, but, yes, I'm afraid that comes with the job."

The twinkle vanished from Lillian's eyes. "Speaking of which, is there any news on Cynthia Alexander? Or is that question taboo?"

"It's not taboo," Sloane answered carefully. "You've read pretty much all there is to know in the newspapers. Leads are great—if they actually go somewhere. Right now they're not. But we're working on it."

"That must be driving you crazy," Luke commented. "Spinning in neutral isn't your virtue under the best of circumstances. And these are the worst."

"True," Sloane acknowledged. "I'm having a hard time with this. Especially when I have to update Cynthia's mother. The poor woman just wants news about her daughter. And I have nothing to offer."

"Now, *that's* not true," Luke countered. "I've seen you deal with people—even when the circumstances are more horrible and less hopeful than these. You have a way of getting through to them like no one else can."

"Thank you," Sloane replied with simple gratitude. "I hope you're right."

"He is," Derek affirmed curtly. "It's what made you such an incredible hostage negotiator, and an exceptional agent. And it's why your leaving was such a huge loss to the Bureau."

Sloane started, glancing up at Derek and blinking in surprise. He wasn't one to dole out compliments. And he sure as hell didn't want to open up this particular Pandora's box in public. So where was this coming from?

"Turning in her badge was a huge loss to Sloane as well." Poor Luke was walking straight into the minefield, unaware of the detonator he was about to step on. "You were still in Cleveland at the time, so you and your team probably didn't realize how torn up she was."

"Three surgeries and continuing physical therapy. Yes, I heard."

"I wasn't referring to her hand," Luke clarified. "Although she coped with enormous amounts of pain, and rarely uttered a complaint. No, what I was referring to was her life. She loved being an FBI agent. And suddenly her career was yanked out from under her. Starting over is never easy. But she pulled it off. She's got a will of iron."

"That I knew." Derek's tone was conversational, but his jaw was clenched so tight, Sloane wondered if it might snap. "Just as I knew about her reluctance to turn in her badge. What I didn't know was that you two were such close friends."

Internally, Sloane winced. She could actually feel Derek's surging testosterone, manifesting itself in primal male possessiveness. Not only was it totally unnecessary, but it was embarrassing and infuriating.

It was Elliot who came to her rescue. "It was easier for Sloane and me to stay such good friends. I have tons of her high school secrets stored away up here." He tapped his head. "If all else fails, I can resort to blackmail." He gave Sloane an affectionate hug. "So far, I haven't needed to. She's one hell of a friend."

"I agree." Luke's gaze flickered from Elliot to Derek. Clearly, he was groping for a way to clarify his friendship with Sloane, even as he struggled to get a handle on what the relationship was between her and Derek.

In the end, he opted to try forging a kinship with Derek. "Sloane mentioned that before you joined the FBI, you were an Army Ranger."

"Sure was," Derek confirmed.

"I served in the army, too, although nothing as elite as the Rangers. I was a combat medic, stationed at Camp Casey in South Korea. But I'll tell you, I got more training there than I did from all my anatomy and physiology classes and clinical experience combined."

"I can believe that."

"Enough army talk," Lillian said abruptly, reaching up to grip her son's arm. "I don't like reliving those days. I worried every moment Luke was overseas."

"Well, I'm right here now." Luke dropped the subject like a stone, hell-bent on not upsetting his mother. Instead, he glanced at his watch. "Time to take your pills," he informed Lillian, giving her shoulder a gentle squeeze. "I'll get you a glass of water and some food. You haven't eaten a thing since noon." He gazed questioningly at Sloane, Derek, and Elliot. "Can I get you anything?"

"Thanks, no. We're all set," Sloane assured him. "The food is fabulous and the punch is spiked just enough to give it a zing." She smiled. "But wait for my strawberry cheesecake. It'll blow the rest of the meal out of the water."

"I've been anticipating it all week," Lillian assured her.

"On that note, I'll be right back." Luke went off to get his mother her sustenance.

"Thanks for bailing me out," Sloane murmured to Elliot as he wolfed down his food. "I owe you one."

"So does Luke," he muttered back. "The poor guy was *way* out of his league, and he had no idea why. He just knew that Derek was about to deck him. Oh, and FYI—in case you're as clueless as Luke, let me spell it out for you. Derek is crazy about you."

"More like crazy."

"Okay, both."

Sloane and Elliot were laughing when Luke walked back over, carrying a glass of water and a plate of food.

"Did I miss something?" he asked.

"Only my making fun of Elliot's eating habits," Sloane hedged quickly. "The way he stuck his head in his plate, he looked like a horse devouring its oats."

This time, they all laughed.

"So what have you been up to, stranger?" Lillian asked Elliot, after dutifully taking the medication her son gave her and swallowing it down with some water. "I haven't seen you in a while."

"The usual. Slaving over my computer." Elliot grinned. "Although thanks to my high school buddy here, I'm getting the chance I always wanted. I'm turning my new computer system loose to help capture bad guys. It's a real rush." He winked at Lillian. "I'd love to share the details, but they're classified. Now, how cool is *that* to be able to say. I feel like a guest star on *Criminal Minds*."

Lillian's eyes widened. "Are you working on Cynthia Alexander's kidnapping case? Because everything I read suggests it's not an isolated abduction."

Elliot caught Derek's scowl. "No comment," he answered quickly "When it comes to what the FBI deems 'classified,' if you talk, they have to kill you."

A chuckle escaped Lillian's lips. "I can't let that happen. You're way too valuable. But I wish you luck." Her attention was captured by someone across the room, and surprised pleasure flashed across her face. "Speaking of law enforcement, there's Detective O'Donnelly. What a kind gesture on his part, coming to my party. He retired from the NYPD years ago. I'm sure he has better things to do than spend an evening with a bunch of academics."

"He's very fond of you, Lillian," Sloane said. "Remember the debate you had after our last workshop? He probably came to finish it." Sloane turned to Derek. "Jimmy O'Donnelly was with the SVU."

"We know each other," Derek replied, swallowing an hors d'oeuvre in two bites.

"Ah. Well, that saves me an introduction, then."

"Luke, I'd like to say hello. Would that be okay?" Lillian turned to gaze up at her son.

"No problem. I'll take your plate and your glass, and we'll cruise on over there."

"Thank you." She handed both items to him. "Will you excuse us?" she asked the rest of the group.

"By all means," Sloane answered for everyone. "We've already monopolized enough of your time."

"I appreciate that." Lillian waited while Luke slid her stemmed water glass into the mesh compartment of the seatback bag attached to her wheelchair. It was a wobbly fit, but it was anchored well enough for the short distance across the room. That done, he balanced her plate of uneaten food in his left hand and used his left forearm and right hand to steer the chair toward Detective O'Donnelly.

The water glass survived the trip.

The china plate did not.

Halfway across the room, a member of the catering staff blew by, jostling Luke's arm just enough to upset his balance.

The china plate toppled from his hand, spilling its contents, and striking the steel frame of the wheelchair as it fell.

The plate shattered into a half-dozen pieces, all of which flew out in different directions around the wheelchair. Luke grabbed for the broken pieces, deflecting them away from his mother. He actually caught two of the larger chunks in

his hand, then rapidly dropped them as the jagged edges
sliced his palm.

"Damn," he muttered as blood began oozing from the
resulting lacerations.

"Luke?" Lillian realized for the first time what had happened, and she pivoted around, her face white with distress.

"It's okay, Mother. They're just superficial." Instinctively, he calmed her, at the same time scanning the deep
slices in his palm to see if any fragments of china had broken off and were lodged in his hand.

"What can I do?" Sloane asked quietly, walking over,
and desperately trying not to lose it at the sense of déjà vu
that came over her as she stared at his lacerated palm.

"Just get me a few napkins and some water," he requested. "The cuts are clean. No pieces of glass. A little
direct pressure should stop the bleeding. I'll go to the men's
room and take care of it. Then I'll construct a makeshift
bandage and we can forget the whole incident."

Sloane hurried over to the table, grabbed a few napkins
and a glass of water, and brought them over to Luke. "Here."

"Thanks."

"Are you still bleeding?" Lillian asked anxiously.

"Nope." Luke lied through his teeth as the blood soaked
through the first napkin. "It's slowing down."

"Wash it with soap and water anyway." Lillian fumbled
through her purse, and handed Luke a compact first-aid kit,
complete with a bandage and a tube of Neosporin. "Then
use the Neosporin and bandage it up."

"Consider it done."

While Luke went off to tend to his hand, Elliot took
over, wheeling Lillian over to talk to Jimmy O'Donnelly.
She and Jimmy were in the middle of round two of their
heated debate, when Luke rejoined them.

"Thank God." Elliot rolled his eyes in mock exaspera-
tion. "I was afraid your mother and Detective O'Donnelly

were about to come to blows." A quick glance at Luke's neatly bandaged hand. "How's it doing?"

"Good as new," Luke assured him. "I'll take over from here."

"Great. Because my vibrating BlackBerry is telling me that I need to go to my office."

"Feel free. Everything here is under control."

Elliot made his way across the room, stopping near the entrance, where Sloane and Derek were involved in what was clearly a heated, and not amicable, conversation. "I'm dashing upstairs to my office for a quick check-in on our progress," he told them, waving his BlackBerry in the air. "If Deborah, my grad student, is holding up, I think I'll pack a doggie bag—including a whopping slice of your strawberry cheesecake—and go home to get some sleep. I've got the predawn shift. I want to be wide awake during my watch."

"Our follow-up meeting's coming up," Sloane remembered aloud.

"Don't remind me. I'm under enough pressure. My entire life has become watching that damn screen, praying for something useful to appear."

"You're doing everything you can," Derek assured him. "We all are. Something will break." He cleared his throat. "But in the meantime, I do have one mandate I need to reiterate and to stress. I know how psyched you are about applying your program to solve these crimes, but it's crucial that—"

"Yeah, I know, I shouldn't have shot off my big mouth," Elliot finished for him. "You're right, and I apologize. It won't happen again."

"Enough said," Derek replied. "Fortunately, you were pretty vague, and at least we're among friends."

"I appreciate your letting me off the hook." Elliot gave a self-deprecating grimace. "But from now on, mum's the word." His glance flickered from one of them to the other. "Now go ahead and resume your argument. If you don't hear from me, it means there's nothing to tell. I'll see you the day after tomorrow."

Four hours later, Elliot had polished off his doggie bag and was sound asleep, when there was a knock at the door of his apartment.

Half out of it, he shrugged into a robe and went to see what was up. As always, he peered through the keyhole, then opened the door with a groggy, puzzled expression.

"Did I forget something?" he asked, seeing his name typed on the large Tyvek envelope his visitor was carrying.

"Just to press the delete key." Shutting the door behind him, he reached into the envelope with one gloved hand, and extracted a large combat knife. "But not to worry," he said, madness glistening in his eyes. "I'll take care of that for you."

CHAPTER TWENTY-SEVEN

DATE: 30 April
TIME: 0600 hours

This drive never ceases to take my breath away.

The Kittatinny Mountains are exquisite in springtime. Lush, green, towering over the ground below. Gripping the steering wheel, I stare out the window, marveling at the countryside, and the sunrise over the mountains. I downshift, urging my car to climb the steepest incline—the mountain upon which, concealed by a thick cluster of trees, New Olympus stands.

I've made this trip hundreds of times over dozens of months. But this time is different. This time, Gaia and I are finally returning home for good.

My epic journey is almost complete. Like Odysseus before me, I will live on through the stories told about my glorious battles with the forces of evil. By the time the viperous FBI and their lesser messengers, the NYPD, find the shrine I created and left behind, Gaia, Artemis, the lesser goddesses, and I will be transported to Mount Olympus.

I'd let nothing and no one interfere with that.

Which is why I feel so fortunate that I discovered the new serpent that Python sent down to thwart me. I put an end to his poisonous scheme. Despite his cleverness, Python has failed. His messenger has died, knowing he'd lost, and knowing that virtue had prevailed. Like Python himself, the serpent he'd sent had been evil. And evil had to be eliminated.

And so it was.

I must keep a constant watch over Gaia. I won't tell her about Artemis—not yet. I'll let that be a surprise. Today, I'll awaken her only to acquaint her with her room, and to show her the panoramic view of the heavens that's hers to savor—first by day, then by night.

It's imperative that I infuse her with peace and joy so that her soul will soar with a sense of rightness when the moment comes for her to slip tranquilly from this world into eternity.

Once she's settled in, everything will be in place.

And we'll have only to wait for Artemis to join us.

FBI New York Field Office
26 Federal Plaza, New York City
7:45 A.M.

Derek got the call from Bob Erwin just as he was sitting down to go over his notes and drink his third cup of morning coffee.

He heard only the basics. They were enough. He felt as if he'd been flattened by a steamroller. Slowly, he lowered his cup to the desk, where his coffee sat, forgotten, turning from hot to lukewarm to cold, as Bob provided the details, filling him in on the when, where, and how—which clearly added up to the who.

Derek already knew the why.

"The Crime Scene Unit is already there collecting evidence," Bob concluded. "They didn't know the homicide was part of a federal investigation until they found my card on his desk, and called me. Sorry about that."

"Not important. I don't stand on ceremony. Just contact them and tell them I don't want the M.E.'s office to move the body until I get there."

"Already done. No one's been inside the apartment except the responding officers, the EMTs, the detectives from the Ninth Precinct, and Crime Scene, who've now sealed the place off. They all know you're the case agent in charge. No one else is going into the apartment until you get there."

"Good." Derek was whipping out a pen and pad. "What's the address and the apartment number?" He scribbled it down. "I'm on my way."

"Derek?" Bob inserted quickly. "How do you want to handle this with Sloane? Obviously, she hasn't been notified. I thought you might want to be the one to—"

"I'll tell her." Derek rubbed a palm across his face, thinking about Sloane. Yes, she was tough. Tough and strong. Nonetheless, this was going to be one of those life-altering moments she'd never forget, the kind that would change her forever. Derek had been in that place, and he knew. He also knew it sucked.

"She's home," he told Bob. "Probably preparing for the meeting that's now not going to happen. I don't want to deliver news like this over the phone. I'll drive straight there from the crime scene."

"The meeting—right. I almost forgot. I'll contact Bill and Larry to cancel. Besides, they need to know about this development anyway."

"Yeah." Derek was on his feet, ready to go. The Unsub was unraveling. Every minute that passed gave him more time to kill again. It also increased the risk that Sloane would find out what had happened from someone else.

That spawned another thought.

"What about the John Jay faculty?" Derek asked Bob. "Do they know?"

"Not yet. Only the grad student who called it in."

"Keep it that way until I've talked to Sloane."

"I'll give you as much time as I can. Call me as soon as you've broken the news. And, Derek, tell Sloane I—"

"I will." Derek placed the phone back in its cradle. As he grabbed his case file and his jacket, he asked himself the age-old questions about life and death that had no answers. Taking a gulp of cold coffee, he headed off.

"Hey." Jeff stopped him, and Derek turned, waiting while his partner walked over.

"What's up? You look like shit," Jeff stated, studying Derek's ashen complexion.

"I feel like shit." Briefly, Derek filled Jeff in. "I'm heading over to the crime scene now, and then to Sloane's."

"Anything I can do?" Jeff asked.

"Actually, yeah. Can you contact ERT for me? I need them at the crime scene ASAP." Derek's mind was racing, figuring out the fastest way to get his answers. And alerting the Bureau's Evidence Response Team was definitely step one. Since the NYPD's Crime Scene Unit had gone in first, the New York field office's ERT would work with them to expedite things. Then they'd take all the bagged evidence, bar-code it, and chopper it straight to the lab at Quantico for immediate processing.

Jeff gave a tight nod. "You do what you have to. I'll call ERT now. I'll also tell Tony what's going on. He'll pitch in to coordinate things at this end. Between the FBI, the NYPD, and the locals who are involved in the hunt, this SOB doesn't stand a chance. We'll find him."

"Yeah. I just hope we do it before his kill list gets any longer."

Hunterdon County, New Jersey
11:25 A.M.

Sloane refilled the hounds' bowls with fresh water. Then she made sure that all three of her "babies" were comfy and settled on the sofa with their blankets and toys. She'd like nothing better than to curl up with them, go to sleep, and skip the whole damned meeting.

There'd been no new developments. If there had been, Elliot would have called. The FBI and NYPD would have done the same. So that meant this "follow-up" meeting was going to add up to a big zero.

In the meantime, she hadn't slept in two nights. Between the ongoing emotional battle with Derek since the night of Lillian's party, and the uneasy feeling that something was wrong, she'd tossed and turned both nights. She felt lousy. Nothing with Derek was resolved. And the uneasy feeling wouldn't go away.

With a weary sigh, she looped her tote bag onto her shoulder, plucked her car keys off the kitchen counter, and left the house.

She locked the front door, turned around to head to the driveway—and promptly collided with Derek.

He caught her arm, which had automatically snapped into elbow-strike mode. "Back off, killer. It's just me."

"God, Derek, don't sneak up on me like that. You know my training, and my instincts. I could have broken your nose." Her muscles relaxed, and she raked a hand through her hair. "What are you doing here, anyway? Denny is right across the street, doing his job. The hounds are in constant attack mode, ready to tear out the throats of anyone who comes near me. I don't need an escort to Manhattan. And I don't want to charge into round three—or is it four?—of our argument over what an ass you made of yourself at Lillian's party."

"I'm not here for either of the above. The meeting's been postponed."

"Why?" Sloane demanded.

Derek drew a slow breath. "Can we go inside and talk? I'm limited on time, and I don't want to have this conversation outside."

Sloane took one look at his expression, heard the somber note in his voice, and her chest tightened. Whatever was going on, it was about to explain the uneasy feeling she'd been living with. She didn't ask questions. She just turned around and unlocked the front door, pushing it open.

The hounds, who'd already been dozing on the sofa, leaped up, rushing out to greet Sloane as if she'd been gone for a week rather than for three minutes. Then they spied

Derek, and raced over to jump all over him, demanding attention.

He squatted down, scratching their ears absently and waiting until they'd calmed down enough for him to do what he had to do. Then he rose, urging Sloane into the living room, and gently tugging on her hand until she was seated beside him on the sofa.

"What is it?" Sloane demanded, her body rigid as she faced him. "Whatever it is, it's bad. Derek, tell me."

He didn't mince words. It wouldn't soften the impact, and it would only prolong her agony.

"It's Elliot. He didn't show up at John Jay yesterday—not for his office hours, not for his shift monitoring the AI system, not even a phone call to check on its status. His grad students tried to reach him on his cell, but their calls went straight to voice mail. By dawn this morning, Deborah was worried enough to call the cops."

The color had already drained from Sloane's face. "And?"

"And I got a call from Bob Erwin. The Ninth Precinct in the East Village found Elliot in his apartment."

"Found him." Sloane knew what that meant. "Was he beaten? Stabbed? Worse?"

"I'm sorry," Derek said quietly.

Utter silence filled the room.

"He's dead?" Sloane finally managed.

"The time of death was Tuesday morning, sometime around one A.M. There was no break-in. Either Elliot knew the killer, or he was half asleep, and just let the guy in."

Sloane's throat was working as she fought back tears. "You went to the crime scene?"

A nod. "I just came from there."

"The killer—was it our Unsub?"

"There's no doubt. The murder was committed using his signature style."

"Oh God." Sloane squeezed her eyes shut, pressing her fingertips against her eyelids to try to block out the images already forming in her mind. "He carved Elliot up with a combat knife. Who knows how long he spent cutting him? Who knows how long it took Elliot to die? Did the son of a bitch make him beg for his life? Who am I kidding? By the end, he was probably begging to die, not to live."

She continued, speaking half to herself. "Elliot's such a softie. He's afraid of spiders and horror movies, and he turns sheet white every time I mention my work. Violence scares the crap out of him. He had to be panicked out of his mind. And the agonizing pain . . . being slashed like that . . . the sheer terror of knowing that death was inevitable . . . I can't begin to imagine . . ."

"Don't try." Derek hesitated, then reached for her, drawing her against him. "It was quick. And without prolonged suffering. Not the way you're picturing it. There was no creative carving. The Unsub went directly for the jugular. He didn't have the luxury of time. He had to get in and out of that apartment in a hurry. This wasn't a show of power, it was the elimination of a threat. So he just did what he came to do, and took off."

"The jugular," Sloane repeated. "How many slashes?"

"A few." Derek tried to hedge.

Sloane wasn't buying it. "In other words, at least three. He wanted to be sure that Elliot was very, very dead. Quick and brutal. Which means a roomful of blood, but less torture." Sloane gave a humorless laugh. Then, abruptly, she slammed her fist against Derek's chest—once, twice, before she forced herself to stop. "It's not fair. Goddammit, it's just not fair. Elliot was a good, decent man. He got involved in this project, in part because I asked him to, despite his personal apprehension, but especially because he wanted to save lives. And it ended up costing him his own. Why? Why the hell do things like this happen?"

"I can't answer that." Derek gazed across the room, staring at nothing in particular. "I don't understand it any more than you do. I've tortured myself with that question countless times, and every time I've come up empty."

"Empty. That's a pretty good description of the way I

feel. Empty and sick. And ridden with guilt." Sloane's tough veneer began to crack, and tears clogged her voice as she broke down and began to cry. "I brought Elliot on board. And now he's dead. *Dead*. And that psycho is running around scot-free."

"You're in shock." Derek stated the obvious, his hands gliding up and down Sloane's back in gentle, soothing motions. "Give it time. But start out knowing this was *not* your fault. Don't go down that path. Yes, you approached Elliot with the idea. But he chose to do it—no, he was *excited* about doing it. His murder is an atrocity. But it's the Unsub who's responsible, not you."

"I know," Sloane replied in a shattered tone, her body still shaking with sobs. "But we've known each other since high school. We studied together. We ragged on each other. He got me through Computer Programming. I got him through Spanish. He's eccentric, and he's goofy, and he's got a heart of gold. And now he's gone. I'm never going to see him again. Never. I just can't wrap my mind around that."

Derek wished he had more of the right words to offer. But both he and Sloane knew those words didn't exist. So he gave her the only ones he had. "I'm so sorry, sweetheart."

She nodded against his shirt.

No more words were said. For long, silent minutes, Sloane just wept, and Derek just held her.

Abruptly, she jerked upright, her face streaked with tears that she dashed away. "Elliot deserves better than this. I'm not going to sit here and cry. I'm going to *do* something. No matter what it takes. I'm going to find this son of a bitch and skewer him with his own combat knife."

Derek's gut clenched. He knew Sloane meant every word. And while he didn't give a damn how violent this Unsub's death was, he wasn't going to let Sloane "go vigilante," which would end up putting her life in danger.

"You're not alone in this," he stated fervently. "Every

single one of us is with you. None of us will rest until this bastard is caught." Derek went on, purposely shifting from the emotional to the factual: "ERT processed the scene quickly. Between them and the Crime Scene Unit, they found and bagged quite a bit of evidence, including finger-prints, hair, and, obviously, blood and blood splatter. They even found two shoe prints in the blood. All the forensic evidence is at Quantico by now. The guys there will turn up something."

"The blood and fingerprints will be Elliot's. You know that as well as I do. The same goes for the hair. The blood splatter will confirm that a main artery was severed. Even if the Unsub got careless, a DNA profile will take two days. We can't wait that long." Sloane stopped only long enough to take a breath. "What about neighbors? A doorman? Didn't anyone see anything?" She jumped to her feet. "I want to go down to that apartment. I'll interview every damn person in the building. Someone must have noticed something."

"Sloane, stop." Derek rose and gripped her shoulders. "You can't march into that apartment and start grilling people. You're not FBI, and you're not NYPD. If you cross the line, you could compromise the whole case."

Sloane gritted her teeth, knowing damn well that Derek was right. "You realize what this means," she surmised aloud. "If the Unsub knew what Elliot was working on, it means he's someone who hangs around John Jay. Maybe even someone who works there. He could be anything from a professor to an administrator to a maintenance worker."

"Or he could be someone who was at Lillian's party the other night," Derek reminded her. "If so, and if he heard that Elliot was working to analyze the abductions through his new computer program, he'd freak out."

"You're right." Sloane nodded. "We'll have to question every John Jay employee, and every guest who was at that party. We'll have to get DNA samples from each one of them, too."

"And we will. The arrangements to do so are already

under way. So's the list of people to interview, which is already being compiled. Larry and Bill have been apprised of the situation, too, so they're on board. We'll do it all—and then some. We *will* find this Unsub."

"Before he kidnaps or kills someone else?" Sloane shot Derek a probing look. "This isn't like you. You're the case agent in charge. You have a ton of investigative work to do, and you're aware that you're racing the clock. So why are you sitting here, babysitting me, instead of *doing* something?"

"I'm not babysitting you." Derek answered her bluntly. "The truth is, I'm all for heading right down to John Jay and questioning everyone—starting with Elliot's grad students, who were probably the last people to see him alive. But I asked Bob to hold off notifying the college so I could have time to get to you first."

"You lost me."

"One second." Derek held up his index finger. As he spoke, he groped in his jacket pocket for his cell phone. "Let me call Bob right now. Once I do, he'll take the gag order off Deborah and inform the college of what happened so they can notify the staff and students."

Sloane blinked. "No one at John Jay knows yet?"

"No. I asked Bob to wait until I'd told you. I didn't want you hearing this news from anyone else."

Abruptly, Sloane realized how much trouble Derek had gone to for her—from leaving the crime scene—and the investigation—to drive all the way out here, to sitting with her and absorbing some of her grief, to halting the red tape of bureaucracy in its tracks to give her time to absorb the shock. "I didn't think about . . ." She blew out a slow breath. "Thank you."

"You're welcome."

"You knew just what I needed."

"I usually do." Derek found and whipped out his cell. "I know you, Sloane," he informed her as he punched in Bob's number. "*Really* know you. And, even though this isn't the time to get into it, that's the reason we've been fighting." He waited while his call went through.

Sloane's brows rose, and she struggled for humor. "Really? I thought we were fighting because you were an over-possessive jerk."

"Were we?" Derek wasn't laughing. "Or were we fighting because we're living a pretense we can't keep up anymore, but you can't let go of because the outcome scares you to death?" His chin jerked down so he could speak into the mouthpiece. "Bob, it's me. I'm at Sloane's." A pause. "Pretty much the way you'd expect. But she's tough, just like I told you. She's determined to come down there now to question some of the staff and students who were closest to Elliot. I think it's a good idea. Right now we've got the element of surprise on our side. The less time people have to prepare themselves, the more likely they'll be to say something they wished they hadn't—assuming any of them has something to hide."

Another pause. "We'll head down together—yes, in my car and with me at the wheel. My question is, if we leave now, does that give you enough time to alert the administration so they can inform the college community and get started doing any necessary damage control?" Derek listened for a minute or two. "Good. We'll meet you there." He glanced up as Sloane gestured for him to hand her the phone. "Bob, hang on a minute. Sloane wants to talk to you." He passed his cell over to her.

"Hi, Bob. Thanks for worrying about me, but I'm fine. I *will* let Derek drive us into the city, but not because I'm an emotional wreck who'll fall apart at the wheel, but because it's stupid to take two cars when we're going to the same place."

She swallowed hard. "The reason I wanted to talk to you is to provide some personal information that will save you time, if not pain. Elliot's family is small. He's got a sister, Patty, who lives in Portland, Maine. And his parents moved from New York to Conway, South Carolina, when he left for college. They're still living there, so you shouldn't have any trouble finding them. You're welcome. See you soon."

She hung up the phone, and looked at Derek. "Bob says you have news?"

"Two detectives are already questioning the residents of Elliot's apartment building. Also, Bob is going to press the decision makers at John Jay to allow mouth swabs to be conducted starting later today."

"Good. The sooner, the better."

Derek walked over, tipped up her chin. "I'm the case agent, as you pointed out. I can handle this part, and fill you in later. Are you sure you want to do this?"

"I'm not sure of anything. But I *am* going to do it. So, let's go." Sloane was about to head for the door, when she paused, giving Derek a guarded, slightly baffled look. "What did you mean before—about us living a pretense that we can't keep up anymore?"

"That's the prelude to a pretty heavy conversation. Maybe we should shelve it until later."

Sloane nodded. "You're right. We've got to jump on this investigation."

"That's not the reason. Impatient or not, we've got to give Bob a little time to alert the John Jay administration, and deal with the initial fallout. It's you I was thinking about. You just lost a close friend. You're in emotional shock." Derek paused. "Or maybe that's all the more reason for us *not* to shelve this talk. We've shelved it too damned long already."

"Fair enough," Sloane replied, turning to face him. "Go for it."

"I plan to." Derek's midnight gaze held hers. "Only this time with no holds barred. The fact is, life is short—*too* short, as tragedies like Elliot's murder remind us. We have to seize every moment, and not get bogged down in crap. The past is the past. The future is a big question mark. The present is all we've really got. So, yeah, you and I screwed up back in Cleveland. You were wrong. I was wrong. Whoever was the bigger jackass is irrelevant. We both paid the price. We lost over a year of time, and threw out a relationship that comes along once in a lifetime—if you're lucky. So now that fate or circumstances has given us another shot to make it work, why are we throwing it away?"

"We're not . . ."

"Yes, we are. We throw it away every time we pretend we're nothing more than great sex partners with a little something extra and a steamy past. Why don't we grow the hell up and call it what it is?"

"Because, like you said, I'm scared to death," Sloane answered flatly.

"Get over it. Because if you don't, you're exactly the coward I accused you of being when you quit the Bureau."

"That's low."

"No, it's honest. Back then, I was wrong. Now—I don't know. Let's find out." Derek framed her face between his palms. "I love you. I did then. I do now. You're a high-maintenance pain in the ass who always needs the upper hand and never gives an inch when you think you're right—which is always. Then again, the same applies to me. So we're going to fight—a lot. We're also going to make up—a lot. But no more of this pseudo-relationship crap. I want *all* of you, not just your incredibly hot body. These feelings are real, and they're not going away, whether or not we talk about them. Maybe we took them for granted, or I would have spent more time understanding the trauma caused by what happened to your hand, and you would have forced me to listen instead of shutting the door in my face and then running away. But, like I said, that's the past. Now's the present. So you want me to stop acting like a jealous asshole when we're at parties? Give me a reason to."

He spread his arms wide, as if to emphasize that he'd kept nothing hidden. "That's it. That's all I've got. I've laid all my cards out on the table. Now it's your turn. So, tell me, are you a coward or not?"

"Not." Sloane stated her answer without so much as a

flinch. Having just stared death in the face, life seemed all the more precious—far too precious for stupid insecurities to get in the way. "You want the words? You've got them. I love you. I'll even tell you that you're right—at least this once. The facade was a cop-out. I was terrified of ever again going through the hell I went through when you and I were over. But after being punched in the gut with a day like today, I realize there are no guarantees." She blew out a long, slow breath. "Life is a gift. It's also fleeting, so emotional self-protection is a waste of time. And life gives us choices. So I choose you, even if you do push every one of my buttons, and drive me bonkers."

Derek's smile was slow, but it spoke wonders. "That's all I needed to hear."

TWENTY-EIGHT

DATE: 1 May
TIME: 0623 hours
OBJECTIVE: Artemis

I have to admit I admire Artemis's hounds. They wanted no part of Mr. Ford Focus. They growled whenever he started to jog beside them, until finally he'd agreed to keep a considerable distance away, and watch her through his binoculars.

True, they're small, not the formidable hounds always depicted with Artemis in my tomes of Greek mythology. But that doesn't inhibit them. They're loyal, fearless, and fiercely protective. They know who and what is right for their mistress.

Someday, they, too, will join us at Mount Olympus. I'm convinced of it. And Artemis will welcome them home.

She's now on her last lap. Which means that Mr. Ford Focus is at his most relaxed.

Today, that will prove to be his undoing.

Sloane's breath was coming in hard pants as she and the hounds took the final lap of their run. She'd run more aggressively today, a natural way to relieve some of the tension that was gripping her.

Yesterday had been an endless day of nothingness. None of the other tenants in Elliot's apartment had seen anything unusual. No one at John Jay had acted the least bit suspiciously. And no one the NYPD had approached had either refused or been reluctant to offer a DNA sample.

Quantico would finish the DNA profile by tomorrow. Then they'd have proof of what Sloane already knew—that the same sick pervert was responsible for this entire crime spree.

That was the easy part. Finding the Unsub himself was the ultimate challenge. And damn him to hell, she was going to do it.

Mr. Ford Focus is in for the surprise of his life.
  I raise my tranquilizer gun, aim, and fire.

Hank felt the stinging pain in his butt, and jerked around, looking everywhere at once. He reached around, pulled out the dart, and examined it. He knew what it was—and what it did.

His time was limited. He had to find his assailant, and fast.

He drew his pistol and raised it, sweeping the area with an alert eye. No sign of anyone.

The bushes across the street rustled.

"Come out with your hands up!" Hank ordered.

No motion whatsoever.

"I know you're in there. Come out or I'm coming in."

Again, nothing.

From down the street, Hank heard the low sound of a car motor. No, it was deeper, throatier—more like a truck or a van. The sound was moving toward him, as, obviously, was the vehicle.

He turned, still aiming his pistol, ready to fire. But at what—the vehicle or the bushes?

The numbness started in his legs, then crept up his body,

until keeping his arms raised was too much of an effort. His head began swimming, and he rubbed his eyes, trying to erase the cobwebs. Dammit. He had to get this guy before whatever drug he'd injected into his bloodstream took over.

Hank glanced back at the bushes, which were now totally still. And the sound of the approaching truck or van was gone, too. So he had no idea where the hell this maniac was.

His only hope was to warn Sloane—now, before she got too close to the assailant to escape. He'd also call for backup. That way, the local cops would be here within minutes.

He twisted around in the direction Sloane was coming from. His turn was executed in slow motion. He could feel it. And Sloane was still way off in the woods, too far away to spot him unless he gave her reason to.

He tried to yell. Nothing came out. His lips were numb and unmoving. So was his brain. The dizziness was winning. He couldn't feel his fingers, so he groped wildly for his cell phone. If he touched it, he never knew.

He raised his other arm to wave Sloane down. It only made it up halfway.

With a choked sound, he fell to his knees, then collapsed onto the street, unconscious.

Once I see Mr. Ford Focus hit the ground, I know I'm home free.

I press my foot to the accelerator, closing the distance to Artemis's house. I park adjacent to her driveway.

There's no time to waste. I jump out of the van, and run over to the stocky bodyguard, who's crumpled in the road. I grab him by the legs and drag him over to his car. He's a heavy SOB. But I'm more than up for the challenge.

Once I complete my job, I step back and admire my handiwork. To any passerby, it looks as if Mr. Ford Focus is taking a nap.

Which he is. A long, long nap.

Lost in thought, Sloane rounded the final curve of her run. As she neared her property, the hounds abruptly began barking and whining, running back and forth in an intertwining fashion until their leashes were tangled. Sloane squatted down to untangle them, her brows drawing together in puzzlement. It was unusual for her dachshunds to be so hyper. Especially after a three-mile run. No, not hyper. Agitated. Clearly, something was wrong.

She raised her head, surveyed the area.

There was a strange van parked next to her driveway. But that wasn't unusual. Landscapers and other outdoor laborers who had projects on her block often left their vehicles wherever it was convenient. From where she stood, she couldn't tell what type of tradesman the van belonged to, but she could tell that the van looked empty.

Nonetheless, she exercised caution. She approached the vehicle slowly, circled it, and confirmed that it was, indeed, devoid of passengers. She peered through the tinted glass, holding her hands on either side of her face so she could see better. Not that there was much to see. Just the usual trunk-type stuff—a gym bag, something that looked like a collapsed bicycle, some tools, a cooler, and two cases of bottled water. Nothing threatening there.

She glanced across the street. Hank was in his car, obviously too tired between quarter-mile sprints to check up on her with his binoculars. The poor guy. Twelve-hour shifts with a combative subject and a royal pain in the ass—namely, *her*—were rough.

Hank was a pro. He'd obviously checked out the van before returning to his car. So it was clear that he didn't view it as a threat either.

The hounds, on the other hand, were still riled up. They were tense and growling, but they were staring away from the van and Hank's car, their gazes angled toward a different spot on the street. Hank himself wasn't a dog person, so he didn't place much stock in the hounds' superior awareness. But Sloane knew better. She knew how keen their instincts were. She wasn't about to ignore their warning—even if it turned out that the only thing they were alerting her to was a nearby skunk on the verge of spraying her.

Sidestepping the van, she tightened her grip on their leashes, and began sprinting toward her house.

She was a short way down her driveway, when she felt the sharp sting in the back of her left thigh. She started, her first thought being that she'd been stung by a wasp. It hurt, a lot, and the sticking sensation warned her that the stinger might still be in there.

Carefully, she reached around, her hand coming in contact with something more cylindrical and substantial than a bee's stinger.

It was a dart—the kind that was shot from a tranquilizer gun.

Someone wanted her unconscious. And there was only one someone that could be.

Her first instinct was to go for her pistol. She reached for it—simultaneously recalling that it was nonexistent. Her days of carrying a weapon were temporarily suspended.

She turned toward Elsa's house, trying to peer through the thick cluster of evergreen trees that separated their properties. She couldn't see anything—or anyone. But she did remember that Burt's car had been parked in the driveway when she ran by earlier.

Could he really be their Unsub?

Feeling a wave of dizziness, she realized she was wasting precious time. Wrapping the hounds' leashes around her wrist, she reversed her steps, weaving her way toward Hank's car. She needed help—and she needed it now. Already her body felt as if it were moving in slow motion. She was on the verge of passing out, and she had no intention of doing so on a secluded parcel of land where her attacker could kidnap her and take off without being seen.

"Sloane!"

Someone was calling her. Blinking the cobwebs out of

her eyes, she tried to focus. A man was approaching. He
was smiling and waving.

Luke? Yes, it was Luke. Thank goodness. A friend.

"Sloane!" he called to her again.

"I'm hurt." She managed to push out the words. "I need
help."

"I know." With an understanding nod, he sped up his
steps, until he was jogging toward her, just yards away.
"I'm here to give you that help."

Maybe it was the odd reply, or the unnatural quality of
his tone. Maybe it was the weird look in his eyes. Or maybe
it was because, as if on cue, all three of her hounds burst
into a round of snarling, growling, and baring their teeth.

Whatever prompted it, the hair on back of her neck
stood up.

And, suddenly, she knew.

Even before she caught a glimpse of the silver object
tucked inside the front facing of Luke's open leather jacket,
and realized it was a knife, she'd planted her feet, tensing
for a fight.

The drugs in her bloodstream were traveling faster than
she was. Her mind was woozy. Her body wouldn't respond
to her commands. And her muscles were freezing up, refusing to react. She didn't stand a chance.

An instant later, Luke caught her around the waist,
steadying her, then half guiding and half dragging her to
his van. "It's all right," he said in a soothing voice. "I'm
taking you home."

"Home?" She wished she could think straight. "I am
home."

As they reached the road, the fuzzy outline of the Ford
Focus swam into view, along with Hank, still sitting in the
driver's seat, still leaning against his window in the exact
same position. "Hank," she muttered. "What did you do to
him?"

"He's sleeping," Luke supplied. "He'll be fine. The only

lasting effects will be some leftover grogginess, a wicked headache, and a slew of guilt. Time for us to go now."

With that, Luke unwound the hounds' leashes from around Sloane's wrist, and tossed the straps to the ground, releasing the dogs as he pulled open the door to his van. "Go on. Run. Go back to the house," he ordered.

They ignored him completely, continuing to bark and snarl, and nip at his feet. "I understand," Luke assured them, as calmly as if he were addressing three distraught children. "You'll miss her. But it won't be for long. You'll join us at Mount Olympus very soon. Artemis will decree it. She needs her hounds."

Mount Olympus? Artemis? Sloane processed that. Whatever it meant, Luke was insane.

Struggling to hold on to her rapidly fading mental faculties, Sloane tried to come up with a counterstrike maneuver. Her Krav skills were useless. Her strength and coordination were gone. She needed a weapon of some kind. Squinting, she peered around inside the van, hoping for something she could use.

The tools. No. They were too far out of reach. The cooler. Again, no. She couldn't get to it, and she didn't have the coordination to grab it and swing it at Luke's head.

There was only one item within her grasp, because it was folded and stacked in the backseat rather than the trunk. And that item was way too large and cumbersome to lift. It was what she'd originally thought was a bicycle, but now realized was a wheelchair. Lillian's wheelchair.

Dazedly, Sloane remembered the retirement party. Luke had been able to store a wine goblet in the seatback bag that was attached behind it.

It was a long shot, but it was the only plausible idea Sloane could come up with. It wouldn't help her now, but later, when he was driving or occupied with something else—maybe.

She cocked her head to make sure Luke wasn't watching

her. At that moment, he was wildly throwing sticks across her lawn for the hounds to chase, and grinding out commands for them to shut up and go away. Sloane knew he could kill all three of them in one fell swoop. But for whatever reason, he seemed to view them as godly, and refused to harm them. She thanked God for that blessing.

However, his patience wouldn't last forever. Even in her drugged-up state, Sloane could see that he was reaching the end of his rope. She had to act now, use these last coherent moments to save her pups, then try to save herself. She reached into the kangaroo pocket of her jogging suit, palmed her cell phone, and shut it off. Then she dropped it directly into the mesh section of the seatback bag behind the wheelchair.

Luckily, they blended, black against black. And her phone was tiny. Now all she could do was to pray that Luke wouldn't spot it.

"Run, Moe," she slurred, waving the dogs away. "Larry, Curly—you, too. Peanut butter . . . kongs . . . inside house . . ."

She saw them take off, heard their excited yips as they raced toward the house, assuming she was behind them.

Then she fell to the floor of the van, and was swallowed up by the darkness.

As had become his habit since moving back in with his mother, Burt stepped out of the house and walked across the front path to scoop up the morning newspaper. It was on his return trip that he heard the hounds. They were making an enormous racket. And it wasn't their customary barking, signifying play. These barks were sharp and frantic, and they were scratching violently at Sloane's front door.

What were they doing out here alone, and why couldn't they get in?

Burt headed in that direction to find out. "Moe? Larry? Curly?" he shouted as he pushed his way through the evergreens.

At the sound of Burt's voice, they came bounding toward him, their leashes dragging behind them, creating such a din that there was no mistaking this for anything but urgency.

"Where's Sloane?" he asked them, already stooping to grab hold of the looped handles of all three leashes. They responded by half dragging him across the lawn and back to their front door.

Burt rang the bell three times. No response. He then knocked until his knuckles turned white. Again, nothing. Finally, he used the spare key Sloane had given him and his mother for those times when they needed to get in for "hound-sitting." He unlocked the front door, and pushed it open. "Sloane?" he yelled.

Silence.

He checked every room, only to find them empty. In the kitchen, a mug and today's newspaper were laid out on the table. And the coffeemaker, which had been program set for six-thirty, had already brewed four cups.

Burt didn't waste another second. He picked up the phone and dialed the police.

FBI New York Field Office
26 Federal Plaza, New York City
7:05 A.M.

Derek wasn't happy. He'd wanted to spend last night with Sloane. Stoic as she was, she was badly thrown by Elliot's murder. And after a long day of grilling people and hearing the gory details of Elliot's death over and over, she needed comfort, not a train ride home—accompanied by one of Manny's people—and a night alone with the hounds. But Derek had been tied up with frantic meetings, phone calls, and paperwork until 3 A.M. He'd never even gone home, just crashed in the office for a few hours, then showered and changed clothes.

Now back at his desk, he glanced at his watch. Sloane should be back from her morning run. He was just about to call and check up on her—under the guise of determining what time she was meeting him at John Jay for day two of mouth-swabbing and interrogating—when his phone rang.

"FBI," he answered briskly.

"Agent Parker?" It was a young woman's tentative voice.

"This is Parker. Who am I speaking with?"

"Deborah Culmen. I am—I *was*—one of Dr. Lyman's graduate assistants. There were two of us helping him monitor his AI system. The instructions he left us from the beginning were that in the event he was unreachable, we should call you if any results materialized."

"And have they?" Derek leaned forward, his body taut with anticipation.

"The computer system just spit out a model based on all the information Dr. Lyman fed it. I think you should come over here and take a look at it right away."

"I'm there."

Derek left the federal building and drove his Bureau car up to John Jay in record time. He took the steps two at a time and strode through the door to Elliot's office.

Deborah was waiting. White-faced, she handed him the screen print. She was actually shaking.

It took Derek three seconds to figure out why.

What he was looking at was a chilling, one-page analysis in the form of a table:

Goddess Name	Characteristics	Date Taken	Victim's Name
Aphrodite	Beauty	April 14	Penelope Truman
Hera	Mother	June 2	Eve Calhoun
Actraeus	Bestower of Wealth	September 12	Lauren Majors

Goddess Name	Characteristics	Date Taken	Victim's Name
Hestia	Nurturer	December 5	Lydia Halas
Athena	Warrior	March 19	Cynthia Alexander
Tyche	Fortune & Luck	April 5	Tina Carroll
Demeter	Agriculture	April 20	Prof Helen Daniels
Persephone	Springtime	April 20	Abby Deniels
Artemis	Hunter, Archer, Keeper of the Hounds	May 1	Sloane Burbank ?

NOTES:

(1) Coin signifies battle between good (goddess) versus evil (Python).

(2) Apollo killed Python and assumed guardianship of Delphi (Greek mythology).

(3) Tai Kee is phonetic pronunciation of Tyche, goddess of fortune, luck, and prosperity.

A hard jolt of awareness shot through Derek as some of the crucial pieces fell into place while triggering a whole new set of questions. Those he'd turn over to the BAU to decipher.

His own attention was fixed on the final table entry—the one that made his blood run cold.

The last victim's name: Sloane Burbank.

And worse, the "date taken" listed beside it: May 1.

That was today.

He flipped open his cell phone and punched in Sloane's number on speed dial. It went directly to voice mail. Dammit. He hung up and tried her home phone. Same thing. She couldn't still be out running. Maybe she was in the shower? Outside?

He was clutching at straws and he knew it.

With his jaw tightly clenched, he checked the time. Hank was still on. He would have some answers. He never left Sloane unattended. During his shifts, he kept a perpetual, full-time eye on her.

Hank's cell phone rang and rang. No one picked up. Eventually, it went to voice mail.

It had to be bad cell reception. Hank never ignored a call, not when he was on duty. Unless he was in trouble.

No. Derek refused to go there. He'd wait a minute and try again. This time Hank would answer.

There was sweat beading up on his forehead, trickling down his neck.

As if on cue, Derek's cell phone rang.

"Hank?" he said into the mouthpiece.

It wasn't Hank. It was the local cops in Sloane's town. Burt Wagner, Sloane's next-door neighbor, had suggested they call him.

Derek listened to the entire story.

He was already in motion as he issued a few terse orders to the local police.

Then he turned back to Deborah, recited Jeff's phone number, and told her to call him, then send him a fax of the printout and have him fax copies to Bill Mann at the BAU and Larry Clark at his New York hotel. He blew out of the office faster than he'd come in.

When he arrived at Sloane's house, the local police were still on the scene, one interviewing Burt inside the house, three others checking the outside grounds and street.

Hank's car was parked in its usual spot. As the cops had told Derek on the phone, the bodyguard had been out cold when they arrived, thanks to a well-placed tranquilizer dart. He was now in the hospital, being treated and, hopefully, regaining consciousness.

Derek would head over there next.

First, he strode into Sloane's house. Burt was in the kitchen with the hounds, who were whimpering and vitally aware that something was wrong. Burt looked grateful as hell to see Derek, and turned his attention to him, answering every one of his questions while the local cop waited.

None of his answers helped. They only reiterated the facts that Derek already knew.

Sloane was missing.

And he was too late to stop the serial killer who'd taken her.

TWENTY-NINE

DATE: 1 May
TIME: 1145 hours

She looks so peaceful on that bed, so utterly right in this room that I built for her. Truly, this is where she belongs until we ascend. I know I have to move her, but locking her in a lifeless cell is going to take a Herculean effort on my part.

But I have no choice. Until I know her intentions, I can't afford to let sentiment cloud my judgment. I must contain her, limit her awareness of where she is. More important, I must limit her access to anything she can use to retaliate or escape.

She's highly intelligent and equally resourceful. But she's also strong—in will and in strength—and stubborn. As goddess of the hunters, she's dedicated to the chase, and she'll do all she can to outwit me so she can regain her freedom.

No matter how difficult she becomes, I must demonstrate patience. She doesn't understand yet. She still views me as the enemy.

It's up to me to convince her that I'm her salvation.

Sloane's house
Hunterdon County, New Jersey
1:05 P.M.

Sloane's living room had become the meeting place for Derek, Jeff, Bill, and Larry, who'd spent the past two hours reviewing evidence, and refocusing their strategy and analysis based on the information Elliot's computer system had spit out.

At Derek's urgent request, Bill had flown immediately up to New Jersey to join the team.

Jeff had been added to the team as well. It was Tony who'd informed Derek of his decision. And Derek offered no argument. Tony was right. Derek knew his objectivity was severely compromised based on this latest development in the case. Plus, Jeff's Violent Crimes experience would be beneficial.

All Derek cared about was getting this Unsub—*now*—before he hurt Sloane.

Unless he already had.

He shoved that thought aside, forcing himself back into special-agent mode. Anything less, and he'd be no good to anybody.

"Okay, so now everyone on this list is accounted for," Larry was saying, having just hung up the phone. "I've now confirmed all the facts on Eve Calhoun, who was our only unknown." He counted off on his fingers. "Worked at the Manhattan D.A.'s Office with Sloane at the outset of Sloane's career. Now a matrimonial attorney. Was last seen doing laps at the NYU pool. Divorced, no family. Just a pissed-off law firm. The victimology fits."

Bill nodded thoughtfully, steepling his fingers together and leaning forward on the sofa, rereading his copy of the table for the umpteenth time. "Eve Calhoun being a matrimonial attorney correlates with Hera being the 'mother.' Not only is she the goddess queen, she's also the goddess of love and marriage." Another thoughtful glance at the printout. "This Unsub has certainly captured an eclectic bunch of women. But there's more than one motherly type. The pattern does demonstrate a maternal fixation."

"Agreed." Larry perched on the arm of a chair. "I'm not up on my Greek mythology, but I did some quick research. As queen of the goddesses, Hera ran the show. My guess is that our Unsub needs his 'Hera' as a strong guiding force. And his 'Hestia,' Lydia Halas, is the calm goddess of home and hearth. The real Lydia Halas is a healer, a nurse. Our Unsub needs her for security and comfort."

"So we have two maternal figures here—one to nurture, the other to parent," Bill concluded.

"What about the other victims?" Jeff asked. "I see the whole mother-complex thing you're referring to. But that only explains two of the nine women our Unsub went after."

"Look, guys." Derek interrupted before Larry or Bill could reply. "This is all very fascinating. But we're racing the clock here. How does all this psychological analysis help us find our Unsub or his victims?"

"As opposed to doing what?" Bill asked, leveling a calm stare at Derek. "Racing into the field, guns blazing? Analysis produces a more focused pursuit, which will lead to quicker success. By knowing who this Unsub is, how he thinks, and what motivates him, we can zero in on him and his intentions."

"But what solid information have we come up with?"

"For one thing, that there's a better chance than we originally thought that the kidnapped women are alive. The coin the Unsub leaves at each crime scene shows the strong dichotomy in his mind between the bad women he murders— the 'Pythons'—and the good women he kidnaps—the 'goddesses.' If he feels he needs these goddesses, then he's keeping, not killing, them."

"For what? And for how long?"

"I can't answer that—*yet*. But some trigger is compelling him to act each time he kills a prostitute or kidnaps a goddess. The prostitutes are an outlet for his sexual fantasies, so the trigger could simply be pent-up sexual need that he loathes and is ashamed of, but can't control. So he takes control by killing the prostitutes, as violently as possible, after he's through with them. But the goddesses—that's the unknown. This isn't a harem, it's a specific collection of revered women, all with virtuous traits and preexisting relationships with Sloane. Once we figure out the Unsub's reason for collecting them, I'd be willing to bet we'll figure out his plan, his timing, maybe even where he's imprisoning his victims."

"So we all agree that the key lies with this list of Greek goddesses," Larry murmured thoughtfully. "We need detailed information. That takes time. Maybe we can shortcut the process." He shot Derek a quizzical look. "Not to sound callous, but can you get a hold of Lillian Doyle? I realize she's terminally ill. And, yes, I realize she's a sociology professor, but that woman knows her ancient history. She's gone into long dissertations on the roots of violence in ancient civilization. I'm not sure if she's an expert on Greek mythology, but I know she's referred to it more than once during the workshop panels we've done together at John Jay. It's possible she'd see a connection here, or, at the very least, know someone who would."

"It's worth a phone call." Derek was already dialing. "Bob," he said into the mouthpiece. "I know you're swamped interviewing the John Jay faculty and students. But you've got personal contact information on the entire John Jay staff, and I need a home number fast—as in, yesterday."

"Whose number are you looking for?" Bob asked, sounding as ragged as the rest of them.

"Professor Doyle's. Also, I'll need her son Luke's cellphone number, since I assume he's taking her calls."

Bob grunted. "You can have the numbers, but they won't do you any good. Neither Dr. Doyle nor her son, Luke, has answered either their home or cell phones. And I've tried each number several times. I hope that's not had news, healthwise."

"How many voice mails did you leave?"

"None. Both their voice-mail boxes are full."

"*Both* of them? That's weird." Something about that didn't sit right with Derek. And when he got that unsettled feeling, he acted on it. "Dr. Doyle. Do you know the name of her physician, or, given her condition, her oncologist? I could call and make sure she's all right."

"Sorry. Don't have access to her medical info. But it shouldn't be hard to finagle. Dr. Doyle lives on West a Hundred and Seventy-first Street near Broadway. I'm assuming her pharmacy is close by. Hang on for a minute." Bob called out to someone who was summoning him into the interrogation room. "I've got to go," he told Derek. "I'll call you later. Let me know if you reach Dr. Doyle."

"Will do." Derek disconnected the call, then called Tony and explained what he needed.

"What are you hoping to find?" Jeff asked, once his partner had hung up.

"I don't know." Derek scowled. "But this feels wrong. And I can't get what I need by phone, because no pharmacist or doctor is going to release patient information to me without seeing proper authorization. So Tony's sending someone out."

He spent the next half hour on the Internet, searching for experts in Greek mythology.

He was about to contact a local college, when his cell phone rang.

"Yeah, Tony, do you have something for me?" Derek listened, then punched "off," an odd expression on his face.

"What is it?" Jeff asked.

"The agent Tony sent out located Dr. Doyle's pharmacist and her oncologist. Evidently, she's no longer refilling her meds, and she's no longer a patient at that—or any other—oncologist's office."

"Since when?" Bill demanded.

"Since yesterday. According to her oncologist—who was very forthcoming, once he heard the circumstances—she delivered this news to him by phone. It came as quite a shock. She'd been following his health regimen from when the cancer had originally been diagnosed—which was, apparently, long after it should have been. The implication was, she hadn't been going for regular checkups, or this might have been caught early on."

"What kind of cancer are we talking about?"

"The doctor's not at liberty to say. But Tony said that our agent spotted a number of consult reports in Lillian's file when the oncologist was going through it. Most of those consults were with an ob/gyn."

"Got it."

"Her oncologist said that Lillian's always had an incredibly strong will to live—even recently, when the prognosis was at its grimmest. So her phone call and abrupt turnaround came out of the blue. He strongly advised her that she was making a rash and ill-advised decision, especially with regard to the pain medication. But she was adamant. She announced that she'd decided to go off to her country house and spend her last days in peace. No meds. No doctors." Derek's head came up, a glint in his eyes. "Only her son."

After that, Derek was like a dog with a bone. He was onto something and he knew it. Now all he needed was proof, and enough probable cause to get it.

Ninety minutes later, Bob Erwin was summoned out of a meeting for an urgent phone call.

"This is Erwin," he said.

"Bob, get a detective over to Lillian Doyle's apartment *now*," Derek instructed. "The landlord will let him in, since the apartment's now officially vacant. You don't need a search warrant; Dr. Doyle broke her lease. According to the landlord, she and her son dropped off her key and enough cash to cover the remaining months of the lease. They then promptly left, for good. ERT's heading over there now to sweep the place and to get a DNA sample from Luke's comb or his toothbrush, and helicopter it down to Quantico.

"And one more thing. Luke Doyle didn't take a leave of absence from Bellevue. He quit. Said he was taking his mother and relocating—permanently. Coincidentally and on the same day, a shitload of morphine and Nembutal disappeared. But this time there were prints. I guess when you're planning to disappear, you get careless about using gloves. His loss, our gain. I had the M.E.'s office compare those prints to the ones on Luke Doyle's coffee mug and stethoscope. Game, set, *match*. We've got more than enough to arrest him." Derek gritted his teeth. "Now we just have to find him."

CHAPTER THIRTY

Consciousness returned in painful waves as she averted her face from the repugnant smell of the mattress she was lying on.

Where was she?

Memory filtered back, first in broken flashes, then in chunks, until it was all there.

Luke. All this time it had been Luke. A serial sexual killer. A stalker. A madman.

Her first reaction was overwhelming rage.

Luke Doyle had killed Elliot. And maybe Penny. And Lydia. And Cynthia. And the list went on and on. Including helpless Asian women who'd been sold into prostitution and then brutally butchered by her dear friend Luke.

Rage transformed into guilt. How could she not have seen it? How could she not have known? If only she had, all those people might be alive today.

Usually, she was an excellent judge of character. But not this time. Then again, Luke had never acted abnormally around her. They'd had lunch together, taken walks together, faced a world tragedy together.

But when she got right down to it, how much time had they *really* spent together? Talked?

Not a hell of a lot. Not alone and not in any depth.

He was a medical assistant. He healed people. She'd watched him do so with her own eyes. He'd been caring, compassionate, gentle.

And that same man whose gentle hands had healed the wounded had slashed people's throats and carved up their bodies. How was that possible?

Even now he was a walking contradiction. He had put his entire world on hold to care for his mother during her final days. He'd even moved in with her to be the best caretaker possible. He'd literally given up everything in his life to ease her passing.

What life?

The thought suddenly struck Sloane like a ton of bricks. Whenever she and Luke *had* talked, it had been about work, about 9/11, about her recovery from her hand injury. Never a word about his friends, never a mention of a date, never a funny story from his past.

And, lately, never a word about anything but Lillian.

Because Lillian *was* his life.

Mentally, Sloane reviewed the detailed profile Larry had developed of their serial sexual killer.

An abnormal bond with his mother. A screwed-up view of other women—the "good girls" and the "bad girls." A built-up rage that needed only a trigger to set him off.

That trigger was Lillian's cancer.

It made perfect sense. When Lillian was first diagnosed, Luke had freaked out. The result had been Penny's abduction. Others had followed. Then Lillian had gone into remission, so the kidnappings had stopped. That was the classic "cooling off" period ascribed to serial killers when their stressor ebbed. And now, when he knew his mother's cancer was terminal, when he was about to lose her forever, he'd gone completely over the edge.

That explained the why. The rest of what was going on here was up to her to decipher.

Sloane shifted, trying—and failing—to change position,

so she could get a glimpse of her surroundings. Abruptly, she realized why she couldn't move. Her arms and legs were in shackles. Evidently, Luke didn't trust her.

Smart man.

He knew how advanced her Krav Maga skills were. He wasn't taking any chances, especially not after the ass kicking he'd taken from Tina.

With an iron will, Sloane fought the last vestiges of medication, forcing her head to clear. She couldn't see much, but she could see that she was alone. That was a temporary luxury she couldn't afford to waste. She had to assess her surroundings, her resources, and her limitations, plus work out her strategy, all before Luke came back.

Dark, cramped room. One blackened window separating her from the world. One dimly lit, freestanding lamp. One wooden chair. Concrete floor. Dirty mattress. Rough wool blanket. Definitely not the Ritz-Carlton.

Resources—none.

Limitations—plenty. Shackles. The excruciating pain in her hand. Being held prisoner by a serial sexual killer who had definite plans for her.

Conventional escape were out. Luke had a combat knife, a traveling drugstore, and a twisted mind. If she fought him, he'd slash her throat or drug her. Either way, she'd die in minutes.

Her only hope of survival was taking a more subtle approach—at least until she figured out what Luke had planned. Not just for her, but for any other victims who might still be alive. Sloane had to find a way to comfortably ease him back into the friendship they'd shared. Maybe then she could earn a modicum of his trust, get the information she needed to fully assess the situation, and look for the best, one-shot opportunity she'd have to escape.

Footsteps sounded from down the hall, followed by a key inserted in her door lock.

Sloane took a slow, deep breath. The Bureau had trained

her as a hostage negotiator at Quantico. She'd honed her crisis resolution and active listening skills in the field.

Time for the ultimate test.

This time the life she was negotiating for was her own.

Luke stepped into the room. His gaze immediately darted to Sloane. Illuminated by the hall light, he was fully and clearly visible for one brief moment before he shut the door behind him. In that moment, Sloane saw an opaque emptiness in his eyes that told her that the Luke she'd known—the one who could at least feign sanity—was gone.

"You're awake," he observed, crossing over to sit on the chair. "I wanted to be here when you woke up so you wouldn't be afraid. But Gaia needed me. She was in pain. I couldn't allow that. You understand."

"Of course." Sloane nodded. "May I ask who Gaia is?"

A soft smile curved Luke's lips. "The supreme goddess. Goddess of the earth, the core of all creation. She rules over the sky, the mountains, and the sea."

"The supreme goddess," Sloane repeated, as if it were the most natural statement in the world to make. "And you said she was in pain. Are we talking about your mother? Is Lillian Gaia?"

"In this world, yes. But all that will change very soon."

"Were you able to relieve her pain? Is she comfortable now?"

A startled look, but one of gratitude and pleasure, crossed Luke's face. Not a surprise, given his attachment to Lillian.

"That's very kind of you to ask," he responded. "Yes, she's resting peacefully now. I had to administer additional morphine." A pause, during which Sloane noted the tiniest flicker of sanity in his eyes. "I didn't expect this to happen so quickly. Of course my plans are in order, but . . ." He shrugged, and the sanity was gone. "Nature works as she chooses. All I can do is relieve her pain, sit by her side, and let her know how precious she is. I take solace in the fact that, although her life here on earth is about to end, her life on Mount Olympus will last forever."

Sloane had no clue what all these references to Mount Olympus meant, but it was time to find out.

"Gaia is fortunate to have a son who cares so deeply, *and* one who's medically trained to ease her suffering," she said aloud.

"It's I who am blessed. I'm proud that I could become a son who's worthy of her. Gaia devoted her life to enlightening me. She taught others conventional knowledge, but she taught me the difference between good and evil, and stressed all the attributes that would make me deserving of my place on Mount Olympus."

This time the reference to Mount Olympus caused a sliver of memory to flash in Sloane's mind. Something Luke had said just before she'd blacked out, when he was shooing away the hounds.

You'll miss her, he'd told them. *But it won't be for long. You'll join us at Mount Olympus very soon. Artemis will decree it. She needs her hounds.*

Artemis. Gaia. Mount Olympus.

The connection gave Sloane a good starting point.

"I'm not an expert in Greek mythology," she told Luke truthfully. "But you keep mentioning Mount Olympus. And I remember your calling me Artemis earlier in the day. Is that because I'm an archer and because I have my hounds?"

Again, pride and pleasure. "Actually, it's the other way around. It's because you're Artemis that you act as you act, and do as you do. But I'm glad you see the correlation."

"Is this Mount Olympus?"

Luke looked amused. "Hardly. This is a dungeon. And I'm sorry you have to be confined to it. It won't be for long. As soon as I'm convinced I can trust you, I'll move you to your room."

"My room?"

"The other goddesses have concrete basement rooms like this one. But you, you're above that. As am I. Artemis and Apollo. Once we reach Olympus, you and I will sit at Gaia's feet and the others will serve us."

Others? Sloane had to fight to keep the hopeful leap her heart gave under wraps.

"Who are these others?" she asked carefully.

"They're the lesser goddesses. The ones who'll be accompanying us on our journey."

"I see. And they're all here now? None have gone on ahead of us?"

"Certainly not." He seemed astonished that she'd even ask. "No one precedes Gaia. All the goddesses, and myself, must wait for her to lead the way. Until she passes, which I expect will be in a day or two, each and every one of the lesser goddesses will wait right here with us. You, as a supreme goddess, are my last addition, the perfect complement to my role serving Gaia. Now we'll be ready, whenever she is."

Thank God. That meant the kidnapped women were alive. Including Penny.

Sloane squelched her relief. She was itching to probe deeper. But her negotiator's instincts sensed that Luke was becoming emotional, and that he was already at the edge of his comfort zone. So she'd wait, stick with more basic, non-inflammatory questions, and revisit the gray area later.

"Apollo. Is that what I should call you?"

"Not yet." He visibly relaxed. "Not until our ascent. Here I'm Delphi."

Delphi. Sloane racked her brain. If she remembered her ancient history correctly, Delphi was a sacred Greek temple or shrine, probably dedicated to either Apollo, Artemis, or Gaia. It made sense. Luke saw himself as the central vessel through which they would ascend to Mount Olympus.

"You're angry." Luke either made that assessment from her silence or her pensive expression. "And I know why. Professor Lyman. I'm truly sorry for your pain. But I'm *not* sorry I killed him. He deluded you. He made you believe he was your friend. He wasn't. He was Python's messenger, an evil serpent sent to destroy the purity of our upcoming journey. I had no choice but to kill him."

This was the toughest moment of Sloane's performance. She wanted to gouge out Luke's eyes for what he'd done to Elliot. But what point would there be to lash out? It wouldn't bring back her friend, and it would only condemn her and the rest of the women here to a certain death.

"I see your dilemma," she said calmly. "And I'm not angry, just confused. I believe you about Python. But these other, lesser goddesses—who are they?"

His expression hardened, and Sloane realized she'd pushed one of his buttons. "You know who the other goddesses are. You've been tracking them, and me, for weeks now. Don't toy with me, Artemis. I won't tolerate it."

"I'm not toying with you," Sloane assured him. "I just wasn't making the connection. Are you saying that the lesser goddesses are the women we classified as kidnapped?"

"They weren't kidnapped. They were rescued. All except that bitch Tyche, who spurned the gods and will be condemned to a lifetime of hell. I wanted to make her pay for what she did to me. But the gods chose to handle it after I'm gone. So be it."

Tai Kee. They'd all assumed it had been a Mandarin or Fukienese phrase. But it was just what Tina had said it sounded like—a name.

"Again, forgive my ignorance," Sloane said ruefully, "but what is—Tai Kee, did you say?—the goddess of?"

"It's Tyche," he corrected her pronunciation, then spelled the name for her. "And she's the goddess of fortune, prosperity, and luck. Or rather, she was. Now she's just a dirty slut like the rest of them."

It was the first time Sloane had heard or seen the brutal Luke, the man capable of being a serial killer. His gaze darkened to near black, and his features twisted with a rage so intense, it seemed to vibrate through him. The transformation was terrifying.

"If this Tyche is really that unworthy, it's good that she's not joining us and the others in our ascent," Sloane said carefully.

"You're right. I communed with the gods and they said the same thing." As Luke spoke, the serial killer receded, replaced by the hollow-eyed Delphi.

"It sounds as if the gods have treated you well."

"Always. It's the demons sent by Hades who forced me to do those dirty, sickening things." Luke pressed his hands to the sides of his head, gave it a few hard shakes. "I won't think about that. The demons are gone now. They've lost this hard-fought battle."

Luke was talking about the prostitutes he'd raped and killed. It didn't take a psychologist to figure that one out.

Sloane took the opportunity to probe an area that Luke might now be receptive to, if only to supplant the dark voices in his head with something he considered light and beautiful. "Can you tell me the details of our ascent? The process sounds intriguing."

"The process is secondary. The destination is everything." Luke lowered his hands, but he was still shaking from whatever emotional upheaval had just taken place inside his mind.

"You mean Mount Olympus."

"It's exquisite—pure, unscathed, perfect. I've heard stories about it all my life."

"From Gaia?"

"Yes. She read to me every night, long stories of splendor and eternal life. If you had seen the way her face would light up when she'd read, she was totally transformed. I always swore to myself that someday I'd see that euphoria on her face again, this time for good."

"So you're facilitating it." Sloane smiled. "What a loving son you are."

"I try."

"Does Gaia know all the details of our ascent?"

"No. I want to surprise her. Actually, no one knows, not

even Hera. I usually talk things over with her. But this time . . . I chose not to."

"Would you be willing to talk them over with me?" Sloane asked. "I'd be happy to listen."

He became very calm, as a soft, peculiar smile touched his lips. "You're always a good listener. Even when I didn't speak, you heard me. I called just to hear the sound of your soothing voice. I'd been deprived of that joy since I realized your FBI friends must have put a trace on my cell phones. That's why I took your name off the invitation list to Gaia's retirement party. I needed a reason to call you. To connect with my twin. And to make sure you were coming. I had to reinforce my connection with you, even though I knew we'd soon be connected for eternity. That's why I visited your home, lay on your bed. Does that make any sense?"

"Yes." Sloane feigned understanding. "To strengthen our connection, would you please share your plans with me? Tell me about our upcoming ascent."

Luke paused, considering her request. "I'm not ready to fully trust you—not yet. However, I do trust you to guard a secret. Also, you're strong. You don't scare easily. So, as my twin, I believe you're the right one to share this with." His gaze flickered over her. "But first, you need a chiton. There are several in your closet upstairs. I'll bring one down, since you're not ready to be transferred upstairs. I'll also bring you some lunch. You slept through the usual hour that it's served."

"What time is it now?"

"Three forty-five. Lunch is served promptly at noon, unless I'm away. In that case, provisions are made."

The mattress Sloane was sitting on was lumpy and uncomfortable. She wriggled a bit, then winced. "Delphi, I understand why you don't fully trust me yet. But is there any way you can keep me confined to your satisfaction without using these shackles? They're cutting into my flesh, especially my injured hand."

That bothered him. "Your injury—I didn't think of that. Very well. When I return, I'll bring an alternative to the shackles." His gaze hardened again, his fists clenching and unclenching at his sides, emanating leashed violence. "Let me state this in advance. I know how intelligent you are. And also how skilled you are at Krav Maga. In fact, I know everything about you. So don't try anything. Not now. Not when I return. Not at all. You won't succeed and it will break my heart to have to kill you. But don't doubt that I will, *if* you force my hand."

"I don't plan to do that," she assured him. "I'm resourceful, but I'm not stupid."

"Very well, I'll be back shortly."

Lillian Doyle's Apartment
West 171st Street, New York City
4:55 P.M.

Derek pulled on his gloves and entered the apartment. ERT was already doing its job. There was music playing from somewhere inside. The Pachelbel Canon, Sloane's favorite. He headed toward it, then paused as one of the ERT agents came up to him.

"Parker, you won't believe this," he said, pointing. "Go take a look. I didn't touch a thing so you could get the full impact."

Derek walked into the spare bedroom, where the music was coming from. Empty. Except for the desk positioned directly across from the doorway. But that desk said it all.

Stunned, Derek came to a dead halt, his gaze glued to the images on the laptop screen.

A slideshow of photos synchronized with the music. Images only of Sloane. Not just at work and at home, but everywhere. And not just current photos, but some that went way back, starting with her days in the D.A.'s office. Luke had obviously become obsessed with her from the very first time they met. He'd kept a month-by-month digital photo album of all her activities, all her meetings with friends, all her time in her backyard—romping with the hounds or shooting at her archery range.

He even had pictures of her in Cleveland—both on the job and off—and at Quantico, where he'd filmed her arriving and departing. The psycho had followed her everywhere, living her life, capturing it for posterity.

There were even a few shots of Sloane and Derek together, strolling, talking, and laughing. A big white "box" had been superimposed over Derek's portion of the photo. Fortunately, Luke hadn't gotten any intimate shots, but just the fact that he'd been stalking and obsessing over Sloane for all these years made Derek want to puke.

The segment ended with a blank frame that simply said: *For Artemis.*

The next segment began.

To Derek, it looked like a Discovery Channel special on viruses and how they invade healthy cells. Then the scene appeared to dissolve to white as if someone poured liquid disinfectant to "bleach out" the contents. In its place were highlights of Luke killing and dismembering the Asian prostitutes. It ended with *For Gaia, with Love.*

And finally, the home video concluded with Luke reading from a prepared script . . .

"Welcome, serpents. By the time you see this, you're too late to stop the Ascension. Gaia, Artemis, the lesser goddesses and I have gone to Mount Olympus, leaving this despicable, disease-ridden world for Python and his FBI underlings to rule. Bow to your superiors and accept your defeat."

With that, the final frame burst into flames, disintegrating into a pyramid of pictures. At the apex was a picture of Lillian—younger, vibrant, and obviously in good health—with a simple caption: *Gaia.* Below that in the hierarchy were pictures of Sloane and Luke, captioned *Artemis* and *Apollo,* respectively. At the bottom of the pyramid was a picture of each of the kidnapped women, captioned with the name of the goddess she embodied.

A moment passed, and the entire sequence started again.

Forcing himself to keep it together, Derek crossed over and examined the desk. Beside the laptop stood only one other object—a children's book on Greek mythology. Derek picked it up and opened it. The inscription read: *To my little Apollo.* Obviously, a gift from Lillian when Luke was a boy. The book was well-worn, signifying it had been read often. There was a chapter on each goddess, complete with an illustration. It was like a textbook, except presented with clear, elementary school simplicity.

At this point, Derek had every drop of proof he needed. The lab in Quantico had called earlier and confirmed the DNA match. So they now had both fingerprint *and* DNA evidence. And now this sick, twisted video.

The problem was, he had no idea where Luke Doyle was.

The bastard was smart. There wasn't a shred of information on him in this apartment that Derek hadn't already obtained elsewhere—his military record, his school transcript, his employment records from Bellevue. Not a damned thing that could provide a clue as to his whereabouts.

Ditto for the phone records they'd obtained by court order. Neither Luke's nor Lillian's phones had revealed anything. No calls had been made, either to or from their home or cell phones, since Sloane's disappearance.

A credit search on both the Doyles had proven equally useless.

No addresses that the Bureau didn't already know about. So if that country house really existed, it hadn't been bought under either Luke's or Lillian's name. Piles of bills and credit-card statements in the kitchen—all with one word scrawled in large, red letters: PAID. No outstanding balances. None.

Eerily, it looked as if the Doyles were paying off each and every one of their debts to society.

Its finality made Derek's skin crawl.

THIRTY-ONE

They were out of time.

Judging from the amount of morphine Luke was administering to his mother, and his own statement that he expected her to pass in a day or two, it was clear that Lillian had made a rapid downhill slide since the evening of her party. And it didn't take a rocket scientist to figure out that once "Gaia" had moved on, the rest of them would follow close behind.

They would be sacrificed in an elaborate ritual, no doubt dismembered piece by piece using a combat knife. Luke had been honing his carving skills on those prostitutes he'd killed. And the fact that he'd implied that Sloane was the only "goddess" strong enough to listen to him describe the details of their ascension didn't bode well for his planned methodology.

Sweat broke out on Sloane's forehead, drenched her back, as she visualized the thick blade of a Bowie knife and what it could do. A hell of a lot more damage than a switchblade.

Vivid recall took over. The excruciating pain of razor-sharp metal piercing her flesh, severing her nerves and blood vessels. The intolerable agony, the sickening sight of blood gushing from her palm, flowing onto the ground until she blacked out—it was a nightmare she'd carry with her forever.

And that was only her hand. This time the ritualistic killing would involve not only a combat knife, but the puncturing of vital organs and a torturous, drawn-out death.

Stop it. Sloane nipped her thoughts in the bud. She wasn't letting her mind go there. It would only paralyze her and waste valuable time. None of the women in this house was going to die. She would come up with a means of escape. She had to.

The Bureau had provided her with the finest, most sophisticated training in the world. But no handbook, no amount of education, innate ability, or years of crisis resolution experience could prepare her for a situation like this—where she was negotiating for her own life and the lives of others—with no help. And, given the circumstances, it felt as if everything was happening at warp speed, with Lillian's impending death being an imposed, but intangible deadline—like a bomb with a lit fuse, set to go off at some imminent but imprecise hour. There was no opportunity for her to make gradual progress, foster developing trust. And there was no margin for error.

Sloane's mind stepped through the salient points of crisis negotiation, extracting those techniques that would work in this high-stress situation. She prayed she had the right answers.

That brought her to the cell phone she'd slipped into the seatback bag of Lillian's wheelchair when Luke had kidnapped her. Obviously, she'd been incapacitated and unable to access to it during their trip. But the phone still had to be in that bag. If Luke had discovered it, he would have slit her throat by now. Fine, but had he brought the wheelchair inside the house? Was it with Lillian? Sloane had to find out. She had to get into Lillian's bedroom—or rather, convince Luke to take her there.

He'd intimated that he'd created a room for "Artemis"

upstairs, one she had to earn the right to move into. She'd
be willing to bet that Lillian's room was on the same floor.
So if she could convince him to move her, she'd be one step
closer to the wheelchair and the phone.

She'd have to do this as subtly as their limited time
would permit. Maybe she could request a peek at the room,
and a brief visit with Lillian—just so she could cheer "Gaia"
up. That would definitely earn her brownie points.

Even if she pulled it off, Luke would never leave her alone
with Lillian. He'd be supervising her every move. But she *had*
to get to that phone, find a way to snatch it as well as a private place to use it—and then pray that wherever the hell
this place was, she would have enough cell reception.

Then there was the problem of rehiding the phone.
While she'd never seen a chiton, she had a funny feeling it
wouldn't be rife with pockets. So she'd have to stash the
phone somewhere where Luke wouldn't spot it, *and* without him noticing she was doing it.

The hurdles seemed impossible.

But impossible trumped death anytime.

When Luke returned, he was carrying a tray and a small
gym bag. He put the tray down beside Sloane on the mattress. There was a bowl of tomato soup, a mixed green
salad, and two grilled cheese sandwiches.

"I'm sorry it took me so long," he said. "You must be
starved. It's five-fifteen and you haven't eaten in twelve
hours, since you wolfed down that power bar before your
run. I truly apologize."

The details he knew about her were getting eerier and
eerier.

"No apology necessary. I assumed that whatever kept
you was important." Sloane gave him a worried look. "Is it
Gaia?"

He sank down on the chair, steepled his fingers. "One
minute she's practically incoherent, and the next minute
she's begging me for a bath. She can't hold down food, her

lucid moments are fewer and fewer . . ." He interlaced his fingers and tightened the grip. "I'm not equipped—"

Abruptly, he broke off, realizing he was revealing far more than he wanted to. "Anyway, I hope that meal is suitable. I remember that you like cheese. Especially Cheddar. So I bought a block of imported white Cheddar. That's what I made your sandwiches with."

"That was very thoughtful of you. Thank you." Sloane leaned forward, instinctively attempting to reach for the tray. This time she couldn't stifle a whimper. There was no blood circulating in her wrists and ankles, and her palm was beginning to throb badly. "Delphi, please, can we unlock my shackles first? I'm losing feeling in my limbs, and my hand is in excruciating pain."

One look at her white face confirmed she wasn't lying.

"Of course." Luke knelt down beside her and unzipped the gym bag. "It's just as well that we're dealing with the shackles. You can't eat or change clothes with your hands chained together."

The first thing he took out was a pistol, which he tucked loosely into his belt. "I don't want to use this. But I'm an excellent shot. So, please, for both our sakes, don't make me prove it."

"As I told you before, I have no intentions of it."

Nodding, he pulled out a key, unlocked and removed her arm and leg shackles. "There. Better?" he asked.

"Much." She rubbed feeling back into her limbs, flexed her fingers, and did a few quick hand exercises Connie had taught her. "Thank you. I was starting to get frightened. After all I've been through with my hand, I'm very protective of it."

"I understand. But there's no need to be frightened or protective." He smiled faintly, that faraway look that gave Sloane the creeps reappearing in his eyes. "Your injury will be healed when we get to Mount Olympus. There's no pain there. Only joy."

With that, he pulled a shapeless, white linen, tuniclike

garment out of the gym bag. "Your chiton," he announced. "Please put it on before you eat."

"All right." Sloane took the garment and rose, unzipping the hooded jacket of her jogging suit.

Instantly, Luke rose and turned his back, rigidly facing the opposite wall. "Let me know when you're finished."

"I will." Interesting. Luke's regard for the goddesses extended to honoring their modesty and virtue as well.

That could work very well in her favor.

If he couldn't watch the goddesses change, then how could he ever bring himself to bathe his mother? He couldn't. Which explained why Lillian had been begging for a bath.

The idea began to take shape. By the time Sloane was belting the chiton with the white rope Luke had provided, it was a full-fledged plan.

She set aside her running clothes, placing them at the very bottom of her mattress. "I'm dressed," she announced.

Luke turned, smiling in approval. "Excellent. Now sit and eat."

Sloane did as he asked, taking a sip of her soup. "This is delicious. Will you join me? I've always enjoyed our lunches together."

He smiled. "As have I. But I've already eaten."

"Then tell me about the ascension while I enjoy this lovely meal you've prepared for me."

He sat down again, propped his elbows on his knees, and stared straight ahead. "Gaia is drifting closer to the end of this life and the beginning of eternity. When the time comes, all the goddesses will be summoned to the ritual room, where they will bathe and dress in ceremonial robes. They will be brought upstairs so they are gathered around Gaia's bed as she ascends. There will be spiritual music and goblets of wine. All of us will drink and bless Gaia as she rises into immortality. Then, one by one, the goddesses will join her, in the order in which they arrived. By the gift of my knife, they will be carved with the requisite exalted symbols, leave this wretched planet, and move on to the wonders of Mount Olympus, where they will serve Gaia and be rewarded with joyous eternal life."

Sloane forced herself not to flinch, but instead continued eating her soup. "So the lesser goddesses will precede us?"

"Yes."

Putting down her soup spoon, Sloane's brow furrowed. "I know of six, excluding myself."

"There are seven."

"Followed by me."

"You, and then me. As the last to ascend, I will perform the sacred and sacrificial rites on myself. I'll have to forgo some of the ceremonial incisions, since I need to ensure my own passing. But I'm well equipped. I've been preparing for this for over a year. Last will come our funeral pyre. In a blaze of glory, any remnants of our earthly existence will be consumed in a towering inferno."

Inferno? Sloane began choking down her sandwich. Her stomach was tied up in knots, but she needed some nourishment. "Like a pillar of fire? How will we manage that, if we've all ascended?"

"Timer. It will ignite the funeral pyre in perfect synchronization with the culmination of our ceremony."

He planted an incendiary device. Shit.

"It sounds like an exalted experience worthy of Gaia." Sloane forced out the words, hoping her food wouldn't come up at the same time.

Luke actually smiled—no, beamed. "I knew you'd understand. I knew it. The others would be afraid, but not you. You know I'd never do anything that wouldn't bring you the ultimate joy. This is salvation, not death."

"I understand." Sloane put down her sandwich. "Would you describe Mount Olympus to me?"

She barely listened as he launched into an elaborate description of opulent buildings and marble walkways. She was too busy figuring out the details of her plan.

He'd given her a golden opportunity.

She wasn't going to blow it.

"You're very quiet," he observed, watching her closely.

Clearly, he'd finished speaking and she wasn't responding to his satisfaction.

"Forgive me. It's just that I'm taking in a great deal at once." Sloane put down her sandwich and gave him a wistful smile. "It's hard to imagine a place so beautiful, or accept that I'm worthy of living there."

His utopian mood returned. "You are. As for taking it all in, I understand. I've had years to visualize Mount Olympus. You're first learning about it." Abruptly, he fell silent, staring at the floor and chewing his lip as if contemplating whether or not to say something.

"Tell me what you're thinking," Sloane urged softly. "We've always had such ease between us."

A faint smile. "That's precisely what I was thinking about. How right it feels to share all this with you. How I knew from the first moment I saw you that it would be this way. You were different from the others. You were pure of heart, kind and decent and good. Together, we stopped victims from suffering, brought families together. I remember thinking what a cruel and ugly place this world has become, and how someone like you deserved so much better. You deserved to be worshipped, and to always be surrounded by beauty."

"I was awed by your selflessness and your sensitivity that day," Sloane heard herself say. "Especially with the children. I've never seen anyone so kind and gentle. You really did seem godlike." There was irony in her statement, but there was also truth. Luke had been amazing. How he could be such a dual personality was a complete mystery to her.

His next words came as a total surprise. "You're thinking about all the things I've done—not with the goddesses, but with the whores. And you're wondering at the paradox."

It was a statement, not a question. So Sloane responded truthfully, qualifying her answer with a nonjudgmental, open-ended question. "Yes. And I'd really like to understand. Can you help me do that?"

He sighed, and his shoulders drooped. "I've sought absolution from the gods for my weakness. There was no excuse for my succumbing to the base and sinful needs of mortal men. My only excuse is that the demons wouldn't relent. They pounded at my brain day and night, until I did as they commanded. I'm ashamed of giving in. But the remainder of my actions? The utter obliteration of those whores' filth and immorality, that was my mission. It was bestowed upon me by the gods."

Sloane watched him as he spoke. He was truly ashamed of his sex acts, but he truly believed that he'd been empowered by some supreme beings to desecrate those poor Asian women, slash them into nonexistence.

It was mind-boggling.

"So you were doing as the gods commanded," she paraphrased.

"Yes. But also as *I* commanded. I did it for me. And for Gaia."

His whole demeanor had changed again. His face was a mask of pure hatred, and icy bitterness laced his tone.

"How did your killing those women appease you and Gaia?"

"Gaia didn't need appeasement. She has the kindest and most forgiving heart in the world. But I needed it for her. And for me. I was young—but not *that* young. I understood a lot more than what I was told. He was an unfeeling, immoral son of a bitch. With all his bravado, he was a weakling. He devastated us, and died without suffering a single consequence. My only prayer is that he's facedown in the River Styx, relegated to the dark realm of Hades."

Sloane listened, then asked, "Are you talking about your father?"

"Did you know that the River Styx means the River of Hatred?" Luke asked inanely, as if he hadn't heard Sloane's question.

"No, I didn't. How old were you when your father died?"

"Twelve." A hollow laugh. And, true, he was half

responsible for my creation. But my father? No. So don't refer to him as such."

"Fair enough. I can see that you hate him. There's obviously a reason for that. Did he abuse you?"

"If you mean, did he crawl into bed with me and commit perverted sexual acts, the answer is no. He saved his sexual perversions for Gaia."

Sloane drew a sharp breath. "He sexually abused your mother?"

"When he was with her. The rest of the time, he humiliated her, reduced her to nothing." Violent enmity glittered in Luke's eyes. "Conventional marriage was an inconvenience to my *father*." He spat out the word. "He had a sick fixation for whores. Particularly Asian whores. He spent half his life with them, catching and spreading their diseases, becoming addicted to their depravity, and then bringing it all home to Gaia."

A vein was pulsing at his temple. "She's a loving, purehearted woman. And he turned her into a receptacle for his filth. What do you think caused her cancer? HPV. A viral infection she was far too embarrassed to have checked. A lady like my mother, confiding in anyone that her cheating husband had contaminated her? Never. By the time she could no longer ignore how ill she was—or hide it from me knowing I would force her to see a doctor—the cancer had spread to the rest of her body. All her pain, her suffering— it was because of him."

Poor Lillian, Sloane mused silently as the truth struck home. A psychologically disturbed son and a sexually abusive husband, whose deviant behavior resulted in her developing cervical cancer that was now fatal. Luke's warped actions now had an explanation.

"I'm very, very sorry," Sloane said sincerely. "You and your mother deserved better."

"He didn't even have the painful, drawn-out death he deserved," Luke added, his hands balling into fists. "The bastard just died of a heart attack. Instantly. He never felt a thing. Worse, he was in bed with one of his Asian whores when it happened. Talk about irony. He should have suffered. The way she's suffering now. *He should have suffered!*" Luke leaped to his feet, picking up the wooden chair and crashing it against the wall.

It splintered into pieces.

Luke stared down at the slices of wood, his chest heaving with emotion. Slowly, he brought himself under control.

"Forgive me," he said, turning to Sloane as if he hadn't just lost it entirely not two minutes ago. "I hope I didn't scare you."

"You didn't," she lied. "You helped me understand you better."

Luke gazed steadily at her. "I've never told that to another soul."

"I'm honored." Sloane gave him a reassuring look. "But then, Apollo and Artemis are siblings. Twins. It's only natural that we share confidences."

A tight nod. "As I said, I knew you were different from the start. I truly believed that all women, other than Gaia, were sluts. But you were everything that was good, strong, decent, and beautiful. I knew right from then that our futures were meant to intertwine in some sacred capacity."

Sloane heard his words, felt their fervor, and she knew her opportunity had arrived.

"May I share a secret with you in return?" she asked.

"Please do."

"Ever since what happened to my hand, I'm terrified of knives. I can barely slice a tomato without starting to tremble. I know it's irrational, but I can't help it." She leaned forward, as if sealing the bond between them. "When we get to Mount Olympus, I'm hoping that phobia will be gone."

"It will," Luke assured her. "There is no fear there."

Sloane hesitated, then rushed on, as if what she was asking was a very difficult thing for her to do. "I have a request. If you could grant it, I'd be grateful beyond words."

Only a flicker of wariness this time. "Go ahead."

"The ceremonial ascension you described is beautiful. I wouldn't change a single aspect of it. Unfortunately, it also means I have to face my greatest phobia. Would it be possible for you to sedate me enough so I don't feel the pain of the blade? That would go a long way toward easing my fear."

The wariness vanished. "Of course. Anything I can do to ease your way. Just ask, and it's yours."

"Thank you. Thank you so much." Sloane gave him a radiant smile. Then a thoughtful look came into her eyes. "It occurs to me that a tortured soul would not be worthy of Olympus. Also, Gaia deserves the most peaceful of transitions, something she won't have with a group of terrified women gathered around her. Perhaps you should sedate all the lesser goddesses as well. It will ensure their cooperation, enhance Gaia's ascension, and relieve the need for you to restrain them. The entire experience will be much smoother and more tranquil."

Luke pursed his lips, thinking. "What you say makes sense. And it does nothing to violate the rites of passage. It's a good idea. I'll get the necessary medications ready tonight."

"That's wonderful. It's a kindness I know all the goddesses will appreciate." Sloane's first victory was a hollow one. She'd ensured minimal pain for all the kidnapped women during this supposed ascension to eternity. But that ease of suffering would need to be implemented only if she failed in her efforts to save them, meaning they were all doomed to die.

It wasn't victory enough.

"Delphi, your morality and decency are rare," she said, moving toward her ultimate goal. "Not just toward us, but, most importantly, toward Gaia. I'm sure the idea of a son bathing his mother seems indecent to you. I fully understand that—and I agree. But I also understand that a woman's spirits are greatly lifted when she's clean and well groomed. If it's all right with you, I'd like to give Gaia the bath you said she was begging for. Not only am I female, but I'm not a stranger. Gaia already knows me. She should get to know me even better if I'm to sit beside you at her feet when we reach Olympus. I'll follow whatever instructions you give me." Sloane went for the clincher, gesturing at the pistol tucked in Luke's belt. "And if you want to aim that at me through the entire bathing ritual, I'll understand. My only goal is to make Gaia comfortable."

There was an expression of almost childlike bliss in Luke's eyes. "What a loving, gracious offer. I'm sure Gaia will be delighted. What's more, you and I can take a short detour once we're upstairs so I can show you your room. I constructed it specifically for you. You'll stay there from now until the ascension. It's just down the hall from Gaia's room, and it will be far more comfortable for you than this jail cell. You've more than proven your trustworthiness." He extended his hand, helped Sloane climb off the mattress and onto her feet—then quickly broke off all physical contact. "Come. Let's leave this place."

Sloane accepted his assistance, at the same time making note of his reluctance to touch her. Her legs were wobbly, but her adrenaline was running high. She'd earned Luke's trust. She was gaining admittance to Lillian's room.

Now she had to get her hands on that cell phone.

THIRTY-TWO

I'm so very proud of Artemis.

I know what it cost her to relinquish her freedom and commit herself to paradise. She has no reason to believe in its existence, other than her faith in me.

I'm honored.

And I won't disappoint her.

If I'd thought she'd even consider bathing Gaia, I would have returned to her that much sooner. Gaia's pleas to be bathed had broken my heart. But I could no sooner remove my mother's clothing and touch her body than I could turn my back on her request. So I was stuck in an untenable position.

Artemis had rescued me.

She was as superb as I'd surmised. The perfect Artemis. I'd chosen brilliantly.

Before we went to Gaia, I'd show her the palace I'd built for her.

I could think of no better way to show her how I feel.

Luke was right behind her. Sloane could feel his presence as they climbed the stairs. So she kept her demeanor upbeat, and her step as steady as she could. Her body still hadn't shaken off all the drugs. But, on the whole, she was in pretty good shape.

The house—at least as much as she could glimpse of it—looked like an old stone mansion that had been unoccupied for God knew how long. It had that musty smell that accompanied a place that had been vacant for ages, and an eerie silence that accentuated the fact that most of the expansive space was unused. The basement, which was where Sloane had been and where the other woman presumably still were, was below ground level, which was why it felt like a tomb. The main floor was clean but sparsely furnished, and as Luke guided her toward the second flight of stairs, Sloane got a glimpse of the practically bare living and dining rooms. She also noticed that there were several other rooms located behind them. She wondered what was in those rooms, and then abruptly decided she didn't want to know. Not unless they contained the incendiary device he'd assembled to burn this place to the ground.

When they reached the top of the second-floor landing, Luke stopped her.

"Gaia's room is that way." He pointed to the left, a short corridor that appeared to contain two bedrooms. Sloane's best guess was that one of them was Lillian's and the other was Luke's. "Yours is directly across to the right."

Of course it was. Luke would never allow those in his charge—be it loved one or prisoner—to be too far from his watchful eye.

He led her over there, halting in front of the room's polished mahogany door.

"I can't tell you how long I've waited for this day," he confessed as he unlocked the door and pushed it open. "Go in. See the opulent quarters I built for you."

Sloane's jaw dropped as she walked across the threshold. White marble floors. Lavish walls—decorated with murals of Artemis, her hounds, and her bow and quiver of arrows. Polished, ornate pieces of mahogany furniture that Sloane suspected were all antiques, probably worth a large sum. A four-poster bed, with a bedspread and canopy of lime-green silk, with matching pillow shams. And tall, hand-painted urns on either side of the bed.

"I don't believe this," she managed.

Taking her reaction to be one of stunned pleasure, Luke urged her to check out the bathroom. She indulged him, walking through the adjoining door, her jaw dropping even farther. Pale pink marble everywhere—floor to ceiling. In the center of the room, an antique alabaster tub. In a smaller inner room, a pale pink marble sink and commode, all with gold faucets. Two Ancient Greek sculptures graced either side of the tub.

Sloane was speechless. Luke had spent an astronomical amount of money, time, and effort on a room that was never going to be used. At best, Sloane would spend one, maybe two, nights here. Then, if Luke had his way, she'd be dead and living in the eternal splendor of Mount Olympus. While this earthly grandeur would be reduced to ashes.

Luke considered her chambers a masterpiece.

Sloane considered them an atrocity.

"You're astounded," he deduced with a broad grin.

"I'm speechless." She reverted back to her masquerade. "You built all this for me?"

"Every bit of it." Luke walked around, reverently touching each piece of furniture, each pottery accessory as if it were a priceless treasure. "I've spent days and days in here, not only building it, but imagining your reaction when you saw it. It became my retreat, the place I went to for solace. Even when the demons threatened to swallow me whole, I found some semblance of peace being here, being in your spiritual presence. Can you understand that?"

"Of course." Sloane was on the verge of throwing up. Instead, she faced him, pasted an expression of utter awe on her face. "Thank you. I can't begin to express my gratitude. I truly don't know what to say."

"Say nothing. Just seeing you in here, watching your elation, is more than enough. Tonight, you'll sleep between silk sheets. Knowing you're lying in the luxury befitting you will make me rest easy." He waved his arm toward the door. "Shall we go to Gaia?"

"Yes. Let's."

Lillian didn't look quite as bad as Sloane had expected— although she had to agree with Luke's assessment that his mother's time on earth was nearly at an end.

Propped up in a large bed on a pile of feather pillows, Lillian seemed small and frail, but awake and coherent. Her coloring was sallow, and her breathing uneven. But at least she was breathing on her own, without the help of oxygen. The only apparatus at her bedside was an IV drip, presumably containing morphine, and a commode.

And one more essential item that nearly made Sloane weep with relief—her wheelchair. Assembled and ready for use, it was on the far side of the bed, away from the IV drip—*and* the view from the doorway.

This was Sloane's luckiest break so far.

"Mother, we have a guest," Luke announced.

Sloane noticed he didn't call her Gaia. He obviously knew she'd be totally confused by that.

"A guest?" Lillian turned her head toward the door, and her pained expression brightened when she saw Sloane— although she did look somewhat baffled. "Sloane. What a lovely surprise. I had no idea you were coming. Did you drive all this way?"

Choosing her words with great care, Sloane replied, "Actually, Luke picked me up. He knew how much I wanted to visit with you, so he made the trip."

Lillian beamed. "That's my wonderful son." Weakly, she raised one arm to gesture at a velvet-cushioned chair. "Luke, would you bring that over so Sloane can sit down and chat?"

Luke shot Sloane a helpless look.

"Actually, before we have our visit, I had another sug- gestion," Sloane interceded quickly. "Luke mentioned to me that you'd like a bath. I'd be delighted to do the honors." She leaned forward conspiratorially. "You know how bad men are at figuring out which product is which. Half the time, they confuse hair and bath gel, or body wash and lotion. You end up with a creamed but unbathed body, or hair that's conditioned but unwashed."

Soft laughter eased the lines of pain around Lillian's mouth. "You're right. And Luke is overly respectful, on top of that. He deals with patients every day, but he can't bathe his own mother. I guess I raised him with an overabundance of good manners."

"You can never have too many good manners. You've done an amazing job with Luke. He's a truly fine man."

"Thank you, my dear, for the compliment and the offer." Lillian was eager to accept. It was written all over her face. "You're very kind. And I'd so like to feel refreshed. Are you sure you don't mind helping me with my bath?"

"Not a bit. It would make me feel useful. And we could chat at the same time."

That did the trick. Lillian raised her head from the pillow, and gazed over at her son. "Some female companionship and a bath would be a double blessing."

"Of course." Luke looked so relieved, it was almost pitiful. "I'll fill the tub with warm water, and bring it over with the soap, bath sponge, and towels." He paused, smiling faintly. "And I'll bring out all the bath and hair-care products so Sloane can choose the right ones."

Once again, Sloane noted he used her real name, not Artemis's. As over the edge as he was, he was still moving in and out of lucidity.

A few minutes later, the bath was set up and ready, and Luke was practically running out of the room.

"I'll be just on the other side of the door." He spoke to both of them, but his stare was fixed on Sloane.

She got the message. He trusted her, but he wasn't taking any chances—not with Gaia.

"That's fine," she replied calmly. "We'll let you know when we're finished."

Finally, finally, he was gone. The door was shut, but not completely. It was slightly ajar, presumably so "Delphi" could listen to every word that was said.

Sloane had anticipated that. She didn't care what he heard, only what he saw.

She started the bath on the far side of the bed, where the wheelchair sat to Lillian's right, knowing that the sooner she got to that cell phone, the better. She'd had Luke set up the tub in that very spot, and she now stooped over to dip in the sponge, soak it with water.

"Let's see which soap you'd prefer," she said aloud, sorting through the products with one hand, groping in the wheelchair's seatback bag with the other. "We have lavender or vanilla. We also have a coconut-scented body wash."

Bingo. Her fingers closed around her cell phone.

In one swift motion, she pulled it out, palming it until she brought it down to the floor, where the bed hid her and what she was doing. She flipped open the phone and slid it down the front of her chiton, hooking it over the front clasp of her bra, then snapping it shut like a clamshell.

Her phone was thin and small. The billowy chiton would keep it well hidden.

The next part of her mission was accomplished.

"Lavender is so relaxing," Lillian was saying. "I think I'd like to use that."

"I agree." Sloane rose, the wet sponge and bar of lavender soap in her hands. "Lavender is known to soothe the senses and relax away stress."

She undressed and bathed Lillian with the dignity and gentleness due the poor, dying woman. All the while, she chatted with her, filling Lillian in on current events, and updates on her favorite soap opera. Anything she could do to help Lillian die in peace made Sloane's heart feel good. She'd lived a hard personal life, and Sloane was almost relieved that she would die without ever knowing how unbalanced her wonderful son really was.

"Aren't the mountains beautiful?" Lillian murmured at one point. "They make me feel closer to God."

For the first time, Sloane looked around and really took in the room. She'd been so focused on getting her cell phone that she'd barely noticed anything else.

The bedroom was a suite, filled with all the things Lillian held dear, from photos of Luke to gifts she'd received from her John Jay family. Her bed, which had its headboard against the wall adjacent to the door, faced a panorama of windows that spanned the entire far wall. The scenery was breathtaking, overlooking tall, lush green mountains. Sloane turned to scrutinize them, as much for her sake as for Lillian's. She was looking for any landmarks that could tell her where they were.

"I can understand how this would make you feel close to God," she replied. "The mountains are exquisite." As she spoke, Sloane noticed something that looked like a mini Washington Monument in the distance. Whatever it was, it made a great landmark.

A short while later, the bath was finished, and Lillian looked exhausted, and yet happier and more peaceful than even Sloane had expected—as close to glowing as a dying woman could be. Sloane wasn't naive. Lillian was on the verge of passing. And yet, it gave her pleasure that her skin and hair were clean. That, in turn, brought Sloane pleasure.

"Come in, Luke," Sloane called as she finished brushing and drying Lillian's hair.

The door opened instantly, and Luke hurried in. One glance at his mother, and his entire being lit up.

"You look lovely," he told her. "Ten years younger than you did before."

Lillian mustered a smile. "Then perhaps I should bathe more often." She turned her head toward Sloane. "Thank you so much—for the bath and for the chat. I've missed that . . ." Her eyelids were drooping.

"Well, I'll be spending the night," Sloane told her. "So we'll have more time to talk."

"Really?" Hope flickered in Lillian's eyes, even as they started to close.

"Really. So get some rest. I'll visit you later on this evening."

Out in the hall, Luke turned to Sloane. "I haven't seen her this happy since the night of her retirement party. I can't thank you enough."

"Just seeing her reaction was thanks enough. But I do have a request." Sloane feigned a tad of embarrassment. "I haven't used the facilities all day. Plus, I feel so grungy from all the hours I spent in the basement. Would you mind if I used that magnificent bathroom you built for me?"

Luke frowned. "How rude and thoughtless of me. Of course you need the facilities. And I want you to use the tub." A brief hesitation. "I have to prepare dinner. So I won't be able to stand guard outside your bedroom door. I'll have to lock it from the outside. But don't worry. I'll check on you in a short while."

"That's fine. Remember, I ate later than you and the others. So I'm not famished. I'll soak in the tub until you come back."

Five minutes later, Sloane was locked in "Artemis's" room. She went straight to the bathroom, used the toilet, and simultaneously turned on the bathtub faucets.

The combined sounds of the flushing toilet and the running bathwater were more than enough to silence the tones of her cell phone as she turned it on.

Dammit. The reception was practically nil.

She walked all around the bedroom, including as close to the window as she dared to go, to see if she could get more than one bar. No change.

She had to try something. Her voice would be garbled with only one bar. If a call wouldn't go through, maybe a text message would.

Swiftly, she navigated the phone's menu to text messaging, punched in Derek's number, and pressed OK. Then she typed the following:

luke. 12–24 hr ? live. mtns. c wash monmnt 2 e. BOMB.

She pressed send.

The chances of him getting the message were bleak, not without a stronger signal.

She'd have to get outside and resend it where the reception was better.

And she knew just how to accomplish that.

THIRTY-THREE

I thought Artemis might enjoy having dinner with me. Not locked in her room, but downstairs, in the dining room. I had never actually eaten in there. What better occasion than this?

So I came up to invite her.

I knocked on the bedroom door, and when there was no answer, I unlocked it and pushed it open a crack. "Artemis?"

No reply.

Now I was worried. I shoved open the door and stalked in, half worried that something had happened to her, half panicked that she had tried to escape.

As I opened my mouth to call her again, the bathroom door swung open, and she stepped into the room, wearing nothing but a bath sheet. It was wrapped securely around her, revealing nothing, but that didn't excuse my intrusion on her privacy.

I froze.

Her gaze widened as she saw me, her hand instinctively grasping the knot at the top of the towel. "Delphi. I wasn't expecting you. I . . ."

She was mortified. How could I blame her? She was a goddess of virtue, a maiden in every way. Having a man walk in on her bathing ritual was akin to blasphemy.

Recovering myself, I averted my gaze at once, feeling utterly ashamed. I lowered my head and retreated from the room, shutting the door behind me.

"I deeply apologize," I told her through the door. "I had no idea you were indisposed. I called your name. When you didn't answer, I got worried. I have no other excuse."

"It's all right, Delphi," she assured me calmly. "I trust you. I know you would never do anything indiscreet. It was an error—mine as well as yours. I should have been listening for your knock. Instead, I was savoring my time in that magnificent bathtub you gave me. I must not have heard you over the water draining from the tub."

I bowed my head, feeling both relief and esteem. She was as forgiving as she was gracious. I was indeed fortunate.

"Thank you for your tolerance. I'm glad you know I'd never invade your privacy. Never."

"I do know that. Let's forget it ever happened. Besides," she added, "I had a wonderful idea, and I wanted to seek your approval."

"By all means."

"I heard sounds coming from Gaia's room. So I assume she's awakened from her nap?"

"Yes. Unfortunately, the pain doesn't allow her to sleep for long periods. The sounds you heard were my attempts to give her dinner. But she has no appetite. And very little strength. Her only joys were your visit, her bath, and a view of the mountains."

"Then my idea should be perfect." Artemis sounded exuberant, and I could hear her rustling around, getting a fresh chiton from the closet. "Why don't we take Gaia for a stroll? The fresh air will do her a world of good. The mountains at twilight will be breathtaking." A pause. "And it will be a wonderful final memory for her to carry with her to Mount Olympus."

A walk. Why hadn't I thought of that? Gaia loved nature,

and she'd been deprived of it since she'd arrived. And Artemis was right. As goddess of the earth, Gaia deserved a beautiful final memory of this planet to take with her.

"Your idea *is* perfect," I said to Artemis. "Gaia would love that. She even has a favorite garden out back. I'll suggest this to her right away."

"If she's up for it, I can be ready in two minutes," Artemis called back. "I'll carry the wheelchair so you can carry Gaia. Once we're outside, she can sit back and revel in nature."

I was so eager to tell Gaia, I could scarcely contain myself. "I'll be right back," I promised Artemis. "That way, I can share Gaia's response with you."

"I promise to answer this time when you knock."

Sloane heard him go, and released a huge sigh of relief. Now all she had to do was hope that Gaia's desire to drink in the natural world one last time would supersede her physical weakness from the disease that was claiming her life.

By the time Sloane's chiton was on and belted, and her hair was dry and brushed, Luke was back at her door.

"We're ready," he said as he knocked.

"As am I." Sloane quickly palmed her cell phone.

He unlocked the door and beckoned for her to join him. "Gaia is elated," he told her as they crossed the hall to her room. "I'm so glad you came up with this idea. She's so weak she can hardly sit up on her own, and yet she's smiling, eager to be pushed through the gardens, to breathe in the scent of the flowers. And it is a perfect twilight. Clear, warm, with a full moon to light our way."

"It sounds as if it was meant to be."

Transferring her cell phone to the wheelchair was easier than Sloane had expected. Luke was so preoccupied with lifting his mother, removing the IV bag so he could carry it downstairs and hook it onto the wheelchair, that he barely noticed Sloane. She dropped her cell phone into the seatback bag, folded the wheelchair, and hooked her arm around it to carry it downstairs.

Soon they were strolling through the gardens. Lillian interrupted to ask Sloane to push her wheelchair. Sloane was puzzled, but pleased to agree.

"Luke is exhausted," Lillian explained, indicating the signs of fatigue etched on his face. "He's done nothing but care for me for weeks on end. He won't take a break unless he trusts whoever's with me. I know he trusts you. Would you mind taking over for him just for this walk? It would do my heart good."

"Of course not." Sloane glanced at Luke to seek confirmation that the arrangement was okay with him.

His nod gave her permission, although he did pat his jacket pocket to remind her he had his pistol.

Sloane didn't need a reminder.

With Luke sitting on a stone bench, scrutinizing them carefully, she had to be just as cautious as if he were walking beside them. Well, almost. At least this situation afforded her the benefits of distance and camouflage.

She wheeled Lillian through the lush garden the older woman loved most, then glided her wheelchair along the path, moving to a beautiful, serene spot. She angled the wheelchair so Lillian could smell the flowers, and simultaneously gaze at the mountains that surrounded them.

"Are you familiar with these mountains?" Lillian sounded half out of it, partially from the morphine and partially from the weakness. "They're so majestic, tall, and green. Or snow-capped in the winter. I've always loved it here. It's like being halfway to heaven."

"You're right. It is." Sloane slid her fingers into the mesh compartment of the seatback bag, retrieved the phone, and flipped it open. Four and a half bars. It didn't get much better than that.

Keeping her hands shielded from view by her body, she accessed the phone menu, entered Text Messaging,

and went to her out-box. Then she selected the last message sent, clicked Options, scrolled down to Resend, and
pressed OK.

The whole process took less than thirty seconds.

With such good reception, Sloane assumed the message
would go through.

Or maybe it wasn't an assumption. Maybe it was a prayer.

But whether or not she'd succeeded, she had to get rid of
the phone before Luke found it. And the best way to do that
would be to leave it on and leave it out here, where nobody
would venture after this evening's walk was over, and where
the reception was ideal. Because once Derek realized the
message was from her, he'd work with the cell-phone company to triangulate on the location of her cell phone.

She glanced behind her. Luke was leaning back on the
bench, his right hand in his jacket pocket. His gaze kept
shifting from Sloane and Lillian to the beauty of the sunset
over the mountains.

Sloane bided her time. Then, when Luke was looking up
at the sky, she grasped her cell phone and tossed it into the
row of hedges just beside her.

Done. Now it was up to Lady Luck.

Second Avenue, New York City
May 2, 12:30 A.M.

Derek hadn't shut an eye. In fact, he'd barely sat down.

He didn't plan on slowing his efforts. Nor did he plan on
giving up or considering the worst. He was best when he
was active, doing things to bring about resolution.

Feeling helpless was *not* his forte.

Goddammit, he was going crazy.

From its spot on the night table, his cell phone gave a
short beep. He snatched it up and glanced at the display. The
text message indicator was on. He flipped open the phone,
which informed him that he had a new text message, and
inquired if he'd like to read it.

He punched in yes.

His heart began pounding as he read the abbreviated words.

luke. 12–24 hr 2 live. mtns. c wash monmnt 2 e, BOMB.

Sloane was alive. She'd managed to use her cell phone. And she was trying to give him the information he needed to find her.

Derek didn't waste time, and he didn't go through channels.

He called his ADIC—the head of the entire New York field office—at home. Frankly, Derek didn't care what time it was, or what protocol he was violating. Sloane had sent the message at seven-thirty. That was five hours ago. Anything could have happened since then. He was down to the wire. And he wasn't about to let Sloane, or any of those other women, die.

He relayed the situation and the contents of the text message to the assistant director in charge.

"What do you need?" was his response.

"For starters, a SWAT team and a bomb squad. I'll also need topology experts from New York, New Jersey, and Pennsylvania." Derek wasn't screwing around. "Also, specialists from Parks and Recreation. Former Special Agent Burbank is telling us that she's in the mountains and that she sees something resembling the Washington Monument to her east."

"At one A.M? That's not going to be easy."

"With all due respect, sir, I don't care how hard it is. I don't care if we have to wake up the governors of all three states. This is a serial sexual killer who's brutally raped and carved up half a dozen victims. Right now he's got seven kidnapped women, all of whom could still be alive, but with only a few hours left to live. Among those seven women is one of our own."

"I'll make the calls."

DATE: 2 May
TIME: Dawn

Sloane had lain awake all night, jumping every time she heard the slightest sound, in the hopes that it was SWAT breaking down the doors and initiating a rescue.

But weak sunlight was starting to filter into her room, telling Sloane that another day was beginning in which she was on her own.

Worse, she'd heard Luke going in and out of Lillian's room all night. His step had been urgent, and the frequency of the visits was increasing. Which could only mean that Lillian was nearing the end.

If a rescue team didn't arrive soon, Sloane would be combating Luke's psychotic group sacrifice alone and unarmed.

She sat up at the sound of Luke's racing feet. He was headed downstairs. She wished she knew for what.

Just to be on the safe side, she went to the bathroom, used the toilet and brushed her teeth, then filled the tub up enough so she could kneel in it and wash herself. There was a method to her madness, because instinct told her that Luke was coming unglued. And *that* meant that she had to be ready on a dime.

The goddesses have been alerted, and are in the ritual room, bathing and dressing.

Now I must initiate the final phase,

I'd amassed everything beforehand. I'd known that, when the time came, my emotions would be too erratic and too overwhelming.

I wasn't wrong.

My hands are shaking as I turn off the furnace. A necessary precaution. Nothing can ignite prematurely. Right beside the furnace is the plastic garbage can I'd dragged in from the garage. Into that, I empty the fifty-pound drum of dry chlorine pellets I'd bought from a local pool-supply company. I then fill an empty, half-gallon ice-cream container with several cans of cheap brake fluid, tape an electric match to its side, and place the ice-cream container inside the garbage can, on top of the pellets.

I pause, forcing myself to take a few deep, composing breaths. I can't spare another second, not with Gaia hovering on the brink.

Still trembling, I continue.

I connect the leads from the electric match to a digital timer. I set the timer.

The countdown begins.

With Gaia entering her final moments of life, there is precious little time to waste. I must hurry. She needs me.

I conclude my final preparations, arranging three propane barbecue tanks symmetrically around the room, cracking open the valve on each until I can hear and smell the propane escaping.

The funeral pyre is ready.

Sloane had just finished tying the rope of the ceremonial gold-trimmed chiton Luke had set aside in her closet—trying not to picture it covered with bloodstains—when his rushing footsteps pounded up the stairs. A brief lull, probably as he checked on Gaia, and then the running resumed, this time in the direction of "Artemis's" room.

His fist hammered against the door.

"Artemis? Artemis, please wake up."

Sloane knew in her gut that the moment of truth had arrived. And that meant there was no rescue team, placing the ball squarely in her court.

Seven women were depending upon her. That, in itself, would have to give her strength and purpose.

"I'm awake," she replied, going to the door. "I'm also dressed."

Luke fumbled with the key, finally unlocking the door and opening it.

He'd obviously stopped off in his room as well, since he was freshly shaved and impeccably groomed. He was dressed in a long chiton, also embroidered with gold, with the pistol tucked in his rope belt. But his face was whiter than his chiton, and he looked like hell.

"It's time," he announced, and Sloane could hear his voice quaver despite all his attempts to appear calm. "All the goddesses are in the ritual room, washing and dressing. I've prepared them for what lies ahead." He swallowed. "You were right. Sedation will be needed. A few of them are weeping hysterically, and a few others are putting up a fight. I can't allow Gaia to be exposed to that negative energy. This must be a peaceful, sacred passing."

He glanced toward Gaia's room. "I have to get back to her. The music and candles are in place, as are the goblets of wine. But I . . ." He turned back to Sloane. "You have to prepare as well. Wash. Dress."

"I've done both." Sloane kept her voice low and respectful of what was about to occur. "I heard you dashing around. I assumed it was Gaia. So I rose, bathed, and put on the ceremonial chiton you left me."

For the first time, Luke seemed to actually see her. "You knew. I shouldn't be surprised. You look every bit the goddess."

"I wanted to braid my hair."

"Yes. Good. That is fitting and proper." Luke was talking more to himself than to Sloane. "The gods will give me the strength I need. She and I will only be separated for minutes."

"Of course." Sloane considered touching his arm, then thought better of it. "Delphi," she asked, gazing directly into his vague, empty eyes. "Would you like me to sit with you at Gaia's bedside—at least until it's time to bring up the other goddesses? Because I could keep vigil with you. It might ease this transition."

Another of those rare flashes of sanity. "I'd like that. So would Gaia. She feels deeply bonded to you. The walk you two took last night is all she talked about during her lucid moments. You made her happy. And that brings me more joy than you can imagine." He stood there for a moment, like a lost boy.

"Check on Gaia," Sloane urged. "Then sedate the goddesses. Leave them in the ritual room until they've calmed down and their presence is required upstairs. I'll braid my hair. I'll be ready for you when you return."

"Right." Robotically, he walked out of her room, shut and locked the door.

Sloane sank down on the edge of the bed. She'd just bought herself a little time alone with Luke. She'd have to use that time, and his grief, to her advantage. Because once Lillian was gone, any trace of Luke would be gone. At which point Delphi would take over, and he'd do away with the goddesses, one by one, culminating with her and then himself. Shortly thereafter, the entire manor would burst into flames and be reduced to cinders, along with their bodily remains.

Pistol or no pistol, this would be her last chance to save them.

High Point State Park
Kittatinny Mountains
Sussex County, northwest tip of New Jersey
May 2, 7:05 A.M.

"There's the monument," one of the New Jersey state troopers pointed out. He, along with a dozen other New Jersey state troopers, and the local police, were part of the FBI-led search team. "It's over eighteen hundred feet above sea level. It's the tallest point in New Jersey. You can see everything for miles from up there."

Derek was wearing his forty-pound SWAT vest and all his protective gear, carrying his assault rifle, with his pistol strapped to his thigh. So were the fifteen-plus other members of New York's enhanced SWAT team who'd been available and were now assembled under the command of John McLeod, their team leader. Joining SWAT were two SABTs, who were on standby, ready to suit up in their heavy-duty EOD-9 bomb suits at a moment's notice, and equipped with the disruption tools needed to deactivate any explosive devices.

"We're going door-to-door, covering the grid, starting with the buildings due west of that monument," McLeod announced to the group. "Derek, fill us in on the topography."

Derek nodded, grateful as hell that Sloane had managed to leave on her cell phone, allowing Verizon to triangulate on the area where she and the victims were located.

"Most of what you'll find are small farms, and *all* of them are spread out," he specified. "Some are hidden by trees for privacy. Be especially interested in those. Our Unsub is intent on keeping his hideaway as close to invisible as he can. But we're going to find it—and we're going to find it *fast*." A quick glance at his watch. "Time's working against us. Let's go."

Sloane leaned past Luke and tucked a blanket beneath Lillian's chin, talking softly to her as she did. Luke stood on Sloane's right, directly beside his mother's face, holding her hand in both of his, and murmuring to her about eternity and beauty and reverence.

Over the past hour and a half, Lillian's breathing had gone from labored to erratic to almost nonexistent—so much so that, several times, Sloane had to stare at the rise and fall of her chest for what seemed like forever, just to see if she was still alive.

This was torture.

And Luke wasn't taking it well.

He was experiencing major mood swings. One minute he was a compassionate, loving son, the next minute he was a delusional soon-to-be Greek god, and the next minute after that he was a violent, angry killer who wanted to seek vengeance on a world who was taking away the only person he'd every truly loved, and who'd ever been there for him.

It was the last of those moods that worried Sloane most.

When the rage took over, Luke was irrational and unreachable. He stalked around the room, waving his pistol and his combat knife, and ranting about justice and decency and the annihilation of society. He kicked furniture out of his way, blotches of red staining his cheeks, and describing the horrific ways he'd killed people and the even more horrific ways he wanted to kill more. Sloane didn't need convincing. She was already worried sick that the wrong provocation—like a defiant remark from one of the soon-to-be-retrieved goddesses—would result in his going off on a shooting and stabbing rampage, and then deferring his own ascension to Mount Olympus long enough to continue that rampage elsewhere.

During those moments when Luke went berserk, Sloane remained very still, just stroking Lillian's hair and adjusting her pillows. Fortunately, the poor woman was totally out of it, so she didn't have to witness her son's depravity firsthand.

But unless Sloane could find the right moment to attack Luke and win, or, at the very least, defuse his murderous rage, this was going to be bad.

Then, as quickly as it had started, the rage ended, transforming Luke into Delphi, who went on ad nauseam about the nobility of Mount Olympus and what awaited them there.

And then, every once in a great while, it would be Luke standing beside Sloane, watching with tears in his eyes as his mother slipped away.

Oddly, it was during one of Luke's tirades that Lillian opened her eyes and very clearly said, "Luke."

He whipped around, staring at the bed, recognizing the fleeting moment of lucidness in his mother's eyes.

Instantly, he lowered the knife and the pistol, walking around Sloane to resume his place at the top part of the bed. "I'm here, Mother." He put the knife and pistol on the floor, and took her hand, clasping it tightly between his.

An expression of wonder crossed her face. "It's beautiful. The other side is beautiful." She drew another slow, shaky breath. "Don't grieve. It's my time." Her lids were slowly drooping. "I'll always be with you. Don't forget that. And don't forget . . . how much I love you."

Her eyes closed, and she was gone.

Luke just stared for a moment, paralyzed with disbelief. Then he lost it, leaning forward until he was lying across his mother's lifeless body. "I love you, too," he wept, his whole body trembling. "Don't leave me . . . I can't be here alone." He was openly sobbing now, sliding to his knees, his head, neck, and shoulders bowing over Lillian as he clutched the blanket Sloane had tucked under her chin.

Sloane knew this was her moment. Luke was consumed with shock and grief, distracted from everything but Lillian's passing, and devoid of weapons.

She might have tried to grab for the pistol in the hopes of stopping him without causing him further pain. She *might* have, if he hadn't muttered his next words: "I'm coming soon, Mother. We all are. To serve you on Mount Olympus."

That clinched it.

Self-preservation took over. So did her Krav Maga training.

Fisting her left hand, Sloane delivered a devastating blow to the back of Luke's neck where his brain stem lay beneath the skin. Without pausing, she followed her left punch with a strike from her right elbow to the same spot on his neck. She couldn't see his face, but she knew her abilities. She'd knocked him momentarily unconscious.

As if on cue, Luke slumped to the floor, making her job that much easier. She caught his shoulders as he went down. There was no time to waste. She had no idea how long he'd stay unconscious.

Using the core strength she'd built up over years of training, Sloane pulled Luke toward the post at the foot of Lillian's bed. She forced him into an upright position, propping his back against the bed. She then untied the rope that was looped around her waist as a chiton belt. Fortunately, it was thick and sturdy. Yanking it off, she used it to tie Luke's feet securely together. Then she pulled both of his arms behind him and around the bedpost. Once they were in position, she untied the rope belt from his chiton, and used it to bind his wrists together.

She rose, surveying her handiwork. Even if Luke came to, he wouldn't be able to get out of here, not without taking the whole bed with him.

Swiftly, she reached down to where Luke had been standing and picked up his combat knife and pistol. As an extra precaution, she dashed quickly down to Luke's room. Sure enough, the room keys were on his night table, where he'd placed them after he'd changed into his ceremonial garb. Sloane took the whole ring of them and ran back to Lillian's room.

Luke was still out cold.

Sloane paused for a brief second next to Lillian's body. "Rest in peace, Lillian," she murmured. "Luke will get the help he needs."

With that, Sloane turned and left the room, shutting the door behind her. Placing the knife and the pistol on the floor, she rapidly tried each key on Luke's key ring until she found the one that fit the lock on Lillian's door.

She slipped it in and turned it, listening for the click that assured her the bolt had engaged. Once she heard that, she jiggled the door handle just to make sure it was locked.

Retrieving the two weapons, she dashed down the first flight of stairs. She had no idea when Luke had set the timer for. But she had to get those women out of here before the place blew up.

As she neared the first-floor landing, there was an enormous thundering crash, and the entire house shook. The front door practically exploded from the impact of the ram, and SWAT breached the entry, pouring inside.

"Gas," someone yelled.

The SABTs were immediately on it, heading toward the basement steps and, ultimately, to the furnace area, where experience told them the bomb would most likely be.

"Half of you go with them and free the victims," John McLeod said to his SWAT team as the muffled cries of female voices begging for help reached their ears. "The rest of us will split up so we can secure the remainder of the house—this level and upstairs."

"The upstairs is clear," Sloane announced, reaching the bottom of the stairs and addressing SSA McLeod as she raised her hands high—pistol and key ring in one, combat knife in the other—to demonstrate her nonthreatening status. "I'm Sloane Burbank," she said. "The subject is unconscious, tied up, and locked in the first bedroom upstairs on your left. I have the exact key isolated." She jiggled her appropriate hand. "May I?"

"Of course." It was Derek's voice, and she'd never heard a more welcome sound in her life. "Lower your hands, Sloane."

"Thanks." She managed a weary grin. She then placed the weapons on the floor and handed the SWAT team leader Luke's key ring, gripping the key to Lillian's room between her fingers to keep it isolated.

"You said the subject was unconscious?" McLeod asked.

"When I left him, yes. My guess is, he'll be out for a while. I slammed his brain stem pretty hard—twice."

"With his weapon?"

"With my fist and my elbow."

"I see." McLeod looked a little taken aback, and Sloane could see Derek's lips twitch.

"The only other upstairs occupant is the subject's mother, Lillian Doyle," Sloane continued. "She's deceased. Natural causes; end-stage cancer. Her body is in the same room where you'll find her son."

"Nice work," McLeod commented, gesturing for several of his men to go upstairs and carry out the secured subject and his deceased mother. His gaze returned to Sloane. "Are you hurt? Or is that a stupid question?"

"I'm fine." Sloane was already heading for the basement. "But there are seven hysterical captives down there, who've been sedated, and are terrified they're about to be carved up."

"Sloane, stay the hell away from there," Derek ordered as he and the rest of the team blew by her. "Let us do our job. We'll evacuate the victims. The SABTs will take care of the bomb. And *you'll* get your ass out of this house."

"I don't know how much time is left," Sloane called after him, ignoring his command to leave.

"Then we'll have to move fast." He and his team were halfway down the steps. "Are they all alive?" he yelled over his shoulder.

"Yes," Sloane yelled back. "Somewhere on your right. Just follow their voices."

"Come with me, Ms. Burbank." One of the state troopers was easing her toward the open space where the front door had been. "We need to keep the area clear so SWAT can do their job."

Reluctantly, she complied. She could hear the SWAT team moving from room to room, securing each of them as they progressed toward the women.

In the meantime, the SABTs had spotted the propane cylinders, proceeding with caution toward the garbage can. They assessed the bomb, then radioed for the disrupter to be brought down ASAP to the basement. If the numerical display on the detonator was correct, they were almost out of time.

When the disrupter arrived, they positioned it carefully at the crude incendiary device Luke had constructed, and fired it. With the detonator deactivated, one of the bomb techs carefully removed the liquid-filled ice-cream container, making sure not to spill its contents. With the bomb and its components secured, he and his partner then focused on closing the valves on the propane tanks and dispersing the explosive gas that had accumulated in the basement.

Having conducted a final search to ensure that no other incendiary devices had been placed, the SABTs resurfaced, and gave the thumbs-up to SSA McLeod.

"Great work, guys," McLeod said.

A second later, Sloane heard Derek call out to the victims. "FBI. We're going to get you out of there. Step away from the door." Another loud crash as the door gave way from the impact of the ram.

One by one, the women were carried up the stairs and out to freedom.

Sloane moved to the side of the porch, counting and matching names with faces. She recognized Lydia Halas right away. Striking Mediterranean coloring, a serene expression on her face. She looked drawn and gaunt from her ordeal, but she was still the same kind-looking RN who'd cared for Sloane at the hospital. Even now, drugged and dazed, Lydia spotted Sloane and managed a weak smile as the agent carried her outside.

Another of the state troopers hurried over. "I called the EMTs. They'll be here in ten minutes to take these ladies to the hospital, and have them checked out."

Next, came Cynthia Alexander, whom Sloane identified from her photos. She was trembling violently. "My parents . . ." she whispered, tears filling her eyes.

"Your mother's been in New York ever since you disappeared," Derek, who was carrying her, reassured her at once. "I'll call her now and send a police car to pick her up. She'll meet you at the hospital."

"Thank you," she managed.

Sloane didn't recognize the next three victims. Two were older, more mature-looking. One was a college kid.

"Eve Calhoun," Derek reported from behind her. "You worked in the D.A.'s office at the same time. Helen Daniels, and her daughter, Abby—a professor and a student at Penn State."

"My first workplace . . . and my alma mater . . ." Sloane shook her head in disbelief.

"You have no idea how warped Luke Doyle is."

"I think I do," Sloane replied softly. "That's Lauren Majors," she murmured as a woman in her late twenties, who looked shell-shocked, was carried to freedom.

"There's one more," the agent who was transporting her reported. "She's in bad shape emotionally. Even sedated, she's cowering in the corner."

Derek met Sloane's gaze. "I'll go."

"I'll go with you."

He didn't argue. The two of them reentered the house, descended the stairs, and went to the anointment room.

Penny was shuddering and cringing in the far corner, her gaze hollow, her arms wrapped around herself for security. After a year in captivity, she was severely traumatized.

Sloane went right to her, speaking softly, saying familiar and soothing things. "Penny? It's Sloane. It's so good to see you. It's been forever." She squatted down beside her friend. "We have so many years of catching up to do. Your mom and I had tea the other day. She served me ladyfingers, just like old times. She looks wonderful. But she's very worried about you. So's your dad. Can we take you home to them?"

Slowly, Penny tilted back her head, gazed at Sloane with a flicker of hope and recognition. "Sloane?"

"It's over, Pen." Gently, Sloane caressed her hair. "We got him. You're free. The nightmare is over."

Tears began sliding down Penny's cheeks. "Really?"

"I promise. We can carry you out of here right now."

Penny continued gazing at Sloane, and it was obvious the reality had only partially sunk in. She was somewhat heavily sedated, and between that and the effects of her long-term confinement, she was pretty out of it. Still, she stopped shaking, willingly accepting their assistance. "Okay."

She sounded like a child. That broke Sloane's heart. But she reminded herself that it could have been a lot worse. Penny was alive. Alive and physically unharmed. The emotional healing would come—with time and counseling.

Sloane and Derek made a chair with their hands, and together carried Penny outside. Penny gripped Sloane's chiton the entire time.

"You won, Penny," Sloane said adamantly. "And so did all the other women. Everyone's fine."

Sloane's words were swallowed up by the sound of approaching ambulances.

"Great timing." Sloane waited, then she and Derek carried Penny over to the trained medical techs who would transport her to the hospital. "I'll call your parents," she promised her friend. "They'll probably charter a helicopter and fly to meet you."

A tiny flicker of amusement touched Penny's lips—the first human reaction Sloane had seen her show.

"Aren't you coming, ma'am?" the medical tech asked Sloane.

"It's not necessary. I'm fine." She shook her head.

"She'll be there," Derek amended. "I'll bring her myself."

He shut the doors so the women could get to the hospital ASAP.

"Is everyone out now?" one of the state troopers asked Derek.

"Yes." Derek nodded. "Everyone's out."

The trooper trudged back to the scene as the ambulances drove off and the tension began to ebb.

Once the din had died down, Derek turned to face Sloane. She looked disheveled, pieces of her braid having come loose to dangle down the sides of her face. Her ridiculous tunic-thing was hanging on her like a queen-size sheet, with no belt to hold it in place. She was a total mess—and Derek had never seen a more beautiful sight in his life.

"You got my text message," Sloane breathed in relief.

Derek tugged her against him, held her tightly. "Are you really okay?" he asked in a rough voice.

"Now I am." She pressed her face against his SWAT vest, wrapped her arms around his waist.

"You scared the shit out of me."

"I'll try not to let it happen again."

"I'm holding you to that."

"Okay." Sloane's adrenaline was rapidly dropping as the full impact of what she'd been through sank in. "If I promise to go and get checked out at the hospital later today, can we just go home now? I'm going to have to answer tons of questions for the Bureau and the NYPD anyway. For now, all I want is a hot shower to wash away the past twenty-nine hours, and an afternoon in my bed—complete with a pint of Ben & Jerry's, all three hounds, and you."

"You know," Derek speculated aloud. "I did an awesome job solving this case. So if I ask for a few days off, just this once, I'm pretty sure I could get them."

"*You* did an awesome job?" Sloane leaned back to stare at him in amazement. "I'm the one who—"

Derek shut her up with a long, bone-melting kiss. "I know. But you know what an arrogant hard-ass I am. I have a reputation to uphold."

"True." Sloane's eyes sparkled with provocative amusement. "Actually, you have several reputations to uphold. Two of which are performance related—one for the Bureau, the other for me. I should warn you, my standards are even higher than the Bureau's. Think you're up for it?"

"Definitely. Besides, I like a challenge."

"Good. Because, Special Agent Parker, you've got one."

And now a sneak peek at
Andrea Kane's latest thriller

DRAWN IN BLOOD

Coming September 2009
from William Morrow
An Imprint of HarperCollinsPublishers

The front door of the apartment was opened a crack. That meant Matthew was home.

Generally, Rosalyn preferred being the first one through the door at night. It gave her time to unwind, to transition from work to home. To savor a glass of wine and a hot shower before starting to think about dinner.

But tonight she was just as happy Matthew had beaten her to their Upper East Side apartment. The two of them needed to talk.

Something was weighing on her husband's mind, and had been for weeks. She'd waited for him to approach her and broach the subject. He hadn't. That was way out of character. Matthew wasn't big on secrets. Neither was Rosalyn. It was probably one of the reasons their marriage had successfully endured for thirty-three years. And what made this situation worse was that whatever Matthew was keeping from her was significant. He wasn't himself. He was quiet and pensive, and he tossed and turned all night, every night.

Rosalyn was really starting to worry.

Tonight she planned to clear the air.

"Matthew?" She elbowed the front door open the rest of the way, and stepped inside, shutting it behind her. "It's me. You forgot to close the door behind you again. Not the smartest idea. One day, someone's going to . . ."

She never finished her sentence.

She heard the footsteps rush up behind her a split second before a pair of strong arms grabbed her. A rag was stuffed in her mouth and a rough sack was pulled over her head.

Instinctively, Rosalyn fought back. Enveloped by darkness, she struggled like a wild animal, even when she was backhanded so hard that her head snapped around and she lost her footing, nearly toppling to the floor. She stumbled upright, regained her balance, and swung out blindly with her fist.

Her knuckles connected with what felt like her attacker's jaw, and she heard his grunt of stunned surprise.

She took advantage of the moment, delivering a second punch, hoping to do some serious damage. But this time she missed, and her attacker grabbed her arms, pinning them behind her and anchoring her so her movements were restricted. She still didn't cave, but continued to battle him with sharp defensive jerks of her body and as many clumsy kicks as she could manage.

When her knee connected with his groin, she knew she'd pushed him too far.

He swore viciously, then barked out a terse, unintelligible command in another language—some Asian tongue. Pounding footsteps ensued, and a second intruder burst out from wherever in the apartment he'd been. The two men started arguing in a guttural Chinese dialect. An instant later, Rosalyn was dragged through the foyer and into another room—Matthew's office, if her sense of direction wasn't completely off-kilter. There, she was shoved into a chair, her wrists were bound behind her, and her ankles were tied together on the floor.

She tried to let out a scream, and only succeeded in gagging from the rag that was crammed in her mouth. The garbled sound that emerged was muffled by the burlap sack. Before she could try again, a heavy, solid object struck her head and pain exploded through her skull.

She saw stars and heard herself whimper. Pinpoints of light flashed behind her eyes. The voices . . . just two? No, maybe three. Male voices. All speaking in the same rapid Chinese. Dazedly, she found herself wishing she'd joined Matthew and Sloane all those years ago when they'd taken their trips to the Far East. Then maybe she could decipher what was being said. As it was, all she could make out was the urgency of their tones, the sound of slamming drawers, and what was probably a lifetime of possessions being hauled off.

With her tongue, she managed to maneuver the rag to one side—far enough so she could scream.

That was a mistake.

A drawer thudded to the floor. A whiz of motion. And then another blow that connected solidly with the side of her head.

This one was too much.

Blinding pain. Then dark silence.

It had started to drizzle when Matthew Burbank got out of the taxi and paid the driver—a cold autumn drizzle that left you feeling chilled, inside and out.

Matthew didn't notice it.

He didn't notice anything.

He was paralyzed with shock and worry.

He'd walked into a Chinatown restaurant to meet his partners, the same group of men who also happened to be his oldest friends. It wasn't a social dinner. It was a strategy session. *All* their necks were on the line—even the two of them who hadn't been at the crime scene—and it was crucial that they nailed down the details of the story they'd be giving the FBI during their individual interrogations. No hesitations. No deviations. It was the only way.

Matthew had arrived late and on edge.

But he'd left panicked, punched in the gut with the very basis for this meeting, and sucked into a memory he'd long since buried—or tried to. Suddenly, the past was the present. No. Worse. Because now what he feared for was his life.

He'd stepped out for a smoke. The Mercedes had pulled up to the curb, parking directly in front of the Cadillac Escalade, not fifteen feet away from where Matthew stood. Two Mediterranean guys, who looked like thugs and were built like linebackers, had gotten out of the Escalade and waited on the sidewalk, as the driver of the Mercedes, burly and Asian, hurried around to open the back door for his passenger.

The man had emerged, emanating power, despite being dwarfed in size by the linebackers. He'd greeted them with a nod, waited for his driver—who was clearly a bodyguard—to be glued to his side, and then led the way, keeping his head down as he walked.

He raised it just as he reached Matthew. He stopped. A long moment of eye contact. The recognition had been mutual and indisputable.

It was more than enough to tell Matthew he was living on borrowed time.

He barely remembered greeting the doorman at his building or entering the high-rise on York Avenue and 82nd Street. He summoned the elevator on autopilot, riding upstairs as he alternately freaked out and berated himself for being a prisoner to his own stupidity.

The elevator doors slid open, and he headed toward the apartment. Never had he needed a drink more than he did right now.

He unlocked the front door and flipped on the light as he stepped inside. His gaze swept the living area, and he froze in his tracks.

The place was trashed, furniture shoved aside, empty recesses where the flat screen TV and entertainment center had been. Kitchen drawers were dumped upside down, minus all the unique Art Deco silverware they'd contained. Two hand-crafted sculptures that Matthew had bartered for in Thailand were missing, as was the Monet that had hung over the sofa, and the one-of-a-kind ivory chess set he'd bought in India. And one of Rosalyn's diamond stud earrings was lying in the corner, clearly having been dropped. That meant they'd been in their bedroom and cleaned out her jewelry box.

None of that meant jack. It was the painting. That's why they'd come. The rest was just an added bonus. They'd broken in because of the painting.

Not the Monet. It was one of his lesser known works, not one of his masterpieces. But the Rothberg—not the painting itself—but its paperwork. *That* was what was invaluable. And timely. Especially after Matthew's encounter tonight.

He flung down his portfolio and raced to his office—where he'd find his answer.

He found a lot more than that.

Rosalyn was crumpled on her side in a corner of the room. She was bound to a toppled chair—hands and feet—and her head was half-covered by a cloth sack. One of the heavy wooden bookends he kept on his mantel lay beside her. A pool of blood was oozing from inside the sack, staining the Oriental rug beneath his wife's head. She wasn't moving. Her unnatural stillness was terrifying.

"Roz." Wild with panic, Matthew dashed over, squatting down and easing the sack off her head, dreading what he'd find.

She was breathing. He released his own breath when he saw that. Thank God. She was alive. The shallow rise and fall of her breasts confirmed it. So did the thready but definite pulse at her wrist.

To hell with the Rothberg.

He pulled the rag out of her mouth and unbound her wrists and ankles, scrutinizing her as he did. There were nasty gashes just above her ear, which was where the blood was seeping from. Whoever had done this had struck her at least twice with the bookend. Hard.

"Roz!" Matthew gripped her shoulders and shook her, realizing he was being an ass. He shouldn't be jarring her body, shouldn't be wasting precious seconds before calling 9-1-1. But he needed a sign—*any* sign—a word, a flicker of recognition—*anything* that told him she was okay.

He got both.

After his second "Roz! Honey, can you hear me?" she cracked open her eyes.

"Matthew?" she managed, blinking up at him. She stirred, then moaned, sinking back into the carpet and squeezing her eyes shut at the pain.

"Don't talk. Don't move. I'll get help. It'll be okay." Matthew knew he was reassuring himself more than his wife, who'd slipped back into unconsciousness.

Groping in his jacket pocket, he snatched up his cell phone and punched in 9-1-1.

"This is Matthew Burbank," he announced the instant the emergency operator answered the call. "I live at 500 East Eighty-second, at the corner of York. Apartment 9B. My home's been broken into. My wife is hurt. I need an ambulance—fast." His gaze was darting around, taking in the wreck of his office as he spoke. "She was struck on the head. At least twice. I don't know how bad it is. She's bleeding, but she's alive. Please . . . hurry." Dazedly, he supplied the other customary answers, then hung up.

He forced himself to scan the room, taking in the ransacked drawers of his myriad file cabinets. Even though he didn't label the cabinets themselves, he had a system, and he knew which cabinets were which. So he knew exactly where to direct his scrutiny. The cabinet that was thoroughly trashed, with a specific drawer pulled out to the max, was the one holding his pre-electronic business records of promising modern artists.

Neatly placed across the open drawer was a now-empty file folder. No surprise as to which one. *A. Rothberg's Dead or Alive* was printed on the tab. And resting on top of the folder like some kind of menacing paper weight was a fortune cookie. He picked it up. The slip of paper that had the fortune printed on it was sticking out from inside the cookie. Matthew eased it free.

Devote tomorrow to silent reflection, it read.

Bile burned Matthew's tongue. It wasn't a suggestion. It was a threat. This is what they'd come for. Not his possessions.

Matthew stared at the objects in his hands. Then he shoved the empty file folder, fortune cookie, and fortune into the inside pocket of his trench coat.

The cops couldn't see these. If they did, the whole situation would explode wide open.

It was already too late for him.

But now his whole family was in mortal danger.

The evening rush hour had come and gone, but the cars were still rumbling through the Midtown Tunnel, making the apartment vibrate and sleep impossible.

Fortunately, sleep was the farthest thing from Sloane Burbank's mind.

Lying alone in Derek's bed, she pulled the sheet up higher, gripping it tightly between her fists and wondering for the dozenth time if she was jumping the gun, making a huge mistake. Was this happening too fast? Was it premature? Would it solidify things, or blow them apart?

The step she was making was huge. How did she know if it was right?

She was still pondering that when the key turned in the front-door lock and Derek's voice reached her ears, accompanied by the sound of short, racing paws. An instant later, three bright-eyed dachshunds scrambled into the bedroom, dragging their leashes behind them. They pounced on the bed and on Sloane with a vengeance, licking her face and burrowing in the pillows.

"Hey." Sloane greeted Moe, Larry, and Curly—or the hounds, as she affectionately called them—with alternating scruffling of their necks. Their enthusiasm was infectious, and she had to grin as Larry stuck his head inside one pillowcase and emerged with two feathers on his snout. She plucked them off, pivoted to her side, and propped herself on one elbow. "That's quite a greeting, you three. And you've only been gone a half hour."

"It feels like a lot longer." Derek Parker entered the room, shrugging out of his lightweight jacket and hanging it neatly over one of the two suitcases near the bedroom door. "We jogged half a mile up Second Avenue. I think we marked every fire hydrant along the way. Twice—once going, and once coming back."

Sloane laughed, sitting up to unsnap the hounds' leashes. Curly was panting the least. Then again, he was her little frankfurter, with almost no hair to weigh him down. Larry was curly-haired, and little Moe—actually, Mona, the only female of the trio—was long-haired and silky. She was panting the most, and took the opportunity to gaze at Sloane and emit a plaintive whimper.

"Oh, cut it out," Derek muttered as he stepped into the galley kitchen to refill their water dishes. "You're such a drama queen. You were the one who dragged us into that mud puddle to play—*and* refused to leave for five minutes. So cut the violins-playing-in-the-background act."

Moe gave a pointed snort and jumped off the bed, leaving to join the others for a long drink.

"Thanks for taking them for their evening run," Sloane said to Derek. "You know that when I'm home I take them for a three-mile jog every morning and a shorter run at night. But I hate running in the city. I'm too Type-A to make my way over to a park before I cut loose. And other than parks, there's no room in Manhattan to move and no air to breathe."

"Not a problem."

Sloane watched as Derek guzzled a bottle of water, then stripped off his shirt and tossed it in the hamper. That was the one good thing about a small apartment—everything was within reach.

The man had a great body. There were no two ways about it. From his broad, muscled shoulders to his six-pack abs, he was as hot as they come. And he didn't owe that body to the FBI. He owed it to the military. As a former Army Ranger, Derek still rose at dawn and worked out like a demon. When the rest of the world—and the sun—were first rising, Derek was finishing up a workout that would knock most people on their asses for a week. No collapsing for him. After the workout, Derek showered, ate a power bar, and drove down to the FBI's New York Field Office to start his work day.

Tonight the two of them had cut short their regular workaholic hours. They'd quit work by six and headed over to Derek's apartment to pack. The packing had been minimal. They'd spent most of the past few hours in bed.

Now Derek was bare to the waist, and, knowing the effect they had on one other, Sloane held up her palm. "Much as I'd love to see the rest of the striptease, it'll have to wait. I ordered up Italian. It should be here in ten."

Derek gave her that sexy grin that made her insides melt. "We've burned up the sheets in five," he reminded her. "And that included getting our clothes off. You're already naked, and I'm halfway there. Plus we both love a challenge." His smile faded. "Of course, we also know that's not the problem. The problem is you've used the past half hour to freak out and consider changing your mind about my moving into your place. Kind of puts a damper on the mood."

Sloane blew out her breath. She wished he didn't know her so well. "Guilty as charged," she admitted. "And it's not because I don't want to live together. I just don't want to screw things up—again."

"We weren't living together when things fell apart," he

reminded her. "And you know damned well that, even if we had been, it had nothing to do with what happened. We shut each other out. We let our pride outweigh our love. We won't make that same mistake twice."

"No," Sloane agreed softly. "We won't."

She was being ridiculous. She knew it. It had been six months since they'd found their way back to each other. They'd worked out the obstacles—at least the big ones. What they had together was unique. She loved him. He loved her. An emotional connection like theirs was rare as hell in today's world.

Which was why she was terrified.

But, like Derek had just said, she never walked away from a challenge. Living together was going to be a biggie. It meant relinquishing another piece of her freedom and lowering another protective wall.

He was worth it. *They* were worth it.

The buzzer sounded, sending the hounds into a barking frenzy.

"Dinner's early." Derek walked over, tipped up Sloane's chin, and kissed her—not just a kiss, but one of those slow, deep kisses she felt down to her toes. "Pity. We could have put those ten minutes to good use."

Her eyes were smoky. "I'll owe them to you. We'll tack them on to dessert."

"Deal." Derek yanked his T-shirt back on. "I'll get the food."

Sloane scooted over to get out of bed. "I'll set the table."

"Don't bother. We'll eat out of the tins. Less dishes to wash, more time to pack. And whatever." With a wink, Derek went to buzz the doorman and tell him to let the delivery kid upstairs with their food.

Pulling one of Derek's oversized sweatshirts on, Sloane combed her fingers through the layers of her dark, shoulder-length hair, then padded into the kitchen to grab some forks and knives. She took an extra minute to pour two glasses of Chianti.

The wine wasn't meant to be savored. Not tonight.

Her cell phone rang.

With a quick sip of Chianti, Sloane retraced her steps to the bedroom. One of her clients, no doubt. With something that couldn't wait until morning. She was used to that. As an independent consultant, with credentials as a former FBI agent and crisis negotiator, she had a client list that consisted of law enforcement agencies and companies who needed round-the-clock availability. So adaptability in her personal life was the name of the game.

She wondered what tonight's interruption would be.

Scooping her phone off the nightstand, she punched it on. "Sloane Burbank."

"Sloane, it's me."

"Dad?" Her brows drew together. It wasn't that hearing from her father was unusual. She and her parents touched base a lot more since they'd moved back north to Manhattan from their Florida condo. But her father's tone, which was normally smooth and upbeat from all his years in sales, was shaky and strained. Not to mention the disturbing background noises Sloane could make out through the phone. The institutional bustle. The clear, unwelcome echo of a doctor being paged. The sounds were sickeningly familiar.

Her father was calling from a hospital—a setting she'd had more than her fair share of experience in.

Her gut clenched. "Dad, what's wrong?" she demanded. "You're in a hospital. Why?"

A hard swallow. "It's your mother. She's been hurt."

"Hurt—how?" Sloane was already rummaging around for her clothes. "And how bad is it?"

Another swallow, as her father struggled to keep himself together. "Our apartment was robbed. Your mother must have walked in and surprised the intruders. She was tied up and knocked unconscious. The good news is that by the time the ambulance got us to emergency, she was coming around."

"So she's conscious?" Sloane snapped on her bra and stepped into her thong, simultaneously reaching for her slacks and sweater.

"Conscious and in pain. I'm waiting for an update from the doctors now."

"Which hospital?"

"New York Presbyterian."

"I'll catch a taxi and be there in ten minutes."

"Wait." Matthew interrupted her. "Ten minutes? Where are you?"

"At Derek's place."

"That's what I was afraid of." An uncomfortable pause. "Sloane, I need you to come alone. Not with Derek. Not with anybody. The NYPD is already handling the break-in. They've got detectives here asking me a hundred questions—most of which I have no answers to. The last thing I need is to escalate the situation by having an FBI agent join this three-ring circus. Your mother needs her rest. She also needs you. So do I. Please, come alone."

"All right." Something about her father's request didn't sit right. Sloane sensed it, despite her shock and worry over her mother. She just couldn't pinpoint what it was—not yet.

But now wasn't the time to argue.

She grabbed her pocketbook. "I'm on my way."

"Alone?"

"Yes, Dad. Alone."

Snapping the phone shut, she was halfway through the bedroom door, when she collided with Derek, who'd come to announce that dinner was served.

He frowned, taking in her drawn expression and the fact that she was fully dressed. "What's going on?"

"My mom's in the hospital. I've got to get over there."

He snapped into take-charge mode. "Is it serious?"

"Someone broke into their place. She surprised them. They knocked her out. That's all I know."

"I'll go with you." Ignoring the tins of lasagna, Derek headed for the door.

"No—wait." Sloane stopped him, shrugging into her coat as she spoke. "My dad asked me to come alone. He sounds really freaked out. The cops are in his face, asking questions. I think he and my mom have had all they can take."

Derek went very still. "I'm not going to interrogate them. I'm going to offer my support. And to be there for you."

This was going to be tough. "I realize that," Sloane carefully replied. "And I'm grateful. But think of it from my dad's point of view. Right now, he doesn't see you as my boyfriend. He sees you as yet another law enforcement official. I don't want to upset him any more than he already is. So I'll do it his way. He and my mom are right here at New York Presbyterian. I'll be there in a flash. And I'll call you with updates."

"Fine." Derek wasn't happy. But he didn't argue. "My doorman will hail you a cab."

"Thanks for understanding."

"I don't. I'm accepting."

"That works, too." Sloane's gaze flitted to the kitchen table. "Go ahead and eat. I'll warm mine up when I get back."

"Right. Sure. Send my best to your folks."

"I will." Sloane was already halfway out the door, waiting only until Derek had reined in the hounds before she took off.

Derek shut the door behind her. He parked himself at the kitchen table, but ignored the tins of food. He wasn't hungry. He was bugged. Sloane had a hell of a poker face. But he knew her. Something was up. What had her father divulged about the break-in that he wanted kept under wraps? It couldn't have been too detailed, given the brevity of the conversation. Regardless, he'd managed to convey that he didn't want Derek around. And Derek wasn't buying into that I'm-too-overwhelmed excuse. There was more to this whole scenario than that.

He was still brooding when his phone rang.

Hoping it was Sloane, he snapped up the receiver. "Parker."

"It's me."

The "me" in question wasn't Sloane. It was fellow agent, Jeff Chiu, Derek's friend and squad-mate on the Asian Criminal Enterprise Task Force.

"Listen," Jeff continued in his no-BS tone. "The squad just picked up a weird conversation from our wiretap on Xiao Long's phone. Something about finalizing a deal with an old art dealer on East Eighty-second."

"Shit." Derek's fist struck the kitchen table.

"So I *am* right. I remember your mentioning that Sloane's parents live on the Upper East Side, and that her father's a retired art dealer."

"Not so retired."

"Meaning this involves him. And you don't sound surprised. What do you know?"

"Only that the Burbanks' apartment was just hit. Sloane got a call from her father a little while ago. He's at New York Presbyterian with his wife. Evidently, she interrupted the burglary. She was roughed up and knocked out."

"Just knocked out?"

"Yup. That means she didn't see Xiao Long's guys, or she'd be dead. That's all I know—at least until I hear from Sloane. She's over at the hospital now. I'm assuming C-6 will be getting official details soon. In the meantime, from what Sloane said, it sounds like the Nineteenth Precinct is all over this."

"I'll have one of our task force detectives contact them and make sure they're aware we have bigger fish to fry. But I doubt that'll come as big news. The NYPD knows we're closing in on Xiao Long. He's the Dai Lo. His gang members are superfluous. If the cops want to make a couple of independent arrests, so be it."

"I doubt they'll find enough to do even that. Like I said, I'd put money on the fact that Rosalyn Burbank never saw her assailants, or she wouldn't be alive to say otherwise. That eliminates a description or an ID. And, based on the previous break-ins, there'll be no physical evidence. All that adds up to nothing."

"Yeah." A pause. "But from what Xiao Long said on the phone—this break-in wasn't random."

"No," Derek repeated darkly. "It wasn't."

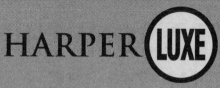